Rachel Lee was hooke and practised her craft all over the United State author now resides in F full-time.

USA Today bestselling author **Barb Han** lives in north Texas with her very own hero-worthy husband, three beautiful children, a spunky golden retriever/standard poodle mix and too many books in her to-read pile. In her downtime, she plays video games and spends much of her time on or around a basketball court. She loves interacting with readers and is grateful for their support. You can reach her at barbhan.com

Discover more at millsandboon.co.uk

CONARD COUNTY: KILLER IN THE STORM

RACHEL LEE

MURDER IN TEXAS

BARB HAN

MILLS & BOON

First Published in Great Britain 2023
by Mills & Boon, an imprint of HarperCollins*Publishers* Ltd
1 London Bridge Street, London, SE1 9GF

www.harpercollins.co.uk

HarperCollins*Publishers*
Macken House, 39/40 Mayor Street Upper,
Dublin 1, D01 C9W8, Ireland

Conard County: Killer in the Storm deals with topics that some readers may find difficult, including rape, sexual assault and domestic violence.

Conard County: Killer in the Storm © 2023 Susan Civil-Brown
Murder in Texas © 2023 Barb Han

ISBN: 978-0-263-30748-1

1123

This book is produced from independently certified FSC™ paper to ensure responsible forest management.

For more information visit: www.harpercollins.co.uk/green

Printed and Bound in the UK using 100% Renewable Electricity at CPI Group (UK) Ltd, Croydon, CR0 4YY

CONARD COUNTY: KILLER IN THE STORM

RACHEL LEE

Chapter One

Sheriff's Deputy Artie Jackson's headlights picked out the man with a backpack. He strode beside the desolate, dark highway in Conard County, Wyoming.

She didn't want to stop, but she did.

She'd just come from the most brutal domestic violence scene she'd ever witnessed. The bleeding woman lying beneath the beast who was trying to strangle her. The man refusing to listen to Artie Jackson. Ignoring the gun she threatened him with.

Reaching for her baton and beating the man with it repeatedly, feeling flesh and maybe bone crushing beneath it.

The moment when he'd reared up and come at her, ignoring her baton and pummeling her. Backup arriving just in time. Stumbling outside and vomiting until she had only dry heaves to give, dry heaves that wouldn't quit. The medevac chopper arriving to take the woman, still barely alive.

The struggling, yelling monster handcuffed and needing three deputies to wrestle him into the SUV cage.

The paramedic offering her help that she refused. Giving a brief official statement to another deputy.

She knew she'd done the right thing, but now she'd have to recover from it and live with it.

Ten miles down the road her stomach still roiled, her

body shook, her mind refused to let go of the images, the sensations of that baton striking. She hardly noticed her own bruises.

Now there was a man walking along the dark roadside. God, she wanted to drive by, to leave him to deal with his own mess, to just get herself home. To warm herself, drink some brandy, try to forget.

The last thing she wanted to deal with was another man. Any man.

But the night, the approaching blizzard, wouldn't allow her to ignore him.

She flipped on her roof lights, blared her horn just once. He stopped walking and faced her as she approached. She rolled down the window on the passenger side.

"Get in," she said, her voice flat, revealing nothing of her inner turmoil.

"Why?" he asked, calmly enough. "I haven't done anything."

"Damn it!" she said, her frustration and anger erupting. "It's starting to sleet. A bad storm is moving in. You'll freeze to death if you don't get shelter. Now get in. I'll take you to the motel in town."

So close to home, but now delayed by a fool who didn't have the sense to take care of himself.

"I'm fine," he answered, still calm.

"Like hell you are. Get in or I'll call for backup. Out here we don't drive past people who might freeze to death from exposure."

He looked away briefly, then returned his attention to her. He was tall, his square face rugged. A dark watch cap tugged down over his ears. His eyes nearly invisible.

He spoke, his voice deep. "In the back?"

In the cage. She drew a deep breath, reaching for reason. "Passenger seat. You're not under arrest. Yet."

When she unlocked the doors, he threw his pack on the back seat. A huge backpack, maybe seventy pounds. Steel frame. The kind a hiker carried on a long trek.

Her mind still functioned clearly enough to take in even the small details. She clung to them.

As soon as he was safely belted in beside her, she hit the gas, wanting to hurry, knowing that her official vehicle would keep her from being stopped. Wondering if she should keep her flashers on.

But only a fool would be out driving right now. Conditions were getting dangerous. Those conditions applied to her, too.

For the first two miles, she said nothing. He sat quiet and motionless beside her.

"What are you doing out here?" she asked, as if she gave a damn, but it was a cop question and the cop inside her was still working.

"Walking," he answered.

"I could see that. Where are you going?"

"The next mile."

Well, that was no freaking answer at all. "Are you homeless?"

"No. I'm just walking across the country."

Beyond that, Artie didn't care. She didn't question why he would do such a thing. Merely a confirmation, perhaps, that he wasn't the smartest guy.

Or maybe he was on the run. She ought to check him out. But just then, with her sickened stomach twisted into a knot so hard it hurt like hell, she didn't care.

Get him to the motel. Drop him off with a warning. Deal with him in the morning.

She wanted that brandy. She wanted to build a fire in her fireplace and stare into it. She needed to check on her dad. Important things. More important than the jerk sitting beside her.

But when she pulled up at the La-Z-Rest motel, the only motel in town, the no-vacancy sign glowed in red neon. Well, yeah, she thought. With the storm coming in over the mountains, nobody was moving, from truckers to random tourists who were always heading anywhere but Conard City.

What was she supposed to do with the jerk sitting beside her? Throw him out? Drop him at the truck stop diner and tell him to drink coffee for the next four days?

For the second time that night, reality crashed in on her.

Gritting her teeth, she jammed her Suburban into gear. "You've got a choice, make it fast. I can put you in a holding cell at the sheriff's office. You won't be locked in, not that that'll help much. It stinks of too many drunks."

"And the other choice?"

"You can sleep on my couch. And no, I won't be alone with you. So decide."

"You don't want me at your place."

"Of course I don't," she snapped. "But those holding cells have been used for a century and even bleach can't clean out the stench. So I'm giving you a choice. Take it, one way or the other."

"I'm a stranger," he replied. "Are you sure you want me in your home?"

"I'm a cop. I have a baton, I have my service pistol and I have some tae kwon do. You step out of line and you'll get more trouble than you bargain for." As she'd learned of herself tonight.

"Your place," he said finally. "But just for the night."

Right, she thought. Well, maybe someone would leave the motel in the morning. Another fool who might cause some other deputy the kinds of nightmares that came from an auto accident scene.

"I'm Boyd Connor," he said.

"Artie Jackson." As if she cared what his name was.

Right then she felt the world was populated by jerks and monsters and she'd have been happy never to see another soul again.

Ten minutes later, she pulled into her own driveway. Lights poured from the windows, along with a flicker of the television screen. The sleet had begun to sting with the rising wind.

"Come on," she said.

The man followed her, backpack in hand. Into a space she'd called home her entire life. Shabby around the edges but clean. She was something of a clean freak, ordering as much of her world as she could.

Her dad sat in his recliner, intent on the TV. She wasn't reassured to find him watching a cartoon.

"Hi, Dad," she said, going to kiss his forehead. Beside him on the end table she saw a plate of food. "I see Clara brought you dinner. Was it good?"

"Fine," he answered with a vague smile. Then his gaze tracked to the man. "Who?" he asked.

The man dropped his backpack near the door. "I'm Boyd Connor, sir."

"Herman," her dad answered. "I'm Herman."

"Boyd's going to sleep on the sofa tonight," Artie told her father. "Bad blizzard."

"I saw the news." Then her dad returned his attention to the TV.

Artie headed for the safe in her bedroom where she

stowed her pistol. She left her jacket lying on the bed. She wasn't worried about the Connor guy. She already knew what she could do with that damn baton, and she kept it with her. The gun was another matter. She didn't want her dad to ever get his hands on it.

Artie returned to the living room and looked at Boyd Connor, really taking him in for the first time. A strong, square face, darkened with several days' beard growth. Brown eyes. Dark hair, a little messy when he pulled off his watch cap. A powerful build with narrow hips, long legs. Taller than average. Her mind stored those details.

Artie picked up the dinner dishes, reaching for some normalcy. She pointed with her chin. "That's the sofa. It has a pull-out bed, but after all these years I can't guarantee it'll be comfortable."

"I'll be fine," Boyd Connor answered. "I appreciate the hospitality."

Civility reared its head even in the midst of her inner turmoil. "You must be hungry. I know I am. I've got some frozen dinners."

"Thanks. Whatever you have."

She turned again to her father. "You want anything, Dad? Still hungry? Maybe some milk or coffee?"

"I'm fine."

He was always fine, a situation that frustrated Artie because she needed to do more for him. But he didn't seem to want or need any more than the basics. God, she loved that man so much her heart ached with it. Her daddy. Slipping steadily away.

"Can I help?" Boyd asked.

She shook herself free of her endless, growing sorrow. "I'm just going to pop the meals in the microwave. I eat out of the containers, unless that's a problem for you."

For the first time he smiled, a faint smile but still a smile. "If you had any idea what I've been eating for years you wouldn't even ask."

Well, that sparked a dull interest, but she didn't pursue it. "After we eat I want to see your ID."

"I'd be surprised if you didn't."

She entered the same kitchen her mother had used, the same pots and pans and dishes. The dishwasher, her mother's pride so long ago, had died and Artie hadn't replaced it. Who needed a dishwasher for two people? She'd added a few things over the years. A small air fryer oven that served for baking or toasting for two. An induction coil for her dad to cook quickly on and safely. And the induction carafe to boil water. She didn't want her father to use the gas stove for any reason. In fact, she often thought about permanently turning off the gas supply to the stove.

She pulled three meals out of the freezer, two for Boyd. As big as he was, his appetite must be large. Basic frozen ziti. She also grabbed a box of frozen Texas garlic toast. Her dad liked that and it would toast quickly in the air fryer. Maybe he could be coaxed to eat a slice or two.

While she waited on the microwave and the coffeepot, she looked around her at a room full of memories, good memories. The white-painted cabinets that had begun to dull with age. The ceramic tile countertops, also white, that her father had installed so many years ago. Artie's reluctance to change anything had good reasons. Emotional reasons, not only for herself but for her father, as well.

Focusing on happy memories was good. At least for a while. Her most recent memories needed to be buried in the deepest darkest hole she could find.

Except she knew they wouldn't be. One way or another she was going to have to wrap her mind around it all.

BOYD CONNOR HAD learned something about Artie Jackson in the brief time he had known her. She was forceful, prickly. Something bad had happened to her before she picked him up.

Then there was her father. Boyd didn't need a road map to see what was happening there. A huge grief for her. He was familiar with grief.

He dropped his backpack on the floor by the sofa and sat. Understandably, Artie hadn't wanted him in her kitchen. He was already encroaching enough and he didn't feel good about it. Maybe he should have chosen the holding cell after all.

She was a pretty woman with inky hair bobbed to her shoulders, and bright blue eyes. A heart-shaped face. And as she'd doffed her jacket he'd seen a good figure despite the gun belt around her hips. Other than the baton, the gun belt was gone now, a brave decision considering she'd invited a total stranger into her home. He felt a flicker of admiration for her.

The two of them ate at her dinette in the kitchen, served out of the containers as she'd warned him. In the living room, in front of the TV, Herman Jackson ate garlic toast and accepted a cup of coffee.

Conversation at the table was limited. Artie evidently had things she didn't want to discuss. Boyd had plenty of things he didn't even want to *think* about.

He let the silence continue, giving them both space. Casual conversation seemed out of place.

But still, he felt the need to make some minor connection since she'd picked him up like a lost dog on the roadside.

"How long is this weather going to last?"

"Until winter is over." Then she raised her head. "They're predicting maybe three days. Then it'll take time to thoroughly clear the mountain roads to make them safe for trucks. So I can't say for sure. You in a hurry?"

A hurry to continue his own self-imposed penance? He supposed he could do that as well here for a few days as anywhere. But it wouldn't help with his fury and despair. Walking had been helping that. He didn't answer her.

He cleaned up what little there was from their dinner. Then Artie said, "I need your ID."

"It's in my pack. I'll get it." Not that she would find out very much. He didn't exactly have a big profile out there on the internet. The invisible man. He preferred it that way, especially now.

She took his driver's license and passport, then retrieved a laptop to place it on the kitchen table. She checked once more on her father, then said, "You might as well make yourself comfortable on the couch. You can take a shower after I get mine. If you want."

It had been a couple of days since his last truck stop shower. He definitely wanted another one, but using her bathroom seemed like a huge trespass. She hadn't needed to offer it.

Interesting woman, conflicting urges. A clear need to be left alone while extending the courtesy of her home. For the first time in a long time, he felt interested in something outside himself, outside his own family.

ARTIE WAS FRUSTRATED. So much for coming home, lighting a fire and drinking brandy.

But she had to learn about the stranger in her home. Her father was vulnerable even if she wasn't.

She logged into her departmental account and started the wheels spinning on a background check. Then she hit the web, searching for anything she could find. Very little was hidden on the web. There *had* to be something.

She burrowed in deeper and deeper until finding a small blurb that had been put out there by someone who was following people who'd served in a certain paratrooper regiment.

Master Sergeant Boyd L. Connor. Retired Army with disability. Three tours in Afghanistan. Maybe that alone was enough to make a man walk alone so far from anywhere. If indeed he was walking far. Clearly avoiding human interaction.

Well, if he had a record of any kind, the background check would turn it up. She closed the laptop and returned to the living room to give Boyd his ID. And now, given his background, she felt a bit foolish for having told him she wasn't worried about him being in her house because she had her police equipment and tae kwon do. This guy probably exceeded her own experience with self-protection.

"Find anything?" he asked as he tucked his papers away.

"You're the invisible man."

Again a smile flitted across his face. "Hard to do these days."

"I'll have your background check sometime tomorrow."

Then she bent to light the fire already laid on the fireplace. She didn't ask Boyd if he minded. He sat on the couch, staying out of the way. Good.

Then she poured herself the long-awaited brandy and flopped on the second recliner. Cartoons still played on the TV. She didn't offer to give Boyd brandy, but eventually awareness of her own rudeness stirred her. "If you want some brandy, help yourself."

"I'm fine, thanks."

Another man who was *fine*. God, she was getting sick of that word.

The crackling fire cast a soothing glow through the room along with some dancing shadows. Between it and the brandy she began to uncoil. It wouldn't last, but she would take what she could get.

But now she felt her own bruises, becoming more painful as they spread. Ice, she should ice them. Hell, no. She didn't need the chill. The internal chill already felt bone deep. Ibuprofen. Later.

Eventually she saw that her dad was dozing. Smothering a sigh, she rose, trying not to wince. She went to him and touched his shoulder. His eyes opened.

"Dad, it's time to go to bed."

He nodded and closed the recliner, sitting up.

"You can take care of your teeth and pajamas, right?"

"Yeah. You know I can, for Pete's sake."

But she knew she'd have to check on him anyway. He could forget between one task and another. Not always. It wasn't that bad yet. But it was headed that way like a freight train rolling down the tracks.

"Teeth first," she reminded him. "Then pajamas."

"I *know* that," he snapped.

Another part of this disease she hated, the times he grew angry when reminded about his memory. The times he grew frustrated when he realized he couldn't remember. One stressor after another.

All of it worthwhile. This was the man who had cared for her when she was a child. Now the shoe was on the other foot and he deserved every bit of care she could provide.

She peeked in after he disappeared into the bathroom. His teeth were getting cleaned. Then she peeked in when he'd been in the bedroom for a while. He slept in his pajamas beneath a comforter. All was well. For a while.

She grabbed some ibuprofen from the medicine chest and,

back in the living room, swallowed them with brandy. She kept trying to turn her thoughts away from earlier events. She knew beyond any shadow of a doubt that they were going to haunt her for a long time.

The phone rang, dragging her back into the middle of her mental and emotional mess. It was Gage Dalton, the sheriff.

"Hi, Artie," he said.

"Give me no bad news, Gage."

"It's not *bad* news. You know the regulations. Don't report for duty tomorrow. We have to put you on leave with pay until the psychologist clears you."

Everything inside Artie clenched. Weren't things already bad enough? "But, Gage, I need to work. I *need* to keep busy. I can do office work!"

"You know the rules," he repeated. "They're the same for everyone. You had a violent confrontation that left you physically battered."

"But how soon will I see a damn psychologist?"

"As fast as we can arrange it. I promise. In the meantime, look after yourself. And your father."

She disconnected without another word, becoming suddenly aware of Boyd's eyes on her.

"It must have been bad," was all he said.

"Bad enough," she answered shortly. "But I could still work."

He didn't answer for a moment, then said, "I know how bad it can get. Take the time. That's what I'm doing."

Which probably said a whole lot, she thought almost bitterly.

"Have another brandy. Kick back and relax as much as you can."

He had no right to advise her, but she didn't want the effort of telling him off.

"There doesn't seem to be anything else I can do." Then she flipped off the TV, sick to death of cartoons. Sick to death of what they meant about her father's mental state.

Sick to death of herself.

Chapter Two

Artie had gotten her shower; Boyd had followed her a few minutes later. At last, wrapped in her pajamas and a thick black robe, she settled on the second recliner with another snifter of brandy and put her feet up. Her baton remained close beside her, just in case. Outside the wind keened.

Boyd stretched out on the couch, wearing an old gray fleece sweat suit. She ought to get him a blanket. Hunt up a pillow. Well, he could ask if he wanted them. She was in no mood to wait on him.

Feet up on one arm at the end of the sofa, head pillowed on the other arm, he didn't look as if he could be terribly comfortable. Regardless, she heard him fall into the slow breathing of sleep.

Good for him. She wondered if she'd ever sleep again.

She didn't want to close her eyes. It was easier and safer to watch the flames dance. Not that it erased the images that had stamped themselves indelibly in her mind.

God! She didn't know what bothered her more, the images of that man attacking his wife or the feeling of her baton landing on flesh with sickening thuds.

She'd become violent, maybe as violent as that beast. Justification didn't matter.

Violence. Her own violence. A part of her she'd never suspected existed to that degree.

Billy Lauer, having beaten his wife half to death, was trying to steal the last of her life with his hands around her throat. Wouldn't stop even when Artie shouted at him and waved her pistol.

A pistol she didn't dare shoot because he was so close to his wife. Because the bullet could have pierced walls and wounded or killed innocent people on the other side of them.

She'd had no choice, but that didn't make her feel better about herself. Not even a little bit.

Maybe Gage was right about her needing some time off, some time to work through this.

Because, sure as hell, she didn't know if she could trust herself to use necessary force again. Hesitation on her part could cost a life, a colleague's. Her own.

So it was more than internal self-loathing she had to deal with. She had to deal with trusting herself.

Slowly, despite everything, she fell into uneasy sleep. She didn't resist it. Tomorrow would come and all the problems would still be there.

BOYD WOKE DURING the night and saw Artie sleeping on the recliner. The orange glow of the fire danced over her face and he could tell she was sleeping restlessly. What the hell had happened to her?

Not that it was any of his business. Not that he should care. But the look on her face when she'd picked him up had told an ugly story of some kind.

Moving quietly, he went to the bathroom, then peeked out the curtains. The storm had reached full fury, making it almost impossible to see the house next door. In the distance he heard a struggling snowplow, probably almost useless. Primary roads, though, had to be cleared as much as possible for emergencies, even if the task was thankless.

As much as he'd wanted to keep walking, he was grateful that Artie had given him shelter. He could have survived the elements—he'd done so before—but he was thankful he didn't need to.

In the kitchen, he filled a glass with water and sat at the dinette. He didn't sleep well as a rule. Nightmares followed him even into the deepest sleep, rousing him with either panic or fury. Or despair.

He stared at the kitchen window, which gave him a view of the storm's anger, and recognized himself in that wild fury. Because that's what part of him had become. Guilt heaped itself on top of the anger, and his own failure crowned the entire mess. Somewhere inside was a heart that wouldn't stop breaking. It was a freaking wonder that he could still breathe.

Purpose alone kept him moving. He had to get to his daughter. If she'd even see him.

But that was another thing he tried not to think about even though it plagued him constantly.

Briefly, the storm lessened. Flakes glittering in the light through the kitchen window grew larger, gentler, as they feathered their way to the ground.

Maybe he wouldn't be trapped here much longer. Except that all too soon the ferocity returned. Nature venting herself on the world. Teaching lessons about the insignificance of man and animal.

He tried to focus his attention on the problems this storm would cause ranchers or people trying to travel. Like the truckers, always on a tight schedule.

It didn't help. His concern for people had been ripped

away a while ago. Recent events had only hardened the disgust he felt. Not only with them but with himself.

Then there was the cop sleeping in the next room. Whatever had upset her so much that her boss wanted her to see a psychologist hadn't prevented her from stopping to pick him up to save him from the weather. A good soul, whatever she might be feeling. Prickly, angry, but good.

Her father. A man clearly suffering from dementia or Alzheimer's. A man she looked after despite everything else on her plate. A man she deeply loved. That had been apparent even in such a short time, even when Herman snapped at her.

Hard to deal with. Devastating for her. Boyd wondered how bad it had gotten for the two of them.

Then he heard the TV switch on. Rising, he went to look and saw that Herman had returned to his recliner. A weather channel occupied the screen. He hoped it didn't wake Artie.

Herman sat in his recliner, wearing his light blue pajamas and slippers. He didn't look like an old man, rather appeared as if he were in his midsixties. Unshaven face, but he was still good-looking even if his face was lined with age. A thick shock of gray hair. He might have appealed to women of almost any age.

But Boyd was concerned about the TV waking Artie. As restless as she had been, she wasn't getting very good sleep and she needed every decent minute she could find.

He had an idea. Entering the room quietly, he walked around until he could squat facing Herman.

"Herman," he said quietly.

The man looked at him.

"Artie's sleeping. Why don't you come to the kitchen with me and we'll have some cocoa or something. How's that sound?"

"Boyd." Herman's eyes suddenly brightened with full intelligence. He looked toward Artie. At once he clicked the TV off. Then he eyed Boyd.

"Cocoa sounds good."

"Let's go, then."

Herman closed the recliner and followed Boyd into the kitchen where he sat at the table.

Boyd spoke. "Where do I find the stuff to make the cocoa?"

"Artie uses the packets. In the pantry. I'll get them."

Boyd waited while Herman rose and opened the large pantry. He emerged a half minute later with a box of instant cocoa packets.

"I'll make it," Herman said.

So Boyd sat at the table, watching. Herman filled the induction carafe that fit on its own coil and started it boiling. Coffee mugs. Packets opened and emptied into the mugs. Herman might have forgotten some things, but he hadn't forgotten this.

Soon enough they sat across the table with hot mugs of cocoa before them. Boyd stirred his absently, wondering what he could talk to Herman about, needing to fill this man's silence with something positive.

"Artie worries about me too much," Herman said eventually. "I'm losing some of my memory, but I'm not that bad yet."

"I see that. So your memory? You're aware of it?"

"Sometimes. I can remember the past all right. It's stuff that happened a few days ago that gives me trouble."

Boyd nodded and sipped cocoa. "That must be tough."

Herman shrugged. "What you can't remember doesn't hurt you. But sometimes I forget important stuff."

That would probably bother Artie more than anything, Boyd thought. "Artie mentioned Clara. Is she your friend?"

Herman sipped more cocoa, then nodded. "We been friends for a long, long time. Always lived next door to each other. She's a widow. Like me."

Boyd drained his mug, then said, "So Clara brought you dinner tonight?"

"Yep. She does that when Artie has to work. Or we have dinner together. And sometimes all three of us eat together."

"That sounds nice."

Herman smiled. "Better than nice. Clara's a lot of fun. Got two good grandkids, too. Good boys."

Grandkids. Clearly Herman didn't have any, and Boyd wondered if that weighed on him. "Do you want grand-kids, too?"

Herman shrugged. "Artie don't have time right now. Too much with her job and me."

"I don't think she feels you're a job."

Herman's smile faded. "Maybe not. But I still make work for her. Not too much yet, I don't think."

Boyd had no answer for that. How could he? But he was starting to feel sorry for this man who was fading mentally and knew it. A man who seemed to feel that he was becom-ing a burden on his daughter.

The wall clock over the sink said dawn was approach-ing, although with this weather Boyd didn't think they'd get much light for hours yet.

"Some storm," Herman remarked. "We get a bad one or two every winter, but usually it's okay. When the snow is dry, it blows for days, though. Big drifts from only a little snow."

At that moment, Artie entered the kitchen, yawning and rubbing her eyes. "You guys having a party without me?"

"Might could be," her father answered with a broad smile. "Want some cocoa?"

"Thanks, Dad, but I really want coffee. Lots and lots of coffee."

"That's my Artie. Just like her mom."

Artie hesitated, but only for an instant. A hesitation so slight that eyes other than Boyd's might have missed it. Was she still pained by the loss of her mother? Or was it something else?

His gaze followed her as she yawned again and made coffee. While the pot hissed and burbled, she leaned back against the counter, folding her arms.

Herman spoke. "Tell me you don't have to go out in this storm."

One corner of Artie's mouth lifted. "Not today, Dad."

"Then I don't have to worry." Herman looked at his mug. "Guess I want more cocoa."

"I'll make it," she answered. "I'm just standing around waiting on the coffee. You ever think about how much time we stand around waiting?"

"Never did," Herman answered.

"There's different kinds of waiting," Boyd answered. Like waiting for his daughter to be willing to see him. "Sometimes waiting is all you can do."

Artie nodded and filled the glass carafe again. The box of cocoa still stood on the counter where Herman had left it. "You want some cocoa, too, Boyd?"

"Sounds good, if you don't mind."

Her response was dry. "It is *ever* so much more work to make a second cup. I mean, I'll have to tear open another packet."

That brought a chuckle out of Herman, and Boyd saw

Artie's face brighten at the sound. The love between the two was palpable.

Herman spoke. "It'll kill you, won't it?"

"Just about," Artie answered as she took the mugs to the counter with her and emptied packets into them. The induction carafe heated the water in about the time it took the coffee maker to finish brewing.

"Looks wicked out there," she remarked as she brought the cocoa and coffee to the table. She joined them, sitting slightly closer to her father than to Boyd. Hardly surprising. What *was* surprising was that she was being so courteous to him, especially since she probably wanted him hanging around about as much as she wanted a wood sliver under a fingernail.

He was well and truly stuck here, however. After the way she had picked him off the roadside, he suspected that if he tried to leave now that baton of hers might bar his way. Or she might call for backup as she had threatened to last night.

The memory brought an almost-smile to his face. To muscles that had forgotten how to smile. Muscles that had become as frozen as the world outside.

Artie spoke. "How's Clara doing, Dad? I haven't seen her in a few days."

"She's fine," Herman answered.

"Always fine," Artie murmured, her gaze drifting away. Then she appeared to shake herself. "I'll check on her later. Make sure she's all set for this weather."

Herman turned his head. "You *know* she's ready for this, Artie. Lived here all her life."

Artie sighed. "I'm sure you're right, but neighbors check on neighbors, don't they?"

Herman nodded. "Always."

"Right. And it's your fault for teaching me that."

Herman laughed. "Okay, okay. Guess I taught you some things right."

"More than a few. Like you told me once, it was your job to get me to the age of eighteen alive."

Herman snorted. "I said that?"

"You know you did. And look at me. I'm nearly thirty and I'm still alive, so you did good."

"Never got the risk taker out of you, though."

Artie tilted her head. "Did you really want to?"

"Hell, no. Like your granddad used to say, *Kids are born with personalities. All you can do is dent them a little to get them in shape.*"

"I remember that," she replied. "Except the only denting you ever did to me was to raise your voice. Right through the roof."

"Got your attention, didn't I?" Herman's smile remained. "I never wanted to change you, girl. Just screw your head on a little tighter."

Father and daughter exchanged looks that once again broadcast a deep mutual love.

Boyd shifted slightly, knowing he was an intruder. But where could he go? He also hated the feeling that he was like a kid outside a candy store window, unable to experience the warmth of this kind of family. Knowing he never really had.

Herman fell silent, drifting away a bit. Artie frowned faintly when he said, "I think I'll go watch my shows now."

Then, without another word, he rose from the table. Artie watched him go, sorrow slipping across her face.

Boyd, perfectly aware he didn't have the right, asked anyway, "How bad is it?"

Her blue eyes sharpened as she looked at him. "What concern of yours is it?"

"Only that it's in front of me." That was all he could say when she had every right to resent his prying.

After a few beats, she rose and poured herself more coffee. "It's episodic," she answered finally. "For a long time I wasn't even sure it was more than ordinary forgetfulness. Apparently it is."

"Hard on you both."

"Goes without saying." She resumed her seat at the dinette but didn't look at him. She had gone to some dark place inside herself. There wasn't a damn thing he could do about that.

From the living room came the sound of voices. A weather program maybe? It didn't sound like cartoons.

Artie closed her eyes and Boyd suspected that in those voices she heard the future she couldn't prevent.

Life sucks, he thought. The question was whether it ever stopped sucking.

Chapter Three

Eventually gray light appeared, but the storm continued angrily. Artie checked the clock, then picked up her phone and stood looking out the front window while she called Clara.

"Hey, Clara, it's Artie. Thanks for bringing Dad his dinner last night."

Clara's warm voice answered her. "Never a problem, Artie. You know that. That old man and I have some good times together. Does he need me today?"

"I'll be here all day. Mainly I called to see if you were okay for the storm or if you wanted to come over here."

Clara laughed. "I'm okay. I always make sure I have plenty of stores on hand. I'm all bundled up in my fleece, looking at a nice fire. You need anything?"

"We're all set." Artie hesitated. "Do you want to spend the day here?"

Herman surfaced from the TV long enough to say, "Where you gonna put her, Artie, with Boyd here?"

Artie closed her eyes. *Oh, Dad.*

"I can leave," Boyd said quietly.

"Don't even think about it," Artie snapped. "I didn't rescue your butt to watch you leave and freeze it off!"

A long pause. Then Clara asked tentatively, "Is something wrong? What is Herman talking about?"

Artie drew a deep breath. This was going to sound stupid, she thought, but there it was. "I rescued a hiker alongside the road last night. The motel is full so he's here."

Artie could almost hear Clara chewing her lip. Finally the woman spoke. "Is that wise?"

"Was there a choice?"

"I guess not. Just as long as you and Herman are safe."

"We are," Artie answered with more confidence that she actually felt. She still didn't know diddly about Boyd Connor except he'd been in the Army. Thus far, however, he seemed harmless. "Anyway, I called about *you*."

"I'm really okay. I have my books, my fire and my food."

"You'll let me know, though? If you need anything?"

"Hell, yes. And the same goes for you and Herman. Call me every now and then, though. Put my mind at ease."

Artie agreed and disconnected. Then she turned to face the two men. Herman on his recliner, Boyd perched on the couch. The small house suddenly felt crowded.

"I guess I should make breakfast," she said. "We've all got to be hungry."

Boyd rose at once. "Tell me what you want. I'll do the cooking."

Artie looked at him. "You cook?"

One corner of his mouth lifted. "I can clean to white-glove standards, too. Just point me."

Despite herself, Artie felt amused. "Where'd you learn all that?"

His faced shadowed. "Once upon a time I took basic training. Once upon a time I had a family."

Then he rose and headed for the kitchen. "What's the menu?"

Artie stared after him. Once upon a time he'd had a family? She had the distinct feeling that that wasn't a happy story at all.

Nor did she want to hear it. Strangers passing like ships in the night. No involvement needed.

Besides, right now she didn't want to get involved with anyone or anything. She had a serious mental mess of her own she had to find a way to climb out of.

Like quicksand, the memories of yesterday kept pulling her down.

Herman spoke, his gaze still trained on the TV. "I told you Clara was fine."

Yes, he had. Just like he was always *fine*. She sometimes wondered how often her dad meant that, and how often he said it just to soothe her.

She supposed she'd never know.

WHILE COOKING WAS not Boyd's favorite thing, he was glad to be doing it. An unwanted guest in this house, he needed to do more than take up a couch and eat the Jacksons' food. He sure as hell didn't want to be waited on.

Artie pointed out the bacon, eggs, bread. Asked if he knew how to use the air fryer for toast and ran him through a brief lesson. Then she vanished, saying she needed to dress.

Boyd let go of the slight tension that had troubled him since he'd been forced into this woman's life. *Force* was a good word for it, too. He didn't doubt she would have called for backup if he'd refused to come with her last night. Not a doubt in the world. She seemed to have a backbone of steel.

Not that she'd been wrong to insist he come with her. She couldn't know that he'd survived similar conditions in the past. He would have made it through, however uncomfortably.

But being comfortable wasn't part of his life. Not during much of his past, and certainly not now.

He thought of his daughter, Linda, and his heart squeezed until it hurt. He deserved her feelings about him, but Linda didn't deserve what had happened to her. Then fury began to replace pain. The urge to kill had never been personal for him in the past, but it was now. He wanted to kill those who had raped his daughter.

Get a grip. Make breakfast. Be useful to someone.

It was an easy breakfast. A good thing, because he was no chef. But it *was* a meal he'd made for himself plenty of times in the past, and more recently since leaving the Army. He'd always believed that bacon topped the list of comfort foods.

Although comfort had left him in the dust, even with food.

While the bacon was sizzling on the frying pan, he poked his head into the living room. "How do you guys want your eggs?"

"Scrambled," Herman answered promptly. "Artie, too. Sometimes she puts cheese in them."

Cheese? Boyd went back to look in the fridge and found a bag of shredded cheddar. That would do.

He turned the bacon and cracked eggs into a chipped stoneware bowl. Two apiece plus one for the pot as they said. Then he shook his head and threw in a couple of extra eggs. He'd finish any leftovers. All that walking had given him the appetite of a stevedore.

Of course, that might mean he would leave Artie and Herman short on food. He shook his head, sighed and continued. If necessary he could hike through these conditions to the grocery.

He knew his own abilities and limits intimately. He'd had plenty of opportunities to learn.

He was on the second load of bacon, the whipped eggs waiting for their turn. He needed to start making the toast with the loaf of rye Artie had put out. The butter was on a plate nearby. Utensils and dishes easy to find. Another pot of coffee brewing. At least he hadn't forgotten how to time everything.

Artie appeared, wearing jeans, a blue fleece pullover and warm-looking slippers. "How's it going, Boyd?"

"For once everything is going according to plan. But I guess I should knock on wood for saying that."

A small laugh escaped her. "What's that saying? Life is what happens when you're making other plans?"

"I'd guess you know all about that."

She didn't answer. "Want any help?"

Boyd shook his head. "You relax and let me be useful. God knows I need it."

The sound of the TV still issued from the living room. Was that all that Herman had to occupy him? Sad.

Artie sat at the dinette watching him. "What did you mean when I asked where you were going?"

"Huh?" He glanced at her as he used a fork to scoop strips of bacon onto a paper towel.

"You said you were going the next mile."

Hell, he thought. How to explain that while revealing very little of his private demons? "Where do you want me to drain the excess bacon grease?"

"See that small white container near the stove? I keep it there for later use."

He snapped the lid off and tipped the frying pan, watching the grease pour into the container. "Good idea."

"And you're not answering my question."

A cop. He should have known she wouldn't let him slide past it. "I decided to walk from North Carolina to Washington state."

The toaster dinged. He set the pan on a cold burner, waiting for the temperature to reduce for the eggs, and turned to start another round of toast and to butter the current four slices.

"Why?" Artie asked. Inevitably, he thought.

"Because it seemed like the best way to deal with myself, okay?"

Boyd hadn't meant the words to sound harsh, but that's how they emerged. At least she didn't come back at him, questioning him more closely. Although to be honest about it, she had every right to know more about a stranger she'd brought into her home.

He diverted, returning to the current situation. A much safer topic than himself. "Any chance that motel might have a room today?" he asked.

She nodded toward the window. "What do you think? I'll call, but don't expect any escape, not today."

He began to scramble the eggs in the frying pan, topped by a layer of shredded cheese that melted into them. "It's not that I'm not grateful for your hospitality, because I am."

"But it's uncomfortable for all of us," she replied. "I get it. We'll just have to jolt along as best we can."

He stirred the eggs some more, keeping them from browning as they set up. "What happened yesterday?" he asked, even though it was none of his business. "Must have been bad."

She didn't answer until he started to scoop eggs onto the plates. "The worst case of domestic violence I've ever seen."

There was more, he was sure. "Want to get Herman? Or does he eat out there?"

"I'll ask him." She rose.

He pulled the last pieces of toast from the oven and slathered them with butter. Only then did it occur to him that not everyone here might like buttered toast. Oh, well.

Artie returned with Herman, who took his place. She brought out a jar of raspberry jam from the fridge and put it on the table, along with paper napkins. Soon the three of them made a triangle at the dinette.

Herman wasted no time diving in.

Artie politely commented on how good the eggs tasted. The bacon was perfectly done.

Idle chat because neither of them would move past it.

Sewed up tight in their own private hells, he thought. Well, they'd deal with silence today. Maybe one more day. They'd all survive it.

ARTIE WANTED TO do the dishes, but Boyd insisted he'd clean up. Taking the opportunity, she went to her bedroom and, sitting on her bed, opened her laptop again. At least the storm didn't appear to be interfering with the internet.

An answer had come from the office: Boyd had no record, no priors, no nothing. Prints showed he'd been in the Army until recently. The department had sniffed out that until two months ago he'd been employed at a construction company.

Not even a traffic ticket? The man was clean, maybe too clean, but records traced him all the way back to a birth certificate thirty-eight years ago.

Well, maybe he *was* clean as a whistle. Still, she didn't like his opacity. The guy was walking like this for a reason. His years at war? That was entirely possible.

Deciding she could look no further, she logged out of the department's connection.

Then she leaned back on her elbows and stared into empty space. She didn't want to be alone, she realized. She didn't want to let her thoughts keep spiraling around with only one destination. She wanted to be working, to be busy.

Except that she knew Gage was right, that she needed

time to find the person she had buried late yesterday, to learn to live with the person she had discovered herself to be.

Her own actions kept her from taking any pride in saving the Lauer woman's life. Necessary actions to be sure, but they disturbed her deeply.

The only bruises weren't the ones on her body, that was for sure.

The wind still keened like a banshee. She didn't need to pull back the heavy curtains on her bedroom window to know the storm was still enjoying itself at a huge cost out there. She didn't need to look to know that it was unlikely she'd have even been able to patrol today. No, she would have been called out only if something bad happened, and she couldn't face another bad thing yet.

So what was she supposed to do? Anyone who thought stewing around inside your own head, while waiting for a psychologist to supposedly clean up the mess, was nuts.

But maybe diversion wasn't a good thing, either. Sooner or later she would have to face it.

Quietly growling, she sat up and tried to figure out what to do with this day. A stranger in her living room might have been a distraction, but he seemed as disinclined to talk as she was.

Not cool. He needed to tell her more about himself. Something other than that he'd taken it into his head to walk across the country. Talk about strange. People only did that when they were fundraising. To get headlines and TV coverage.

Boyd Connor did not strike her as someone who wanted any kind of attention. He was marching off something mile after mile. That backpack of his was carrying more than supplies.

She thought of her dad again, thought about how his life must seem to him now. He knew he was losing his memory, an awful thing to know. But on days like this, he couldn't seek activity at the senior center in the basement of Good Shepherd Church. He couldn't meet up with friends to pass the time with card games and conversation and endless coffee. He was stuck in this house with only the TV.

For a man who had been active all of his life, a man who had never been fond of watching TV except in brief spurts, this must feel like hell.

"Damn!" The word escaped her explosively and she jumped up.

Three people trapped by a storm that didn't show any sign of blowing itself out. One was a stranger.

Heck, she thought with an unexpected burst of amusement, didn't that sound like a plot for a movie?

Just as long as none of them stepped out into that blizzard to meet an axe killer.

Finally a laugh escaped her.

She was going to be okay.

ALTHOUGH BY EARLY AFTERNOON, she began to wonder if they *all* would be okay. Her dad started pacing the house restlessly. He was a man who needed physical activity, and sitting in front of the TV wasn't cutting it.

Artie watched him pace and wondered how many times he had paced for hours while she was at work, hours during which he might not have gone to the senior center for some reason. Maybe he sometimes forgot about going.

Realizing that neither she nor her father could be certain of his memory was a downer. More than once she'd thought about cutting off the gas to the stove because he might turn it on to make oatmeal or something else, then forget he had turned it on.

She *thought* he was used to using the induction coil, the air fryer, the coffeepot. But what if they slipped his memory, too?

Maybe she should scrape together the money to get an induction stove. At least it was less likely to cause a serious problem.

Damn it all. Worry forever nibbled at the edges of her mind but she wasn't ready to put her dad in a facility far away. It wasn't as if there was one near Conard City. Making time to visit him would be tough by itself. And tearing him out of his home, the only house he'd ever lived in, might nearly kill him. It sure wouldn't make him happy.

He might even feel abandoned. Nor was his state bad enough to justify such a thing. No, she'd just have to keep on worrying about him and hoping he didn't deteriorate too fast or too much.

Home care? Maybe. If he could tolerate having someone to watch him all the time Artie was working.

Clara was a lifesaver, though. The two of them got on like a house on fire. The time they spent together plainly cheered Herman up. Clara seemed to enjoy it, too.

So she watched her father pace. Then Boyd took over part of the floor and began to do push-ups and squats. He clearly wasn't used to all this sitting, either.

Artie felt no urge to join them in the activity. Everything inside her felt drained, as if someone had pulled the plug.

Her dad, however, chuckled as he stepped around Boyd, who was busy working up a good sweat. He even teased the stranger in their midst. Artie couldn't help smiling when her father accused Boyd of being a masochist.

"That's one good word for it," Boyd retorted. "The other thing is I'm no layabout. Gotta keep moving."

Always moving, Artie thought, wondering about him again.

When the two men settled, Artie brought out a folding table and a pack of cards. Mental stimulation for her father. Distraction for her and Boyd.

Briefly the blizzard eased, but before hope of its end grew too much, it resumed blowing. Artie cussed as she heard the keening renew.

"Have you checked the motel for me?" Boyd asked quietly.

"Not yet. It'd be pointless anyway. As soon as the plows move through, the snow fills the roads again. We'd just get stuck out there trying to cross town. Only a fool would leave the La-Z-Rest while this is going on. How far would they make it out of town? Half a mile?"

She dealt another hand of cards and realized she hadn't been paying close enough attention to remember what game they were playing. In a moment of wryness, she wondered if her memory was going, too.

Then her cell rang. Hoping for word that she could hike her way into the office and answer phones or something, that one of the deputies with a plow on the front of his Suburban might show up to take her to work, she knew before she answered that no such word was about to arrive. The departmental vehicles with plows would be out in more distant areas to handle emergencies.

The voice she heard was unfamiliar.

"You're gonna get yours, Deputy. Better watch your back."

Then the caller disconnected. She checked her recent calls, but this one was labeled Unknown.

"What?" Boyd asked.

She hesitated, then answered truthfully, "I think it was a threat." Then she shrugged. "I've had them before. No biggie."

Except she'd never had one over the phone. All the other threats had come in the middle of an episode, like a bar fight out at one of the roadhouses. A chill crept through her scalp and neck. Watch her back?

As if anyone could threaten her in this blizzard, she reminded herself. She pushed the threat aside and returned to the card game. Some bully. Bullies talked tough but seldom acted because they were cowards at heart.

Nothing to worry about. Hell, she didn't need one more damn thing to worry about.

FROM WHAT HE'D seen briefly in Artie's expression, Boyd knew she was more disturbed by the call than she was admitting. He wanted to know exactly what was said but couldn't ask.

In some ways this current situation was more than uncomfortable: it was annoying.

Herman, studying his cards, said, "Artie's name is special."

"Oh, Dad." Artie sighed.

"No, it's special. Your mom chose it specially." He lifted his gaze and looked at Boyd. "Letitia, my wife, had a thing for Greek mythology. I swear she could rattle off the entire pantheon without taking a breath. Could tell you what all the gods and goddesses represented."

"She could," Artie agreed. "She did it from time to time."

Herman smiled, his gaze growing distant with memory.

"A smart woman, well read. She was always on me because I didn't read much."

"Because you were too busy as a mechanic," Artie said. "She always made you use that special soap."

"Three times at least. She wanted clean towels." Herman chuckled. "Had to use shop rags until she thought I was clean enough to use the good towels."

"And you complained every time."

Herman looked at her. "A working man gets dirty hands. Goes with the job."

"True." Artie folded her cards, clearly quitting the game.

Boyd spoke. "Letitia sounds like a wonderful woman."

Herman nodded. "She was. Always gentle. I can't figure out where Artie got her bristles and steel from."

"From you, Dad," she answered dryly. "Where else? But don't forget Mom had a strong backbone. She stood up to you, didn't she?"

Herman grinned. "That, too." Then he shook his head and proved he didn't forget everything that happened just minutes ago. "But Artie's name. Care to hear, Boyd?"

"Absolutely," Boyd said with a glance at Artie. "Unless she objects."

"Gonna tell you anyway. Letitia picked the name *Artemis*. Artie here has been spending most of her life trying not to use it. I think she hates that it's on her driver's license."

Artie sighed. "I don't hate it. It's just strange."

Boyd started to smile. "I like it. So, Herman, who was Artemis?"

"I'll never forget *that*," Herman answered. "Among other things, she was the huntress, the protector of nature. Figure how that goes together."

Artie clearly gave up. "Mom said that different towns

and villages added traits to the gods and goddesses they
most liked."

"That's right. I remember now." Herman nodded. "Anyway, she thought it was perfect for you, and I think she
was right."

"Why?" Artie asked. "Do you think I wouldn't be me if
she'd chosen another name?"

Herman laughed out loud. To his amazement, Boyd felt a
grin on his own face. These two could be a trip. Even Artie
had started to smile.

"Okay, I'm me," she said. "And the Romans stole Artemis and turned her into Diana. Why didn't Mom choose that
name? It would have been easier to live with."

"Because Artemis was also the protector of animals, children and childbirth. I think she hoped you'd become a protector. And you did, didn't you?"

Artie didn't answer. Her face darkened. What was going
on? Boyd wondered. Something about yesterday, whatever
was troubling her? Something to do with being a protector?

Herman spoke again. "There's one trait I don't think your
mom wanted you to have, though."

"Which is?"

Herman eyed her, then dropped a bomb. "Artemis was
the goddess of virginity."

For endless seconds, except for the storm outside, you
could have heard a pin drop. Boyd wished he could remove
himself somehow. Make a quick bathroom call? Where had
that statement come from and why had Herman mentioned
it in front of him?

Artie sure as hell wished he'd kept his mouth shut. It was
written all over her.

When she spoke, she kept her voice level. "Well, Dad,
you don't have to worry about *that*."

It grew so quiet again that a pin drop would have sounded like a thunderclap.

All of a sudden, Boyd wished he could laugh. *These two.* They were something else.

Chapter Four

Dinnertime approached eventually. Artie wondered why she'd let her dad get her goat, but he sometimes had a way of doing that. The worst part was that she'd let him. And in front of Boyd. Why hadn't she just let it go?

Well, she hadn't. Her answer had flopped out there in a moment of annoyance and there it sat. Boyd Connor must be wondering if she was nuts.

Maybe she was headed that way. Especially after yesterday. She could feel the hair trigger of her emotions and had probably pulled it with that stupid announcement.

She hated to admit it, but Gage was probably right in not letting her come back to work yet. If she could respond to her *father* that way, simply because he'd irritated her, she shouldn't be driving around the county with a loaded Glock.

Hell, she was apparently loaded herself. Like a cocked pistol.

Pawing around in the pantry, looking for something to make dinner for the three of them, she paused a moment.

Nothing quick, she decided. The longer it took her to cook, the longer she could avoid her big faux pas. The gaze of a near stranger who didn't need to know such things about her. Oh, what was she thinking anyway? Boyd didn't need to know it, but he'd be leaving as soon as he could. It was her *dad* who didn't need to know that. For once, she hoped his memory problems would come to her rescue.

Leaning her head against a shelf, she knew she had to get a grip. Then there was Boyd. She could feel his desire to get on the move again. Whatever was tugging him along his trek wasn't easing any now because he was trapped by nature.

What the hell had happened to him anyway? What was *his* story?

She was used to living in an area where she knew most people and had all her life. Some acquaintances were just that, acquaintances. Some were people she wished she'd never had to meet, but they were a decided minority.

Regardless, she had a story of some kind or another about nearly everyone. Their families. Their troubles, their concerns, even their fears. The point was, she knew about them.

Now here she was with a man she knew almost nothing about, a man whose story was opaque to her, and she was uncomfortable with that. The guy didn't have any kind of pigeonhole.

It wasn't as if strangers never came to Conard County. They did, of course. Many stayed long enough that their stories became known. Others moved on so fast it didn't matter.

But never had she taken in a true stranger. Never brought one into her home. So naturally she was uneasy.

Sighing, she straightened and started scanning shelves again. She had plenty of food stocked in her upright freezer on the mudroom, stocked against bad weather, or times when running to the grocery became difficult. She also had plenty of dry goods in her pantry. Cooking wasn't her favorite thing, but she could do it when Clara didn't run over to rescue her and her dad.

Only now she *had* to cook because she was damned if she was going to serve up frozen meals again. Because she needed to escape into a task that would require more than reading a label and punching buttons, or shoving it all into the oven to do the work for her.

Egad. How was she ever going to deal with her enforced leave from duty? But maybe it wouldn't be as bad when this blizzard blew itself out. At least she'd be able to get around, do things, see people.

A trickle of amusement came out of nowhere. And she thought Boyd was antsy? Look at her. Worse, look at her total self-preoccupation.

Sheesh.

She resumed her search but wasn't exactly thrilled with what she found. Okay, so it wasn't frozen meals, but the parts she'd have to put together would come mainly from boxes, like boxes of dried potatoes au gratin.

Suzy Homemaker she wasn't. Clean freak, yes, but chef, no.

Six cans of Spam? Seriously? Why so many? But she pulled one down anyway. Meat without thawing, which at this point in the day had become a requirement. Maybe she should thaw something for tomorrow?

Oh, heck, she thought, and put the Spam back on the shelf. Instead she got two boxes of red beans and rice, feeling certain she must have andouille sausage in the freezer to round it out. At least browning and slicing the sausage would require some of her degraded cooking skills. And a little time.

Was she really spending all this time thinking about cooking?

"Aagh," she groaned aloud. Was she coming to this?

"Everything okay?" Boyd's voice came from behind her.

It bothered Artie that she hadn't heard him approach. It bothered her that she was still standing in the pantry with the boxes in her hands. In an enclosed space where she could easily become trapped. "Red beans and rice okay by you?" she asked instead of answering his question.

"That's great. What can I do to help?"

Put him to use, she decided. He probably needed something to do as much as she did. Maybe even more.

"There's a freezer in the mudroom. Could you check and find a package of andouille sausage?"

"You got it."

She carried the boxes back into the kitchen and pulled out her rice maker from a lower cabinet. Another convenience. Another thing to keep her from standing over a stove. Hah!

Boyd returned with the package of sausage. "Success," he said. "Now what?"

"I need to thaw that. Could you put it unopened in a bowl of cold water?" She nodded to the cupboard with the larger bowls. Her mother's mixing bowls, some stainless steel and others glass.

"The whole package?"

"Yeah. Thanks. It won't take long." And while that thawed she would have to wait to make the rice. Great. Back into the pantry, but this time she emerged more quickly, with a box of blueberry muffin mix. Although she always turned it into a quick bread because it was easier.

The sausage was thawing and Artie pulled out a loaf pan. How many times had she watched her mother spend a day making bread dough, then turning a wonderful loaf out of that pan?

She grabbed another mixing bowl and started.

The silence was getting heavy again, she thought, so she

spoke about something safe. "Do you know why I have to stand here adding eggs and other stuff to make a batter?"

He leaned back against the counter and folded his arms. "There's a reason?"

"Oh, yeah. My grandmother told me about it. Back when box cake mixes first appeared, all you had to do was add water. But the mix wasn't selling. Anyway, they finally figured out that women didn't feel like they were really baking when all the ingredients were already mixed. Success came when the companies altered the mixes so that anyone using them has to add eggs and oil and so on."

He tilted his head. "That's fascinating."

Artie merely shook her head. "It says something about women's roles at the time. Me, I'd be glad not to have to add anything but water."

Boyd chuckled, a pleasant sound. "I'd eat more baked goods if they were that easy to make."

While she was pouring the batter into the pan, he startled her with a question. "That phone call disturbed you, didn't it? But you say you get threats all the time."

She didn't want to answer. It seemed ridiculous to make a big deal out of a single phone call when she was perfectly able to look after herself. She answered anyway. No biggie, and she was getting tired of silences.

"Only that the threats I've received in the past have been in face-to-face confrontations. People get angry or drunk and say all kinds of things." She shrugged. "Just a bully wanting to make a point."

Boyd didn't reply immediately. It seemed to her that he frowned faintly. After a half minute or so he said, "I can see why that might be disturbing. I'd be disturbed."

Given his background, Artie doubted it. He'd faced bigger threats than a phone call. One call was meaningless.

Until the next one came. Right after dinner.

DINNER TURNED OUT OKAY. The browned sausage, sliced neatly into bite-sized pieces, added some wonderful flavor. She'd made extra because of Boyd and his healthy appetite. The meal went over well and she was glad to see her dad eat heartily. Sometimes he seemed to forget to eat at all unless someone put food right in front of him.

If not for Clara, Artie would have spent all her time at work worrying about him. Maybe she should check on Clara again. A glance out the window, however, warned her that trying to get Clara over here would be difficult and maybe dangerous. In that wind with these low temperatures, people could get frostbite or hypothermia fast, especially older people like Clara.

She sighed.

Her dad spoke, becoming aware of something besides his meal. "Artie? What's wrong?"

"Being stuck in a blizzard is all. You know I'm not good at staying inside."

Herman smiled. "Never were. I used to have to pull you out of that tree in the backyard to get you inside for bedtime." He turned to Boyd. "Quite the tomboy."

"Quite the woman," Artie retorted. "Just because I was a girl didn't mean I wanted to be inside cooking and sewing."

Herman laughed. Boyd smiled.

"Anyway," Artie continued, "don't let your sexism show."

That drew another laugh from Herman. "Feminism started with your mother."

"In this house anyway."

Herman's gaze drew distant with memory, but his

smile remained, although it had grown a bit sad. "I miss her, Artie."

"We both do," she answered quietly. Sorrow once again slipped into her heart.

"Sometimes I think she's going to walk back in the front door."

Artie stilled, wondering if he meant that literally or as a recognition of his grief. The former would be another step in the wrong direction. Man, this wondering was awful.

Then the landline rang. She looked up. Boyd looked at the phone. "Still have one of those landlines?" he asked.

"Cell towers out here aren't always reliable. The weather gets to them. But it has to be the sheriff. No one else has that number."

She rose, expecting to hear Gage Dalton's rough voice at the other end. Instead she heard a stranger.

"This is a warning," a male voice said. "We'll get you." Then he disconnected.

Okay. Now she couldn't dismiss the trickle of uneasiness that ran town her spine. Someone had gone to the trouble to get this phone number. Maybe someone serious. She closed her eyes briefly, trying to shake it off, then hurried to clear the table. *Keep busy.*

She might be stuck inside, but that didn't mean no one could get to her if they were determined enough. Her dad. She was more worried about him than herself, though. If someone tried to get into this house…

She couldn't complete the thought. She couldn't bear to. Images of herself running around to bar doors and check windows began to plague her.

She was not the type to worry excessively about her personal safety or she couldn't be in law enforcement. This was not the time to start, not because of two phone calls.

Boyd grabbed some of the remaining dishes and followed her to the sink with them. From the living room came the sound of the weather on TV.

"Another threat?" he asked quietly.

"Yeah. Meaningless."

She went back to get the last of the dishes, but Boyd forestalled her.

"I'll do the cleaning up, Artie. Least I can do. Go sit with your father."

And watch the unending, pointless broadcast.

It seemed to be enough for her father, though. He stared at the screen as if it were the most important thing in the world.

She wondered if he was trying to escape from his own condition or if he was really fascinated by that endless loop.

"How about a movie?" she asked him presently. "Something you want to see?"

"I want the Christmas tree."

"Okay," she answered promptly, although it was the last thing in the world that she wanted to do. "I'll get it out of the attic."

"And those acrylic ornaments Letitia likes so much?"

His use of the present tense was another thing to trouble her. "Of course," she answered. "They meant so much."

Herman nodded. "She'll like that."

Boyd spoke from the kitchen doorway. "Need some help with the attic?"

"If you wouldn't mind." Ordinarily she would have asked one of her friends to help get that big, long box down. Too awkward for one person. It was about the only help she ever needed, though.

Her phone rang again, this time her cell. She didn't want to answer it after the earlier calls, but it could be the office. Maybe they needed some help despite her being on leave.

But it was Guy Redwing, one of her colleagues. "How are you and your dad getting by right now?"

"We're doing well." She watched Boyd put another log on the fire. He seemed to have taken over that chore. "You guys need any help?"

Guy chuckled. "Just can't stay away, huh? But there's little enough we can do right now. I hate to tell you how many deputies are stuck around the county right now. We'd better not have an emergency."

"Fingers crossed."

Guy's voice, usually unrevealing, grew warm. "You call if you need anything. We're bedded down around the office now. I got five people I can send over if you need anyone."

"Where's Gage?"

"The place any sensible man would be. At home."

Despite herself, Artie laughed. "What about the rest of you?"

"We're all nuts. You call, hear?"

"I will," Artie promised. She thought about mentioning the phone calls, then decided against it. It wasn't good for Guy to be sending someone over, not in this messy weather. Besides, she could take care of herself.

And if Boyd was half the man she'd begun to believe he was, he'd help protect Herman. She looked at him again and wondered if *stalwart* was a good description. It was beginning to seem like it.

He stood there waiting for the trip up to the attic. Putting down her phone, she led him to the back of the hallway. "Up there," she told him, pointing to the ceiling. "Drop-down ladder."

She usually had to get on a step stool to reach it. Boyd had no such problem.

He followed her up the ladder. She pulled the string that

turned on three overhead lights and revealed the detritus of three generations. Old furniture, boxes full of items she couldn't remember because she'd never looked and they weren't labeled. Someday, she promised herself. An old promise she still hadn't kept.

"What needs to go down?" he asked.

She started pointing, and one by one she lowered boxes for him to reach for at the bottom and move out of the way.

"The tree is a beast," she warned him. "Mom wanted this big one that's flocked with snow. Unfortunately, stringing the lights is practically a whole day's work."

Boyd came up to help her wiggle the box to the attic door.

"I'll catch at the bottom, okay?"

"No argument from me," Artie answered. "Just be ready for the weight."

The easy part was tipping the box over the edge and urging it to slide downward. Not nearly as easy on Boyd's end because he'd not only have to stop it at the bottom, but he'd have to slide it out of her way.

Naturally he made it look easy.

It only took a half hour to set the tree up in the corner where it had always stood, in front of seldom-used book-shelves. These days she read on her tablet.

"You know," she remarked, making casual conversation as they spread the branches, "I never read those books any-more. I have duplicates of the ones I love on my tablet."

"I would, too."

Would, not did. She wondered if he read at all. "Do you read much?"

"I used to. Lately I haven't felt much like it."

Again she pondered about his story. Again she wanted to ask. Again she didn't.

She began to pull lights out of the boxes. "These darn

things get tangled even with the reels. I can't imagine how it happens."

One by one, they spread out strands and checked the miniature lights. All of them burned brightly. All of them blue. Just as her mom wanted. It was all just as her mom wanted.

And now just as her dad wanted, but this year he didn't help. This year he watched the weather.

Boyd was a great help, though. She never asked for help with this part. Because she ought to be able to decorate one damn tree by herself.

As soon as Boyd saw how she was trying to string the lights along each branch, just not once across each, he followed, helping with each strand. One tree and eight strands. It was always beautiful, though. The snow on the branches was clumped so that it didn't look artificial.

It was well worth doing, she admitted to herself. Every bit of it.

Putting it all away after New Year was when she wanted to rebel. Every year.

Amused, she realized she was smiling.

"This is fun," Boyd remarked.

"So you can still have fun?" The question maybe had more bite than she'd wanted.

He answered with apparent truth. "Occasionally. In patches."

Her, too, since her father's illness had become unavoidable, but she didn't say so. Instead, she said only, "This year I might be a Grinch."

"And that might be understandable."

Amazingly, with Boyd's help, the lights were on the tree by her dad's bedtime. He nodded approval as he passed by it. "Mom will like it. Great surprise for her."

Artie bit her lip, then said, "I'm sure she will, Dad."

After her father disappeared into his bedroom with the requisite checks from his daughter, Artie turned to Boyd, who was sitting on the floor. "I'm going to decorate this tree tonight, unless I'll keep you awake too late."

"Go for it," he answered. "It'll be a nice surprise for Herman in the morning."

BOYD, HOWEVER, had seen quite a bit that evening, and he was sorry as hell.

He hadn't missed the way Artie's father had shifted into the present tense when speaking of his late wife. Hadn't missed Artie's pained reaction, though she had tried to conceal it.

Then there were the threatening phone calls. Artie might pretend to shrug them off, maybe tried to tell herself they were meaningless.

But Boyd could read faces. He had spent a lot of time with people in tight-knit units. He'd learned to tell when some guy's game face tried to conceal that he was about to crack. To tell when someone was growing more fearful than usual. To know when someone seriously needed a break. At his rank, he'd been something of a father to all of them.

A better father to his unit than to his daughter. He yanked himself away from that black hole and focused on his present circumstances. He was also good at that when necessary.

Right now he was seriously worried about Artie. The thing with her father couldn't be helped. That was happening regardless.

But those threatening calls? He wasn't about to dismiss them. For the first time he considered how to remain in this house if Artie didn't get protection from her fellow officers. If she never told them about the calls so she wouldn't *get* that protection. He wouldn't put it past her. To him she seemed too self-reliant. Too unwilling to seek help even for something that might be a serious threat, or she would have called already. She'd have told that officer who called earlier.

He felt sorrow for her, for having to watch her father fail like this.

Watching Artie open the boxes of tree ornaments, he decided he might have to be her protector. Lousy at protection as he was, given the situation with his daughter.

Self-loathing rose in him again, bringing bile to his throat. Well, he might be able to do a better job here, at least for a brief time.

Then he rose from the floor. "What can I do to help?"

BOYD WOKE TO an excited exclamation in the morning before the sun came up. He sat up immediately and looked around. He found Herman standing in front of the tree, wearing a tattered old plaid robe, smiling from ear to ear.

Artie appeared quickly, still tying her black robe around her waist. "Dad?"

"The tree," he answered. "Pretty like it always is. I guess Letitia finished it while I was sleeping."

Oh, God, Boyd thought. Artie appeared to nearly shrivel. He felt renewed pain for her. The blizzard still raged outside, but he felt as if it had come indoors. A storm. For an instant it all brewed inside.

ARTIE FELT EVERYTHING inside her clench at the way her father was speaking about her mother. God! Was it getting worse? Was he slipping his place in time more often? How could she be sure?

These instances had been happening for a while, but were they coming closer together? Or had the approach of Christmas, heralded all over the TV, simply triggered the problem?

Taking Herman to the doctor and to a therapist wasn't very helpful. Crosswords? Herman had always hated them. No word games for him. Memory puzzles? If she could keep him working on them for longer than two minutes.

She went to stand beside her dad, staring at the tree. "It's beautiful, isn't it?" She couldn't bring herself to join him in his belief that her mother would return at any moment. Trying to jostle him back into the present would only make him furious.

Maybe it was better to just let him enjoy his happiness right now. God, how did she know? She just didn't want to anger him or hurt him. Either would be awful.

After a few minutes, she looked at Herman and said, "I'm going to make breakfast. You hungry?"

He nodded, still staring at the tree. "Oatmeal."

"You got it." There were plenty of packets of the instant stuff in her pantry because her dad liked it so much. Personally, she hated it.

Boyd followed her, still dressed in the gray sweatshirt and pants he must have slept in. Socks on his feet.

"What can I do?"

For an instant she felt angry. He was so underfoot with his offers to help. So at loose ends, reminding her that she was at loose ends, too.

"Slice the blueberry bread for me?"

"Gladly. Will your dad eat any?"

"If it's there," she answered quietly. "If it's there. Do you like oatmeal?"

"Love it."

"Then you and Dad make a club of two. I hate it. I don't like any hot cereals."

More pointless conversation. This was going to drive her

mad, although in the current situation she didn't know how she could escape it.

As she served oatmeal for the two men and blueberry bread for herself, she remarked, "I wonder if this storm is ever going to blow through."

Now reduced to talking about the weather. She closed her eyes briefly, then went to get her father.

It occurred to her that she wasn't being a very nice person. Not since the domestic. Not since Billy Lauer. Not since she was facing a truth: she hadn't swung her baton simply to protect Bea Lauer. She'd raised it in rage.

She'd lost her self-control.

Two MEN, Willie and Joe Lathrop, hunkered down in their small house far outside town.

"Time to make another call?" Willie asked he stirred the embers of the fire on the hearth.

Joe shook his head. "Tain't smart, Willie. I could git in more trouble."

"How? That cop's gonna testify against you, and you'll get years for a bar fight? Mack's angry, too. She took away his license. Now Billy Lauer. You gonna let her testify against him, too?"

Billy was a good friend of theirs. They didn't exactly approve of the way he beat Bea, but they could see the sense in it. Damn woman wouldn't stay in line for nothin'.

Joe said, "Cop bashed Billy up pretty good, too, from what I'm hearin'."

The men poured some more coffee from the tin pot resting on the stones in front of the fire. They had some standards. No beer before noon. Maybe.

"We gotta stop her from testifying," Willie said firmly. "Scare her off."

"She don't seem like the type to scare easy."

"We'll do it. Just gotta keep on."

"Call some of the others that's mad," Joe said finally. "See what they think about it."

Willie scratched his head and rocked in the old wood chair. "We know what they think. Mack's still seeing red. Ain't nothin' changed."

Joe shook his head. "I mean about another call this soon."

Willie grunted. "Mack said to make some calls, maybe scare her."

"I mean it, Willie. We might could do this all wrong."

"We got good enough heads."

"Remember what Ma used to say? About more heads being better?"

Willie grunted again. "Okay, okay." But he sounded more annoyed than agreeable. "You remember we might have to do more."

"I 'member. Can't hardly forget."

The beer came out early, as soon as they finished their coffee.

Chapter Five

In the late afternoon, the wind quieted down like a baby who was through screaming. Outside, some snow still fell, but not much. Behind them, a movie ran on the big-screen TV. Something with sled dogs abandoned in an Antarctic winter. Herman had asked for it.

"Looks like the storm is almost over," Boyd remarked as he stood beside Artie at the front window.

"The weather said three days. But you must be in a rush to get out of here. Not that I blame you."

Surprisingly enough, he wasn't. Why, he couldn't really say. Something about that protector urge, which might not even be necessary since another call to Artie had failed to come. Or was it something else? He sure didn't seem to be able to avoid noticing how attractive Artie was. She'd probably hate him if she knew.

Then the wind screamed again and almost instantly the house across the street disappeared in the whirlwind.

"I thought it was about to stop," he remarked.

"I don't know, but this looks like a whiteout. You know, when the snow is dry enough that it blows around. It's hell when it hits and you're on the road."

Since he could no longer see the house across the street, he knew she was right. And he'd seen whiteouts in Afghanistan.

She turned her head and offered him a crooked smile. "As long as these keep happening, no one should move anywhere. Although if the blowing stops long enough, people might think it's safe to go out in their cars. It might not be."

She turned to look back out the window. "It just takes a few strong gusts and there it is."

As well he knew from experience, but he didn't tell her so. She was talking, not silent with worry, and he didn't want to stop her. "But no one can stay hunkered down all winter."

"No. When the sun comes out again it'll help, hardening the snow on top. Until then..." She shrugged. "Guess you're stuck here a little longer."

Which was far from the worst fate, Boyd thought. Awkward as it was for him, and for Artie, he had no desire to hit the road again. Not yet.

Besides, he could get the phone calls he was hoping for as well from here as from the road. He just couldn't hike out his roiled emotions, not when he was here.

Artie's cell phone rang. She answered it without hesitation, maybe because she could read the name of the caller. She put it on speaker. "Hi, Clara. How are you making out?"

"I'm doing just fine. I wanted to ask about that old man of yours."

"Oh, he's doing great. Watching one of his favorite movies, happy the Christmas tree is up."

"Is that Clara?" Herman asked. "I know that voice."

Artie closed her eyes. "Yes, Dad, it's Clara. Want to talk to her?" But Herman just went back to his movie.

After a pause, Clara said, "Like that, huh?"

"Sometimes. We're okay, though. And you stay tucked inside."

"Saw the whiteout. I am *not* going to attempt to shovel my walk."

Artie laughed. "I'd recommend that."

"You shovel that dang stuff and it just blows into a heap nearby anyway, and the heaps keep getting deeper."

"I've noticed that."

"I think we all have," Clara said dryly.

"When are you going to hire someone with a snow-blower?"

"It's getting sooner with every year. This may be the year. I'm getting tired of it. Thinking about Florida. Not seriously, though."

"I'm glad to hear that."

When Artie disconnected, she almost seemed to relax. One concern off her mind, Boyd supposed.

Then he spoke. "I'll walk to the grocery when this lightens. You need some fresh veggies. Other things. Give me a list."

She tilted her head and wasn't smiling. "What did I say about not going out until the sun crusts the snow?"

He looked out the window again. "If it'll make you feel better, I'll wait until tomorrow. But I've been through this before." He turned his attention to her again.

"And just how much will you be able to carry in that backpack of yours?"

"I'll manage. Get me a list from Clara, too."

A snowplow groaned its way past on the street, as they had been nearly since the start of the blizzard. Waging a tireless and mostly useless battle to keep streets clean enough for emergency vehicles.

Boyd spoke. "I imagine they're plowing outside town, too."

"They are. But do you have any idea how many hundreds of miles of road there are out there? They keep the plows stationed at intervals along the state highway to make it faster, but it's still going to be a while."

She faced him. "Talking about going to the grocery? You're not planning to leave in the morning, then?"

"No." But he didn't tell her why, because she'd be furious if she knew he was staying out of concern for her. "I'll get a room at the motel as soon as one becomes available." Even though that would put him too far away from the current situation, but if it helped Artie to be more comfortable, he'd find another way to keep an eye on her.

Her lips compressed. "Like hell," she said. "Like hell."

He didn't pursue the matter. No point. But he was relieved she didn't seem to be in a hurry to throw him out.

ARTIE LOOKED AT the stranger in her home, still wondering about his story. So he knew whiteouts? She hadn't felt as if she was giving him any new information, so why had she rattled on?

The movie was over. Her dad began pacing again. She couldn't bear to watch it. He always looked so alone when he did it. Memories? His despair over his diminishing capabilities? She didn't know how to ask, or if she should. Always that tightrope between dealing and hurting.

At least he paused occasionally to look at the tree. His face relaxed when he did. Was he still expecting Letitia to come through the door? If so, he didn't appear distressed by the fact that she hadn't yet.

She went to the kitchen to make some more coffee and try to plan another meal. God, she wasn't good at meal planning, either. She'd been able to justify it because of work, but there was no justification now.

Boyd came with her. "Thinking about dinner?"

"How did you guess?" Her voice held an edge of bitterness. She hated the sound of it.

"Why don't you let me root around? Maybe I can cook it tonight."

"When did you become a chef?"

One corner of his mouth tipped up. "No chef. It was just survival."

"Have at it." Her voice sounded more natural this time.

A few minutes later, he emerged from her pantry with a jar of chipped beef. "This and cream gravy? On toast?"

She noted he didn't use the military slang for it. Probably because he didn't want to use the impolite word in front of her. As if she hadn't heard it a million times. "Sounds good. My dad loves it. He doesn't get it often because I'm lousy at making cream gravy."

He nodded. "Takes a little practice. Anyway, you're getting low on bread. You wouldn't happen to have one of those machines?"

Her personal nod to her mother's homemade bread. She almost never used it and felt like a slug for not kneading the dough herself. "I have one." Down in the cabinet with the rice cooker.

"How long does it usually take?" he asked, looking at the clock. "Because I'll be using your last loaf."

"An hour and a half maybe. Or two. I can't remember."

"Good enough. It'll be ready soon enough for morning."

"Have at it." She pulled out the machine and told him the recipe was inside it. Then she started moving toward the living room to check on her dad. To avoid seeing a stranger in the most comforting room in the house.

Boyd's voice stopped her. "Artie? What happened that got you put on a leave?"

Internally, she swore. Quite inventively. "How is it any business of yours?"

"It's not. But I can tell you were upset when you picked me up. Saved me from myself, maybe."

Well, she didn't want to talk about it. She shifted direction. "You can't possibly carry many clothes in that backpack of yours, big as it is. I can show you my washer and dryer."

"I'm used to grungy clothes." Then he chuckled. "Of course, you might not like the smell. Thanks."

Then Artie at last made her escape to the living room. To one of the most troubling problems in her life.

Used to grungy clothes? She added that tidbit to the story she was beginning to build about him.

Then she returned to her dad. The movie was long over and he was watching cartoons again. She ought to be grateful he still remembered how to use the remote. Maybe the memory was so old that it didn't leave him.

The complexity of Alzheimer's was difficult to grasp. The death sentence it gave him troubled her beyond bearing.

"Dad? Would you like another movie?" Even in his state he must be growing sick of cartoons. But maybe the simplicity of them gave him some pleasure without taxing him.

"A Christmas movie," he said presently. "One your mother likes."

So the slippage in time continued. Maybe Christmas wasn't such a good idea after all.

BOYD HAD THE chipped beef soaking and was putting ingredients in the bread machine when the wall phone rang. He looked up as Artie came to stand before it. At least he hadn't put the flour in with the liquids yet.

She stood for a few seconds looking at the phone, then answered it.

"Jackson," she said briefly.

Not long after, he saw her face pale. Okay, this was going beyond enough.

She hung up with a slam.

"What was that?" he asked.

Instead of telling him it was none of his business, she answered sharply, "Another damn threat. This time the creep said it could get worse than phone calls."

Boyd forgot the bread. This was indeed beyond enough. "Damn it, Artie, you can't keep ignoring this."

"Just a creep. A coward hiding behind phone calls. They're easy enough to make." But her color hadn't returned.

"You keep telling yourself that. But it isn't quitting. Could it have anything to do with that incident before you picked me up?"

"*That* beast is still in jail."

"How do you know?"

"Because of the blizzard. Nobody's going to make it to court in this mess. Not his lawyer, not the prosecutor, not the judge. They probably won't arraign him until tomorrow or the next day."

"That's a bail hearing?"

"Yeah, and possibly a plea. Which will be *not guilty* because he's such a bastard he probably doesn't think he's done anything wrong."

"I've known that type. Total sociopaths."

Now he saw the unspoken questions on her face. She didn't need to know about *him*. There was a more pressing matter anyway. "You need to call your department. Tell them about this."

"Like hell. I can take care of myself."

"Like hell," he retorted. "Not when you don't know what's going on."

Anger seeped out in her voice. "What can they do about some damn phone calls? God, Boyd, you're making a mountain out of a molehill."

He'd had enough. "I've also been in situations where I had to depend on the eyes and ears of other people! They might have some ideas. They have more resources than you do at home."

"They're already overstretched and this storm is creating a mess for them," she snapped at him. "Stay out of my business!"

Then she stormed out of the kitchen.

That was it, Boyd decided. Nothing was going to drag him away now.

He wondered if she'd even considered that her father might be at risk, too. That he might be the one most at risk. There were a lot of ways to get to someone.

HERMAN WAS INVOLVED in *Miracle on 34th Street*, the original version. A movie Artie had once loved, too. Now it held reminders of grief, reminders of how much her mother enjoyed it. Mom had always put it on at a time when there would be no interruption and, if there was one, life would have to wait.

Grief stalked her footsteps, Artie sometimes thought. Grief about the past, grief about the now, grief about the future.

She shook herself and watched a bit about Santa playing Santa at the department store. About the little girl who spoke Dutch, which Santa of course understood.

Then she thought ahead to the courtroom scene. A moment when sheer joy would burst from the video. She wished she could find something like that in a real court.

But then her thoughts darkened again, remembering Billy Lauer, about the merciless way he was treating his wife when she found them. About her own damn baton. Couldn't she have handled it better?

She closed her eyes, hating to remember it, but unable to stop second-guessing herself. Moment by moment she replayed the entire atrocity, wondering what she could have done differently.

There had to have been a better way. But Lauer had seemed hell-bent on killing his wife. Beating her bloody wasn't enough. Nothing would have stopped him from strangling Bea. She wondered if she could have pulled him off. But even one hit from her baton hadn't stopped him. It had taken repeated blows for him to turn his fury on Artie.

With her eyes closed, she could still see Bea with only a few seconds left in her miserable life. The blood. Lauer's hands squeezing the breath from her.

God, what made people do things like that? She could understand a drunken brawl. Tempers fueled by booze. Anger during a squabble between neighbors that resulted in blows, usually after the quarrel had been going on for a long time. Usually because nobody would compromise.

This was different. Something in Lauer wasn't right. Was dangerously wrong. Something in him made him an innate murderer. Who might he take that rage out on when he could no longer get at Bea?

But he couldn't be the one threatening Artie. He was locked in a cell where he'd probably had his one phone call. His only phone call. A phone call that wasn't even required by law. A courtesy only.

Maybe the deputies who'd arrested him had been mad enough to refuse that call.

It was possible.

She opened her eyes, unable to find a resolution to her conundrum. She hated what she'd done, but she didn't have to hate herself for failing to find another way.

Behind her, Santa Claus was still insisting he was Santa Claus. What came next to entertain her dad? *How the Grinch Stole Christmas*? Why not. A better cartoon for her father than the silly ones he'd been watching.

When the aroma of baking bread reached her, she returned to the kitchen.

BOYD HEARD HER light footsteps as she approached. He glanced at the clock and saw it was almost time to begin toasting the remaining loaf of bread and making the cream gravy. But that wasn't critical.

His sense of urgency had grown. This woman needed some kind of help to deal with the mess on her plate, but he couldn't imagine what. Her dad's disease was inevitable. Whatever had happened to her on the job was bad enough she'd been placed on leave. All he could do was hang around waiting for some way, any way, to help.

Her face was smooth but her eyes were pinched. "That baking bread smells really good," she said.

"I love the smell. I ought to get one of these machines eventually."

"See what you think when you taste the results. When I get around to it, I only make simple white bread."

"Hot and fresh, it's the best."

More dancing around. Artie sat at the table, chin in hand, and simply stared. At him. At empty space.

* * *

LATER, AFTER A dinner that had pleased Herman enough to eat two huge helpings, Artie insisted on doing the dishes.

Boyd left her to it, saying only that he wanted to step outside for a few minutes, just to see how the weather was doing.

But what he needed to do was make a phone call to his ex-wife, Shelley, to find out how Linda was. Not that he expected any good news. He'd made Shelley promise to call when matters improved, but she hadn't called and the demons riding his back wouldn't let him trust for long.

The connection went through. He waited through six rings, his heart sinking with each one, his stomach knotting. Had something else happened?

But then Shelley answered, sounding impatient. "I told you I'd call, Boyd."

He closed his eyes, ignoring the frigid wind that blew around the porch, its fury blinding with dry snow. No improvement there, either.

"Shelley, I just need an update, about everything."

"Like you wanted updates ever before."

Bile rose in Boyd's throat. That wasn't entirely true, but he let it pass. He didn't want an argument, but he still needed news.

"Look," Shelley said. "I'm not going to pressure her. She's under enough pressure. She's torn up enough. She still doesn't want to press charges."

Boyd's breath locked in his throat. Before long, he could find some air. It was so cold it made him want to cough. "I think I can understand that."

"I'd like her to realize that putting this damn man behind bars would make her feel better."

"A trial might not."

Shelley's voice tightened. "How dare you? You aren't here, you were never here! You don't have a right to an opinion!"

His hand tightened around his cell phone until his fingers might have crushed it. "The counseling?"

Shelley's anger shot across the miles. "She still doesn't want to see you. The psychologist says a lot of that may have to do with you being a man. Your long absences didn't help, either. Linda doesn't trust you."

He drew a shuddering breath. "Got it."

"Anyway, I know you, Boyd. It might make things worse for Linda if you get here feeling like you want to tear Seattle apart. Deal with your own mess. You're not ready to help with anyone else's."

Boyd closed his eyes. There was more than his fury he needed to deal with, but he didn't mention it. They were his problems, not something he needed to burden anyone else with. And yeah, he still wanted to rip things apart. Drop bombs. Clear out every sleaze who occupied that city.

Then she floored him. "How's your PTSD?"

He answered frankly, "I don't have room for it now."

"I don't know if I should be glad about that. I remember how it could get."

So did he. "Don't worry about it."

"Well, you sure took a helluva way to deal with all this. I keep feeling you're bearing down on us like a rocket-propelled grenade."

He gritted his teeth so hard his jaw hurt. Then he squeezed out the words. "Tell Linda I love her."

Shelley disconnected without another word, the silence on the line as deafening as a bomb.

After the call, Boyd remained on the front porch, risking frostbite, letting the icy wind batter him. It was all he deserved.

But soon the door behind him opened and he heard Artie's voice.

"Boyd, get in here. I don't want to be dealing with any frozen corpses."

What an invitation, he thought as he turned. *That woman!*

She sparked a lot of things inside him, not all of them bad. In fact, little about her was bad at all.

Amazing.

Unlike his phone call with Shelley.

WILLIE AND JOE LATHROP remained hunkered down in the ramshackle house they'd inherited. From experience, neither of them needed to know that the wind was probably building a drift six or more feet high on one side of the house, and probably around the front corner, too. Onto the porch.

Both knew they'd be fools to leave the house. Even after it all settled, neither of them was going to want to try to tunnel out. Sometimes Joe remarked that they might as well stay put all winter.

Impossible, of course. Plenty of food in the house, though. Plenty of coffee and beer, too. Even a couple bottles of whiskey for times when longnecks weren't enough. But not for all winter.

Worst of it was their phone wasn't working. Not the landline or the cells. No more calls to that cop, not now.

Willie popped the top on another beer. Joe tossed a log onto the fire. No central heat in this old house.

They were pretty much stuck together in this one room unless one of them ventured to the kitchen for peanut butter and crackers. Tempers might fray, but from long practice they knew not to take it too far with each other.

"Can't even call Mack," Joe muttered.

"What good'll that do? We can't git outta here, we can't make a call. Mack's prolly stewing as much as we is and he still thinks we're fools."

"Can't argue that." Joe took another swig of his beer. "Woulda liked a football game or somethin'."

Both men stared at the big flat-screen that had betrayed them early during the blizzard. The only splurge they'd made in this place.

"Lucky we still got power," Willie said.

"Can't figure that out nohow. No landline but we still got power?"

"I'm not complainin'."

"Nah. Just seems weird is all."

"Got that right."

More silence. More beer guzzled.

Then Joe spoke. "I keep sayin' we need a woodstove. Less wood to chop every year."

"Got any idea how much they cost?"

"I ain't no fool. Seems like I was with you when we looked. Don't mean we don't need one."

Willie nodded. He'd started thinking about their whiskey stash. "We can't do nothin' about that damn cop right now."

"They's time," Joe answered. "Court ain't for a coupla weeks now."

Willie nodded. "Time. But they ain't too much of it." He rose. "How about some *real* booze while we do some thinkin' about that cop."

BOYD AND ARTIE sat up after Herman went to bed. Before them on the TV, the weather station chatted cheerily about more hellish weather. This was one blizzard that wasn't going anywhere in a hurry, probably one to be talked about for years to come.

They sipped brandy. Artie enjoyed the blaze from the fire. Ordinarily she'd rely on the central heating, but Boyd seemed content to keep loading the fireplace, and it *was* more cheerful than anything else around here.

Well, the Christmas tree added some cheer, too. Especially now that Herman had moved back into the present.

Boyd eventually spoke quietly. "How bad is it with Herman? Or just tell me to mind my own business."

Artie shook her head. Boyd was seeing it. Hardly a secret. "I can't really be sure. No one can. A year ago he started having problems with recent memories. Conversations we had that he'd totally forget two days later. But it wasn't often."

"And now?"

"More often. And you've seen it, those slips into the past. They're a recent development. No one can tell me how fast this is going to worsen. Nobody. Varies with everyone, everyone has their own slope. For periods he's just fine."

"And you live for them."

Artie nodded. "I sure do." She looked straight at him, feeling the corners of her mouth tug down. "I'm already starting to miss him."

"That's gotta be hell."

"Pretty much. If I didn't have so many wonderful memories of when he was himself it might be easier." Her hand shook slightly and she put her brandy on the side table. "I've got to cling to *that* man. Hang on to those good days. I don't want to lose them. I've also got to cling to what I still have with him. Much harder." The true hell of it. Today versus yesterday. Both important.

Boyd nodded and fixed his gaze on the fire.

Well, Artie thought, what could he say? Nothing. Not for something that no one could help.

BOYD STARED INTO the fire, thinking over his phone call with Shelley. She'd reminded him of every one of his failures. She'd brought up his PTSD, not that she'd ever evinced a smidgen of sympathy for it. No, it had frightened her and angered her and he couldn't blame her for that.

But she'd brought it up. A spear meant to pierce him, then that bit that she felt like he was an RPG aimed at her.

God, was that really how he made her feel? Just by walking across the country, hoping like hell that Linda would reach the point where she wanted to see him? Hating himself with each stride for all his failures?

And if that was how Shelley felt, how could he ever be sure that she'd allow Linda to see him? To allow Linda to trust him enough to *want* to see him?

For the first time it occurred to him that he might be on a true fool's errand. In the end it might not be Linda's feelings about him, but Shelley's that would prevent him from hugging his daughter.

What in the hell could he possibly do about that? How could he know if, or when, it might be safe to find a way to approach Linda? He was being held behind a solid steel wall, and despite Shelley's earlier promises that she would let him know when Linda was ready to see him, he could no longer believe in them.

She had just stripped him of his last hope.

Working his jaw, he stared into the fire, facing a hopelessness that wasn't new to him. Just a new kind.

But he was damned if he was going to give in to it.

First he was going to settle in his own mind that these threats Artie was getting were just blather. That she was really safe from harm. That her dad was safe, too. He was growing fond of the old man as well as Artie.

Then he was going to resume his trek to Seattle and figure out what to do once he got there. Once he had dealt with the demons inside him.

As Linda's legal father, as a father with shared custody, there had to be ways around the wall Shelley was building.

If indeed she *was* building a wall. How the hell could he know? Nasty comments didn't necessarily mean a permanent state of affairs. Shelley was under a lot of strain after all.

But he still wanted to hurl his brandy glass against the hearth and listen to the satisfying sound of it shattering.

He closed his eyes and drew a deep breath.

That was *exactly* the person he never wanted to be again.

Focus on Artie and Herman. There must be something useful he could do here.

Chapter Six

Artie sensed the terrible tension in Boyd since that phone call he'd made from the front porch. He'd returned with a darkened face, a stiffness to his posture she hadn't seen before.

In fact, until then he'd turned into a comfortable companion, one who left her alone with her self-disgust, her struggle with capabilities she'd never suspected in herself. A painful journey to acceptance.

Gradually, despite all that, she'd felt a growing awareness of him as a man. An attractive man, despite him being bottled up as tightly as she was at the moment.

In the midst of all this she could feel sexual attraction? Once again she wanted to shake her head at herself. Talk about an emotional mess. Her brain felt as if it had been in a blender since the Lauer incident. Her gut, too, come to that.

But wanting sex with this stranger? God, she was losing it. Or maybe the idea of a stranger felt safer. He'd be moving on as soon as the storm and travel conditions would allow. No continuing complications.

She had enough complications in her life just then.

Sighing, she rose and went to refresh her brandy. She spoke to Boyd, who had grown even more silent than usual. "Would you prefer a beer or more brandy?"

He looked toward her. "Beer?"

She shrugged. "I keep it for when the guys drop by. Never liked it myself. But maybe you'd prefer it. I didn't think to ask."

"I'm hardly an invited guest," he answered dryly. "But a beer would be great."

She didn't keep the beer in the fridge but on a closed shelf against the wall of the mudroom. Just inside the kitchen so it wouldn't freeze but it wasn't taking up room in her small fridge. She brought him an icy bottle and returned to her seat. For some reason, despite the growing lateness of the hour, she felt no desire to turn in.

The heat from the fire felt welcome after her venture into the colder kitchen.

Boyd surprised her then by speaking once again of the off-limits topic. "Artie? What's had you so upset since you picked me up? Why did you get put on leave with pay?"

She nearly glared at him. "Suppose you tell me about that phone call that upset you so much?"

"Touché," he answered after a half minute. "I guess we both got our own secrets."

"Seems like." Feeling grumpy now, all relaxation gone, she scowled. "Why'd you have to bring that up?"

His voice took on an edge. "Because you've been getting threats."

She drew a deep breath, seeking her self-control, usually an easy thing, but suddenly difficult. Her own voice grew sharp. "Has it occurred to you that all those calls have come since you got here?"

Chapter Seven

Oh, hell, Boyd thought, feeling almost gut-punched. There it was. An idea that hadn't occurred to him but had sure occurred to her. How could he answer without telling her too much about himself? How could he reassure her? Her accusation filled the air like a suffocating smog.

Then the moment of shock clarified. "You know I haven't been making those calls. Have you seen me use my phone? Haven't I been here when you received every call? Do I somehow know the number of your landline? It's sure not written on the phone. What could I have against you any-way?"

She didn't answer, but she didn't look at him, either.

"I'm on a mission," he said presently. God, with this woman worrying about everything else she didn't need to be worrying about a threat inside her own walls. "I've got one thing on my mind and it isn't you. You know damn well I only just met you, and there's nothing on your offi-cial records about me being any kind of danger to you—or to anyone else. In fact, I'm the biggest threat to myself." It hurt to admit that, but it was true. Too true.

"You're the invisible man, like I said."

"Is that what has you worried?" He was certain it was, and he ached as he realized he wasn't going to be able to remain invisible with this woman. The urge to move on was growing again. His demons were his own.

"All I know is you spent too much time in Afghanistan. That you have medals and a reasonably high rank and that you're retired with disability. That you had a job with a construction firm you quit two months ago."

His fists began clenching. "That's quite a bit, don't you think?"

"You know a hell of a lot more about me."

"Do I? I know you're a cop, I know where you live and I know your dad now. That's not much."

"You think not? Where do you live? Where's your family? What do you do now except trek around like a nomad?"

This was probably not a good time to continue this conversation, Boyd thought. He was knotting up inside again. Getting up and walking away, even out into the storm, seemed like a good idea. Just go and never return.

Except some kind of tendril seemed to be growing between him and Artie. Some need on his part to ensure she was okay. A need to help in ways he couldn't help his own daughter.

A need to be something more than a useless guy trying to walk off bottomless rage and a sense of failure that would haunt the rest of his life.

"Okay," he said finally. "Okay."

"Okay what?"

"I was in Afghanistan. You read that. Too many times, maybe. I was good. Maybe too good. There was a crying need for experienced NCOs."

Once again she put her brandy snifter on the table beside her chair, this time twisting to look at him. "That war has been endless."

"Until lately. You've heard they call it a generational war?"

She shook her head. "No. What's that mean?"

He wanted to throw his beer bottle. His hand clenched around it until it should have shattered. "It means," he said heavily, "that I found myself leading young men and women whose fathers and mothers I had served with. Did I know who they were? Hell, yeah." He drew a deep, steadying breath. "Kids. Following their parents into uniform and the same damn war."

"Oh, my God," she murmured.

"Yeah. *Oh, my God.* Almost nobody thinks about it that way. Almost nobody. I thought about it every damn day for the last few years of my career. It might not have been so awful if some of these troops hadn't been only four or five when the damn war started. Hell, a few of them had barely been toddlers back at the beginning."

"I can't imagine," she said quietly.

"I didn't have to imagine. I saw it too often. Frankly, Artie, it haunts me." There. He admitted to it. To someone, for the very first time. He had a lot of ugly, brutal memories stamped into his mind, but that one...that one brought an infinite sorrow of a different kind.

"I'm so sorry, Boyd." Then she asked, "Is that why you're on this hike?"

"I've got a lot of things to deal with, but I didn't need to deal with that one by walking."

"So this is different?"

"Yeah." He had no intention of telling her more than that. She didn't need to know about his daughter, about his abject failure as a father. That Linda didn't even want to see him.

Nobody needed to know that outside Shelley, Linda and himself. Well, and her counselor, apparently.

Time to turn the tables on her. "Your turn," he said. "What the hell is going on apart from Herman?"

"You don't need to know."

"Maybe not. But you didn't need to know that about me, did you?"

She shook her head, looking down as if she never wanted to raise her head again. Serious trouble, he judged.

"Artie?" He kept his voice quiet. "Do you think you've seen or done anything I haven't?"

Her head jerked up at that. Despite the glow from the firelight, he saw her face pale.

"Something got you put on leave," he said. "I heard the call. Leave with pay. That usually means a terrible event. That you were involved in violence. Am I right?"

She rose from her recliner and began pacing. "I don't want to think about it."

He nodded, leaning back, making himself as unthreatening as he could. "I can sure understand that."

"So you talk about it?" she demanded, turning on him.

"I just did."

"How can you talk about it without thinking about it?"

"You can't." He waited, knowing she might not speak another word to him, but determined not to press her any further.

One thing for sure, he was hurting for her. With all his problems, he hadn't become immune to feeling for others. He had the worst urge to reach out, just draw her into his arms, encircle her in a hug. As if that would do her a damn bit of good. Embraces were hardly a bulwark against an internal enemy.

"Okay," she said finally, still pacing. "When I picked you up, I'd just come from the most horrific domestic violence scene I'd ever responded to." Her arms now wrapped around herself, holding herself tightly.

"Pretty remarkable you gave a damn about me," he offered. Maybe it would remind her that not everything was violent. Although he knew damn well that little could erase brutality.

"It's my job," she said sharply, facing him at last. "Like I was going to leave you out there to freeze regardless of what else was going on. By the way, it's the law. The law says I have to stop. *Everyone* has to stop. Doesn't mean anyone has to force you to accept help."

"But you kinda threatened it."

At that a small smile curved her lips. "I kinda did, didn't I?"

"Something about calling for backup. Gets attention every time."

"Got yours, I guess." Then she resumed pacing, still hugging herself. "I never saw a man so determined to kill his wife."

"That bad?"

She nodded shortly. "I've seen plenty of drunken fights. You can break them up, usually. The sound of racking a shotgun works pretty good. Failing that, a pistol shot into the ground. I've seen armed ranchers in a standoff ten feet apart over a stream arguing about who had water rights. That at least is a life-or-death problem, unlike a bar argument, but can usually be quieted without injury. But what happened the other night..." She shook her head and fell silent.

"What happened that night," she said eventually, "was pure evil and I was a part of it."

Then she turned her back. "I'm going to bed, Boyd. You need anything you know where to find it."

Boyd watched her disappear down the hall. A few minutes later he heard her showering. He hoped the heat helped ease the stiffness he'd seen in every part of her slender body.

After a bit he went to the kitchen to empty the beer bottle

and rinse it in icy water. Leaving no trace of his passing. The lesson of long years in uniform.

Returning to the couch, the fire burning to embers in front of him, he looked into those dying flames that opened a door to memories he tried to avoid. Nights when he and his unit would have given almost anything to warm themselves by a fire. To sit around and shoot the breeze. The rare nights when they'd been able to, feeling like kings in their small, protected area.

Fire could mean a lot to a human. Everything. Warmth. Protection against wild animals. Hot food. Companionship. A barrier against the night. He'd never really thought about it until he'd been so often denied one.

Now here he was in a safe place, one where he could look into a fire and feel satisfied with life, just for this brief time. Reality always returned. Always. Usually with an explosion of bombs, grenades and bullets.

Or in this case an unwanted desire for Artie. A growing, strengthening need that made him despise himself. Hell, his timing sucked. He had to force his thoughts away from her curves and pretty face, her bright blue eyes, and return himself to the here and now.

There were those phone calls, which wouldn't leave him alone. He couldn't dismiss them the way Artie was.

In his experience bullies made threats. He was certain she was dismissing them as exactly that, and she might be right. But then there were those who enjoyed playing cat-and-mouse with only one ending for the mouse.

Not simply bullies full of big talk. There was never a way to be certain which kind you were dealing with, not until they gave themselves away through action or inaction.

He closed his eyes briefly, considering the kind of mind

that would want to threaten Artie in the middle of a blizzard that had this entire county frozen like a Christmas display.

Just threats, but headed where? To accomplish what? He wished he'd gotten more information from Artie about the content of the calls. Some little bit might give away the entire show.

Then there was Artie's determination not to involve her colleagues. Stretched to breaking by the storm? Yeah. Maybe thinly spread over a county this size. But if she thought they wouldn't care... Well, she was wrong about that. They might not be able to put a guard on her house. Hell, at this point that wasn't even necessary. Artie was her own guard.

But what about trying to trace any of those calls? Find the originating cell tower or landline? He had no idea how long that might take, but did it matter if they put a lid on this?

Because Artie sure as hell didn't need this crap in her life.

He closed his eyes briefly, watching the flickering orange light through his eyelids. Fire. Sometimes it surrounded everyone's life, emotionally or in reality.

So she had experienced evil? He suspected that was a strong word for Artie to use. She had to have seen an awful lot as a cop, but this case had cut her to her core. It followed her even when she was trying to think of something else. He watched the flicker of pain or distress pass over her face even when she wasn't worrying about her father.

Evil. It had touched her somehow and it wouldn't leave her alone. Was she trying to find a way to do penance just as he was?

Sometimes the only penance, he was beginning to discover, was learning the lesson, never doing it again.

But what could she possibly have done? She'd broken

up a domestic violent enough that the sheriff wanted her to take some time, to talk to a psychologist.

But that meant she'd inflicted some violence herself, didn't it? Had she needed to shoot someone? That would seriously rattle most people, at least until they became used to it, unfortunately.

Getting nowhere at all, he finally banked the fire, then stretched out on the couch. Sleep came easily and quickly to someone who'd had to take advantage of every possibility to cadge some.

But that didn't mean he wasn't alert. His ears never turned off, not anymore.

But all that filled them was an endless wind nosing noisily around the house.

No human threat out there.

Yet.

Chapter Eight

The morning brought silence. The sky remained leaden, the temperature looked frosty enough to cause dogs to shiver in their front yards, but there was no wind. Maybe the lightest of breezes.

And gently falling snow. Evidently it wasn't over yet. Nearly, but not completely.

Eventually the silence was broken by the snowplow passing in front of the house, clearing the street yet again. No one had yet ventured out to shovel walks or driveways. No one moved a car.

The world was hushed with expectancy.

Herman ate his oatmeal. Boyd and Artie toasted the last of the bread he'd made.

"I'm going to the store," Boyd announced. "Give me a list. Get me a list from Clara, too."

Artie put her hand on her hip as she stood near the counter and shook her head. "It's not over. The whiteout could whip up again."

"I'll manage. If not, you'll be free of an unwanted boarder."

"Damn it, Boyd!"

He shook his head and managed a crooked smile. "I've made my way through worse and you know it. Now get me those lists. And don't let Clara cheat, okay? Not every day someone gets a willing mule."

Twenty minutes later he had two lists tucked into the pocket of his arctic jacket, his empty backpack settled into place, and then headed out the front door.

God, the air smelled clean, with that particular scent that could come only from fresh snow.

No one was out and about except one man walking a Belgian Malinois who had black booties on his feet. They both looked as if the weather offered them no surprises.

The man's upright stride and the dog's attention told a story, Boyd thought. He paused, eyeing man and dog.

"Military?" he asked.

"Marines. Kell McLaren. This is Bradley, retired K-9."

Boyd thrust out a gloved hand. "Boyd Connor, retired Army, no K-9, sadly."

McLaren laughed and shook his hand. "Good to meet you. Staying awhile?"

"The storm got me thrust into Artie Jackson's house. No room at the inn and she took me in."

Kell nodded. "She's that kind of woman. Where are you off to?"

"The grocery. I need to replace some supplies. I'm hoping they're open."

"Open but not busy. Not sure how much is still on the shelves."

"Maybe my luck will hold." Then he paused, knowing he was probably breaking Artie's confidence but feeling the need to anyway. "Do you know if anyone might have a serious grudge against Artie?"

Kell McLaren stiffened, almost invisibly. "You got a concern?"

Boyd shook his head. "Just something she said."

"Well, a cop is going to have a lot of grudges against her, isn't she? People she arrested, helped put behind bars. It'd be weird if no one bore a grudge."

"Makes sense."

Kell nodded, but his gaze remained sharp. "Let me know if there's a worry. Give me your phone and I'll put my number on it."

Once the transaction was completed, Boyd moved on.

Well, that encounter had made him feel a bit better, Boyd thought as he resumed his hike toward the store. But then, so did being out in the air, on the move. Being on the move had been part of him for a long time.

And he liked that marine. Liked the way he appeared to believe that a military man might have a decent reason for a sixth sense operating overtime. Yeah, a good man.

Then he continued his trudge, trying to stop the images of Artie that persisted in bugging him. Damn, she was too attractive for his own good, and he had no place in his life for that now. Sure as hell not when the only place he wanted to be was in Seattle with Linda. Hiking toward some kind of healing with Linda.

Now he was trekking emotionally away from Artie. Hell.

THE HOUSE, Artie realized, felt surprisingly empty with Boyd gone. Not that he left much of a footprint, but his absence was more than that. A loneliness she'd never felt there before, except for a year or so after her mother died.

She sat with her dad before the fire that Boyd had conscientiously built early that morning.

"That man," Herman announced, "is going to burn through the entire winter's store of wood."

Artie laughed quietly. "So? I can get more from Jimmy."

"Yeah, I know. Long as we don't get caught in another

blizzard that takes out the power before he gets another cord here."

Artie shook her head. "Come on, Dad, you know we have plenty out there already. Some of it's been there for years we burn it so rarely. But if you want to worry about it, I'll get Jimmy to deliver as soon as he can get here."

Herman waved an impatient hand. "Just being a grumpy old man and you know it. I always liked sitting in front of a fire with your mom."

Artie felt her heart clench. "Should I put it out?"

He nearly glared at her. "And take away that memory, too? I'm losing enough of them. It's a good memory. Let me have it."

How was she supposed to take that? Did he blame her for his memory losses? The idea that he might terrified her. She didn't know whether to apologize, so she left the subject alone. "What do you think of Boyd?" she asked after a while.

"If you had to drag in a stray, you couldn't have done better. Fine man, I believe, but dogged by something bad. Nothing he did, I don't think, but something sure has him unhappy as hell."

"Seems that way to me, too, Dad."

Herman nodded slowly. "Don't let him run off too soon, hear? Might be good for you to have someone around who doesn't have one foot in a grave."

"Dad!" Artie was appalled and jumped to her feet. "Dad! Don't say that!"

His gaze sharpened as he met hers. "It doesn't do any good to deny what we both know. I see you worrying all the time and I'm sorry I'm causing it. But it's the truth, Artie, and you can't keep trying to evade it, especially with me."

"I haven't been evading it," she said quietly, refusing the

description. Wasn't she dealing with the situation day in and out? There was no evasion possible.

But her father disagreed. "Yes, you have. You won't talk about it with me. You watch my every mistake, my every sign I'm better, as if that's going to change a damn thing. You're living on tenterhooks because of me, swinging from hope to despair."

Artie's throat tightened until it hurt.

Her father continued, "You know, I'd kinda like to be able to talk frankly to you about it all. Not hide it so I don't upset you."

Artie's breathing became labored, shaky, as she took the punch of his words right in her solar plexus. "Dad..." she said weakly, then nearly ran into the kitchen where she gripped the edge of the counter and leaned over the sink as huge tears began to roll down her cheeks.

Dad. Oh, God, Daddy.

THE WIND RETURNED as Boyd walked to Artie's house. His backpack was full, and he carried several plastic bags, as well.

As the wind kicked up, visibility diminished. His balaclava didn't exactly do a great job, either, as it blew icy crystals into his face until his eyelashes were weighted with ice and his body chilled rapidly from every cold breath he drew.

He knew it all. He was used to it from the past. That didn't mean he liked it.

He entered Artie's house with his load and noted that Herman was sitting by himself in his recliner. No TV, just a small fire before him. And the Christmas tree, a tree that had at first given the man so much pleasure but now appeared all but invisible to him.

Cussing under his breath, Boyd headed for the kitchen

and found Artie standing by herself, looking out the window at a world that had began to spin itself into another whiteout.

"How was it?" she asked. Her voice sounded thick, as if she'd been crying. Not that she'd ever want him to know that.

He started unloading onto the table. "The store wasn't terribly empty. They must have prepared, too. Anyway, I got everything on your list. If you want to start putting things away, I'll take Clara's over to her."

Artie nodded, keeping the back of her head to him. He hesitated, then decided to just shut up. The woman rarely spoke about anything unless she chose to. It certainly wouldn't help anything to prod her when she was clearly already disturbed.

"Back in a few," he said after he gathered Clara's items in a plastic bag. "Which house?"

Artie pointed in the general direction.

Then back out into an increasingly ugly day. God, this weather ought to break soon, shouldn't it? A little bit of sunlight and maybe some quieter air would sure be welcome.

Clara Bateman must have been watching from her window. She opened the front door before he'd barely kicked the snow off his boots.

"You must be Boyd," she greeted him warmly. "Come in. I can't thank you enough for going to the grocery for me."

Boyd managed a smile. "I was going out for a walk anyway."

"Hate being cooped up?"

"Believe it."

She led the way into her warm, bright kitchen. When he'd placed the bags on her table, she looked through them. "I think," she said dryly, "that you brought me some things that weren't on my list."

"Everybody deserves a treat. I just hope you're not diabetic."

She laughed. "I missed that, thank goodness. Tea? Coffee?"

He might have accepted. This cheery, plump woman, with a thatch of gray hair that looked as if it never took orders from a brush, was inviting. Warm. Bright. Unlike the gloom in the Jackson house. But he understood the gloom over there and didn't expect the Jacksons to put on some kind of performance for him. Especially since he was an invader.

Besides, he was worried about Artie, about her mood when he returned from the store. He shook his head at himself. She didn't need *him* to get her through a day. Clearly she stood on her own two feet.

But that didn't prevent him from worrying. Besides, welcome as Clara's cheer might be, the darkness inside him wouldn't yield to it for long.

"How's the old man doing?" Clara asked as she put the Danish on the counter. "Do you have any idea how long it's been since I treated myself to a pastry?"

"Of course I don't." He summoned a smile. "You're talking about Herman, I gather."

"Yeah, that old man. The only one I worry about. You aren't getting to see much of it, but we have some great times, him and me."

"Been friends for a long time?"

"Most of our lives. Both of us even married our high school sweethearts. Don't hear much of that these days, do you?"

"I wouldn't know. High school was a long time ago."

She flashed him a smile. "For all of us." Then she eyed him. "You want to run, don't you? Won't even sit for a minute."

He opened his mouth to apologize, but Clara forestalled him. "I'm not offended, Boyd. You get on back and tell Herman I'm going to beat him at dominoes the next time I come over."

"Will do." Boyd straightened and pulled his balaclava down again, wet from melted snow and his breath. Good thing it was wool.

"And, Boyd?" Clara said as he turned to go.

"Yeah?"

"Look after Artie as much as she'll let you. I swear she refuses help almost like it's an insult. Anyway, you don't much know her, being here only a short time, but please do what you can."

He nodded. "I can promise that, Clara."

He was a man who kept his promises, even when they conflicted and he had to balance them out. But he kept them.

ARTIE HAD UNPACKED the groceries by the time Boyd returned. He'd gone beyond her small list, too, bringing home some sugary treats that were sure to please Herman. More packets of cocoa. More canned soups. He'd not only replaced whatever they'd used while he was there but had brought enough to make sure they were stocked up for a while to come.

Was he planning to stay? She was nearly appalled to realize that she hoped he would. But then she remembered the wanderer, the man who said his destination was the next mile. No, he'd move on as soon as he could.

"Hi, Herman," she heard him say in the next room. "Clara says she's going to beat you at dominoes next time she comes over."

Herman laughed. "She always says that. Rarely does."

Artie smiled faintly. She was fairly certain her dad was exaggerating.

She hesitated to join the two men, though. The sting from what her father had said remained with her. Worse, it was one of those instants that changed her self-perception completely. An emotional whiplash.

Like what had happened at the Lauers'. Man, she was trying hard not to think about that. Could an effort to avoid thinking about something become physically exhausting?

Then her phone rang. She froze.

AT HOME, the Lathrop brothers discovered that their landline once again functioned. The first thing they did was get on the horn with Mack Murdo, their friend in just about everything.

Mack's voice poured out of their speakerphone. "Look," Mack said roughly, "you gotta be careful 'bout calling me. It's not like I can get out of this here house right now. The woman and them brats is all over. A man can't get no privacy."

"We still gotta do something more to scare that woman off," Willie argued. "Can't let this go on till she sends Billy or Joe up."

Mack growled. "Didn't help my DUI none. Didn't need no cop." Through the phone came the shrieking of kids in the background. "Damn it," Mack swore. "You ain't been listening!"

Joe hammered his hand on the arm of his chair. The beating he'd given it over the years had fractured some of it and now it drove a large splinter into the palm of his hand. Joe jumped up, cussing loudly and kicking at the door frame, which only made two toes hurt like hell.

The dogs of the world, wherever they were, would be grateful that the Lathrops had never wanted one of them. Damn dogs were too much trouble, always needing somethin'.

"Just shut the hell up," Willie growled. "You freakin' fool, hurtin' yourself. Can't talk to Mack with you shoutin' yer fool head off."

Joe shut up, then hunted for a pair of pliers to pull out the splinter. It hurt coming out, but the drops of blood afterward gave him an excuse to suck on it. He'd always liked the taste.

"Okay," Mack said. "Can you listen now? I told you what that damn fool lawyer told me, if'n I can remember exac'ly. Said they had me because of a blood test and the camera on the damn cop car. Told me not to fight cuz they might get harder on me. As if takin' my license twern't bad enough, but least tain't jail."

"Yeah, yeah," Willie answered. "We heard all that. But we ain't talking about you. You keep sayin' it's bad if that damn cop testifies. We gonna scare her off with the calls."

Mack growled. "Keepin' you from being more stupid is all them calls do."

"Hey, it was your idea."

Mack snorted. "I didn't say to keep it up. My cousin, the lawyer in Gillette?"

"The one who works all them fancy deals for the oil companies. Yeah. Crooked like all of 'em."

Mack didn't argue the point. Seemed obvious to all of them anyway. Lawyers were crooked.

"Like I was sayin'," Mack said, lowering his voice. "God dang it, hang on. I gotta get into the garage afore the rug rats drive me nuts. And Marilou's ears be flapping around listening."

The Lathrop brothers waited, hearing doors slam. Hearing the wind blow into the phone's speaker, hearing another, heavier slam.

"Damn it all to hell," Mack said finally. "Put me in mind why I didn't never get that space heater out here?"

"Fire," answered Joe promptly. "You was worried about all that old dust."

"I *know* that," Mack snapped.

"Then why…"

Willie spoke. "Shut up, Joe. That was one of them questions that ya don't answer."

"Oh." Joe went back to nursing his hand.

"Anyways," Mack said, after a loud cough, "my cousin says you either gotta deal or go to court. You wanna deal for a manslaughter charge, Joe? You at least got a chance for that, just a brawl is all. Gonna be worse for Billy, mark my words. I hear he banged up that woman of his pretty bad. Near killed her. You ain't likely gonna get a bargain on that."

Willie froze. "You asked him about *us*? You let him know?"

"I told him I was asking about something I read. He don't know this is for real. My feelin' is he don't *want* to know nohow."

Willie relaxed somewhat. "Okay."

"Anyway, he said they might deal on Joe cuz bar fights happen alla time and Joe didn't mean no harm, 'ceptin' to punch the guy. Ain't Joe's fault the bozo hit his head on the bar. Bad side of that is ever'body liked that damn cowboy and them prosecutors might decide not to deal. Anyhow, my cousin says they bargain that alla time, might this time. Mebbe. You gotta get 'em to bargain. Ain't gonna bargain Billy's case, though."

"Why the hell not?" Willie demanded.

"Headlines," Mack answered, voice heavy with inside

knowledge. "Can't let headlines be that the effing state went easy on a guy who set about killin' his wife. My cousin says they'll take Billy all the way to court, and they's gonna need that damn deputy to do it. She's what my cousin said is the eyewitness. Somebody who saw it happen."

For a minute, the line crackled almost emptily.

"Meaning?" Joe asked finally, his hand forgotten.

"Meaning that bitch is gonna testify. She can't refuse. They can force her. Meaning Billy Lauer ain't got no excuses, 'ceptin' maybe that cop is blind."

More silence. Willie cleared his throat. "You sayin'?"

"You know exac'ly what I's saying. They got enough on Billy. Don't go makin' it worse by tryin' to stop that cop. They won't deal then, not with you, not with Billy."

Willie hung up with a slam. Like he was ever going to listen to that wimp Mack. "We're gonna call again."

"Mack was sayin' twouldn't be smart."

"Like I care."

Chapter Nine

When the phone rang again, the landline, Artie didn't want to answer it. Not this time. With the storm quieting down at last, this house didn't feel quite as secure as it had before.

It was now nearly accessible to a determined person.

For the first time, she couldn't just dismiss the threats. They were clinging to her back like cold, wet leaves even though they were so unlikely. But another one?

She could feel Boyd's gaze on her as she didn't reach for the phone. Did he think she was a coward? What did that matter? The worst thing about ignoring the call was that it might be the office. Someone who needed her.

She was just screwing herself up to reach for the damn thing when Herman called out, "Aren't you getting that, Artie? Your business phone I thought."

"Want me to get it?" Boyd asked almost inaudibly. He stood in the kitchen doorway.

"No." God, she was being an idiot and making herself look like a coward in front of a man who'd probably *never* been a coward. She reached for the receiver and said in a clipped tone, "Jackson."

Then she heard the ugly voice again, but this time ice ran down her spine. "You better forget," the voice said. "Forget ever'thin' you seen. Cuz I can *make* you forget. Or maybe you should be worrying about your old man."

Then the click of a disconnected line. Artie punched the buttons to call back, but only a beeping answered her. Nor would the punch buttons give her the caller's number.

God! She slammed the receiver onto the cradle and closed her eyes. A threat against her father. And what the hell was she supposed to forget?

"Artie?" Boyd had stepped closer.

She squeezed the words out. "Another threat. This time he mentioned my dad."

Boyd closed the distance between them and without asking wrapped her in his arms. Strong arms. She gripped his sides and let her head fall against his shoulder.

All of a sudden she didn't feel alone. This stranger no longer felt like a stranger. He had begun to feel like a friend.

"You don't need anyone telling you what to do," he murmured, holding her close.

Yeah, and she was grateful that he didn't try to tell her what she needed to do. Now that her dad had been threatened, she knew she could no longer ignore this bastard.

Reluctantly she freed herself from the surprisingly welcome embrace and called the office number. Guy Redwing answered immediately. "What's up, Artie?"

"Sheesh, are you guys still bedded down there?"

"Might be getting some relief later today, if the weather keeps improving. So, you have a problem?"

"Threatening phone calls. Four of them now, and this one mentioned my father. Can you track the calls to my landline and cell? Find out, maybe, where they're coming from?"

"You got it," Guy answered, suddenly sounding all business. "You want someone to keep watch at your place?"

"You guys are already understaffed and overworked. I

can protect myself and my dad. Other people are gonna need you more after this storm."

"Your call," Guy answered, but he didn't sound pleased. "You let us know if anything at all happens, including another call. Got it?"

"Got it. And, Guy? Somehow my landline number got out there. I've kept it private for official use only."

Guy swore. "You better believe I'm gonna look into that."

When Artie hung up, she felt marginally better. Marginally.

"Think they can locate the numbers?" Boyd asked.

She turned to face him. "I don't know. The cells can be tracked to a nearby tower but given all the wide-open space out there, cell towers haven't sprouted like weeds. Satellite phones are more useful but I don't know about tracking them. Then there's the possibility of pay-as-you-go phones. Might not be registered to a real person. Guy might do better with the landline."

He nodded.

She started to walk past him, to go put her eyes on her father and ensure herself he was still there, still okay. That call had seriously set her on edge.

Boyd spoke before she'd moved two feet. "Maybe you don't want it, but I can help. I used to be pretty good at what I did."

She didn't need a road map to understand that he referred to his Army experience. To his combat experience.

She looked at him again with fresh eyes. This time she saw a strong, tall and determined man with a square face chiseled by weather. A face that right now seemed to have a hard edge.

He might be hiking to nowhere, but she had no doubt he'd know how to help defend her father.

Which, in the end, was all that mattered.

* * *

STILL NO SUN to melt the top layer of snow. Still gray clouds that continued to sift down new flakes. Still occasional gusts that whitened the world.

To hell with it. Boyd went hunting in Artie's small shed and emerged with a snow shovel. He passed through the house with it after kicking off the snow from his boots in the mudroom.

"You and Herman be okay if I go shovel some? Clara needs to be able to get help if she gets sick and as far as I can tell the plow has been dumping a lot of snow on the edge of walkways and driveways."

"We'll be fine," Artie answered, bristling.

He liked the sight of that bristling and smiled. "Figured you would, but asking is polite. Besides, I'll have my eyes on the surrounding area. In case."

She answered dryly, "Whenever you can see, that is."

"There is that."

Outside, though, felt like momentary freedom. If there was one thing he'd learned about himself during his long trek, it was that he no longer found the outdoors to be threatening, like during the war. No, now he felt the expansive beauty of it all.

Thanks to the leaden sky, twilight was settling in earlier than usual. He headed directly for Clara's place, determined that if she needed help an ambulance stretcher would be able to get to her door.

The work felt good to nearly every muscle in his body. He wasn't used to being as inactive as he'd been the past few days.

The snowbank along the street in front of Clara's house and driveway was hard-packed and heavy. At least he felt as if he were accomplishing something with each heft of the shovel. Using his muscles felt good, but the cold was getting to his injured knee, stiffening it, bringing the pain to the fore. He ignored it.

He kept scanning the area, too. Few people were emerging, although he saw a guy a few houses down tackling the snow. Someone else walked a dog in the front yard, leaving a yellow stain behind. He tossed a friendly wave in their direction. Life moving on again, bit by bit.

He ought to be moving on, too. Dealing with the realities he might have faced during his last call with Shelley. Was she really trying to keep him from Linda? Or was Linda so estranged from him she just didn't want to see him? Especially not during this time when men must all appear awful to her.

He shook his head, scattering the useless wondering, and kept on with the snow. By the time he reached Clara's porch the snow had become lighter, drier. The wind might undo every bit of his work along the walk to her porch. He mentally shrugged. Then he'd just do it again.

Clara appeared briefly to thank him and offer him a hot drink, but he shook his head. "You just get inside and stay warm. I gotta get on to Artie's house."

More heavy labor, every bit of it making his body happy. The rest of him not so much. He *had* to find a way to stay here, especially since a threat had been made to Herman. Artie probably *could* take care of herself, but her father at the same time? It could turn into a real mess.

Maybe he could use Shelley as his excuse for not moving on right away. She was sure a damn good excuse for a lot, including some of the disappointment he felt for himself. Some of the self-hatred. He hadn't built that pile entirely on his own, although he was only just beginning to admit it to himself. No, the poisoning hadn't started with his PTSD. It had started earlier in their marriage.

Not everyone was cut out to be a military wife.

FROM HER FRONT WINDOW, Artie watched Boyd perform the yeoman's work of clearing all that snow. He was being generous doing Clara's walk and driveway, too. Hell, at the rate he was going he might do more of her neighbors' houses, as well.

Except the twilight had abandoned the sky. The only light now was reflected off the snow by the streetlights and some coming through windows of houses. Everyone but Boyd had disappeared inside.

At last Boyd reached her porch, shoveled a bit more, then stomped his way around to the back of the house with the shovel. To return it to the shed. To enter through the mudroom. Always considerate.

Then she went back to her dad who was now playing checkers with himself. It had always amused her that he could play both sides objectively, mainly because, as he always said, he didn't care which side won.

For a lot of years, though, he and Artie's mom had played checkers together. And dominoes. Neither had seemed especially interested in card games although they played them from time to time. When they did, they placed bets with paper clips.

"Dad?"

He looked up. "Wanna play?"

Artie shook her head. "No. I just suddenly wondered why we never got another dog after Maple died." A thought that had sprung out of nowhere, catching her by surprise.

Herman's face saddened. "Your mom couldn't bear the thought. Just couldn't. Losing animals is hard, Artie."

Artie nodded, accepting it as fact. She'd seen her friends grieve after they lost a pet but somehow apologetically, as if they felt it shouldn't be as big a deal as losing a family member.

For some, she would have guessed, it was every bit as bad. She sure had grieved for Maple, even as a small child.

"Why'd you ask?"

"Just crossed my mind. Who knows why?" Except she suddenly knew why. A dog on alert would have been a comfort right now. To hear barks of warning.

But there was no dog. And she realized she was relying on a man who really *was* a stranger. A few days and a glimpse of his war service didn't change that.

Yet his presence had begun to comfort her.

Man, she was a mess. Thoughts of the Lauer incident kept pressing at the corners of her mind, demanding attention. Attention she couldn't afford to give it right now.

Maybe that psychologist would be a good thing after all.

OUTSIDE, HEADED FOR the shed, in the very dim light where only streetlamps bouncing back off snow gave any light at all, Boyd stopped dead in his tracks.

Those darker shadows in the snow were footprints. And they weren't his.

Someone had been out here. Not to go to the shed as he had. He could still see his own prints clearly. Straight from the shed to the mudroom. These went crossways, as if someone had walked along the back of the house.

Seeking a way in? Moving close enough to the house where the snow hadn't become as deep thanks to escaping heat. Where the crust had begun to build, making the prints as clear as if they were stamped there.

He put the shovel in the shed, then went to follow the

footprints. Easy to see they had come from the yard next door. Had passed right behind Artie's house, then continued toward the alley behind the house.

Who the hell would be walking there?

He looked sharply around, knowing it was too late to see anyone, but needing to look anyway. He followed the prints to the alley, then lost them. Snow several feet deep had blown into the narrow alley, obliterating everything.

Any hope that Artie might cherish about this all being empty, bullying threats had just vanished.

Someone wanted her badly enough to come out in this weather and get near her house. Maybe scoping the place out.

Hell.

Chapter Ten

Knowing Boyd had been out in the cold for a couple of hours, knowing someone had to do it, Artie cooked dinner. They all needed to eat, Boyd most of all.

The need didn't change her feelings about cooking. She sometimes wondered why she hated it so much, then always thought about her mother. Mom had buzzed around in the kitchen a lot, making it her domain, always in the midst of preparing something delicious.

A life as far away as any Artie had wanted for herself. She'd never wanted to be a housewife, or anything approaching it. Cooking must symbolize the worst of it for her, somehow.

At least the desire for a spotless house hadn't caused her a problem. No, cleaning was a good way to stay busy and it was something everyone needed to do, not just a housewife.

Or so she rationalized all of it.

Regardless, she cooked that night. A jar of marinara, browned hamburger, shredded mozzarella, ricotta and uncooked rotini with a couple of cups of water. All in one pan, simmered for a little less than half an hour. The rotini came out cooked, the meal cheesy and thick.

Where the heck had she learned that from? Mom, of

course. In some distant recess of her memory, she'd recalled this dish. Amazingly enough, she even had the cheese.

But Boyd had been shopping. If he had plans for some of this food bursting out of her fridge and pantry, he was out of luck now.

Distraction. Cooking at least provided some. Distraction from the Lauer incident, distraction from the phone calls.

The threat against her father. God in heaven, who would do that? What reason could there be?

While dinner simmered, while she heard Boyd come back in through the mudroom, she gripped the edge of the counter and stared out into the blackness of the window over the kitchen sink.

All her life she'd liked the night. Until now. Now it loomed, pressing in against the glass. Full of threat.

"That smells good," Boyd said as he entered the kitchen. The night's cold entered with him.

Before she could summon some kind of response, the kitchen phone rang again. She exploded.

"Damn it! Damn it, damn it, damn it!" Someone kept walking into her house through that damn phone connection. They might as well have entered through the front door. Worse, they came with a threat.

"I'll get it," Boyd said before she could move.

She wanted to stop him. It was *her* phone, *her* problem. But he'd already reached for the receiver.

"Hello," he said, his voice level.

After a moment, he turned and handed her the phone. "Gage Dalton. The sheriff, he said?"

Relieved, so relieved that Artie's legs momentarily weakened, she took the phone from him.

"Hi, Gage," she said, her voice fairly steady.

"Who the hell just answered your phone, Artie? That wasn't your father."

"Uh, no." Lord, how to explain this in less than a thousand words? And to Gage, who parented his deputies as if they were his own family?

"Artie," Gage said. Just her name. Letting her know he wouldn't let her off the hook.

"It's Boyd Connor. When I was coming back from the Lauer incident, I found him walking along the road. The storm was just beginning. The motel is full. So he's staying with me."

Gage fell briefly silent. "This is the man you had Guy do a background on?"

"Yes. He's clean."

"And when did those phone calls start?"

There it was again, the suspicion. Except that Boyd had been standing right there when some of those calls came. "It wasn't him. He was right here."

Gage again fell silent. "I'm going to come over. Be there in an hour or so."

"The roads…"

Gage's answer was dry. "It's been a very long time since I worked out of Miami. I'm pretty sure I've learned to handle these winter roads."

She replaced the receiver on the hook and looked at Boyd. "Sounds like you're going to get interrogated before long. We'd better eat before it gets cold."

If Boyd felt one way or another about Gage coming over to question him, he showed it in no way. But then Boyd could become amazingly impassive sometimes.

Herman shuffled in from the living room, a smile on his face. "Smells like something your mother used to make."

"I think it is." And Herman was still in the present, a good thing. Some of Artie's tightening tension eased. Too much, she thought. Sometimes it all felt like too much, and since Billy Lauer, that feeling had become stronger than ever.

Herman was in a good mood. He chatted throughout dinner, telling a few of his well-worn jokes, all of which appeared to entertain Boyd. Or maybe Boyd was just being polite.

Hard to know at this point. But she remembered his embrace earlier and she knew for certain that his hug hadn't been merely polite. He'd been offering genuine comfort insofar as she would let him.

Maybe her dad was right about her when he sometimes said she was a prickly pear cactus. What had made her that way?

Damned if she knew or cared. Just being herself had always been important to her.

Except she was beginning to wonder if she was becoming a train wreck.

Lauer. Her thoughts kept returning to that beast, much as she tried to bury him. Returning to his savagery. To her own. Losing her self-control. Beating a man with every ounce of strength in her body.

She didn't much like that Artie Jackson.

GAGE TURNED UP just after the last dish had been washed, while a fresh pot of coffee was brewing. As usual, Gage wanted the coffee. Sometimes Artie thought he lived on it.

He settled onto the couch, his smile crooked because of the burned and grafted skin on the side of his face. The man winced nearly every time he moved, limped with nearly every step, and never once complained. He'd been crippled by a car bomb that had killed his first family but had learned to live with it all.

Artie frankly admired him.

Boyd leaned against the wall, arms folded, wearing his gray sweats again, leaving room on the recliners and couch for the other three. Herman looked pleased to have company, and he'd always liked Gage.

Sipping coffee from his mug, Gage looked at Artie. "Got the report on Bea Lauer."

Artie drew a sharp breath. Her last image of that woman was of her lying in a pool of her own blood while her husband tried to strangle her. Too vivid. "How is she?"

"She's going to survive. Physically anyway. Emotionally is another thing."

Artie nodded, staring down into her own cup, drawing in the aroma of coffee, seeking to hold at bay all the terrible feelings that were trying to flood her. "She's going to have to overcome a whole lot."

"Years of abuse, I hear. One of those situations we don't hear about until it's almost too late. Or already too late."

"I can't disagree." But Artie was tensing again with a different concern, waiting for Gage's inquisition of Boyd. Maybe she'd learn more about him. Or maybe she'd discover he had something important to hide.

But Gage didn't turn immediately to Boyd. He wasn't done with Artie yet. "So how'd you get a stranger in your house?"

"I told you."

Gage nodded thoughtfully. "Coulda put him in an unlocked holding cell."

Boyd interrupted, "Given her description of one of those holding cells versus her house, when she offered her house I took it."

Gage's dark gaze settled on him. "Risky, maybe?"

"Risky for who? *I* knew I wouldn't hurt her. As for what

she said when I pointed out that taking me home with her could be dangerous…" Boyd shrugged. "She said she was a cop, she had a gun, a baton and tae kwon do. That I'd get more than I bargained for if I gave her any trouble."

Gage astonished Artie with a loud laugh. "That's Artie, all right. But all that protection might not have been enough against you, would it?"

"Probably not."

Gage offered another one of his crooked smiles. "Military, I hear."

"Army."

"Four tours in Afghanistan."

Boyd leaned forward, settling his elbows on his knees. "Yeah." His face had darkened a bit.

He wasn't liking this direction in the conversation, Artie thought. But why?

"A nice set of medals," Gage continued. "A hero, I guess."

Boyd shook his head. "No hero." Then he straightened a bit. "My military record is no secret. You want to know something else, so ask it."

"I want to know what you're doing walking through my county, nearly two thousand miles from your last known address, in the dead of winter with nothing but a pack on your back."

OH, WOW, Artie thought. Now she was wound tighter than a drum skin, her hands clenched around her coffee mug. How would Boyd respond to that? The insinuation was there, however subtle: Boyd must be up to no good.

She realized she was chewing her lower lip and forced herself to stop. She glanced at her dad and found him intensely focused on what was happening in his living room. As welcoming as he had been to Boyd, evidently he had some doubts of his own. Some doubts that probably revolved around his daughter's safety.

Was everyone in this room thinking she must be some kind of fool? She'd wondered that initially when she brought Boyd home, but the wondering hadn't lasted long. Her only excuse for offering him shelter in her own home had to do with her own mental and emotional state after Billy Lauer. A lousy excuse if ever there was one.

She wasn't one to defend her choices, though. She made them and lived with them. Like Billy Lauer. Sometimes it was harder than other times, though.

"You gonna answer my question?" Gage asked after a pregnant pause.

Boyd shook his head slightly. "How much do you really need to know, Sheriff?"

"Start with why you quit your construction job after only two months."

Artie caught her breath. Gage sure wasn't pulling any punches.

Boyd's mouth tightened. "Family emergency."

Gage lifted the one eyebrow that was still mobile. "How much of an emergency when you're walking across the country? I hear planes are faster these days."

Boyd unfolded his arms but remained relaxed. At least on the surface. Artie thought she saw something hard glitter in his eyes.

"I don't know how much you think you have a right to know about my personal situation, Sheriff."

"Just enough to know you aren't trouble on the hoof."

Boyd looked down, drawing a deep breath. When he raised his face it hinted at sorrow. "Some families get broken pretty badly. So do some vets. I'm walking off a lot of personal trouble."

That seemed to satisfy Gage. It only whetted Artie's curiosity. She wanted to know the story behind this trek of Boyd's. She wanted to fill in all the blanks. But, like Gage, she had no right to anything Boyd didn't want to share.

Unable to hold still any longer, she went to get the coffeepot and freshen mugs.

Herman spoke for the first time. "Seems to me like there's a lot of problems a man's got to work out on his own. By himself."

Boyd nodded faintly. Gage settled back a bit on the couch, wincing as he did so. He gulped more coffee.

"Now," he said, facing Artie, "I want to know more about these phone calls."

Artie immediately glanced at her dad. She didn't want him to know about any of this. Gage followed her gaze and gave a brief nod as if to himself. "Alrighty, then. I'll just finish this coffee, if you don't mind, Artie, then I'll be on my way. And Guy's running down those calls for you, okay?"

"Thanks." Artie was surprised by how much gratitude she felt. It was as if her colleagues were steadily closing ranks around her. Like Gage coming over here on icy streets to check up on the situation.

Even though she kept insisting she was fine, that she could take care of herself, she couldn't deny that it was comforting to know she wasn't facing this all alone.

HER DAD WENT to bed shortly after Gage departed. Once tucked in, he opted to turn on his bedroom TV, this time to a movie, some kind of drama. The kind of movie her mother had preferred. Sound and motion to block him off from the rest of the world, maybe from his memories. Or maybe a deep dive into them.

Artie felt another wave of sorrow. Herman had lost his

wife and now he was losing himself, piece by piece. Could anything be more awful?

Well, it could: someone hurting him to get even with her about something she couldn't begin to imagine. What had that guy meant by telling her to forget? Forget what?

Her spine stiffened and by the time she settled in her recliner, she was beginning to feel very angry. Some sicko was forcing his way into her life, threatening her father. For the first time in her life, she actually *wanted* to use her baton, and would if anyone broke in here.

Boyd sat on the couch, leaning back, legs casually crossed. "What's going on?" he asked eventually.

"About what?" She was in no mood to be questioned, or to feel obligated to answer those questions.

"The threats. Any ideas?"

"None. Too opaque, too general." She put her chin in her hand and had to admit she liked Boyd's attention to the fire. It was more soothing than a blast of central heat, more relaxing by far.

"But your father? Does Gage know that?"

"He picked up on it, didn't you see?" She shook her head. "Gage misses almost nothing."

"I've been worried Herman might be at risk since you told me about the first call."

She turned her head, scowling at him. "You think that didn't cross my mind? Now it's overt."

Then she had a feeling. A strange feeling that seemed to come out of nowhere. Her entire attention focused on Boyd. "You know something and you'd better tell me."

His lips compressed and he appeared to be preparing to tell her nothing at all. Finally he said, "I don't lie. Unfortunately."

"Except by omission, evidently. So what are you omitting?"

His frown deepened. "When I went to put the shovel back

in the shed, I saw footprints. Walking close to the back of your house, headed for the alley. They disappeared there. The snow must have blown over them."

Artie rose from her seat, anger starting to burn in the pit of her stomach. "You didn't think I needed to know this?"

"I think I didn't have a time to tell you, Artie. Damn it, it's not as if we're hiding ourselves away in some private part of the house. You wanted me to say this in front of Herman?"

Her anger seeped away like the air from a punctured balloon. "God Almighty, this sucks."

"I'll second that." He rose, too, and began pacing the small living room. "I'm glad I'm here. You won't accept any backup from your department, so you're stuck with me. I'm your backup."

She wrapped her arms around herself as if trying to ease a deep chill. Her legs were planted firmly, however. The fight in her was far from gone.

"I don't need backup." But she didn't sound quite as certain as she had when all this started.

"Maybe *you* don't," he said evenly. "But what about Herman? Sounds like you're going to need an extra fist in this house."

She liked the way Boyd phrased that. Not as if she needed protecting, but as if she might need help protecting both herself and her father.

As well she might.

Then Boyd stopped pacing in front of her. "What's Gage's story? It must be a bad one from the look of him."

She nodded, trying to uncoil the tension in her neck, her back. Tension that hadn't left her since Lauer.

"He used to be undercover with DEA. A car bomb killed his family and nearly killed him, as well."

"My God," Boyd murmured.

"Yeah. I admire the hell out of that man."

"I can see why."

Then Artie pinned him with her gaze. "So what's *your* story, Boyd? Not just the bits and pieces."

Chapter Eleven

Willie was still trying to warm up in front of the fire, practically sitting on top of it. "Gotta get a better parka soon." Then he waved away the cold beer Joe tried to hand him.

"For hell's sake, Joe, coffee. Ise freezin'!"

Joe hurried to obey, stacking the percolator and putting it on the hearth. It wasn't long before they could hear the bubble of the coffee perking.

"Booze is s'posed to warm ya," Joe said.

"Sure. Coffee does it better."

Joe didn't argue. Arguing with Willie when he was in a certain mood could be rightly dangerous. "So what'd you see?"

"A woman and her old man livin' in a house like we thought. One kink."

Joe didn't like the sound of kinks, even just one. "Yeah?"

"Got a man livin' with her. Don't know him, never seed him afore. Mebbe just because of the storm."

"He a problem?" Joe asked nervously.

"I dunno. He was out shoveling snow when I first seed him." Willie shook his head and reached for the coffeepot, not caring if it had finished perking. "Point is, it don't matter."

"Why not?"

"Cuz they ain't much that can stand up against a gun."

Joe liked the sound of that. He began to smile.

But Willie never left Joe very happy for long. "Been thinkin' though."

"Bout what?"

"Looked easier afore this storm. Now that damn cop is stuck to her house like glue. We gotta get her away from there."

"Why?"

"Damn it, Joe, whatsa matter with your brain? You wanna leave evidence all over that house?"

Joe felt unhappy again. "This is gettin' harder."

"Never was gonna be easy."

"But that was good, say'n about her dad. That's gotta scare her."

"Mebbe."

Willie returned to brooding and Joe wisely shut up. Whatever Willie said, it *was* getting harder. The easy plan they'd started with, of scaring that cop off, was springing up problems like weeds. Like them damn dandelions that showed up every spring.

MORE COFFEE. Boyd made the pot. They settled at the kitchen table for some reason. Maybe because it was less comfortable, suited for a difficult conversation. Or maybe because it was farther from Herman. Artie had a strong feeling neither of them wanted this story to be overheard.

Artie waited, but when Boyd didn't speak, she looked into his tight face and said, "Well? Gage was right, this hike of yours doesn't sound like a family emergency."

"It is." He wiped his hand over his face, calluses scratching a bit on the day's stubble. "Except I can't do a damn thing about any of it."

"Except walk?"

"Walk and wait." He turned his face away a bit, staring at something only he could see. "I don't talk about this."

"You told me once it could be helpful to talk." Except tossing his words back at him seemed a little harsh on her part. Seemed too pushy, although she believed she had a justifiable need to know more about Boyd Connor.

"About some things. Not everything." He fell silent again.

And once again, Artie waited. Some things couldn't be pushed. No way. Some things had to come in their own good time. At least now he seemed willing to talk, a little anyway. So she waited.

Eventually Boyd spoke again. "I made a hash of my life, I'm a huge failure, and now I'm wondering if my ex will ever let me see my daughter again. She was supposed to, but that last phone call with her..." He shook his head, allowing the words to trail off.

Artie felt her chest begin to tighten. This guy was carrying more than a backpack. It sounded like a hell of a mess.

After a bit, Boyd's gaze returned to her. It was utterly naked, hiding nothing of his anguish. "I blew it, Artie. All of it. I lost my marriage, I guess I lost my daughter, I sometimes lose my mind, and if I got any angrier I'd be a cinder."

Artie didn't know how to reply. Any words that sprang to her mind seemed trivial. She didn't want to trivialize any part of what he was saying or feeling. Rightly or wrongly, this man must feel gutted.

The only thing she could do was reach across the table and rest her hand over his. To her great surprise, he turned his hand over and gripped her fingers gently. Warmth. Human touch. So very important. It felt good to her, too, bridging the gap she'd been trying to place between herself and the world. An important bridge.

"Tell me," she said quietly. She wasn't sure she wanted to hear this, but she needed to. Needed to better understand this man who had blown into her life on a blizzard and was now insisting he would stay to back her up. That meant he was caring, right? The way he treated her father, so kindly, as if Herman had no problem at all. And now he wanted to help look after both of them. That caring on his part called out the caring in her.

God, the two of them were a hot mess!

He rubbed his free hand over his face again, as if trying to wash something away. Then he spoke, his voice carrying an edge.

"I was in the Army, right? You know that. What you don't know is how rarely I was actually home. Shelley—my ex—didn't want to live anywhere near where I posted, so it wasn't like I could just drop in when I had a couple of days."

Artie blew a long breath. "Why didn't she want to live near your posts?" When she thought of being in love, she didn't imagine choosing to live apart, at least not for long. Was this weird or something?

"Her family," Boyd answered. "She wanted to be near them, to stay in the town where she had all her family and friends. Especially after she became pregnant with Linda, it made perfect sense to me."

"Sense maybe. But difficult anyway."

He shrugged one shoulder and looked at her again. "It was the way she wanted it. I could understand her not wanting to move to some strange place where I was the only person she knew. I thought it was best for her, too."

"Then?"

"Maybe not the best for the two of us. For our marriage. I came home when I could, but I wasn't exactly overwhelmed with free time. I got thirty days a year for leave, but it didn't always come in a huge block. Sometimes just a week or two, depending on my unit's orders."

Artie could already hear what was coming. The ache in her heart deepened a bit. "Did she ever come visit you?"

"A couple of times. She didn't like it, especially when Linda was small. I got it."

Artie bet he got it. Whatever had brought about the marriage in the first place evidently had begun vanishing quickly.

"Anyway," Boyd continued after a minute or so, "I was busy. It was the way things were and I didn't give it a lot of thought. Making Shelley happy, I thought. Only I wasn't. And I saw so little of my daughter I'm honestly not sure that I was ever much more than a stranger to her."

"That's sad," Artie said. Very sad.

"Worse than sad. I failed her. I failed my daughter."

Artie felt a flicker of anger. "Just what were you supposed to do? Quit the Army to move home to be near your ex's family and friends? When she wouldn't even consider doing the same for you?"

One corner of his mouth lifted, but the crooked smile lacked humor. "You know the worst thing we can do in life is run on automatic? Thinking everything is as it should be? Not evaluating? I'm evaluating now, and I'm not liking what I see of myself."

Artie sighed, then rose to freshen their coffee. "Funny how life makes us reevaluate ourselves."

"You, too? Is that what was going on that got you put on leave?"

"You could say that." She nearly slammed the mugs on the table, then remembered that Boyd had bought some kind of apple cinnamon coffee cake. She pulled it out of the fridge, opened it and put in on the table with a knife and two plates. "Remind me not to let you do the shopping again. You buy too many treats."

He shook his head, that lopsided smile remaining. "You deserve it, especially if this crap keeps up."

"Hah! Seriously, Boyd, does the crap ever stop?"

"Guess not." He cut himself a healthy portion and put it on a plate. "Just depends on what kind of crap."

"No kidding."

"And some is worse than others."

He ate half the cake he'd cut for himself and pushed the rest of the cake toward her. "You need some, too."

She took a small slice but stared at it as if it were alien food. It *did* smell good, however. Probably would have been better if she'd heated it.

"So the hike," she pressed, wanting the rest of the story while he was still talking. Before he clammed up.

He just shook his head. "The brain is an amazing thing. Especially when it gets screwed up. Or maybe the gut. God knows which one rules the roost at a given time."

"Don't I know it." Memories of her baton striking Billy Lauer. Purely a gut reaction, just as her continuing reaction to it was in her gut, squirming around like some creature trying to break loose. She could hide it in the recesses of her brain but the rest of her body wasn't letting her forget.

"The hike," he said, taking another piece of cake. "My penance. Working off a fury that seems boundless. Waiting for something to ease the pain, frustrated that I can't get to my daughter. Dealing with a whole load of stuff from my past that there's no way to fix now."

"That sounds like a heck of a lot." More than the things she worried about. A lifetime of regrets? Because that's what it sounded like and she simply couldn't imagine the burden.

He shrugged. "I'll get through it. I always do sooner or later, but this is a big one. A messed-up life."

"You didn't mess *everything* up!"

"Maybe just the really important parts, like marriage and fatherhood." He eyed her. "Was Herman always there for you?"

She looked down, feeling oddly embarrassed, perhaps by her good fortune. But she wouldn't lie. "He is, was, always there for me."

"And *that*," Boyd said, slapping his palm on the table, "is exactly what Linda never had from *me*. I was almost never there. And I sure as hell wasn't there when she was raped two months ago."

"Oh, my God." The words seeped from Artie, barely passing her lips. She screwed her eyes shut, turned her hands into fists and let the pain slice through her. *Rape.*

"Yeah," he said roughly. "Yeah. Brutal. She's only sixteen, for the love of God, and all I want is to be there with her but she doesn't want to see me. Can you blame her? I sure as hell can't!"

He jumped up and she heard the front door slam behind him.

Her eyes remained squeezed closed, her hands fisted until her nails cut into her palms.

No words. No way to comprehend the magnitude of what this man was facing right now.

No wonder he was walking from one end of the continent to the other.

OUTSIDE, JACKETLESS AND not caring, Boyd kicked savagely at snowbanks and got little pleasure from it. He needed a punching bag. Something to hit really hard. Something to be on the receiving end of his fury.

Because it never stopped seething inside him, making him unfit for any but the most casual company. The PTSD had been pretty bad after his discharge, but it had started quieting, thank God.

But not before it had proved to be Shelley's last straw. He sure as hell wasn't the man she'd thought she'd married, and all those years and miles that had separated them because of the Army had fractured it all, he thought. But the bouts of rage he sometimes felt from the PTSD had been the last straw.

He'd never taken them out on Shelley or Linda, had tried to take the episodes away from them, but apparently he'd never gotten far enough away. But it had grown better, a lot better. Until this.

Like a rocket-propelled grenade bearing down on her? *That* was the feeling he'd left her with? What the hell had he done? What the hell had he forgotten doing during those episodes of black rage? Or the bouts of heavy drinking?

He'd gotten it under control, but too late. Shelley and his daughter were gone.

Now all he could do was hike until he was too weary for self-loathing to overwhelm him. Until he was too weary to be constantly on edge waiting for Shelley's phone call telling him that Linda wanted to see him at last.

Although he wasn't at all sure that Shelley would keep her promise, not after that last phone call. The only thing he could be certain of was that he hadn't been capable of sitting in North Carolina, working his construction job and just waiting. Waiting endlessly. At least this hike made him feel he was heading toward resolution. Toward being able to hug his daughter again. Or just sit with her and listen to her.

Simple things to wish for, things he'd allowed to slip for too long.

He shoved his hands into his jeans pockets and looked up at the sky. Streetlamps caught gently falling snow, turning the flakes into gold, sometimes scattering the light into tiny prisms.

And once again it was Artie who called him back.

"Damn it, Boyd, get your butt in here. No way am I going to let you freeze to death in my front yard!"

Shaking himself, he headed for the door. Somehow he had to find a resolution with Linda. There had to be a way.

In the meantime he had Artie and her father to concern him. He was in no way ready to dismiss those threats, no matter how weak they seemed on the surface. Not when he'd seen those footprints outside. Not when her father had been indirectly threatened.

Given what was going on right under his nose, indulging his own self-hatred—which when he thought about it, might well be self-pity—he had more important matters on his plate right now.

Such as who might intend Artie and her father harm. And why.

INSIDE, THE CHRISTMAS tree still glowed with blue lights. The fire blazed quietly on the hearth. And the instant Boyd hit the warmth inside, the snowflakes that had sprinkled all over him began to melt. A small thing, especially with the fire so near.

Without asking, Artie brought him a hot mug of cocoa. Dropping cross-legged to the floor, he reached for it, thanking her.

For a little while, other than the crackle of the fire, the house remained sealed in winter silence.

Then Artie spoke. "I'm not quite sure I understand the

problem with your daughter. Why didn't you just get on a plane and go? At least then you'd be nearby."

"The thought occurred to me. Believe me." He swigged the hot cocoa, not caring it singed his tongue.

"Then why the hike?"

"Because Shelley, my ex, told me not to come, that Linda wasn't ready to see me, that she was already messed up enough by the rape. Then she told me Linda's shrink said not to come."

"Good God. But if it's like that, why'd she tell you about the rape in the first place?"

He stared off into space, then eventually said in rough voice, "Punishment."

"Cruelty," Artie said sharply. "Stay away but here's the awful thing that happened and we don't want you."

"Yeah. Maybe. Well, I could hardly sit on my hands waiting. Shelley promised to give me a call the minute Linda changed her mind, so I decided to hike off all the feelings that were driving me to no good end. I mean, how would my daughter react if I showed up in Seattle ready to tear the town apart?"

Artie sighed, then slipped off the recliner to sit beside him on the floor. "I see."

"I'm angry, Artie. I want to *do* something for Linda. But what? The cops evidently have the creep, so I'm not needed for finding him. And I'm sure not needed within a block or two like a simmering volcano. No amount of anger I feel is going to fix this, so I need to manage it. Walking is good for that."

"Not gonna tear the creep's face off, huh?"

Boyd felt an unexpected lightening in his chest. An almost-smile reached his face. "Or break his neck. Unfortunately."

"Ah, that's too tame," she replied.

"Nah." He returned his attention to the fire. "What Linda needs from me, if she ever wants any of me again, is kindness and understanding, not fury. Anger seems to have become my general reaction to life."

"I hear that's not uncommon in vets."

His answer took time in coming. "That may be true. There's a lot that has to be bottled up."

"Anger is at least safe."

He turned his head to look straight at her. "Safe for who?"

A GOOD QUESTION, Artie thought. Safe for him, maybe? Not to let in pain if you could hold it away with anger? But safe for others? Probably not.

She also knew she was getting into deep waters here. She didn't have the experience or training to get into anyone's psychology and certainly not Boyd's. Time to back out before she risked appearing judgmental. Hell, she had no business judging anyone else, not after Lauer. Not after what she'd done.

She put her mug aside and leaned back on her elbows, her legs still crossed. "We make a pair," was all she said.

At last a small chuckle escaped him. "Here we sit next to a Christmas tree and I doubt either of us could be any bluer than those lights."

"A pity party?" she asked dryly.

"We seem to be edging into one. In my own case I think I'm spending too much time kicking myself for what I've done. I did it. Time to move and find some way to fix what I can."

"Sometimes easier to say than to do."

"Can't disagree. But when it comes to Linda I got to thinking this afternoon, after talking to Shelley, that I've still got parental rights. For some reason she didn't try to get sole custody."

He paused, then shrugged. "Maybe she didn't think I'd be around enough to become a problem, so why duke it out? And she was evidently right. Until now."

"What will you do about it?"

"That remains to be seen. First I get myself into a more reasonable frame of mind. Linda doesn't need a wreck for a father."

Then he leaned back on one elbow, stretching his legs out, turning toward her. "And what about you, Artie? You're not saying a damn thing about what happened to you just before we met. Not one thing about why someone would want to scare you. Not a thing about how this could involve your father."

But this wasn't the time for naked truths, she thought. Not her own anyway. She wasn't ready to give voice to the turmoil inside her.

But she was ready for something else. Firelight played over Boyd's strong face. Blue light from the tree illuminated the shadows, emphasizing the determination she saw in him.

In that instant, she felt the electric shock of overpowering hunger. It zinged through her, both unexpected and unwanted. Not now. Not this stranger with a huge pile of problems that made her own seem trivial by comparison.

Not a man who'd be leaving in a few days, homing in on his daughter, more focused on helping Linda than anything else in his life.

Not a fling. She'd never been the type to want a fling, a good thing in this small town. Then she wondered why she cared. What was wrong with a romp in the hay, just this once?

Boyd's eyes had narrowed. Had his face come closer to

hers? She hoped so, and realized her breathing had changed, as if the air were being sucked out and she couldn't inhale deeply enough.

Excitement found every nerve ending in her body. She had to force herself to remain still, not to reach for the wonder lying just beside her.

Then he spoke the question that cracked every wall she'd tried to place between them.

"Artie?"

She reached for him.

BOYD WAS ASTONISHED that she wanted him, but even more astonished that despite his self-imposed punishment and anger, he could feel this sudden surge of desire.

In a split second, Artie tugged him out of the real world into a place of hunger and light. Everything else on the planet vanished as he pulled her close, feeling every inch of her slender body pressed to the length of his.

He spared one last hope that neither of them would regret this, but then he didn't care at all.

He just wanted Artie with every fiber of his being. Just Artie. No one else. No other woman. It was all blindingly new, somehow. All of it. All of her.

When she tugged at his sweatshirt, he pulled it away, hungering for the touch of her hands on his naked skin. Her touch everywhere and all over.

He shed his clothes quickly. Hers proved a little more difficult with those damn buttoned jeans, but she gave a little giggle and helped him get rid of them.

Then they lay there on the rug, two gleaming bodies, bare for every touch of eyes and hands.

"God, you're beautiful," he whispered as he began to stroke every inch of her he could reach. Her skin, smooth as satin, warm beneath his palms and fingers. Her curves delicious perfection. Her breasts small and firm with large nipples. They hardened, calling for his mouth.

But he touched them with his hands first, cradling her breast and brushing his thumb across her nipple.

Her breath grew ragged. Her body began a gentle squirming that only aroused him more. As if that was even possible.

A breathless, tiny laugh escaped her as she rolled even more closely to him. "My turn, gorgeous."

He was happy to comply, rolling a bit more to his back, giving her free rein to enjoy him as she chose.

And man, did she choose. He closed his eyes, giving himself up to her spell, feeling her hands search out every bit of him from his own tiny nipples to his swollen groin. The shocks of pleasure ran through him until he felt every nerve of his body burning for her.

"Artie…" His voice had grown thick.

"Yeah, yeah," she said, panting a bit but sounding a little humorous, as well. "Wait a little longer, big guy."

But he didn't need to wait that much longer. Rising up, she straddled him, wide open to his touch. Reaching down, he felt the nub of her desire swollen for his touch.

"God, that's so good it almost hurts," she whispered brokenly. "Boyd…"

No words necessary now. Finding himself, he slid into her moist, hot depths. In an instant the blaze welded them together. She rocked on him and he reached up to cradle her breasts, teasing her more.

They rode in the waves of an eternal sea that carried them from crest to crest, each higher and stronger than the one before.

Then the sea became a tsunami, sweeping them away into a place beyond the mind. Beyond earth.

To a gentler shore.

To a peace neither of them had known in a long while.

RESTING BENEATH A blanket that Boyd had rustled up from the back of the couch, they held each other tightly, limbs feeling weak but oddly strong at the same time.

Boyd caressed her hair, dropping gentle kisses on her shoulder. The scent of their lovemaking perfumed the air around them. Artie sighed quietly, moving her fingers over his smooth skin. She felt one scar, a long one, near the base of his spine, but said nothing. He'd gone to war after all, and she didn't want to remind him. Not now in these minutes out of time, minutes the rest of the world still hadn't intruded on.

"I'm luxuriating," she murmured eventually.

"Me, too. I could stay here forever."

Except forever wasn't going to happen. At last a cold trickle of reality reached beneath the blanket. She wanted to bury it, but it wouldn't go away. Especially when she thought of Herman. Her dad. Now threatened, too. But why?

At last she gave in, sitting up even though moving away from Boyd felt as if she were tearing her own skin off.

"God."

"I know." He sat up, too. "I know."

"Cocoa," she said after the sense of loss eased. She reached for her clothes and pulled them on. He wasn't far behind. But at the last minute he pulled her close and kissed her deeply. "Another time?"

How could she refuse? She wanted time after time with him. "Yes."

Then he smiled, helped her up and walked to the kitchen with her. "Does Herman sleep through the night?"

"Mostly. He gets up earlier than he used to, but sometimes he gets a nap in the afternoon. Things change as we get older, I guess. Clara says that she used to have to be dragged out of bed in the mornings, but now she's up before the birds. You?"

He shook his head briefly. "I have nothing resembling a sleep schedule. I take what I can get when I can get it."

The war, she suspected. And maybe now, too.

Once again they faced each other across the table.

"I'm so sorry about your daughter," she said into a silence that seemed to be growing heavier, the joys of their lovemaking easing away into memory.

"Me, too." He sipped the hot cocoa. "I haven't often felt helpless in my life, but I do now."

She wrapped her hands around her mug, wanting the warmth in her chilling fingers. "You said you might be able to do something? Custody?"

"Yeah." He stared into space. "I still can't imagine why she didn't try to deny me any custody at all, but she didn't. So that must give me legal rights."

"I'd think so." Once again she ached for this man. "I wish there was something I could do to help."

"Nobody can," he answered roughly. "I made this mess. Maybe what I need is a lawyer."

"So you can see your daughter?"

"So I can find out her mental and physical state. God knows I'm not going to force myself on her. But that call with Shelley made me wonder just how much of this problem *she* is. Anyway, I've got to know more about Linda than Shelley's reports."

That revealed a lot. Artie drew a long breath. "You don't trust her."

"Maybe I never should have. Or maybe I should have figured it out sooner."

"I suppose love pretty much blinds us." Not ever having been truly in love, she could only imagine it.

"And maybe we should wait long enough to figure it out. A cooling-off period."

Artie grinned in spite of everything. "How likely is that?"

Boyd returned her smile. "Not very."

"Probably one of the reasons most marriages end in the first year. Eyes open up."

"That's a depressing thought. Think of all the hopes and dreams, how high falling in love makes us feel."

Which was exactly a situation Artie needed to keep in mind right now. Their lovemaking had made her high as a kite. But that couldn't be all of it, shouldn't be if a future were involved. But there was no future here, she reminded herself. Blinders could do little harm.

They were on their second cup of cocoa when Boyd broached the difficult subject. "You changed your mind about those threats."

"When they mentioned Herman, yeah. Why are they telling me to think of him? Not just about myself." Artie looked down, trying to deal with that. "I can't imagine any possible reason."

"Except to scare you," he pointed out. "They must feel they haven't done a very good job of it so far."

"Or maybe it's just one guy. I don't know. I can't tell from the voice on the phone." She looked at him. "Boyd, I don't scare easily, but that last call started to frighten me."

Then there were the footprints behind her house. She didn't want to think about those, either, but she did. "Those prints you found in the snow out back? Who the hell would be out in this weather? And just to scope my house."

"Maybe they thought they wouldn't be detected."

"Well, they sure as hell could have broken in right then. You were out doing all that shoveling."

"That's a point. But maybe the guy isn't brave enough to take you one-on-one."

She thought of her baton and what it had done to Billy Lauer. Maybe that was enough to scare a single attacker. She still couldn't believe she hadn't put Lauer in the hospital, though, as hard as she had hit him. But that was the point of the baton, wasn't it? Nonlethal force.

"So what exactly happened that night you picked me up, Artie? Something sure as hell messed with you."

Her gorge rose; the memory became more vivid. Much as she wanted to escape it, she couldn't. It hit her like a shock wave all over again. She choked out the words. "I nearly beat a man to death with my baton. And I'll never forget the way that felt. I'll never trust myself the same way again because I let rage control me."

Then, unable to hold it in any longer, she jumped up and reached the kitchen sink just before she began to vomit. Just as she had right after the incident. As if she could puke out all the violence she had discovered in herself.

Boyd swiftly came to her side, dampening a towel and pressing it to her forehead. "Let it out, let it all out."

Her retching stopped soon, turning into dry heaves that made her sides and stomach ache. At last she leaned weakly against the counter, at once ashamed of herself, yet still grateful that Boyd was there, helping as much as he could.

"Rinse your mouth," he said when she straightened. "Don't swallow."

She obeyed, then turned, feeling the swelling in her eyes, the continued burning in her stomach. "I'm sorry."

"For what? You think I haven't puked my guts out? Sometimes that's the only answer."

She couldn't have asked for a better man at this time. One who understood. Who made no apologies for her. Gratitude washed through her, along with the first inklings of true friendship.

"Thanks." She made her way back to the table and pushed aside the cup of cocoa that looked revolting now. "God, I guess I'm not dealing at all. I thought I was."

"You've been distracted by other things," he pointed out. "Threats. Your father. But everything gets its due. That's one thing I sure as hell have figured out. We get haunted sometimes. Haunted permanently about some things. When you're ready, talk to me. You don't need to hold it in like a time bomb."

And that was precisely what she seemed to be doing. Holding it in, trying not to face it, trying to avoid her horror. That seemed to be doing no good at all.

Her stomach turned over again. "I don't know if I can."

"You'll have to, sooner or later." Now he reached out and took her hand. "When you're ready. But I'm absolutely positive you can't tell me anything I haven't already done or seen."

She closed her eyes, grateful for his touch, accepting slowly that he was probably right. Her one experience couldn't possibly equal what he'd seen at war. But facing it in herself was a different thing.

"I don't know where to begin," she said eventually, her voice ragged.

"Anywhere will do," he said gently. "These things rarely follow a timeline. Experiences are different from a calendar."

She swallowed, seeking courage. Never before had courage deserted her, but it had right now. For this. "It should be like writing a report."

"If that's what feels more comfortable to you."

She drew another deep breath and blew it out between her lips. He'd shared some terribly important stuff about himself, things that caused him enough anguish to walk across an entire continent in order to deal with them.

"It was a domestic violence call," she said presently. "Get them too often. The Lauers...you could say they're familiar to us. Frequent fliers, we sometimes call them. Bea, the wife, would never press charges and we never saw anything ourselves so we couldn't pursue it."

He nodded. "The victims are terrified, aren't they?"

"That's the least of it."

"But this was different?"

"Oh, God, Boyd, I've never seen it that bad. I was the first to arrive on the scene. Bea was lying in a pool of blood and Billy Lauer was choking her to death. Her eyes were bulging. She couldn't make a sound."

"God!"

"So I pulled my gun and ordered him to stop, to get off her or I'd shoot."

She squeezed her eyes tightly, the images painted in stark detail in her mind. Those images would never leave her. "He didn't listen," she said thickly.

Boyd didn't press her. He let her take whatever time she needed.

"I couldn't shoot," she said, her voice ragged. "They were too close. There were people in apartments around them. I couldn't risk hurting any of them if a bullet went through the walls."

"Smart."

"Smart?" She nearly shouted the word and jumped up from the table. "There was nothing smart about any of it. I should have found a better way."

"What way?"

She sagged against the counter. "I don't know. I keep thinking there *had* to be a better way. Any kind of way."

"But you couldn't find one?"

"I'm not sure I was even thinking at that point. I was seeing red. Scared he'd kill Bea, scared I wouldn't stop him in time and all I wanted was to *kill* that man. Kill. I was murderous."

Again he remained silent, letting her find her way through this morass. As if she ever might.

"I've never wanted to kill anyone before," she said, huge silent tears beginning to roll down her face. "I did the only thing I thought of. Maybe because I was past thinking. I opened my baton and started beating him as hard as I could. I'll never forget the feeling of my baton hitting him. God, it was awful. Just awful!"

"I know."

He probably did. Little consolation in that.

"And then?" he asked, evidently sensing there was more.

Her voice grew even heavier, harsher, approaching sobs. "I got his attention. He came at me. Was reaching for my pistol, punching me again and again. I managed to lock the pistol and throw it behind me, out the front door. Not that it mattered then. Blow after blow."

"He was well past any kind of rationality," Boyd said. He'd risen and was coming closer to her, but not enough to make her feel trapped.

"Then backup arrived." She half covered her mouth, trying to hold all the broken pieces inside herself together somehow. "Almost too late. Outside I just kept throwing up. I couldn't stop. Weakness. Everyone saw it."

"Damn it, Artie, I don't think a single soul saw you as weak at that point."

"I did." The words hung in the air, an ugly miasma of guilt, of fear, of self-doubt.

Boyd drew a step closer, holding his arms out in invitation, but before she could move, she heard her dad's voice.

"My God, Artie, what have they done to you?"

"DAD...GO TO BED."

But Herman was having none of it. "You get out there and sit in front of the fire. Boyd, you make sure it's ablaze. I'll make us all some cocoa."

"Dad..."

"I heard, Artie. I heard most of it. And if you think I'm going back to my damn bed when you've been going through hell, you're mistaken."

Boyd guided Artie to the couch, not to the recliner. He fed more logs into the fire, letting them catch into a brighter fire.

Then he tucked the blanket around Artie and sat close beside her. He'd seen this before, knew there was never going to be any easy solution, but very glad Herman had stepped in. Artie had been too much alone with all this. Way too much.

There was a point, as he knew from personal experience, when you needed some buddies to rely on. Buddies who understood. Boyd understood from the war. Herman understood because this was his daughter.

Damn her self-reliance. It had kept her isolated when she least needed it.

Herman served up the cocoa along with some of the coffee cake. A capable man who'd probably been doing such things all his life. A man who maybe resented having to rely so much on Artie. Like father like daughter, Boyd thought. They were a pair, all right. Inevitably he wondered if Linda was at all like him, and he felt a strong hope that she wasn't. He wouldn't wish anyone to be like him. Not anyone.

Boyd took the bull by the horns, addressing Herman even if Artie didn't want him to. "So, Herman, just how much do you know?"

"Since the blizzard? Since you came walking through my front door? Since I took one look at Artie's face and knew all the way to my soul that something bad had happened to her? And that it wasn't you."

Artie's head jerked a little. "Dad..."

"Quit trying to hush me, Artemis. Just because I lose my memory sometimes, forget where I am, doesn't mean I got stupid. You hear me?"

Artie nodded slowly, looking forlorn, still too pale.

"I don't sleep too well anymore," Herman said. "Littlest sounds can wake me. Not like my younger days when I could have slept through the house burning down. But now...now I wake up. You two think I don't know what was going on in front of the fire out here?"

Artie gasped. "Dad!"

Herman shrugged. "Normal. Expect it from you from time to time. There hasn't been enough of it around here. Always thought you needed a good boyfriend, or a good girlfriend. Never had either. I was beginning to worry that maybe I was part of the cause of that."

Artie shook her head. Boyd watched feeling a mild amusement. His affection for Artie and her father was growing.

Herman hadn't lost himself, though, or slipped his place in time. Right then his memory was as sharp as a tack. "I heard what you were telling Boyd. Why the hell didn't you tell me? Damn it, child, if anyone in this world can be trusted with your feelings, don't you think it's me?"

Artie's voice croaked, almost like laryngitis. "I couldn't trust myself with them."

Herman nodded. "Drink some of that cocoa. 'Bout time you started being human like the rest of us. We all got feelings we can't trust unless we talk to ourselves or somebody else. Ask Boyd, here."

"It's true," he agreed. Although he was guilty of a lot of failure to share himself. Mile after mile of it. Maybe years of it. That didn't make Herman wrong.

"So you saved a woman's life by beating that bastard nearly to death and you're blaming yourself. What for?"

Boyd answered for her, despite realizing she might resent it. *Someone* had to talk about this. "She thinks she lost her self-control. That she should have found a better way. That she let anger rule her."

Artie found enough energy to glare at him. "I can talk for myself."

Boyd sighed.

"Not doing enough of it," was Herman's judgment. "You're turning into a bottle that's about to blow like a Molotov cocktail. Where the hell did you get that from?"

"You," she answered, for the first time showing a genuine spark.

"And you think I never talked to your mother? Guess you weren't listening. Well, you were just a kid. Anyway, at least you talked to Boyd here, and I'm glad I heard."

Artie at last sipped some cocoa. It went down easily this time, but she felt some resentment that her father was trying to tell her how to live, but hadn't he always? Didn't mean she had to listen. She'd been making her own decisions for a long time now.

Herman waved a hand. "You won't listen to me," he said, as if reading her mind. Maybe he could. "Never did. But what's with these phone calls? I knew something was bothering you, but you never said a damn word."

"There wasn't much to say about it," she answered, mostly truthfully. Glad to escape any further discussion about the Lauer incident. She'd already said enough about that, exposed herself quite enough, at least for now.

"Nothing much," she repeated.

Herman harrumphed, a sound that always indicated that he didn't believe her.

"Okay," she said presently. "I've had a handful of calls. One of them told me to watch my back. Another mentioned you, as if you're at risk. That's the one that really set me off, if you want the truth."

Herman nodded. "Anything else I need to know?"

Boyd answered since she seemed reluctant. "A couple of the calls came over your landline."

At that, Herman slammed his recliner into the upright position. "Nobody knows that number except your department!"

Artie shook her head. "It must have slipped out somehow."

"And that's why Gage was here tonight, wasn't it? He's aware. What the hell are they doing about it?"

"Trying to track the calls. Find out who made them."

Herman nodded. "Seems like little enough."

Artie spread her hands. "What else can they do, Dad? They're already overstretched as it is, and since the storm they must be buried in more important things. I can handle this. I always have."

"Nothing like this," Herman grumped. Then he eyed Boyd. "You planning to stay for a while?"

Boyd nodded reluctantly. He didn't want to make Artie

feel any worse. "Just a little backup. Artie probably won't need me at all."

At that, Herman laughed. "No, she'll never admit she might. Even if it comes out that she does."

"Oh, Dad, for Pete's sake! Quit talking about me like I'm not here. You don't know what..."

Her father interrupted her, "Artemis, I been raising you for damn near thirty years and I know you like the back of my hand. I just don't usually remind you of that. All your life you never wanted any help. I *know* you can take care of yourself. You almost always have. But this could be different. Especially with you being all upset about that Lauer and what you had to do."

Artie gave up the struggle. Her dad was turning into a battering ram, not that she hadn't seen that before, and he was in a mood to take charge of her and her decisions. Well, let him. Might as well make him feel better, even if she knew in the end this would all come down to how she handled herself.

Herman settled back on his recliner, rocking it gently as he stared into the fire and sipped cocoa. The fire blazed cheerfully, probably the most cheerful thing in this house right now. The Christmas tree paled by comparison.

Boyd stirred, putting his arm around her shoulders. That felt so right and good that it was all she could do not to turn into him. But not with her father right there.

Boyd, she found herself thinking, might be the best thing to come out of all this.

A while later, Herman spoke again. "You think it's this Lauer guy threatening you?"

"Not likely." She felt Boyd's arm tighten around her a

bit, supportive. God, was she actually accepting a man's support? But she didn't pull away from it. Felt no desire to.

"Why not?" Herman asked.

"Because he's still in a cell. He can't make any phone calls from there. He probably won't even be offered bail until his arraignment. Maybe tomorrow if things get rolling again. So it can't be him."

"Hmm," Herman said, sounding doubtful.

Boyd spoke. "The man have any friends? And why would they be after you anyway? The incident happened. The evidence is there."

Artie shook her head. "Doesn't work that way. If Bea won't press charges, then there has to be a witness who can prove Lauer did all that damage to her himself. I'm the only one who saw it all. So... I'd have to testify at a trial."

Boyd swore quietly. "That could be what this is all about. His friends might be doing this."

"Like they can stop me. If this goes to trial, I'll get subpoenaed as a witness. Even if I quit my job, I can't get out of that."

As she spoke, she felt her stomach sink. *Forget about it,* the voice on the phone had said. *Forget about it.*

Forget what she'd seen? Develop a hole in her memory under oath, or before a trial?

For the second time that night she felt sick to her stomach.

"That leaves only one option," Boyd said.

Artie couldn't disagree. And now her father was a pawn on this creep's chessboard.

A threat against her dad scared Artie more than a threat against herself.

Herman spoke. "Seems like it might be good to have

Boyd stay awhile, Artie. I'm not in the shape I used to be. Although I could probably still do a good job with a tire iron."

The way she had with her baton. God, could it get any worse?

Chapter Twelve

When morning arrived, Artie awoke to find herself leaning into Boyd, wrapped securely in his arms. She felt as if she could stay there forever.

The fire was dying to small flames and embers. From the kitchen came enticing aromas.

Herman must be cooking. The usual concern tried to edge its way into her mind. If he forgot what he was doing…

But she smelled no burning, and maybe she was over-worrying the situation all the time. Her dad still had his good spells. Quite a few of them. And when they came, they lasted awhile.

He was not completely lost in his disease. Far from it. Fear of the future consumed her even more than the present worries, and maybe it was high time that she took the good spells as a gift.

Boyd stirred. "I hope you slept as well as I did," he said, his voice rusty.

She had, better than she'd slept in a while. Much as she hated doing it, she straightened, leaving his embrace behind. *Don't get attached*, she warned herself. Not now. He was leaving as soon as he could, resuming his private march into a hell he was still plumbing, a hell he didn't yet know the depths of.

She allowed the blanket to fall away and stretched. God, she needed a shower. If Boyd did, she couldn't tell. His scents were as enticing as any emerging from the kitchen.

"I need to look in on Herman."

"Okay. If it's all right, I'll take a quick shower and throw my things into the wash. Unless you want to go first."

"You first." She really *did* need to look in on her father. Last night was fresh in her mind, reminding her of the man who had raised her since birth, the man she would love for the rest of her days, whether he was gone or not.

She hoped that man was still with her this morning.

Bright morning light was beginning to pour through the kitchen window. The storm was over.

Herman hummed quietly as he cooked bacon. Rye bread was toasting. Coffee already made.

"Smells wonderful," Artie said.

Herman turned from the stove with a smile. "It should. I swear there's nothing better to start a day than bacon. You want scrambled eggs?"

"Boyd just headed for the shower."

Herman frowned faintly. "The bacon'll keep but I wish I hadn't started the toast."

"He said he'd be quick. I don't think he'd want to interrupt you."

"Probably not. Seems like a thoughtful young man."

He did, she thought, extremely thoughtful considering the baggage he carried. Sitting at the table, she accepted a mug of the fresh coffee.

"So," her father said, returning to the bacon, "did anything I said last night penetrate that stubborn wall of yours?"

"Maybe."

Herman chuckled. "Not likely you'd admit it. But I'd pay attention to these calls if I were you. Somebody's got a burr under his saddle and doesn't seem like he wants to forget about it. Maybe not that Lauer guy, but like I said, he's got friends. Must have. Somebody who might have a big grudge against you."

Artie couldn't deny it, but she shook her head anyway. She was still feeling raw from her revelations last night, from the things she'd admitted to. From her own pain and self-doubt that weren't going away just because someone said they weren't unusual or were even justified. She had to deal with her *feelings*. And they weren't likely to yield to reason.

"Let's talk about something else," she suggested.

"Sure. Then we can all *think* about it while the world gets on the move again. While you become reachable."

"Damn it, Dad!"

"Gotta look it in the eye, and it's not like you to ignore it."

He turned off the burner and lifted the last strips of bacon onto a plate covered with a paper towel. "I'm more worried about you than me," he said flatly. "You don't need to tell me there's only one way you can be prevented from testifying against that monster."

"That might not be what this is all about." But she knew it was. In her heart of hearts, she knew it all revolved around Lauer.

The timing practically shouted it. But with Lauer in a cell, just how far were his friends prepared to go? They might wind up in cells, too, with charges just as bad.

But what else could they hope to achieve? She was the only eyewitness. Her backup had arrived only as she had overpowered Lauer with her baton. No one else had seen that Lauer was the one who was strangling his wife. Lauer could plead that someone had broken into his apartment. Could even claim Artie herself had beaten Bea like she'd beaten him. Not that that would stand up in court, not against a cop sworn to tell the truth.

Without Artie's testimony, there'd be no trial and the prosecutor might have to deal for a lighter sentence for Billy Lauer.

God Almighty. She didn't even want to *think* about what had happened but now she might have to replay it all again. In a courtroom. In front of others who would see her rage, her loss of control. Some who might even feel some sympathy for Lauer's treatment at her hands.

While juries tended to support cops, they didn't always. A lot depended on their overall reaction to the case. A decent defense attorney might even make it sound as if Lauer had suffered the worst harm.

Damn, she should have gone with the ambulance that night. Should have let her bruises be documented in photos and a doctor's report. To substantiate her own claims about what had happened.

She put her head in her hands, trying not to think about the several ways in which she seemed to have lost her mind that night. Something in her had snapped. How could she be sure it wouldn't happen again? How could she be sure she could trust herself to run around this county with a weapon on her hip?

As if out of nowhere, a plate full of eggs, bacon and toast appeared in front of her. For the first time she realized that Boyd was there, too, sitting at the side of the table.

"Man," he said. "Herman, this looks like heaven."

Herman laughed. "I'm not helpless in the kitchen despite what Artie thinks."

She lifted her head and looked at him. She felt not a muscle in her face move. Frozen.

"Of course, maybe she's right," Herman said as he poured

fresh coffee, then joined them. "Sometimes I'm not as well put together as I used to be. Can't guarantee I won't forget I'm cooking and start a fire."

He waved his hand around the kitchen. "See all she's done for me to make this place safer? All that induction stuff. That toaster oven. And didn't I just use the gas stove?"

At that, feeling frozen or not, Artie tipped up one corner of her mouth. "Guess I need to replace that, too."

"Kinda expensive." Herman paused, a slice of bacon between his fingers. "Okay, okay. I get it. Don't have to like it, but I get it. Doesn't mean I can't still start a fire."

Artie just shook her head. "Gas is dangerous, Dad. And that stove is so old, what if the pilot light goes out? Won't matter if you're cooking at all."

Herman grumbled. "Look, can we eat without getting one of us upset?"

Artie nodded. This was a pointless argument anyway. That induction stove would come whether he wanted it. But her dad was right. She didn't want to consider all the reasons over breakfast.

Boyd spoke, carrying them past the awkward moment. "This is a great breakfast, Herman. You can cook for me at any time."

Herman laughed, a sound that was wheezier now than in his youth, but not by that much. "You're on. But the menu is limited. Artie's mom was the kitchen boss, wasn't she, Artie?"

"Definitely."

"She tried to teach you once in a while," her dad recalled. "Not that you were having any part of it."

Artie shrugged a shoulder. "I hated it. I still hate it, but I couldn't tell you why."

"Just wasn't your thing. We all have stuff like that. All

your mom said about it was that one day you were going to learn whether you liked it or not."

"She didn't quite succeed," Artie answered dryly.

"Frozen meals," Herman nodded. "They're good enough."

Of course they weren't, but Artie felt she had quite enough guilt just now and wasn't about to add any over nutrition.

Boyd spoke. "Plenty of times I'd have given my eyeteeth for a frozen meal. Dried food just isn't quite the same."

In an instant, Afghanistan and the Army marched into the room with them.

God. Artie nearly pushed her plate aside, then decided she didn't want to hurt her dad's feelings. She bit into another strip of crunchy bacon, tasting only sawdust.

Herman answered him, "Bet you ate a lot of that. Army, you said?"

"Yeah. Freeze-dried foods are lighter, easier to carry more of it. Of course, when you got back to base, there was plenty of fast food available."

Surprised, Artie looked at him. "Fast food?"

"A few of the chains had outlets there. Like the food court at a mall."

"Wow. I never thought of that."

"It's one way to get young people to eat enough. Besides, it wasn't long before you started craving a taste of home. A burger and fries topped the list. Pizza was pretty popular, too."

"For the most part, the closest we get to fast food around here is Maude's diner or the truck stop. Or that pizza place just outside town."

"Maybe that Mexican restaurant will finally open," Herman said.

Artie spoke. "I'm not holding my breath. They've been

trying for quite a while. I never asked why they were having so much trouble."

"Money," Herman answered bluntly. "It'd be nice if this town ever came out of the doldrums again."

BOYD, PAYING ATTENTION to every detail, noted that the pinched look around Artie's eyes had eased somewhat. At least she'd achieved a few minutes of distraction with the conversation revolving around food.

But he knew damn well the other thoughts would return. He knew damn well how they did, how they simply wouldn't go away until you learned to live with them. That took time.

The Lauer incident and now this fear for her father. There hadn't been a call since yesterday but that didn't mean a thing. Carrying dishes to the sink, he stared out at the brilliant winter day and felt it coming.

The threat was real. No matter how much Artie might try to dismiss it. It was real and now that the weather had cleared, there'd be nothing to get in the way.

The back of his neck prickled as it hadn't since Afghanistan. He could feel it coming.

"ALL RIGHT, GENIUS," Willie said to Joe, "you got a brilliant idea? Once the plows gets here and we gets out easy, what then? Walk up to her door with that there sawed-off and shoot? Like you ain't in enough trouble already."

"We already got to that damn house," Joe said.

Willie couldn't rightly argue that. "Damn near killed ourselves on them roads."

"We still got there."

"And I saw another SOB there. She ain't alone."

"The guy was skinny. Shoveled snow like he got orders. Wimp."

"Skinny, huh?" Willie rolled that around in his brain, his thinking fueled by a longneck. "We ain't skinny."

No chance of that, Willie thought proudly, patting the years of beer on his belly with pride. Some of them football players had bellies even bigger. Thinking about how they crashed through other players made him smile as he swigged more beer.

Yeah, him and Joe had the edge in that department.

As THE DAY brightened and the brilliant sunlight began to crust the snow, Boyd announced he was going to finish the shoveling out front, including Clara's house.

Artie immediately said she'd help. "I'm going stir-crazy."

"I hear you." But for once, Boyd wasn't in the mood to play the polite guest. "But you're going to keep your butt inside and keep an eye on things. Like Herman."

Artie returned a rebellious look but didn't argue. The way Boyd's mind was made up, he figured a fight with Artie right now might turn into a nuclear explosion. He'd seen the spark and fire in that woman. He felt a surprising amount of relief when she gave him a mulish look but didn't disagree. Hell, she even planted her bottom in the recliner near Herman's.

And Herman had gone back to watching some seasonal cartoon or other. Boyd hoped that wasn't a bad sign. And there stood the Christmas tree, always on, with not one cheery thing about it at the moment.

Ah, hell. Boyd left by the back door through the mudroom. Booted up, wearing his parka, he was ready enough for the cold day.

He paused on the back step, though, and scanned for the footprints he'd seen. Nothing toward the alley. Snow must have filled them in. But right behind the house, where heat escaped, the prints remained in the crust.

Boyd went to get the shovel, but the first thing he did was cover up those remaining prints. If the creep decided to take another peek, he'd leave fresh tracks behind.

The sun began at last to crust the snow. It also felt warm on the shoulders of Boyd's parka and began heating the inside. He pulled the zipper down partway and resumed shoveling Clara's walk.

He was doing more than moving snow, however. He was keeping an eye on the activity on the street, looking for anything untoward.

Hard to tell on a street that had become busy with other shovelers like himself. He joined in the long-distance camaraderie, at least by waving to others. No one seemed inclined in these temperatures to gather for a confab. Which was good because he didn't need any distractions. Not now.

Since he could think of only one way the caller could prevent Artie from testifying in a trial, he couldn't afford any distraction, not one. He'd protect Artie and Herman with his life, if necessary. Part of that meant remaining on alert.

But night. When night came the danger would be higher than it was on this bright street. At night he would have to be on highest alert.

Because he absolutely did not believe this was going to end with a few phone calls.

ARTIE FUMED AT being stuck inside, even though she understood Boyd's reasoning. She was also getting sick of the sound of cartoons. Her dad had been so good this morning. Was he backsliding now?

She kept shooting looks his way, wondering if there was

any way to tell. At least he'd dressed himself this morning. Some days he never got out of his robe.

She went to make more coffee even though she didn't want any. Boyd might like it when he came in from the cold.

God, being stuck in the house like this was going to drive her absolutely over the edge. She needed to work. She needed to be out in the world, associating with other people, helping them as she could, protecting when necessary. Her job fulfilled her even on the days when it was boring.

Now this. Yeah, even on temporary suspension she could have gone out, walked around, talked to people, hit the grocery, picked up something at Maude's. Anything except being stuck in this house because of threats, trying not to pace because it might disturb her father, especially if he really was that absorbed in the cartoon.

Which she honestly hoped he wasn't. Stifling a sigh, she *did* pace a little, quietly, away from the TV. God, she needed to *do* something.

Midafternoon, she got a welcome surprise. Boyd opened the door and leaned in. "Look who came to visit. I'm taking the shovel round back."

Then Clara stepped into the house, her cheeks rosy and a huge smile on her face. She wore her calf-length, hooded red wool coat with faux white fur surrounding her face. Maybe not the warmest clothing for this climate, but perfect nonetheless.

She greeted Artie with a hug as Boyd disappeared back out the front door. "You're looking about as well as I'd expect from anyone with cabin fever."

Artie smiled. "How'd you guess?"

"I think I have a case, too." As Clara started unbuttoning her coat, she called out, "Hey, Herman! Am I less interesting that that damn TV?"

Herman turned immediately, first looking surprised, then grinning ear to ear. "Clara!" He rose instantly and opened his arms to her.

Clara shrugged out of her coat, letting Artie take it, then walked into Herman's embrace. "Been missing you, old man. Dang storm froze every bit of life, didn't it? Oh, the Christmas tree is beautiful. Letitia would have loved it."

Artie held her breath, fearing the past tense in her father's reply. Relief filled her as he stayed firmly in the present.

"She would have. Artie and Boyd put it up for me. I like remembering, Clara."

She stepped back, her hands on his upper arms, and nodded. "I like remembering, too."

"You look beautiful today."

"It's all the color the cold put in my cheeks. Don't go overboard there."

But Clara did look great, Artie thought, feeling drab in her jeans and a blue fleece pullover. Clara had managed to put together a green wool suit, dressed to the nines as it were. But then Clara had always had a sense of style even here where jeans were the uniform of the day.

"Now," said Clara, "are you going to turn off that TV so I can whip you at dominoes?"

"Whip me? You wish."

Ten minutes later Artie had set up the folding table and chairs, and brought them both coffee.

Then she wondered where Boyd had gone.

BOYD HAD CHECKED out Artie's backyard again, hunting for even the least indication that someone had been there.

Nothing. He wasn't sure whether that was good or bad. A stalker might keep away for a few days, he supposed. Planning. Or not wanting to leave an obvious trail. He couldn't dismiss those footprints he'd seen, though. Bad weather, too bad for an ordinary stroll. Too close to the house, as if someone wanted to peek through windows.

Whoever it had been was up to no good.

That tightening through his neck and shoulders returned. Gearing up for action, for something bad that lay around the corner. For an unseen threat.

He'd lived a long time with those sensations and he'd learned never to ignore them.

He scanned the houses around that might give anyone a good view of Artie's place, but saw nothing to concern him in the windows.

Then he headed next door to Clara's, her key in his pocket, his eyes scanning constantly. She wanted him to get the large casserole she'd made for dinner and bring it over. Easy enough.

Better yet, he could check another area for anything suspicious.

This threat didn't have to be coming from far away, though. It might be arising from just down this street or a block away. It could come fast.

He started thinking about what he could use as a weapon in Artie's house, because he was damned if he was going to use her baton or service pistol. She needed those. He was trained to use a whole lot of other stuff. Darn near anything, come to that.

Clara's house showed no sign of any unwanted visitors. The last sign had been those footprints he'd seen marching toward the back of Artie's house and they'd been nearly covered at the time.

None to be seen, not even the remains of the first ones. With the snow developing a crust, an intruder would have a harder time concealing his passage.

One good thing to think about. Right now the only one.

Then the wind whipped up and blew snow in his face. So okay, it wasn't all crusted yet. Didn't seem to be getting packed much, either. Footprints might still vanish in minutes.

Damn it all to hell!

THE CASSEROLE WAS warmly received. Artie appeared delighted. "I can't thank you enough, Clara!"

"I know how you love to cook," Clara answered wryly. "Anyway, it's nothing special. Creamed chicken and veggies. It'll need some bread with it. Or mashed potatoes." Clara looked up from the dominoes. "Mashed potatoes," she decided.

"Now that's something I *can* do," Artie answered.

"If it comes out of a box…" Clara laughed. "Just keep the casserole in the oven warming until we're ready for supper. That is, if you don't mind me staying."

"Of course not!"

Well, another person to watch over, Boyd thought. Not impossible, of course, but just another moving piece on the chessboard. He *did* enjoy seeing the happiness Clara clearly gave Herman and there was no question that she took pleasure in his company.

Cozy little scene. He went to stare out the front window at the slowly dimming day. A scene he'd never known. A family and a friend who were close and happy together. Had he ever truly tasted that in his adult life? It would be so easy to just settle in with these people and stay.

But darker thoughts haunted him as they'd been haunting him since he'd learned of Linda's assault. Memories surging from a war, unleashed by the rage he felt toward Linda's attacker. He clenched his fists and reached for his self-control.

Worse, though, he started wondering about Shelley. As little as she would tell him about Linda and how she was doing, why had she called at all to tell him Linda had been raped? Why had she shared that when she'd been doing everything she could to keep Boyd cut out of the picture, even before their divorce?

He closed his eyes, expelling a long breath. Telling him just so he could feel even worse for not being there for Linda, for being an absentee father for so long?

Since that phone call he'd begun to wonder about a lot of things. Trouble was, he wasn't sure of his own reactions, not since PTSD had bitten him on the butt after his last tour. How could he trust himself to be thinking clearly when Afghanistan kept trying to pop up? Trying to take over again?

He wanted to growl in frustration but silenced himself. He didn't want to upset the happy group behind him.

Damn, he needed action. Action of any kind. This waiting crap was going to kill him.

Then he had a thought. Checking his watch, he realized it still wasn't 5:00 p.m. in Seattle. Maybe time to call that attorney he'd used for the divorce. Get some information on just what rights the custody agreement gave him.

Like speaking to his daughter's therapist, to find out how she was really doing.

And whether she had a reason for not wanting to see her father. What were those reasons? Could he help counter them in any way?

He was on this damn trek because he sickened himself enough to want to vomit, because dangerous fury had overwhelmed him. Because he needed to see his daughter and couldn't. Because Shelley had promised to let him know the instant Linda agreed to see him. Because he'd give his life to hug his daughter just once.

Stepping outside into the deepening twilight, hardly aware of the frigid temperature or the growing clouds in the sky, he punched the number on his autodial and turned his back to the street, to break the wind. He hardly heard the truck move down the street behind him. Traffic had become more common throughout the day.

He got the lawyer's receptionist, of course, but she promised the attorney would call the next day, probably after court, mid-to late afternoon.

Good. He shoved his phone back into his pocket and suddenly realized he was close to getting frostbite on his fingertips and nose.

Genius, he thought sarcastically. He knew better. But then he should have known better about a whole bunch of things.

As THE LIGHT dimmed to almost nothing, Willie and Joe drove their ATV along the icy street past the cop's house. Needed to check on who was there.

They didn't get very close before Joe started swearing a blue streak. "Is some guy livin' with her now?" Joe cussed. "You see him out there without a parka? Ain't no weakling."

"We're heavier than him," Willie reminded him confidently. "Like football players. 'Member, we played us a good game in high school." He didn't much like what he saw, either, but that didn't change nothin'.

"Well, yeah. Maybe. And they's two of us."

"Yup. 'Member how we used to knock them linemen down? Nothin' on us and this one guy ain't *them*."

Then Joe cussed again. "They's having a freakin' party in there! Look at all them people." He added a few more cusswords. The man had gone inside so Willie slowed down and looked. The front windows were uncovered, revealing at least four people inside.

Then he started cussing, too.

"Haveta wait," Joe ranted. "Can't take much more, Willie."

"Me neither."

When they got home, he was gonna call Mack again, even though the guy was nothin' but a heap of warnings. Maybe he'd change his mind a bit and suggest somethin' useful.

Sometimes Willie wondered if Mack had the only smart brain 'tween the three of them. Well, mebbe not so smart. Lost his license after all.

Chapter Thirteen

Dinner, served around the kitchen table, proved to be as delightful as the afternoon had been. Herman was at his best, telling old jokes. Clara smiled and laughed. Artie felt a whole heck of a lot better. Boyd didn't say much, but there was evident warmth in his gaze and a slight smile on his face that made Artie feel even better.

This man deserved far better than the cards he'd been dealt.

In fact, she was starting to feel a little disgusted with herself. All that had happened with Lauer didn't amount to a hill of beans compared to what Boyd had been through.

Hell, he'd probably reckoned with a whole lot more than she could begin to imagine. Had learned to live with it all somehow. Now she needed to stiffen up and do the same.

She'd known when she'd signed up to be a cop that violence could become part of her life. What she hadn't imagined was what she could do, repeatedly, with her own hands. Wonder she hadn't broken his ribs.

Why she thought that was any worse than shooting him, she couldn't quite imagine. Except that she had lost control. Control was the one thing she needed to exert when she was walking around with a pistol on her belt and a riot gun in her vehicle. She'd always exercised it before.

Until Lauer. She wondered how long she was going to be scared of herself. Scared of losing her cool and overreacting.

She sighed and smiled at the conversation and felt little of the warmth inside her. The chill wouldn't quite leave her heart or soul. Not quite.

Despite herself, she glanced at the wall phone and wondered if that episode was over. If the bully who'd made those calls had had his fun and was now done.

God, she hoped so. Looking at her father, she knew she couldn't bear to have anything bad happen to him. To have someone willfully hurt him.

Then she realized that Boyd had looked at the wall phone, too, as if following her gaze and her thoughts. Their eyes met, and she felt a flash of lightning zing between them. Electric desire. Oh, God, she wanted him again.

But there was more, the concern that tightened the corner of his eyes. A strange mixture, she thought, as she saw her hunger briefly reflected in his face, along with that concern for her.

What a mess! Of two minds. Threatened or not threatened? Risk ignoring the threat and have it come true? Or give up on the need she felt, a need that was for normalcy as much as anything.

To be free of this whole chaotic situation and cling to one thing from the rest of life. A good thing. Not all the bad stuff that seemed determined to take over.

The chat around the table continued casually until Artie felt the weight of Boyd's warm hand on her thigh, the light squeeze of his fingers. Her eyes leaped to his and she saw again that slight smile, but this one decidedly warm.

She closed her eyes and released a long sigh. His hand slipped away. Herman's attention jumped to her. "Something wrong, Artie?"

She shook her head. "Maybe something right for once."

The sound of Boyd's quiet laugh eased the chill in her heart.

If he could reach past all his misery, maybe she could, too.

BOYD AND ARTIE took over the cleanup duty, sending Clara and Herman back to the living room recliners. The two of them just couldn't run out of conversation. Happy sounds. Good sounds.

Boyd spoke as he began to wash dishes. "Clara's good for Herman, isn't she? The two of them get along like a house on fire."

Artie nodded, smiling. "I love hearing it, watching it."

"I'm surprised they haven't moved in together."

At that Artie laughed. "Clara's definite about that. She said she was leg-shackled to one man for most of her adult life and likes being able to make all her own decisions without discussion."

Boyd returned her smile. "I can see that. Did she really call it leg-shackled?"

"She did." Artie shook her head and brushed hair back from her face with her forearm. "They were in love, though. She might feel free in some ways, now, but she misses Greg to this day. It just gets quieter with time, I hear."

"The grief? That's what I hear, too. Sometimes I don't believe it, but everyone's different."

The wall phone rang. Artie froze, a plate in her hands, and turned her head to stare at it.

Boyd moved toward it but she stopped him.

"No. If it's the station, they know my cell number and I get caller ID."

"You need caller ID on this phone, too," he remarked, returning to help with the cleanup.

"Until now I never did. I guess it's time to change that."

But as the last dishes and pans were dried and put away, Artie eyed that wall phone. White, slightly yellowed by the years. Remembering how her mother was disappointed to have to switch from the rotary dial to the punch buttons because the old phone had died.

Then, without warning, Boyd's arms slid around her, holding her tightly, astonishing her by lifting her onto the counter so that he stood between her legs.

"Boyd?" But suddenly she could barely find breath to squeeze out that one word.

"Shh," he murmured, running one hand over her hair while the other arm held her tight. He moved in a little closer, until their centers pressed and she could feel how hard he had grown for her.

"I want you," he said quietly. "At the worst time possible."

Her heart hammering, her breath coming in gasps. Electricity tingling through every inch of her body. Helplessly, she rocked her hips against him, bringing him even closer. "Your timing stinks."

"Right now it does. And they're too busy to notice."

His hand slipped until it cupped her head from behind, then he pressed her lips into his.

No gentle kiss. A hard, demanding one. Feeling as if it would suck the very heart from her. She raised her own arms, wrapping them around his neck, wanting him closer and closer.

Right now nothing seemed close enough, not even his tongue as it speared into her mouth, teasing exquisitely sensitive nerve endings.

Just about the time she grew certain she'd never be able

to breathe again and didn't care, he tore his mouth from hers and tucked her head onto his shoulder. A powerful shoulder that smelled good of man, of soap, of the outdoors.

"God, I don't want to let go of you," he said roughly.

"I don't want you to let go," she admitted. Odd to feel so weak and so strong all at once, but that's what he did for her. Weak and strong. A heady sensation.

Reluctantly she drew her arms from around his neck, then ran her hands over his strong back and powerful arms. A protector.

That's what he was built for, whatever he might think, and he'd already made it clear that he wanted to protect her and her father. Strangers to him, but that didn't seem to matter. And maybe they weren't strangers anymore.

But however he'd failed his wife and child, Artie was sure it wasn't because he hadn't tried to protect them. Maybe the Army had kept him away too much. Maybe his wife's decision to remain a thousand miles away with her family instead of knitting a home for herself, Boyd and their baby had had a lot to do with it. There was no way for her to know.

All she knew was the man she leaned into right now, and she didn't think he could possibly be the failure he believed himself to be.

Dang, how many men would walk clear across the country hoping to see their daughter again, all the while lashing themselves with guilt? Not many, she'd bet. Most would have either shrugged it off because they weren't wanted, or would have hopped a plane and arrived in an angry, controlling mood.

Boyd had chosen a better option, she thought. He'd given control to his daughter, who probably desperately needed it after being raped.

She wondered how she could talk to him about that? Could she even persuade him if she did? Was it her place at all?

Then the kitchen phone rang again.

Their eyes met, all softness gone. Boyd stepped back, steadying her as she slid from the counter. She tried not to shake as she took the few steps and reached for the receiver.

"Jackson," she said, the word clipped. Then she heard Guy's voice and relief made her knees weak. As if sensing it, Boyd pushed one of the kitchen chairs over so she could sit.

"It's Guy," she said to Boyd.

He stepped back, leaning against the counter, folding his arms. He appeared far from relaxing completely.

BOYD *WAS* FAR from relaxing. It didn't matter to him that it was Guy, that Artie appeared relieved to hear his voice. The idea that she had weakened upon realizing that it was not another telephone threat told him a hell of a lot more than anything she'd been admitting.

Nor did he think this call was going to be stuffed with cheery news like "we've caught the caller." Not likely.

As he watched, he saw tension creep back into Artie, a tension she'd utterly lost when they embraced just now. The softening, the melting, it all vanished within a minute.

He cussed silently and unfolded his arms, unconsciously preparing himself for trouble. Stiffening into readiness, like when he marched out into enemy territory. His fists clenched and unclenched.

"Thanks, Guy," she said finally. "Just keep updating me, please? And no, I don't need a guard outside. I don't *want* one. I already feel like a prisoner, and frankly I'm going to be more at risk when I leave this house."

Boyd spoke, not caring that he interrupted a supposedly private conversation. "Artie won't be going anywhere alone."

Her head jerked around; the receiver came far enough from her ear that he heard Guy's voice say, "Glad to hear it. That Boyd fellow? You couldn't ask for better."

When Artie disconnected, she glared at Boyd. "You're not going to be my watchdog, either."

"Sure I am. Just try to stop me."

They stared at each other, chins setting stubbornly, then at last Artie dropped her gaze to stare at her hands. They rested on her lap, turned upward, looking relaxed.

Boyd doubted they were relaxed at all. This woman was good at hiding inside herself. Probably made her a good cop, not to reveal herself and her thoughts unnecessarily.

It was also maddening. He wanted to scoop her up again, hug her until she squeaked and promised to start talking.

That would turn him into a hell of a brute. Screw that.

He sighed and leaned back against the counter again. "Okay, I get it. Accepting help mashes your ego. But in this case, nobody is going to let you get *physically* mashed, okay? Like it or not. This Guy sure seems to want to protect you. And from meeting the sheriff, Gage Dalton, I think he pretty much feels the same. Wouldn't surprise me if they keep an eye on you whether you want it or not."

At last she blew a long breath, brushed her black hair back from her face and tucked it behind her ears. When she looked up, he saw just how weary her eyes appeared now. She'd hidden it well, but not now. It was as if she trusted him enough to reveal her exhaustion.

He stepped closer and squatted, taking her hands in his. His right knee objected, a long-ago battle injury, but he never let it stop him. Right now, nothing but a fifty-cal bullet hitting him in the chest could have stopped him.

"Tell me," he said quietly, "a little about this Guy. Redwing, you said at some point?"

She nodded. Almost reluctantly she wound her fingers with his. A small hand in a large hand. "Guy Redwing. Our newest detective. He's Indigenous and I'm sure that's given him some trouble over the years, but he's the best. Kinda stoic, but I'd trust him to have my back in the worst situation."

"Sounds like a good man."

"He is." Her fingers tightened. "Boyd, the department can't afford to put any kind of detail on me. I don't know how much I have to emphasize that, but after this storm everyone's going to be stretched to the limit, more even than usual. People still haven't been able to dig out. They may need food or supplies. They may not have heat or water. Some may have gotten injured." Then she averted her face. "When people get locked up like this, well, domestic violence rises, too. Every man and woman in the department is going to be needed all over this county."

He nodded. "I get that. And like I said, I'm not letting you go anywhere alone."

She released a heavy breath. "And my dad? I can't leave him here alone, not after that phone call."

"Then he'll get some out-and-abouting with us. We'll deal. I'll help you deal. For once, damn it, just take the ego bruising."

That brought the faintest of smiles to her face. "I guess you figured me out."

"It's like reading a book I wrote." He watched the astonishment appear on her face, then a small laugh escaped her.

"God, Boyd, you're something else!"

"We try." He released her hands reluctantly and stood

because his knee demanded it and there was no point in annoying it unnecessarily.

"More coffee? Or one of those beers I stuffed in your fridge?"

"Beer," she said after a moment. "I don't need to get any more wound up. I'm doing just fine in that department."

"Or I could get you a brandy?"

She shook her head. "My dad and Clara are having too much fun out there. I don't want to disturb them."

He put two longnecks on the table, and they sat again facing each other. "I'm getting addicted to this table," he remarked, taking a long pull from the bottle.

"No place else right now. I suppose one of these days I should open up the dining room again. It's been closed since Mom died and I just haven't gone in there. Haven't even cleaned or dusted it. She used to make such a big deal of setting a perfect dinner table even for just the three of us. Making it special. It hurts to look in there. But right now I'm wishing for the extra room. You wouldn't have to sleep on the couch."

"I'm fine on the couch."

"And I could offer Clara a place to stay tonight. I don't want her going home alone. Don't ask me why."

Boyd tilted his head. "Then give her your bed, you can take the sofa, and I'll sleep on the rug. Trust me, I've slept in worse conditions. At least there won't be a stubborn rock poking into my ribs."

She smiled at him, sipped her own beer.

Boyd had been letting her find her way past the mood that had struck her during Guy's call, but he couldn't let it go forever. No way. He had to know what disturbed her because it might be important to this entire situation.

"So," he asked slowly, quietly, "what news did Guy have for you?"

Her face sagged. "Nothing, really. They can't identify whoever called me. A burner. They tracked one call to a tower out where the land is so flat the line of sight allows it to work over a huge area. Any number of people out there, some not on the registered deeds. Anyway, they got that one call, then the tower started to fritz. There was another call from a different tower, nearer to town. Again transmission troubles. Storms are good at that. They're still looking. As for the rest…" She shrugged. "Who knows how many records glitched during the blizzard."

"So there's no way to know who's been bugging you."

"Not yet anyway. Doesn't matter where he, or they, are, I guess. They still have to get to me."

"Well, it doesn't make the situation any worse."

That pulled another smile to her face, a small one. "Man, you're positive."

"You know damn well I'm not always. Anything else?"

"Yeah. Bea's gonna recover. Good news. She's refusing to press charges. Not good."

His head jerked back a bit. "You mean that bastard is going to get off free?"

She shook her head. "The prosecutor is filing the charge anyway. Evidence. They have a record of her injuries and they have me to testify that *he* did it to her."

"So it all comes down to you."

"Evidently."

Boyd sat very still, absorbing the news, trying not to get angry with the victim, waiting for Artie to look at him again.

"Well, that explains a lot. Every reason for you not to testify."

She shrugged. "I told you I will. They can't stop me."

"And as we mentioned at the time, there's only one way to stop you."

"But why the calls, Boyd? Why would they think they could scare me off?"

"Because maybe they don't know diddly about the law."

AFTER THE BEER, they went to the living room, where Clara and Herman appeared content in the separate recliners. Didn't keep them from extending their hands across the side table. Holding hands.

Artie felt a bubble of warmth rise in her. Precious moments for the two of them, well worth protecting.

Clara giggled when she saw them, but she didn't tug her hand out of Herman's.

Artie sat on the couch. "I was thinking, Clara, I'd like you to spend the night here. I'd just feel better about it."

Clara shook her head. "No room at the inn."

"We'll make room. You can have my bed, I'll sleep on the couch and Boyd's offered to sleep on the floor."

Clara eyed Boyd and spoke dryly. "The floor, huh?"

Artie nearly blushed at her obvious subterfuge.

Boyd then startled the room. "Is it anyone's business where I sleep?"

After an instant of surprise, everyone burst into laughter, including Artie.

"Well, it's Artie's business," Clara said archly. "But none of mine or Herman's, right, honey?"

Herman was smiling. "No Artemis anymore, huh?"

"Dang it, Dad!"

He laughed.

"What's that mean?" Clara asked.

"Oh, God, don't ask him that, *please*. Spare me. He just likes to yank my chain."

"Tsk," Clara said to Herman. "Don't be bad to your daughter." Then she leaned toward Artie's dad. "I'll just ask later anyway."

Artie rolled her eyes, but there was no escaping this. Nor upon reflection did she really want to. A glance at Boyd told her all was good with him, so she let it go.

Then she rose. "Bedtime snacks anyone?"

EVERYONE WAS AGREEABLE to finishing the coffee cake that was in the fridge. Hot cocoa joined it, all of it prepared and served with Boyd's help.

The two older people looked quite delighted to be waited on, especially Clara, who'd probably spent most of her life looking after a family and now taking care of herself. And Artie's dad.

Eventually, though, as the night deepened, Boyd stood, stretching. "I need some air and I need to get a few more logs in here for the fire. I'll be back in a jiff."

Artie watched him pull on his jacket and zip it up, the balaclava going on over his head. She had the very strong feeling that he wasn't going out just for a breath and an armload of wood.

Okay. So this experienced veteran seemed to be more concerned than she was. Or maybe she just wasn't letting herself face it.

IT WAS TRUE Boyd had more on his mind than wood and fresh air. With the town and parts of the county steadily digging themselves out, the opportunities to get to Artie were increasing. He was on a mission, one of reasonable stealth, to hunt for any sign that a human had been prowling. The emerging moon brightened the snow almost to daylight brightness, making it harder to remain unseen.

But the same would hold true for anyone who tried to approach.

Shoveled sidewalks were covered with boot prints now. It looked as if a mail person had been delivering, sometimes approaching front doors. Awful job, he often thought. But those approaches went straight to front doors, then back to the street.

Most people had cleared enough of the snowbanks away to make their cars and doors accessible. Lots of hard work had been happening that day.

But there was little sign of anything untoward nearby. Kids had been playing in yards, trying to build snowmen, but the ground was all trampled, mostly by small feet, and the partial snowmen stood testament to the activity.

At last he began looking around the back. He circled Clara's house first, wanting the snow to be untouched when he reached Artie's, unless someone else had been out there.

Nothing. Pristine snow, muddled a bit from his own trips with the snow shovel, greeted his eyes. No one had come back, at least not here.

Shaking his head, trying to decide how he wanted to evaluate this noninformation, he scooped a huge armload of wood and returned inside through the mud room. The logs had come from lower in the woodpile, from beneath a tarp that had provided some protection, but they still had snow caught on them.

Messy mudroom, he thought with mild amusement as he mopped up the increasing puddle from the wood and his boots.

Then he lifted his head, thinking. Maybe this guy, the one making the threats, didn't need to hurry. Maybe he could afford to take his time.

Well, hell, wouldn't that be just great?

THE LATHROP BROTHERS had given up and started shoveling. Riding their ATV through town had seemed kind of obvious, and cold, too. Besides, there was that party going on in there.

Beer fueled the process, of course, and from time to time they went inside to warm themselves with some whiskey. Maybe even some coffee.

"Shouldn't gotta work this hard," Joe complained.

Willie didn't disagree. "Could drive to Miami."

Joe snorted. "Like that damn truck'd get us there."

With more whiskey the shoveling seemed less important. Besides, it was warm in front of the fire, and comfy in them old recliners their bodies had mashed into shape over the years.

"Still ain't figgered it out," Willie said finally. "That damn cop gonna be the death of me."

"More likely *me*," Joe groused.

"Worse can happen."

The two brothers glared at each other and appeared ready to come to blows, but then another pour of whiskey and they settled back.

Willie spoke. "At least we gotta look-see."

"Yeah," Joe retorted. "And that guy ain't no twig."

"Anyway," Willie continued. "He don't look like no football player. We got the edge on that, 'member?"

Joe relaxed a bit. "Yeah, we got the moves."

"Tackle good, don't we?"

"Allus."

"That's it. He ain't no problem. Take 'im out, then we get to that cop, and mebbe her damn dad."

"Whadda we want him for? Old guy just get in the way."

"Hostage," said Willie. "Make her do what we want."

At that Joe finally looked appalled. "Things ain't bad enough the way they is?"

Chapter Fourteen

Night blanketed the house, bringing the utter quiet of a town fallen into sleep. Boyd lay on the rug beneath a blanket Artie had found somewhere, using his jacket for a pillow. His gaze followed the flicker of firelight on the ceiling and he dozed on and off. Experience had taught him to sleep like a cat. At a single sound he could wake instantly, be ready.

He hadn't even taken off his boots, because if there was one thing a soldier knew, it was that when you had to hit the ground, your feet needed protection.

He was comfortable in his old gray sweats, though. As he listened, he could hear Artie's quiet, steady breathing. Reassuring. And if he'd had to bet on it he'd have taken odds that Clara was sharing Herman's bed.

The thought made him smile faintly. A bit of pleasure did everyone some good. Life offered little enough of it.

No unusual sounds disturbed him, though. Not a one. The sounds of the old house had become familiar, almost reassuring. Nothing different there.

The fire was dying down, but still splashed flame and light. Cozy.

Maybe not cozy enough. His thoughts kept wandering to Artie, wondering what he was getting into with her. If she'd allow him to get into anything at all.

And Linda. She remained his priority. Maybe he'd hear from the damn lawyer tomorrow with some good news. He could sure use some.

Then, a while later, he felt Artie's hand brush his arm. Probably fell off the couch while she slept, he thought.

But then her hand began to move in a light unmistakable caress. In one mere instant he burned hotter than any fire.

"Artie?" he whispered. "You awake?"

Her answer was to slide off the couch until she rested on top of him.

Oh, Lord, fireworks exploded in his head.

"Boyd," she breathed, then their mouths met in a kiss that was far from gentle. Hunger filled it with strength. A sealing of breaths together.

His arms wrapped around her, holding her crushingly tight. Had he ever wanted a woman this much? If so, he couldn't remember it. She writhed against him, blanket and clothing creating a maddening barrier.

"Boyd," she murmured again when their mouths separated and breath returned. "I need..."

So did he. No time for finesse, though. Not here plain as day on this damn floor when either Clara or Herman could rise for a glass of water.

Boyd lifted her slightly and yanked the blanket away. He found the waistband of her pajama bottoms and tugged them down. Then his own sweatpants. Heat met heat, so sweet, so exciting, crazing.

He found his way into her hot depths, then slipped his hands beneath the blanket, hoping they weren't cold, and cupped her breasts, finding her puckered nipples.

The softest of moans escaped her as she started rocking against him. He bit back his own groans of pleasure and let her take the lead. She'd taken the bit between her teeth and rode him hard, then harder. A lighting storm erupted in his head, driving away everything except the miracle of Artie.

Then soon, way too soon, completion found them, weakening them with total satisfaction. Artie lay limply on him and he could barely move enough to tug the blanket over them, concealing them, warming them even more.

"God," Artie murmured, keeping her voice low. "God, Boyd. You ignite me."

"Same here," he said a bit gruffly. "You set me off like a range fire."

The quietest laugh escaped her. "Maybe you're the best thing that's walked into my life in a while."

"Ditto." He meant it, too. She took him out of himself, carried him to nicer places, places he wanted to reach and remain eventually. She didn't make him forget, but she offered the possibility of better things to come.

Not necessarily with her, he reminded himself. She sure seemed determined to remain self-sufficient. She might well feel that she had enough on her plate without taking on a vet with a passel of problems that seemed to dog his every step.

She had a pretty normal life as near as he could tell. A normalcy he'd never known, not even in his broken childhood home.

But none of that kept him from enjoying these precious minutes while she relaxed on him, sighing quietly, occasionally running a hand over his arm or shoulder. Moments like these should be eternal.

Eventually, Artie raised her head. "I suppose I should get back on the couch."

Boyd snorted quietly. "As if Herman doesn't already know or suspect."

"But Clara..."

"I'd bet ten bucks right now that she's in bed with him."

A soft titter escaped Artie. "I sometimes wonder what those two get up to when I'm working."

"Wouldn't surprise me if it's more than dominoes. You see how they look at each other."

About like Boyd was looking at Artie these days. About like she'd begun to look at him.

"Yeah." She sighed. "It's so good for him."

Good for him, too, Boyd thought, but didn't say so. He had no right to push the issue, not given his other problems.

But reality returned because it always did. Because it *had* to.

Artie spoke quietly. "You said something about calling a lawyer?"

"She's supposed to get back to me tomorrow."

He felt Artie nod against his chest. "You've got to have *some* rights."

"At least to find out the truth from Linda's counselor, not just what Shelley wants to tell me."

"This must hurt like hell."

"It does." Why not admit it? There were all kinds of pain and grief in life, but this one was taking the cake, even more so because he couldn't evade his own responsibility, his own failures as a father. Maybe he had no right to happiness at all.

But he had a right to know how his daughter was doing. How she was coping. If she'd ever want a hug from him.

Then he thought he heard something from outside.

He eased Artie to the side. "I heard something," he said quietly. "Stay here. Keep an eye on your father."

In one, swift easy movement he rose to his feet, pulled on his parka and watch cap, then slipped silently out the front door.

Sitting in a heap of blankets, Artie stared after him, her

heart racing. Then she rose swiftly and went to her bedroom. As they'd suspected, Clara wasn't in there. Which made it easier for Artie to unlock her pistol and grab her baton.

If anyone came into this house tonight, they were going to meet hell unbound.

ACROSS THE STREET, mostly hidden behind the huge ancient trunk of an elm tree, probably one of the very few on this continent that had escaped the ravages of Dutch elm disease, Mack Murdo watched. He had to figure out a way out of this heap of crap Joe and Willie was busy building. He'd tossed a small rock across the street at the side of the cop's house, and now waited for a reaction.

He saw the guy come out the front door, as if he'd reacted. Murdo was pretty sure he'd been soundless, other than the rock, but neither his hearing nor his eyesight were as good as they'd been in his hunting days.

He didn't really have a horse in this race, other than his friendship with Billy Lauer. Good drinking buddies from way back. He didn't much care about Joe Lathrop at all. Man was a stupid sucker. But it might do Mack some good to see that bitch of a cop get her comeuppance.

Now Mack, frankly, didn't want to deal with killing that woman and he was getting a notion that the Lathrops were thinking about it. Nor did he like the idea that the Lathrop boys had threatened the old man. A coward's choice.

Mack Murdo had *some* standards. His grievance didn't reach killing or taking people as hostages.

But he *did* give a damn about Billy Lauer. Man had beat his wife. So what? Men did that. Gotta keep a woman in line. But not to the extent of nearly killing the woman or getting an attempted murder charge for it.

Whether the Lathrop boys wanted to listen to his cousin

the lawyer didn't matter. They didn't freaking get the whole picture.

So while Mack Murdo wanted to teach that cop a lesson, he wanted no part of the Lathrops' messy plans. Not to that kind of extent.

And to make matters worse, they'd called the woman and threatened her father. What good did they think that would do? The few words of sense he'd tried to push their way had gone unheeded or unheard.

Nothing like those two to get obsessed.

Mack was a guy who preferred to take his time when he could. Those two hadn't waited for anything except a blizzard. And their own lack of a plan.

He watched the stranger examine the street, look around, hike toward the back of the house.

Guy was on watch, no doubt of that. None at all.

Skinny or not, something in the way he moved bothered Mack. He could be a threat. A real threat, for which neither of the Lathrops would be prepared. Or even able to handle.

Then there was that cop herself. She'd beat Billy near to death, he'd heard. Except she hadn't put Billy in the hospital. Lucky Billy. He wondered if the Lathrop boys had gotten the measure of that. What that woman might do if her family was threatened.

Mack bit back a sigh and waited, watching. Too many people in that house right now anyway, according to what Joe and Willie had told him. Needed to get the numbers down.

The stranger came round again to the front of the house, surveyed the street, then returned inside.

Okay then. Mack started shambling down the sidewalk, trying to appear aimless, but he wasn't aimless at all.

Hell, no. He was going to talk some good sense into those

boys, then try to get them to make a plan that wouldn't get any of them killed or maimed. And still teach that cop a lesson.

He didn't much care if the Lathrops went to prison, but he damn well wasn't going himself. Which might mean knocking Joe's and Willie's heads together.

Mack shook his head and let an exasperated growl escape him. How the hell had it come to this? Simply because he'd sympathized about the cop. Had he dragged himself into this by being a friend?

Some friends the Lathrops had turned out to be. Heads as thick as blocks of cement, hearing everything wrong.

Everything.

ONCE INSIDE, Boyd saw Artie at the ready, collapsed baton in her hand, service pistol belted to her side. Every line of her was poised for action.

He tried to keep the snow on his boots to the rug in front of the door, saying, "Nothing. No one's been out there. Must have been a branch or something caught by the wind."

Muscle by muscle she relaxed, almost as if unwilling to let go of her preparedness, almost as if she *needed* to act.

He understood that. This waiting for a threat to materialize wasn't sitting well with him, either.

Artie finally uncoiled and began to unbelt her pistol. "Coffee," she said presently.

He had to agree. As much as he'd enjoyed their lovemaking, as much as he wanted to stay cocooned in that blanket with her, neither of them was in the mood any longer.

Tension had invaded and wasn't going to leave them anytime soon.

Before long they sat at the kitchen table, hot mugs of coffee between them.

"I need to make some more bread," Boyd remarked absently.

"That was sure good." She sounded about as enthusiastic as he felt.

Between them on the table lay her baton and pistol. A reminder. No escaping it.

She raised a weary face. "I sure as hell wish I had any kind of clue about who's behind this."

"The wife beater is still in jail?"

"Until tomorrow, at least."

"Then?"

"Then Judge Carter will arraign him. Maybe give him bail."

"A man like that? With what he's done?" That seriously troubled Boyd.

Artie shook her head. "Among other things, bail has to be reasonable for the crime. At this point I don't know what the prosecutor will charge him with. Or be able to charge him with. Right now all Amberly has to go on is my brief description from the scene and Bea Lauer's condition. I'll need to make a statement eventually, but right now?" Artie shrugged.

"So what exactly will happen?"

"Amberly will go to court and present the charges. Lauer will be given an opportunity to plead. He'll plead not guilty of course. Then both Amberly and Lauer's lawyer will argue terms of bail. It's all up to the judge in the end."

Boyd nodded and reached across the table to touch her hand. "Which is ripping you up?"

"No. It's standard. The only things ripping me up are my own conduct at the Lauer scene and the threat against my dad."

He breathed a curse. "What do you think of this judge?"

One corner of her mouth tipped up. "An honest man who

really gives a damn about the cases that come before him. I admire and respect him. He never just runs by the book."

Then she snorted.

"What?"

"The judge's father is Earl Carter, one of our local lawyers. Wouldn't it be something if he got tapped to be the public defender for Lauer?"

Boyd's head jerked up a bit. "Wouldn't that be a conflict?"

"Who knows? Earl is as respected as his son. Honest as the day is long. I guess the only one who might object would be the judge himself. Then comes the question of who else they can tap. Not that many criminal defense lawyers around here. They might have to bring someone in from outside the county. That'd gum up the works."

Boyd nodded, taking in all the complexities, but mildly amused that they were talking about the legalities and avoiding the one thing foremost on both their minds.

But what else could they do? Nothing was more anxiety-inducing than to have no gauge of the threat. Of where it might come from. Running blind into a possible narrow defile, as he had so many times. Wondering who was on top of those cliffs or if anyone was there at all.

Artie spoke suddenly. "You know what I'm never going to forgive? This bastard threatening my father." She slipped her hand from beneath his and balled it into a tight fist.

"I completely understand."

"I'm sure you do." Then she shook her head. "Damn it, Boyd, I'm feeling that violence rising in me again. The same thing that happened when I beat Billy Lauer with my baton. I hate feeling like I can kill."

"But anyone can," he said flatly. "*Anyone* can kill in the right circumstances, and saving a life or protecting family...those are some of the circumstances."

She sighed, blowing the breath straight up her face so that it ruffled her feathery bangs. "I'm starting to hate myself."

"Oh, for Pete's sake," he said sharply. "Don't do that. You have no reason to. Think about it. Lauer had beaten his wife to a pulp and was strangling the life from her. That's what you said. What else were you supposed to do? Hold up a peace sign? You said he wouldn't listen, his wife was on the brink of death and there was only one thing you could do. *Get his attention.* Break his focus and intent. In the process you might have gotten yourself killed."

She closed her eyes. "Maybe."

"No maybe about it. Take it from me. I've been there. And that kind of incident is one of the few that never gives me nightmares. Never. Much as we may dislike it, there are situations that justify that kind of reaction."

"I don't know." She sighed again.

"Think about it. If you feel bad now, how would you have felt if Lauer had succeeded in killing his wife while you stood helplessly by?"

Her head lifted, her blue eyes glistening just a bit. "I didn't think of it that way."

"Of course not. You're a nice, moral, law-abiding person. You broke all three of those parts of yourself. Hard to deal with."

"Broken," she murmured. "That's how I feel." The description cut her to the bone.

"You won't always feel that way, not to this degree. You'll find your footing again."

One corner of her mouth quirked. "Have *you*?"

"A lot more than I had when I came home for the last time."

She didn't answer him, sat there lost in thought.

Then, surprising him, she jumped up and started looking through the fridge. "God, I'm hungry. Cinnamon rolls? They need to be baked."

"I'll help."

As he stood, she faced him again, and something in her face had softened. She asked quietly, "Is that what you're doing on this hike of yours? Finding your footing?"

He nodded, revealing more of himself than he truly liked, but feeling he needed to share part of his innermost self with this woman. "Yeah. That's some of it. Lots of time to think. To deal with things, like the past, like the dark fog of the future. Like the rage I feel about what happened to Linda. Sooner or later, I gotta deal with it all."

Astonishing him, she put down the tube of rolls and walked straight into his arms. "You're a good buddy," she murmured into his shoulder. "A good friend. We'll both get through this, won't we?"

"We will," he answered with more surety than he felt. "We will."

Chapter Fifteen

Morning arrived cloaked in beauty. The snow gleamed and glistened whitely under the sun, the crystals acting like prisms in some places, reflecting the colors of the rainbow. A sight that might be missed by those who believed that snow was only white.

But it was not. It was full of color.

Artie stood looking out at it, thinking how perfect it was. There hadn't even been enough activity yet to gray the white with blown dust or the exhaust of cars or the woodsmoke that rose from many houses, like her own.

Pristine. Unlike the world that was seriously beginning to stir out there. Kids heading to school. People driving to work. Others shoveling, probably with more than a few curses. Down the street a snowblower shredding the silence with its engine.

She couldn't help smiling, even though she knew what lay behind that perfection. Even though she knew the dark depths that lurked below, that to some extent belonged to all human beings. Even though she awaited action from the man who had warned her to forget, had suggested her father might be at risk. One way or another, something bad lurked, and that bad thing would arrive.

All she could do was prepare mentally and emotionally.

From the kitchen came the aromas of baking cinnamon rolls. Clara had taken over out there, in Herman's company. For the moment anyway, the two had become inseparable.

Clara said something to Herman about needing to go home for a change of clothes. Herman objected. Clara responded that he didn't want to smell her in dirty clothes.

"I'll take you covered with mud," he replied.

Again, Artie smiled.

Boyd, near the kitchen, spoke. "I'll run next door and get whatever you need, Clara. Just give me a list."

"And have you pawing around my underthings?"

Herman chuckled. Boyd's response was dry. "As if I haven't seen any of it before."

"You read lingerie catalogs, do you?"

Both Boyd and Herman guffawed.

A wider smile came to Artie's face, but along with it came apprehension. She didn't like the idea that Clara might be caught in the approaching threat. Didn't like it at all.

But she also didn't know what to do about it. Throwing Clara out, however gently she did it, might cause a serious storm of another kind, mostly with Herman. She couldn't bear the thought of her dad being angry with her.

It wasn't as if it hadn't happened in the past, all the way back to her childhood, but now was different. Very different. God help her if they had a fight and Herman keeled over before she could make amends. Yeah, such morbid thoughts troubled her from time to time. Thoughts she could hardly stand.

EARLY AFTERNOON, the county went into a near state of shock. People in outlying areas were still trying to dig out when another blizzard marched in.

Artie watched heavily falling snow through the window and cussed. Loudly enough to be heard.

Boyd came to stand beside her. "Again?"

"Yeah. This is unreal. Make Clara give you that list. I am *not* sending her home tonight in this."

"I'll make a fast trip to the grocery, too. Did I do okay last time?"

"You did a wonderful job." She turned around to face him. "Boyd, I can't leave them alone here. Not now. Do you mind doing this by yourself?"

He gave her a half smile. "I wouldn't allow you to leave them alone."

She reached in her jeans pocket and handed him keys. "My personal vehicle. It's parked beside my official one."

He nodded. "I'll be fast."

It didn't take Clara long to agree to giving Boyd a list of what she needed. She saw what was coming, too, and clearly didn't want to spend another blizzard alone in her house.

Herman turned on the weather channel. A cheerful meteorologist chatted about the unexpected blizzard and the reasons for it.

Clara spoke. "Have you ever noticed how much these guys enjoy a good weather catastrophe?"

Artie had to laugh, whatever her other worries. "It's their bread and butter. Nobody would watch if the forecast was always for perfect days."

Boyd left swiftly, and with amazing speed returned with Clara's things packed in the suitcase she'd told him about. She thanked him profusely, but before she finished he was out the door again.

Artie heard her car start without a problem. One thing not to worry about.

But another blast of Arctic air had escaped. The stratosphere and the troposphere, whatever they were, had messed up the polar vortex. Look out folks.

Six inches of fresh snow, winds at gale force. Artie wanted to collapse in a chair. *More?*

Even worse, it might prolong the threat, hold it off. More waiting to find out the worst. *Damn it all to hell!*

MACK WAS MORE than ticked by the time he got back to his ramshackle house. Another storm? And those Lathrops so eager to deal with that damn cop that they kept making stupid phone calls and hinting at worse? Now the new storm might make them even more impatient.

And likely to die from the elements before they even got near that Jackson woman. Somehow he had to figure out an idea that would keep them all from getting life sentences but settle those two jackasses down enough that there wasn't a string of bodies halfway across the county.

But one thing was for sure. He wasn't going anywhere near those two blockheads. In no way did he want to be considered abetting whatever they did. It was stupid of him to have ever thought that suggesting a phone call would palliate them. Give them chuckles the way they'd shared during their school days by making nuisance calls.

Nope. These jerks had turned this all into a steamroller, and nothing he'd said had slowed it down.

WILLIE AND JOE were having their own thoughts about the coming storm and they weren't silent ones. Joe cussed a blue streak, not very inventive because he only knew some basic cuss words.

Willie threw a bottle of beer across the room. Beer washed everywhere but the bottle didn't break, which was good because neither of them was going to waste time cleaning up broken glass. As for the beer, it didn't matter. Whole place reeked of it along with woodsmoke and unwashed bodies. They were nose blind.

"What now?" Joe demanded. "I ain't gonna wait forever. Dang, we should call Billy, see if he's outta jail yet."

"What's he s'posed to do?"

"*Help!* Mack ain't being much help."

"He don't really want no part of this. Been mad at us since we made the second phone call."

Joe nodded. "Guess so. Said it was a warning to the bitch."

"We was trying to scare her."

"Ain't seen her running yet."

Willy shook his head and grabbed another beer. "Now she got all them people in that damn house. Might be too many even for us." He looked down at his lineman's belly. At least that's how he thought of it.

"Gotta do it anyway," Joe said harshly. "Before we get stuck and can't move again. So think, you bastard. You allus say you got the brain."

Willie had begun to doubt it but refused to say so. He still didn't have a plan, which wasn't making him feel all that smart. "Call Mack."

"What the hell for? He keeps telling us reasons this ain't no good."

"Call 'im anyway. Mebbe he got some idea."

Turned out Mack's only idea was to leave the bitch alone. They'd already gone too far.

Willie and Joe exchanged glances. The words escaped simultaneously. "We gotta kill the broad."

WHEN BOYD RETURNED from the grocery with a trunkful of food, everyone helped put it away. Plenty for another siege.

Then Clara and Herman settled in the living room with the TV still on the weather channel, and Boyd and Artie went to the kitchen for a little privacy. Boyd even started another loaf of bread. That machine sure made a lot of noise.

Artie faced him over the inevitable cups of coffee. "I have to do something, Boyd. I can't sit here waiting and wondering if those calls were from a bully or if they were serious. I've had enough of sitting on tenterhooks, enough of waiting for a bomb or a firecracker. Or nothing at all."

He nodded, his expression grave. "I hear you."

"And with another storm, we'll be locked down again, wondering. If they're really gonna act, don't you think it would be soon, before everything becomes impassable again?"

He nodded again. "That's what I would do. But they're not me."

Artie heaved a big sigh. "No, they're not. I keep thinking that if those phone calls were genuine threats then they must be fools. They put me on guard."

"True." He sipped coffee, then drummed his fingers on the table. "But you said the guy wanted you to forget. Forget what?"

"Something I saw, and I have a pretty good idea. Intent is important in a murder charge. Right now Amberly doesn't feel he has enough for attempted murder. More evidence needed, I guess, although where he's going to get it from I can't imagine."

"You," Boyd said flatly. "You saw most of it. You can testify that beast wouldn't quit."

Artie sighed again. "Yeah." The memories surged to the forefront, making her stomach turn over. "He'll want my full, formal statement before he can go ahead, I guess. At least Bea Lauer is safe in the hospital."

Silence fell. More coffee was poured.

Then Artie said, "I need to make myself an easy target before this storm hits full force. Then if this guy really wants to act, he'll have an opportunity before the whole county gets shut down again."

Boyd's face darkened and he reached across the table, squeezing her hand tightly. "Artie…"

"I need this resolved, Boyd. Somehow. This just can't keep up."

"What if he never shows?"

"Then I'll assume the calls were bullying and I'll get back to normal life."

His hand tightened even more. "And if he does show? Your life may be at risk."

"I know." Her own face darkened. "But, Boyd, I'm a cop. If I'm afraid to face danger, then I should turn in my uniform."

"Well, I can hardly disagree with you about that, considering how many years I spent in uniform."

She offered a crooked smile. "In much more dangerous situations. I'm up against one guy, not an army."

"You assume it's one guy."

She closed her eyes a moment. "I doubt it could be very many."

BOYD COULDN'T ARGUE THAT, EITHER. He totally understood her need to finish this. The storm had created a cocoon in which to be nervous, but not to be truly fearful.

Now there was a break in the weather and any true fear could no longer be quelled. He also understood her need to get this settled before the world became frozen in place once more.

He turned his head, looking out the kitchen window.

The snow fell, but not heavily. The worst was supposed to arrive tomorrow. A narrow window in which to take any kind of action.

He faced her again. "You got a plan?"

"I have to be alone. Clara and my dad have to go to her house. You have to head out. The motel, the truck stop diner, anywhere that makes it appear you've moved out."

He gave her a half smile. "I've really moved in?"

"It's beginning to look like it." But her tone was mildly humorous.

He waited a minute, certain he was about to stir up a hornet's nest. Then he said, "I'll come back because I sure as hell am not going to leave you here alone."

"But he might see you!"

Boyd shook his head. "I know how to be surreptitious. Better than this bastard ever will. But I'm not leaving you alone and you'd better get used to it."

Her blue eyes sparked with anger. "I don't want any interference."

"I won't interfere. I want this finished as much as you do." His own irritation was rising. Part of him admired this woman's stubbornness, but he also didn't want to see it turn into foolishness.

"Then why even tell me you'll come back," she snapped. "How could I stop you anyway?"

"Because," he said levelly, "I will never lie to you."

She drew a sharp breath, then her face started to soften and the anger left her gaze. "Boyd…"

"I mean it. There were things I didn't tell you at the outset because you were a stranger. I just left them unsaid. You did the same, didn't you?"

She nodded.

"But neither of us had lied and now that I know you so

well, I'd be lying by omission if I didn't tell you what I'm going to do."

"Oh, Boyd," she murmured softly.

"And I'll thank you to save that tone of voice for a better time."

At least he got a small laugh from her.

Then she said, "The only question is whether it's enough to make the house look empty of everyone except me, or whether I need to get outside."

"After dark," he said presently. "He'll move after dark for the concealment. But he may be watching right now, so we'll move Clara and Herman while it's bright, and I'll leave then, too."

"But later..." She nodded. "After dark. Maybe I'll try a walk to the grocery if the weather isn't too bad. I'll think about it. But first to clear the house."

Chapter Sixteen

Mack had refused to talk to the brothers, so the two numb-skulls, as Mack had called them before hanging up, set out for town while the roads were still passable enough.

Tonight, they promised each other. They'd shut up that woman's yap before she could do any more damage. Then hightail it before the storm could freeze them in town. How they were supposed to accomplish this miracle when she had a houseful of people, they didn't know.

But fueled by beer, they believed the fates would favor them. A little stakeout to start, make sure she no longer had a houseful of people. Yeah.

JUST BEFORE ARTIE managed to devise an explanation that could get Clara and her father to move next door, Boyd's cell phone rang.

Since he was now trying to be invisible as possible from watchers outside, he took the call in the kitchen.

A woman's voice spoke. "Mr. Connor? This is Deborah Wainsmith, your attorney. My clerk passed on your questions to me. Do you have a moment?"

Boyd's heart sped up until he thought it would leap from his chest, and he plopped down hard on one of the kitchen chairs. He was hardly aware that Artie watched him.

"Thank you for calling, Ms. Wainsmith."

"Well, I'll charge for the time," she said humorously. "Always."

"Of course." *Get to the point*, he thought impatiently even as he dreaded more bad news.

"I did some research into custody issues for you. You know your ex-wife allowed you to have joint custody, although I'm not sure why, given the way she's been acting. For example, she didn't have the right to take Linda out of the legal state of residence you both shared at the time of the divorce, not without your permission."

Boyd drew a sharp breath. "Honestly?"

"I'm going to call this my fault that you didn't know. I'm sure I must have told you, but you were so upset at the time you may not have taken it all in. I should have made a point of ensuring you understood."

Shelley had had no right to take Linda to Seattle. The realization hit him like a sledgehammer. And if she hadn't taken Linda to Seattle... Boyd couldn't finish the thought.

He cleared his throat. "Anything else?"

"Oh, yes. She has no right to keep you from seeing your daughter. She has no right to exclude you from the counseling sessions."

"Oh, my God," he whispered.

"I've already called Linda's counselor and made her aware of that. If she doesn't call you to give you a report, call me. I'll take care of it."

"And Linda?" All of a sudden everything inside him turned into a block of fearful ice.

"She hasn't expressed any objection at all to seeing you, Mr. Connor. Your ex-wife has been lying."

Boyd squeezed his eyes shut and for the first time in

years a tear trailed down his face. "I've been praying," he said thickly.

"Your prayers have been answered. If you want to raise a civil case over this, I will. But if you're happy with knowing the truth, I won't. Just tell me when you make up your mind. And *I* am going to warn your ex that she's crossed some serious legal lines."

When Boyd hung up, he still couldn't open his eyes. His hands shook, whether with gratitude or anger he couldn't have said. Linda wanted to see him. Shelley had been lying.

Oh, God!

Suddenly strong arms wrapped around his shoulders, hugging him tightly. Fingers ran through his hair. "Boyd. Boyd?"

He lowered his head. "I can see Linda," he whispered. "I can see Linda."

ARTIE FELT AS if a hole had torn her heart, but it was a good hole. A hole that had earlier been full of pain had filled now with joy for Boyd. He could see his daughter. As far as she'd been able to determine that had been his primary concern on his trek across the country.

Yeah, he felt as if he'd failed as a father. Maybe he hadn't been around enough because of the Army, but the sense of failure had to come from his daughter refusing to see him. And most of his pain and guilt had arisen from that.

Now he should be free of all that, if he could work his way out of a mental state that had obsessed him for weeks now. He would, she decided. This man had worked his way through a lot of terrible things. He'd find his way now, though it might take time.

She murmured, "So you want to grab a flight out of here

as soon as this storm passes? Admittedly, all we have are puddle jumpers…"

He straightened abruptly, causing her to let go of him, and dashed a hand across his face. When he spoke, his voice was like steel.

"I am not moving one inch from here until I'm sure you're safe."

Wow! She straightened, too. This guy wanted so desperately to see his daughter and now he was going to stay for *her* sake?

"Boyd, I can take care of myself. You go to your daughter."

He turned from the waist, his head at her breast level, and stared straight up into face. His eyes looked hard.

"I don't want to hear that anymore."

Startled, she asked, "What?"

"That you can take care of yourself. I get it, Artie. You're a powerful, strong woman. You're also stubborn as hell. But here's the thing. I'm sure you can take care of yourself in most circumstances. Not a doubt in my mind."

"But?"

"But you don't know what *these* circumstances are. You don't know how many people might come after you. You don't know *how* they might come after you. What if some guy with a damn deer rifle decides to take a shot at you through a window?"

She stiffened. "There's no way on God's earth anyone can prevent that, Boyd."

"Yeah, there is. *I* can. I'm not going to be indoors with you. I'm going to be out there watching anything that stirs where it shouldn't. Yeah, you can take care of yourself, but you don't have two sets of eyes."

"Damn it!" She turned away, inexplicably angry because she knew he was right. She *did* need his eyes.

"What's more," he said, "you're going to tell Herman why you want him over at Clara's. No fishy stories. The man may have Alzheimer's but he's not stupid. He won't argue, bet on it. Because the thing he most wants is for you to be safe, and he'll know that at his age there won't be much he can do. As long as you're not alone."

It was Artie's turn to look down. She grabbed the edge of the counter, squeezed her eyes shut, and faced the truth. Boyd was right. "Okay. Okay."

"WILL YA LOOK at that," Willie said to Joe, who was busily downing a bag of potato chips.

"What?" Joe asked.

"See? The old man and the old woman is goin' next door. They's not gonna be in the house."

"If they stay over there. And there's still the guy." Joe, getting frustrated with this endless watching from a cold, battered pickup just around the corner from the cop's house, reached around to grab another beer from the case behind them.

"The guy," Willie said firmly, "is gonna be up against us two. Plus, it'll be dark. Ain't no one gonna see us comin'."

Joe downed half a bottle of beer.

"Hey, lookee," Willie said with satisfaction. "The jerk is leavin', too. Got his backpack on."

"We ain't called again," Joe remarked. "Mebbe she ain't scared no more."

Willie thought that might be true. Mebbe Mack had been right all this time. He almost hated Mack for that.

THE HOUSE HAD never felt so vacant to Artie before, not even when her father had gone to the senior center with Clara.

Boyd's absence left a new kind of emptiness, one that made her almost sad.

She watched him hike away down the street, then pulled all the window curtains closed, casting the house into near darkness. She wondered how many times she might have to do this before the bad guy showed up. Then she reminded herself that they had concluded this would be the only opportunity for days to come because of the steadily arriving storm.

It *had* to be today. The worry about her father far exceeded any worry about herself. At least he was next door with Clara, and Boyd had assured her he'd keep watch over both houses and the surrounding area.

She believed he could. How many times had he needed to do the same thing in the war? If anyone knew how, *he* did.

When the kitchen wall phone rang, she hesitated before answering it. What if it was another threat? Just an empty one, maybe.

But no, it was Gage Dalton. "How goes it?" he asked Artie.

"Wound up tighter than a drum."

He made a sound deep in his throat. "Do you have a plan?"

She outlined it for him swiftly.

"Good. I agree that if anything's going to happen other than nasty phone calls it'll have to be tonight. Otherwise the creep might get snowed in for a few more days."

"Right." Her hand grew tighter around the receiver. "Gage, I don't want..."

"Yeah, I know. You don't want protection. I get it. And you're going to get your wish, to a point. You know I checked Boyd Connor out and he's all the close-up protection you could ask for, want it or not. But here's the thing. You're not going to be alone, the two of you. I'm going to have some plainclothes out there at a distance watching approaches to your street and alley. Through binoculars, so don't yell at me."

"As if anyone yells at Sheriff Gage Dalton," she managed to say dryly.

He chuckled. "Been known to happen. Anyway, nobody can be sure it's just one creep after you. If someone wants to prevent you from testifying, there could be more than one. And that's your fault for being one of my best cops."

She almost smiled. "Flatterer. You know that's not true."

Gage sighed. "Well, I don't keep useless folks, it's true. Don't have a big enough budget to carry deadweight. Anyhow, if you can contact Boyd about my stakeout, it'll save him a lot of time wondering about the wrong people. If he wants exact locations, have him call me, hear?"

"Will do." She disconnected, once again feeling warm about the sheriff. About most of her colleagues, in fact.

BOYD WAS HIKING back toward the house, keeping to out-of-the way locations, armed with nothing but the Ka-Bar he'd carried for two decades, the one he'd carried cross-country because you never knew, especially when you started to get into real bear territory.

But it had been a while since he'd needed to use it on another human being. He hoped tonight wouldn't break the peace he'd made with himself and the war, imperfect as it was.

When his phone buzzed with Artie's call, he drew behind a thick, snow-covered evergreen and answered.

She explained quickly.

"Okay, I'll call the sheriff. Text me his number. I'll thank him for the heads-up, too. Smart man."

"Nobody ever claimed he was a fool."

"Stay alert, Artie. I feel it coming."

"How can you?"

"Been doing it for a while. I'm going dark now. No incoming calls. I'll phone Dalton now."

He hated going dark because it would prevent Artie from reaching him if she needed help. But there was no choice. A sound from his phone could give him away. Could send this creep and any of his accomplices into flight. No good. This whole thing needed to be done and over so Artie and her father would be safe.

Nothing else mattered. He called Dalton, got the locations of the stakeout, then let the sheriff know where he was and his planned approach. No point causing any confusion on either side.

Then he slipped slowly shadow to shadow among hedges and trees. The bastard would come as soon as he felt he wouldn't be seen by anyone on the streets. Late.

He glanced at his watch. There was plenty of time.

JOE WASN'T HAPPY with the continued wait. "It's dark now," he whined.

"You blockhead, it ain't dark enough. We gotta wait til nobody be lookin' out a window or walking on the street."

Joe cussed and pulled out another beer. Stash was gettin' low, which bothered him some. Damn truck felt like being inside an ice cube because Willie insisted they couldn't run the engine without drawing attention.

Maybe Willie was the real blockhead between 'em. Satisfied with that, Joe settled down again.

MACK MURDO, miles safely away, stewed over his own beer, knowing tonight was the night his jackass buddies were going to get themselves into big-time trouble. Joe might only have gotten three or six months for a barroom brawl. Now he was flirting with the rest of his life. So was Willie, come to that.

And Mack wanted to be nowhere near them when it happened. Nope. But he sure would have liked to hog-tie them two lunks to chairs. Maybe for his *own* good. They'd made too many phone calls after all. Sendin' up a flare for that cop.

Jerks. Screaming damn fools.

He stewed some more.

"OKAY," SAID WILLIE FINALLY. "Another hour."

"Hour?" Joe shouted.

"Shut the hell up. You want someone to hear we're in this truck?"

Joe quieted. "I want *out* of this damn truck."

"Soon, you jerk. Soon. Never had two brain cells to rub together."

It was something their mother used to say, mostly to Joe. Occasionally she added Willie, but not as often. Either way, it had always made Joe shrink more than him.

BOYD, NEARING ARTIE'S house from the north side, saw the pickup parked alongside a cross street, not far away. He couldn't remember seeing it there before late afternoon. A visitor, maybe?

Except that battered, beaten, rusty, nearly ancient truck looked seriously out of place in this general neighborhood.

Then he saw what appeared to be two moving heads in the darkness inside, highlighted by the brightness of the snow all around.

He tensed. Two of them. This might be it.

But he couldn't just pull two guys out of a truck. He had

to catch them in the act. He couldn't even call the sheriff to watch the truck. Not now. Not when he might be overheard.

He just had to hope the loose stakeout had noticed it. And ratchet himself into serious combat mode.

ARTIE PACED THE inside of the house, ready to crawl out of her skin. *Let it be tonight*, she thought. *Just get it over.*

While there was no way to be certain that this guy meant business, that he wasn't simply a bully or a creep getting his jollies with the idea of scaring a cop, the possibility that he was serious couldn't be ignored. Nor did she want to ignore it.

It would be impossible not to fear for her father if this didn't get settled somehow.

She'd been shaken at first. Especially when the guy used her private landline number, but then she'd gotten truly worried. And now she didn't fear even the least little bit for herself. Now it was all about her dad.

So she paced the house quietly. One small lamp burned on the mantel above the fireplace, which now glowed dull red and black with coals, all that was left of the earlier blaze.

Her night vision had adapted. She wondered if the guy outside would have less adaptation because of the snow.

And what about Boyd?

BOYD WORE A set of sunglasses, if you could call them that, purchased soon after snow started falling along his trek. Glasses that protected against the snow's glare. Glasses that sharpened the definition between objects.

Not as good as the infrared goggles he'd once used, goggles that would have made people stand out as red and yellow against the blue background of the snow and other cold things. He wished for IR but he had these glasses and they were good enough not to deprive him of all night vision around the snow.

He waited, not too close to Artie's or Clara's houses, but close enough that he'd see or hear anyone approach.

The waiting was familiar to him. Without truly good intelligence, waiting was the only smart thing to do. Alert, he settled in for however long it took.

Chapter Seventeen

"Okay," Willie said. "You still awake, Joe?"

"Yeah." Joe didn't notice that his speech was a little slurred by too much beer and couldn't see the way Willie rolled his eyes at him.

"Damn it," Willie said, punching Joe in the arm, "wake up. I don't need no drunk in the middle of this."

"I's okay. You don't hav'ta hit me."

"How drunk be you?"

"I ain't seein' double."

Willie cussed repeatedly. "Okay, we wait another hour til you git sober."

"Ain't doin' no such thing. Bein' an icicle ain't useful at all. Git to it."

Grumbling, Willie opened the door and winced as he was reminded how much it squealed.

"Oil," said Joe. "I done tol' you. Oil."

Willie told Joe to screw himself. When the two were outside the truck, they waited to see if anyone moved because of the noise of the truck door.

After a bit, Willie said. "We okay. Now don't be fallin' flat on your face in this damn snow."

Striding forward, Joe proved he could walk okay. Sort

of. Willie stopped him by grabbing his arm. "Slow, you ass. Slow. Don't wanna git attention."

Joe didn't see what difference it made but walked slower anyway.

BOYD HAD BEEN keeping an eye on that truck from near the two houses, and there was no mistaking the screech of the truck's door when it opened.

They were coming.

He got into a crouch and watched, thinking they were either going to come to the front of the house or try the back way. No point in anything else.

Then he noticed how one of the guys was staggering a little.

Boyd grinned into the cold and the wind, his teeth showing. This might be fun, as long as those guys didn't shoot right off.

He was also pretty sure the sheriff's cordon was slowly closing in now. All Boyd wanted was the chance to get to these guys first.

His hands itched to throw a few punches.

AS THE TWO Lathrops edged around to the back of the house, things got a bit hairy. Willie kept glancing around but saw no one on the street. Good.

Then Joe stumbled against the side of the house with an audible thud.

Willie grabbed him by the arm and yanked him up, hard. "You lummox. You too drunk to walk. Stay put."

"Screw it," Joe answered in a whisper. "Anythin' coulda hit the house. She ain't expectin' us. Besides, 'member what she did to Billy? We gonna need two of us."

Willie couldn't argue that. He'd heard about that baton from a friend closer to what had happened. He winced a bit at the thought and hoped Joe took most of it.

"Jest don't trip over your own damn feet."

Joe glared, the expression visible in the reflected light from the snow. Still, he moved more cautiously. He wanted this done tonight, git it over with, and not have to go runnin' like damn fools without gittin' to that woman. He patted the pistol in his belt.

Stupid place to carry a pistol, his dad had once said. *Likely to shoot off your own balls.* So Joe kept it to the side. Mostly.

INSIDE THE HOUSE, Artie heard the thud against the exterior wall. No mistaking it for a branch. No mistaking it at all. He was coming around to the back.

She snapped her baton open and took up station between the fridge and the mudroom door.

Holding that baton again made her feel a little queasy, but no way was she going to allow this guy to hurt anyone. Not anyone. Ready, she waited.

BOYD HAD MOVED in closer once he saw the direction the two men were taking. Fools, maybe, to think they'd be safer coming in the back way.

But Boyd was ready, crouched behind a shrub. Nor did those two men appear to have any situational awareness, any idea that anyone could be watching them.

Oh, he liked the way this was going, as long as he could get to them before they got to Artie.

Then he watched them struggle with the back latch. Artie would hear it. What were these guys anyway? Stooges? Keystone Kops?

ARTIE HEARD THE back latch being fumbled. She tensed, ready to spring. Sure that Boyd couldn't be far away. Sure that this time she wasn't alone.

Then the inner door opened and she caught sight of a gun barrel. Like that? He was coming in ready to shoot anything that moved? Her stomach tightened because he might have shot her father.

Without further thought, she swung her baton and brought it down hard on the guy's forearm. He howled and the pistol skittered across the floor. She moved in, ready to strike again, when there was an explosion of activity in the mudroom.

The next thing she saw was Boyd wrestling with yet another man. *Two?* There were two?

She raised her baton, ready to help, but Boyd preempted her. A couple of punches sounded with resounding thuds and a moment later two guys were lying on the floor, one seeming unconscious, the other writhing in pain.

Boyd looked up. "Got 'em," was all he said.

THE REST OF the night turned into a kind of coffee klatch. The miscreants were carted off to the hospital in cuffs, short statements were given by both Artie and Boyd, then the rest of the surveillance team hung around for pots of coffee and some shared laughter when Boyd described what he'd seen.

"There ought to be a law against stupidity," Gage Dalton remarked, having claimed the nearest chair. He hadn't been five minutes behind his deputies. "Of course, it makes our job easier."

Eventually he rose. "We'll need official statements at the office in the morning, assuming anyone can get there."

With his departure, the group moved on.

Boyd rebuilt the fire into a pleasant blaze, and they sat silently for a long while.

"What's next?" Artie asked finally. "You're going to Seattle?"

"Yes. As soon as the storm makes flying out of here possible."

She nodded, feeling the worst ache in her heart, knowing she had no right to feel it. "I hope it all goes well with Linda."

"I think it will," he said positively, although there was a hint, just a hint, of uncertainty.

"That girl has a father to be proud of."

"One who wasn't around damn near enough." He passed a hand over his face. "Should I go rescue Clara and Herman?"

"All the police activity out here probably said enough, but you're right, I should call."

"Especially since an ambulance went out of here."

She hadn't thought of that and guilt swamped her. Immediately, she reached for her cell and tapped in her dad's number.

Herman answered groggily, "It's okay?"

"Very okay, Dad. I'm absolutely fine, we got the bad guys."

"Good. Good. And Boyd?"

She glanced over. "I think he might have a few skinned knuckles from some punches."

Herman laughed. "I do like that boy. Tell him I'll see him in the morning. Love you, girl."

Then, as easily as slipping into a comfortable bed, Boyd and Artie slid to the floor in front of the fire.

Their lovemaking was hot, fast, ravenous. So little time left, Artie thought. So very little.

BUT THE STORM blew through the next day and Boyd packed his duffel to head to the airport.

"I'll drive you," Artie offered.

He shook his head. "I hate goodbyes, Artie."

At the door he paused and turned toward her. "Can't say when, but I'll be back, Artemis Jackson."

She nodded, managing a smile, and watched him stride out of her life just as he had hiked into it.

All she could hope was that he found the closure he so needed with his daughter. The closure that had set him out on a cross-country trek.

The trek that had wound up tearing her heart nearly in two.

He left desolation in his wake.

Chapter Eighteen

Nearly three months later, Artie had settled back into her routine as a cop. Counseling had helped her deal with the entire Lauer incident and she at last felt mostly free of it.

And with difficulty, she had begun to push Boyd Connor from her mind, if not her heart. Some things just weren't meant to be.

The sense of loss and sorrow began to ease a bit, and she started to feel comfortable in her own skin again. Some you won, some you lost.

It hadn't been meant to be. Get used to it.

But then came the twilight when she returned home in her official vehicle and saw a man sitting on her front porch step. Was that…?

Her heart flipped and nearly stopped. The man rose and there was no mistaking his figure. Boyd. God, it was Boyd!

Her hands started to shake as she wheeled her official vehicle into the driveway. She was almost scared to move. Why had he come back? To tell her in a gentlemanly way that it had been nice but he was returning to his old life? Or only because he had promised to?

Because he hadn't phoned her once in all this time and it had felt as if he dropped off the map.

But here he was. Nearly holding her breath, she switched

off her ignition, opened the door and stepped out into crusty snow. He stood on the porch, waiting as she walked slowly toward him. A magnificent man in an unzipped parka, a watch cap over his dark hair. A face, strong, stern and kind all at once. A face that she cherished more than he could possibly know.

"Hi," he said quietly.

"Hi."

"I guess Herman's not here."

"Uh, he and Clara have something going on at the senior center. You been sitting in the cold for long?"

"About an hour. No big deal."

As she reached him, she thought she saw a deep warmth in his gaze.

He spoke again. "Can I hit you up for some coffee?"

"Sure," she answered, finding a bit of briskness for her voice. "You can tell me all about your daughter and how it went." And this would be as far as it went. Steeling herself, she stepped inside with him.

They settled at the kitchen table after Boyd dumped his jacket and backpack. Artie didn't want to go into the living room. It was now too full of memories she was reluctant to resurrect.

Sitting there in her uniform, she felt an unwanted distance between them. Separate paths into separate futures.

"How'd it go with Linda?" she prompted again.

One corner of his mouth lifted in smile. "Now that was interesting. Very interesting."

"How so?"

"Well, we're in family therapy right now. I had to wait for permission to leave town briefly to come see you. But that wasn't what was most interesting."

She nodded, waiting.

"I had meetings with just Linda and me with the psychologist. And that's what blew me away."

"How so?" She leaned forward a bit.

"Linda's mad at her mother now."

Artie's eyes widened. "Tell me."

Boyd shook his head. "It seems, as the full story came out, that Linda understood why the Army took me away so much. She wasn't happy about it, but she didn't blame me for it, unlike Shelley. But Linda got furious when she learned her mother had been lying to her about seeing me. It seems Shelley gave Linda the idea that I didn't want to see her. That I didn't care."

Artie drew a deep breath. "Oh, my God," she murmured. "Oh, my God."

"My reaction was a little stronger, to say the least. And Linda's was even more powerful. We're going to need some more therapy, Linda and me, but we've passed the critical point. However..." He paused. "However, it makes me sad as hell that Linda feels she can no longer trust her mother."

"That's awful!" Artie ached for a young girl who now had to feel that way about her mother, couldn't help wondering how Linda was going to learn to deal with it. Loss of trust was a *huge* thing.

"I think so, too. The psychologist isn't sure how she can mend the rift, but she wants to try. So do I, for Linda's sake."

Artie nodded, aching for him and the young woman she'd never met. "You're an awfully generous man, Boyd."

She rose and went to get more coffee, topping their mugs. "So you'll be settling in Seattle?"

"Not exactly." He stood up and began pacing the small confines of the kitchen. "I'm probably going to make a hash of all this," he said. "Be patient, please."

"Sure." At least she hoped she could. The idea of Boyd

living in Seattle broke her heart wide open again. Would this sense of loss be with her forever?

"Here's the thing," Boyd said presently. "Linda has decided she wants to live with me. The psychologist wants a few more weeks to be sure Linda is really satisfied with that. I get it. But…" Then, "Ah, hell, you'll probably take this all wrong, but I don't mean it that way."

Artie leaned back, watching him with the tiniest flicker of hope and a bigger dollop of fear.

"Legally it's Linda's choice which parent she wants to live with. And she can live with me if I have a permanent domicile."

"Makes sense."

"Perfect sense. Thing is, oh, hell, Artie, I want to make my home with *you*. I've had more than three months to think about how I've been missing you, how I care about you. I won't be happy living without you. It's what I want more than damn near anything."

He paused again, sitting, facing her directly, holding her gaze with his own.

"I love you, Artie. No ifs, ands or buts. I love everything about you. But I come with a string attached, a sixteen-year-old daughter, and I'd understand perfectly if…"

Artie's heart leaped into her throat as unmitigated joy filled her. Only with effort did she restrain herself enough to say, "Linda has something to say about that."

"Yeah, but I already told her about you and this town. She's eager. We don't have to take a permanent step until you're both sure. It's just… Artie, say yes. Say you'll try."

She could barely breathe. Hope and joy overwhelmed her. "Boyd?" she whispered, hardly daring to risk all that he was suggesting.

"Yeah?"

"I have a string, too."

His face sagged a bit. "What?"

"My job. I won't quit it. I love it too much." A fact that she had at last learned about herself again.

At that his face broke into the widest smile she'd ever seen on it, making him a million times more attractive than ever to her.

"Say it, Artie. I'd never change you. Just say it, please."

"I'll try." She held her breath, trembling on the edge of a precipice as she sought to say what she had never before said. Then the words burst from her. "And what's more, Boyd Connor, I love you with every breath in my body."

Somehow they became tangled together in a blanket on the sofa, hugging so tightly it was almost bruising, kissing so deeply they stopped only to breathe.

"The three of us are going to work together," Boyd said roughly. "It's going to work. It has to."

"It will," Artie answered with utter conviction. "It will. Just don't expect me to be Linda's mother."

His head pulled back a tiny bit. "Meaning?"

"She's too old and I'm too young for that kind of relationship. So friends, okay?"

A quiet chuckle escaped him. "From what I've seen of Linda, I think she'd prefer that, too."

Then Artie laughed, the most joyous laugh that had escaped her in a while. "It'll work," she said again. "It'll work."

Because the most important part was love, and there was already plenty within her to give.

* * * * *

MURDER IN TEXAS

BARB HAN

All my love to Brandon, Jacob and Tori, who are the great loves of my life. To Samantha for the bright shining light that you are.

To Babe, my hero, for being my best friend, greatest love and my place to call home. I love you with everything that I am. Always and forever.

To Shaq and Kobi, the best (and barkiest) writing buddies ever.

Chapter One

A December cold front arrived in Cider Creek at almost exactly the same moment as Liz Hayes. Mother Nature had decided to punctuate the sentence with sleet. Liz turned down her music so she could see better. Clouds covered the sun, making it dark outside for four o'clock in the afternoon. Pea-size hail pelted her windshield as the temperature gauge on the dashboard dropped before her eyes while she sat at the first red light past town.

Liz tightened her grip on the steering wheel. Being in her hometown was hard enough without the weather reminding her that she should have stayed home instead of taking this trip. Houston wasn't far, but she rarely came back to her old stomping grounds to visit. Her jerk of a grandfather was to blame, but she didn't want to think about him right now as she impatiently tapped her thumb on the wheel.

Traffic lights in small towns could last forever. This one felt like it had been red for an eternity. Under normal circumstances, she would appreciate being as delayed as possible. Driving in bad weather had her nerves on edge. The conditions were getting worse by the minute. In fact, she rolled her window down to get a feel for how cold it had become.

A sudden glow from the construction site to her left

caught her attention. The lights must have been automatic, turning on now that it was almost pitch black. There was a noise coming from the area, too. She strained to listen. It wasn't a noise so much as what sounded like a call for help—one that got louder and more desperate sounding the second time she heard it.

Liz tapped the button to turn on her hazard lights before pulling to the side of the road, opening her door and exiting her five-year-old Honda Accord. As she bolted toward what sounded like a male voice, a rogue thought that this could be some kind of setup struck. Setup for what, though? Crime in this small town was almost nonexistent. Her mind was probably playing tricks on her.

Either way, someone was in trouble.

As she neared the voice, she heard the fragility. A twinge of recognition dawned. This person was familiar even though she couldn't quite place him as rain came down like needles against her skin. Wind gusted. She put up an arm to block against flying debris in case it came at her, too.

"Hello?" she shouted against the storm.

Liz reached the open lot. A structure that looked a lot like a small strip mall was in the early stages of development. Strange how she expected everything to stay the same since the last time she'd been here. Towns, like life, moved on.

Scanning the area, she didn't see anyone. No one responded to her, either. She called out again and then listened. A half dozen thoughts fought for center stage in her mind. Was the person unconscious? Were they gone? Was the cry for help an echo that had traveled across the mostly bare lot? She didn't want to question whether or not the person was dead. Were they? Alive yet buried?

A knot twisted in her stomach so tight she could scarcely breathe. Adrenaline coursed through her, causing her hands to shake. Liz reminded herself not to let her imagination run wild.

"Is anyone out here?" she asked. Sheetrock was stacked several feet high in spots near the metal beams that were beginning to look like what the structure would end up being. The person could be lying behind one of those.

There was a hunter-green porta potty in the middle of what looked to be a future parking lot. Wood was staked into the ground, marking something. Liz had no idea what. And there were piles of rocks, big and small, pretty much everywhere.

Maybe she was hearing things, losing her mind. The stress of having her small accessory company's sales take off in the past year was clearly doing her in. Sales had gone through the roof, and she felt like she was paddling against a hurricane to keep up. She'd been handling the business well. Or so she believed. Orders were going out on time. The major retailer who'd picked up her line of *Just Totin'* bags seemed happy so far. She'd had to ramp up production on what had felt like a moment's notice.

Liz and her controlling grandfather might have been opposites in almost every way, but she credited him with passing down incredible business sense. She was building her company from the ground up with no outside help, much in the same way he'd done for his successful cattle-ranching business. Duncan Hayes might have been a jerk, but he'd been shrewd. A twinge of guilt struck at calling him a jerk now that he was gone.

Liz sighed. She assumed the family meeting she'd been called home to take had to do with figuring out what to do with the cattle ranch and inheritances—money she didn't want or need because she hadn't earned it. Her mile-long stubborn streak had probably come from her grandfather as well.

Gravel crunched underneath her boots as she circled the construction site. This wasn't the time to regret wearing heels. At least her feet were dry and warm as another gust of wind snapped around her, whipping hair so dark it almost faded into the night around her. Strands stuck in her eyelashes as Mother Nature's wrath sent larger chunks of hail crashing into Liz.

Turning toward the sedan she'd abandoned, she decided to retreat while she still had a hint of pride left and before her vehicle ended up on the back of a tow truck.

"He-e-e-lp me." The weak voice came from behind her. Liz whirled around to a spot she'd missed when she'd been circling the area. A cold shiver raced through her as she bolted toward the sound.

As she rounded a stack of sheet metal that was backed up to a pile of gravel, a bolt of lightning cut sideways across the sky. There it was, plain as day…a human hand sticking out of the gravel. Was he stuck underneath heavy Sheetrock? Wedged in somehow?

Another wind gust caused wood to come flying from seemingly out of nowhere. Visibility in this area was next to nothing since there was no light in this part of the construction zone. The last thing she wanted to do was step on the hand. She instinctively checked her pockets for her phone, then remembered it was still inside her car.

"I'm here," she said, hearing the panic in her own voice. "Hold on. Okay?" *Please don't die.*

Staying rooted to her spot, she bent down and searched for the hand where she'd last seen it. The second she found it, fingers closed around her. A moment of pure panic struck at the thought she might not be in time to save this person.

Pushing through her anxiety, she offered reassurances as she started digging him out.

A pair of headlights illuminated her vehicle on the road. She shouted and waved, but the truck went around her car and kept going. No one wanted to be out in this mess for longer than they had to.

Resolve replaced fear as she let go of the hand so she could use both of hers to move the gravel. A person was wedged underneath the Sheetrock.

"Hold on, okay?" Liz asked, but it was more statement than question. "I'm going to get you out of here."

In the dark, it was impossible to get a good look at the man's face. Based on the feel of the skin on his hands, he wasn't young. Not old, either. Middle aged? His hand was like ice. She was already shivering from the cold. At least the hail had let up. Bad storms in Texas had a way of blowing right through faster than a roller coaster at Six Flags.

The reprieve from being hit in the face every few seconds was welcomed.

The man mumbled something unintelligible.

The likelihood she was going to get him out at her slow rate of progress was slim.

What else could she find to dig him out? There had to be something around here to work with. This was, after all, a construction site. Wouldn't there be tools? She scanned over by the well-lit areas. Saw nothing.

Since she was in a praying mood, she went ahead and sent up a request for an ambulance and maybe a forklift operator. Trying to lift the heavy construction materials off the man by hand would be impossible. The most she could do was make it budge the tiniest bit.

There was no choice but to run back to her car and call

for help, no matter how much she hated leaving him here alone. Would he understand her if she told him the new plan?

"I have to call for help. I'll be right back," she said, finding the hand again. There wasn't much life to it, but a small squeeze of reassurance gave her hope that he was still fighting. "Hold tight."

Liz stood up and then turned around, ready to make the run back to her sedan. Lightning flashed. She gasped as she stared at the chest of a man.

"Oh, hell no," he said as she fisted her hands at her sides, ready to fight back.

Another voice came up behind her. She felt a blow to the side of her head. And then everything went dark.

DILLEN "PIT BULL" BULLARD paid the cab driver, exited the vehicle and then shouldered his rucksack. On a sharp sigh, he tucked his chin to his chest and headed toward the double glass doors at Cider Creek General Hospital.

Five days had passed since his father's accident. It had taken two days to get word to him where he'd been deployed and three to get back home. *Home?* He almost laughed out loud. Cider Creek, Texas, was the furthest thing from being his real home. He'd grown up here. Hated every minute of a childhood where he hadn't fit in. And couldn't get out fast enough.

There was no reason to feel sorry for himself. He'd found his calling with the United States military as an army ranger. *Rangers Lead the Way.* Considering his father had been fighting for his life for five days with Dillen almost as far away as a person could be, he couldn't help but think he'd failed.

Dillen was here now. He'd convinced his supervising officer to let him skip the normally requisite visit to the alpaca farm in east Texas where he could cool off so he wouldn't reach for a weapon on instinct if someone tapped him on the shoulder in a grocery store line. Coming in hot meant he'd have to manage his emotions. Living in a hot zone for months on end had a way of making a solider prepared for any kind of fight, even when diplomacy was the best course of action.

A receptionist sat behind a bar-height circular counter. A twelve-foot Christmas tree twinkled to his left. Signs of yesterday's holiday were everywhere. To say he wasn't in the yuletide spirit was the understatement of the year.

The attendant's back was to him, and she was playing a game on her cell. He'd been to this place many times in as a kid, always as a patient and mostly because of fighting. Going into the military had given him a positive outlet for his anger. Ranger school had exhausted him and taught him how to channel his rage at something productive—a real enemy and not some kid who'd made a smart remark about how poor Dillen and his father had been. Or how his dad couldn't keep a woman around. Jerks. The grown-up version of him realized that now.

He cleared his throat to get the lady's attention. She swatted like there was a fly buzzing beside her.

"I'll be with you in a minute," she said, clearly irritated by the interruption.

Did she just disrespect him?

A coil tightened in Dillen's chest. He smacked his flat palm down onto the counter. The receptionist jumped. She spun around in her chair, phone still in hand. The *go straight to hell* look he shot her got attention. It probably didn't hurt that he was still wearing full operational camouflage. Her eyes widened as she got a good look at him.

Murder in Texas

"May I help you?" she asked, her voice cracking enough for him to realize she was afraid.

He didn't know how to turn down the level of intensity, so he stood there practically glaring at her. "My father is here. William Bullard. I'm told he isn't doing well."

"Oh, right," she said, like that explained his intense mood. People not doing their jobs while they were on the clock sent white-hot anger roaring through him.

Dillen took in a couple of deep breaths while he watched her roll up to the computer and tap keys on the keyboard.

"The waiting room is on the fifth floor," she said without looking up at him. "You can't miss it." She pointed toward an elevator bank. "Those will take you where you want to go. Just don't forget he's on five, and you'll be fine."

"Thank you, ma'am," he said. His Southern manners were ingrained in him now. *Ma'am* and *sir* were instilled in his vocabulary from his time in the military. He would have thought growing up in a small Texas town would have done the trick. It hadn't hurt. He'd been rebellious enough to fight using any sign of respect.

Dillen walked over to the elevators and then pushed the button to go up. At ten o'clock at night, it didn't take long. The hallways on the ground floor were almost empty, too. The *ding* sounded, and doors opened. Dillen walking inside and pushed the number 5. The ride was short. He could use a cup of coffee. But first he needed to see his father. Too many years had gone by without Dillen keeping in touch in the way he should have. In the way a good son would have.

So many *could haves* and *should haves*.

Dillen bit back a curse, clenching his teeth to keep from saying something he shouldn't and adding to the list of regrets.

The last thing he remembered about being home was how

much he couldn't stand the Hayes family and their holier-than-thou attitude. They were everything he wasn't. The boys had been athletes and made good grades in school. The girls had been picture perfect and way out of his league. Then again, he hadn't had a league back in high school. He'd had raging hormones compounded by the fact he'd lived in a town where he never belonged. His father hadn't belonged. Dillen had been picked on, made fun of and generally tortured until he'd filled out his six-feet-three-inch frame. Then, he'd signed up for the military before he could take out his revenge on the jerks who'd made his life miserable and wind up in jail.

There was one Hayes in particular he couldn't stand more than the others. Liz Hayes had been in his grade and was everything he despised about the small town. She was privilege times ten and knew it. All she'd had to do was bat an eyelash for one of the jocks to rush over to pick up her pencil if it had dropped on the floor. It had been disgusting the way his classmates had been ready to jump if she'd snapped her fingers.

The elevator dinged, jolting him back to reality and out of his quick trip down memory lane. He realized his hands were fisted, and he clenched his back teeth so hard he thought they might crack if he didn't ease up.

So, yeah, he was ready for battle.

Dillen forced a couple of slow breaths as the doors opened. There was a nurses' station immediately in front of him. He assumed the waiting room would be off to the side. Maybe he could swing by his father's room rather than sit in a blue-and-white room with burnt coffee sitting on warmers.

There were two nurses at their station. As soon as he

stepped out of the elevator bank, they studied him as though a warning call had been made from downstairs.

"The waiting room is right over there," one of the nurses said. "We've alerted Dr. Lawrence that you've arrived. He's on his way."

Dillen nodded and thanked them. It might've been best to be briefed by the doctor before he saw his father in person. Although part of him wanted to explain to the nurses there wasn't much that could shock him considering what he did for a living.

He stopped halfway across the hallway and turned. "Coffee?"

"There should be some already brewed in there," the nurse said. The somber tone had him concerned. "If not, let me know and I'll put on a pot."

After thanking them again, he walked into the sterile, white-tiled room with blue chairs. The room was empty save for one woman with a large bandage on her head. She looked up, and his hands fisted.

What the hell was Liz Hayes doing here?

Chapter Two

Liz stood up the minute Dillen Bullard walked into the room, surprised at how quickly her pulse climbed. The man was over six feet tall and built with stacked muscles on top of lean hips. His dark hair was cut tight, and he had the most piercing pair of hazel eyes—eyes that were surprisingly soft on a face of hard angles and planes. Military fatigues made the green hue in his eyes pop. He was all broad chest, solid arms and slim waist. If it wasn't Dillen Bullard standing there, she might've thought he was the sexiest man she'd seen in a long time. Maybe ever.

Chalking up her physical reaction to a stress response at seeing the person who'd mercilessly picked on her growing up, Liz mentally shook it off. Besides, she hadn't backed down then and she wouldn't now as he stood there with his arms crossed, studying her.

"I'd ask what you're doing here, but the bandage on your head tells me you're a patient," he said before heading toward the coffee machine.

For a split second, she debated whether or not to tell him the real reason she'd been in this waiting room for five days straight without a shower and skipped Christmas with her family yesterday. A few spritzes of perfume had kept her from stinking up the place.

Dillen poured a cup of fresh brew and stood rooted to his spot as he took the first sip. She couldn't help but notice he kept one eye on her the whole time.

"True," she finally said, folding her arms and hugging them to her chest. "How do you explain the fact I was treated and released five days ago yet am still here, waiting for Mr. Bullard to wake up?"

The look he shot her could have frozen water on the sidewalk during a Texas summer. She shook it off.

"I was there at the construction site," she said before Dr. Lawrence walked in the room, stopping all conversation. Since she wasn't next of kin, the doctor couldn't tell her anything about Mr. Bullard's condition even though she'd slipped in his room a couple of times when the night nurse was busy.

A look of shock flashed across Dillen's features before he refocused on the man in scrubs. Dillen's jaw muscle clenched like he was biting back something he wanted to say. At his height and with the way he took up space in a room, most people would be intimidated. Not Liz. So, she dropped her arms to her sides and turned toward the doctor.

The look on Dr. Lawrence's face as he made a beeline for Dillen with an outstretched hand caused her stomach lining to braid. Introductions were made after a handshake. The doctor was middle aged and half a foot shorter than Dillen. He was slim and serious with small specs for glasses. Dillen seemed to sense the news wasn't going to be good. His face was stone-cold sober as he asked how his father was doing.

"Mr. Bullard sustained multiple contusions to his frontal—"

"Can you give it to me in plain English, please, sir?" Dillen asked. His deep, even timbre washed over her. It wasn't something she could risk paying too much attention to or she might actually stop resenting the guy. This seemed like a good time to remind herself that she was here for a lonely old man whose son was deployed. Plus, she respected Dillen for his service. It was impossible to hate him. He appeared to have cleaned up his life even though his attitude toward her hadn't changed, which was exactly the reason she had every intention of keeping him at arm's length.

Dr. Lawrence looked Dillen straight in the eyes. He shook his head. "I'm sorry to inform you that your father passed away twenty minutes ago." He paused for a beat. "We did everything possible to save him."

All the muscles in Dillen's body tensed. He took in a breath that looked like it was meant to calm a rage building inside him, as though guilt threatened to eat him from the inside out. "I was briefed as to how he ended up in the hospital, but I have questions."

"According to the file, this young lady found him on a construction site covered in rubble during a sleet storm," the doctor said. "Flying debris may have been responsible."

Dillen nodded and his jaw muscle clenched. "I appreciate everything you did for my father."

"I couldn't be sorrier," Dr. Lawrence said as tears welled in Liz's eyes. "Would you like to speak to someone in the clergy?"

"No. Thank you, sir," Dillen said, his voice even like he'd switched to autopilot. Her chest squeezed and her heart ached.

The doctor excused himself after saying someone would be coming to take Dillen to his father in a few minutes.

Dillen swallowed the rest of the contents of his cup and then crushed the foam in his hand before chunking it into the trash. He dropped his backpack onto a chair and then walked over to the window, raking his hands through his hair.

There were so many things Liz wanted to say, but her mouth couldn't form the words. *I'm sorry* seemed hollow and lacking. Before she could think, he whirled around on her.

"What were you doing at the construction site?" he asked, his tone accusing. Those hazel eyes appraised her, causing heat to flood her.

Considering the fact he'd just been told his father was gone, she didn't feel the need to split hairs about his tone of voice.

"That's a good question," she responded. "The sheriff believes this was an accident."

"You don't?" he asked, studying her.

"I left my car on the side of the road at a red light in a sleet storm after hearing a call for help," she said. "Apparently, someone called 911 but didn't stop because the storm was getting worse. That's as much as I know since I must have also been hit with debris. I can't remember much else about that afternoon other than the fact I was on my way back to my family's ranch."

"But you don't believe it's as simple as that," he said.

"No. I don't," she admitted. "It's strange. Don't you think?"

He shrugged. "I have no idea. I landed an hour ago and made my way here. I was told there was an accident, and that's about all I know."

"I have questions," she said.

"Meaning?" he asked. His posture said he was still a bundle of tension and coiled so tightly that it wouldn't take much for him to snap. She couldn't blame him for his frustration and sadness. He'd traveled a long way to receive devastating news.

"What was I doing at a construction site in the first

place?" she asked. "Not to mention the fact I'm still confused as to what your father would have been doing there when a storm was on its way." She shrugged. "He's not connected to the job in any way. So, why go?"

"What did the sheriff say?" he asked. "I'm assuming you mentioned your concerns."

She blew out a breath.

"I'm not sure why he believes what he does," she said honestly. "I guess it wraps the situation up in a nice bow." She paused for a beat. "It just doesn't scan right for me." She tried to ignore the headache trying to form in between her eyes. Blinking a couple of times didn't help. Neither did the overhead fluorescent lighting in the room.

Her eyes burned. "I'm not trying to cause trouble here. None of the explanations make sense. I mean, I'm supposed to have abandoned my vehicle based on realizing someone needed help, but there must have been thunder and lightning. So how did I hear your father? And then why wouldn't I be the one to call 911 if I had concerns? According to the sheriff, a concerned citizen saw my vehicle and called for help. That much, I can believe based on the weather reports. Your father was supposed to have been buried in debris and I was also hit. But I have bruises that don't match up with what was supposed to have happened to me. Then there's my head injury. Wouldn't I duck if debris was flying at me?"

"Why would you even care about my dad?" he asked with the venom of a snake bite.

She bit back the urge to call him out on his preconceived notion of her. Once again, she reminded herself that he'd lost someone he loved. She knew what it was like to lose a parent, except that she'd been too young to remember much about her father.

"Because when I asked the hospital staff how your father

was doing, they shook their heads. I came into the waiting room to offer sympathy, and no one was here," she said with a little more ire than intended. She couldn't help it. Dillen got under her skin more than she wanted to admit. "No one should be alone over the holidays."

THOSE WORDS WERE the equivalent of knife stabs to the center of Dillen's chest. He stood even straighter and clenched his fists. "I was on my way as soon as I received word."

"And here you are," she said with a curt tone. He was being dismissed by the raven-haired woman—a woman who'd grown up from a spindly-legged child with long hair and dark-roast eyes. She had on jeans that covered long legs and a sweater that hugged full breasts. Under normal circumstances, she was exactly the kind of person he would want to get to know better. But this was Liz Hayes, and her attitude toward him was a bucket of ice water. After all these years, she still looked down her nose at him.

"Then you can go," he said before it clicked that she might've been the only witness to what had happened to his father—a father who was gone now. Those last words were more physical blows.

Dillen issued a sharp sigh as she stood there, tapping her toe.

"But I hope you won't," he said as a nurse entered the room.

"Mr. Bullard," she began reverently, "I can take you to see your father now." Her tone matched the occasion and was a stark reminder of his loss.

Dillen nodded even though he couldn't seem to get his feet to move. He caught Liz's gaze and held on to it. Would she be here when he returned? He didn't have the right to ask her, so he turned and walked out of the room behind the nurse.

It dawned on him that Liz had stuck around when his father had needed someone and Dillen had just treated her like she'd been the one to hurt his dad. Jerk move on Dillen's part. Part of him hoped she would stick around so he could apologize. Based on the bandage on her forehead, she'd been through hell and back. She said she didn't remember exactly what happened. Although that could change. He wasn't an expert at head injuries, but he'd experienced or witnessed his fair share. One of his buddies had forgotten how to speak for a week after being knocked in the head with a piece of metal. His speech had come back as though nothing had ever happened.

Time slowed on the walk down the long hallway. Dillen's mind snapped back to the past, to all those Sunday pizza dinners. They'd always had pizza on Sundays. Every night had had a meal assigned to it. Routine had been the staple of his father's existence. There hadn't been much in the way of money, but there'd been food on the table every night. The government had provided Dillen's breakfast and lunches while at school. It was most likely part of the reason he'd signed up for the military after high school graduation instead of working in town or on a ranch. He'd figured he owed some loyalty, that the government deserved to be paid back for their investment.

Routine had also the bane of Dillen's childhood.

During high school, he'd tried to talk his father into driving two towns over to grocery shop at one of those big box stores. He'd tried to convince his old man that the cheap prices had made up for the extra gas. But Pop had waved him off, saying Tuesdays were for the grocery store in Cider

Creek. Dillen had been embarrassed for his friends to see they'd been on government assistance.

His part-time job cleaning out stalls had earned him the nickname Bullcrap from the jocks at school. It had been replaced by Pit Bull once he'd joined the service for his ability to lock onto a target with relentless force. All the bullying in school had given him the drive to push his body to its limits and become the strongest human he could possibly be.

It also had also him enough anger to last a lifetime. He'd taken some of it out on Liz in the waiting room. Dillen owed her an apology.

The nurse stopped in front of room 501.

"Take all the time you need," she said. "Hit the call button when you're ready." She didn't explain further as she spoke softly. The rest was obvious. His father's body would be taken to the morgue. "Someone from administration will be waiting at the nurse's station for your instructions on how you would like to handle the details."

He thanked her before stepping inside the room. An emptiness filled his chest like when he'd been five years old and had watched his mother walk out and into the cab of a waiting U-Haul. The memory gutted him, even after all these years.

Dillen walked to his father's bedside, sat down and then reached for his hand. Closing his eyes, he could imagine them sitting at the table, talking about all those stupid little things people talked about like gas prices and the weather. Funny how people never discussed anything important or noticed how much they would miss someone until they were gone.

A few tears spilled down Dillen's cheeks as he bent forward and rested his head on their joined hands. He would give ten years off the back end of his life to be able to tell his father the words neither had uttered out loud in his thirty-two years of life. He would tell his father that he loved him.

Minutes passed before Dillen could pull himself together enough to sit up straight again.

"Hey, Pop," he began. It didn't matter that his father couldn't hear. "Remember that time I hid in the closet in your room and ended up trapping myself inside?" He paused for a few beats, remembering all the times he'd been a jerk to his father. The teenage years had been the worst. His temper had raged, and he'd hated everything about their life.

Dillen took in a couple of slow breaths so he could get the next part out without losing it.

"I wasn't scared, even though I didn't like being in tight places back then," he continued, a few rogue tears rolling down his cheeks, dripping onto the blanket one by one.

He squeezed his father's lifeless hand.

"Because I knew that you would come looking for me," he managed to get out as emotion knotted in his throat, making it hard to speak. "I wasn't afraid because I knew you would turn over the whole house until you found me, and I'd be okay."

Guilt and regret slammed into him at all the years he'd missed with his father. It had been too easy to leave Cider Creek and not look back. Keeping himself distracted and busy had made it too easy to lose track of what was really important. It had been too easy to turn his back on the one who'd stuck it out, unlike his other parent.

And now it was too late to get any of the missed time back. Too late to be the son his father had deserved to have. Too late to make it right between them.

His father wasn't supposed to be gone this soon.

Dillen sat there in silence for a long while, no longer counting the minutes as they passed.

Eventually, he stood up and let go of his father's hand. Then he said the words he should have a long time ago: "I love you, Pop."

It occurred to Dillen that he'd been inside the room for an hour. There was no way Liz would still be waiting around after all this time had passed. He didn't blame her, either. There had to be some way to look her up or ask for her number. As he walked down the hallway toward the nurse's station, her words cycled through his thoughts and his anger returned. Because she'd made it seem like there had been foul play involved. And he intended to find out why.

Being a notoriously private person, Hayes would make tracking her down a challenge. Many people lived their lives on social media by "checking in" to every restaurant, park and jogging trail. Not so for the Hayes family—not that he'd stalked them. It was common knowledge.

A man who resembled his father's neighbor stood at the elevators. Mr. Martin must've been getting ready for the cold because his gloves were already on. Dillen shoved the thought aside as the guy stepped into the elevator and then the doors closed behind him.

By chance, he peeked inside the waiting room just in case Liz was still there. As he'd expected, she was gone.

Chapter Three

Liz washed up in the fifth floor bathroom as best as she could and brushed her teeth. The lack of a real shower in more days than she cared to count made her want to soak in a hot bath for an entire evening. She'd slept in fits and starts. A real bed sounded like heaven.

After drying her hands and face, she applied ChapStick to dry lips. She figured Dillen might be in his father's room for a while longer, and she planned to stick around until they could have a conversation about the things that didn't add up. Then she could go home and face the family meeting with a clear conscience. As far as she remembered, Mr. Bullard had been a kind person. He'd never bothered anyone or asked for much. His job as a lab tech assistant couldn't have brought in a lot of money, but he'd managed to make ends meet and bring up a son on his own. He'd been an admirable person by anyone's standard.

The second she opened the door to the hallway, Dillen's masculine voice hit her full force. The deep baritone was smooth as whiskey over ice. She mentally shook off her physical reaction to him.

He stood with his back to her, speaking to one of the administrators. There was no hint of sadness in his tone despite the fact that he had to be torn apart by his father's death. Dillen hadn't made it in time to say goodbye, either. Those were the details that would haunt a man like Dillen for a long time to come.

His earlier anger subsided, most likely buried deep inside while he worked out the arrangements for his father.

The hospital administrator typed on the keyboard as he spoke. He must have heard the door open and close because he gave a sideways glance, performed a double take and then held a finger up to the staff member, indicating he'd be right back.

Dillen turned around. With the full force of those intense hazel eyes on her, Liz had to swallow to ease some of the sudden dryness in her throat.

"You didn't leave," he said with a hint of gratitude, which was another surprise coming from him. He'd been prickly to her a little while ago. It had caused her defenses to respond in kind and they'd had a tense exchange, but that wasn't going to stop her from doing the right thing.

"Bathroom," she managed to say in more of a croak than anything else.

"Will you stick around for a few minutes?" he asked. "I'd like to talk."

"That's why I'm here," she said, croak-free this time.

He nodded and then turned his attention back to the staff member, finishing up their conversation. Him turning his attention away from her was a lot like stepping into a cold, dark cave after being warmed by the sun.

There weren't any chairs in the hallway, so Liz made her way back into the waiting area. Bone weary, she was exhausted down to her toes. In fact, they ached along with the rest of her. The tiredness that she'd been keeping at bay was finally settling in now that Dillen had arrived. It was almost as if her body had gotten the message that she didn't have to push to stay awake any longer. Relief was here in the form of an army ranger.

At one point, a nurse had brought her a pillow and blanket. She retrieved them before curling up in the uncomfortable blue chair and rested her eyes. Before she knew it, she was out.

"Hey," Dillen said. His quiet but masculine voice roused her from sleep. She tried to sit up, but it was like moving in slow motion. Almost like her soul had left her body and she was left in some kind of strange haze. This wouldn't be a good time to ask her to balance the books of her business or stand on her two legs for that matter.

"Everything okay?" she managed to ask as she shook off some of the fog. Her eyelids were the equivalent of sandpaper. How long had she been out? Couldn't have been more than a couple of minutes.

"You need sleep," Dillen said with a hint of frustration in his voice. Excuse her for not being ready to talk after sitting in this room for the past five days. "Are you all right with me helping you to my vehicle?" He muttered a curse. "I just realized that I don't have anything to drive here."

"My Honda is outside," she said, wondering where this was going but too tired to put up much of a fight. "One of my brothers brought it to the hospital."

Dillen glanced around like he expected one of them to be standing around in the background.

"I wouldn't let them stay," she said. "And I don't want to go home this late." She wasn't as ready to face the Hayes family home as she'd believed.

"Would you be fine with me driving?" he asked.

She didn't think she had a problem with it. "To where?"

"A place where you can sleep on a comfortable bed," he

said before adding, "and don't worry, I wouldn't try any-thing with someone like you."

Those last words were the equivalent of half a dozen bee stings on her face. She could ask him what the hell he meant later. Right now, a bed was too tempting to pass up, and she did need to have a serious conversation with the man. It would be easier to do if they were under the same roof.

"Good," she said. "Because I wouldn't let you get away with it anyway. And I can take the couch."

He mumbled something she couldn't quite hear.

"I'm going to help you up now," he said as she struggled to stand up. Dozing off had been a bad idea but she'd be fine in a few minutes. She glanced around. "My purse is over…" Well, hell, she couldn't remember where she'd last put it.

"It's underneath the chair. Do you want me to get it?" he asked.

She shook her head before bending down, with his help, and retrieving her handbag from underneath the chair. She shouldered the strap.

"Thank you," she said before pointing out the keys to her vehicle were inside.

"I have no intention of putting my hand where it doesn't belong," he argued. There was something to his tone that said he'd gotten himself into trouble with that one before. A woman's purse could definitely qualify as sacred ground. However, she'd expressly given him permission, which was a whole different story.

If she'd had the energy, she would have cracked a smile. Instead, she dug inside her handbag for the key fob so she could unlock the doors when they reached the lot. "Got it."

Now he picked her up with almost no effort on his part. The man's arms were like bands of steel, which wasn't something she wanted to focus on as he lifted her off her chair like he was the angry green version of Bruce Banner.

Dillen carried her to the Honda and then managed to place her inside the passenger seat without so much as bumping any of her body parts on the material surrounding the door, which made the huge bruise on her hip happy. Being pressed up against a solid wall of muscled chest caused her pulse to rise, though. She felt his heartbeat against her body, the pace matching her own.

"Go ahead and sleep on the way home if you want to," he said.

She nodded and closed her eyes after he helped her buckle up, not that she needed his or anyone else's permission to rest. When she got settled, she would need to let her family know she'd left the hospital so they didn't bring food or drop by as they had been. She'd had the chance to meet her new sisters-in-law. Even her baby sister had found an amazing person to share her life with, and Reese had been voted least likely to settle down first. Marriage and kids were good for some people. Liz had a business to run—one she'd been accused of choosing over her last serious boyfriend.

Since her mind decided to wander, she sat up a little straighter. Dillen claimed the driver's seat. She wasn't alert enough to trust herself behind the wheel, so it was good that he was the one doing the driving.

"Where are you taking me again?" she asked.

"To my father's house," he said. "I have no idea what condition it's in since I haven't been home in two years."

"Really?" she asked before she could reel the word back in.

"Why would you have a problem with that?" he asked as his face twisted with disdain. "I apologize if my family isn't as good as yours."

Liz wasn't touching that statement with a ten-foot pole.

DILLEN GRIPPED THE steering wheel until his knuckles went white. After his last statement—accusation, if he was being honest—Liz became quiet. Too quiet. It was the seething quiet that told him that he'd crossed a line that shouldn't have been touched.

Rather than address it, he figured he could do better by keeping his own mouth zipped. Besides, his anger shouldn't have been pointed at her since it hadn't been her fault to begin with.

"I'm a jerk for not getting here sooner," he finally said after a long pause. "An absolute waste as a son." His strained relationship with his father would haunt him for the rest of his life. Death was final, and there was no way to make it right now, to tell his father how much he appreciated him for sticking around when, apparently, parenting was optional once a kid was born. "That last comment I made was me taking out my frustration on you, and that's not okay." He wasn't quite ready to absolve her from having her nose into the air for her whole life, but she'd done what he hadn't—made certain his father hadn't been alone on his deathbed.

"I slipped into his room every night," she said. "Since I wasn't next of kin and he was in intensive care, I had to sneak."

"On my count, you spent the holiday in a waiting room for a man who wasn't even your father," he said, realizing he needed to rethink his position on her being a spoiled brat. Time would tell, but he was a big believer in watching people's actions instead of listening to their words.

"Yes," she admitted. "Is that a problem for you?"

Fair point, he decided. He'd probably had that one coming—and possibly more considering he'd shoved her into a category that he was thinking maybe she didn't belong in any longer.

"It means a lot that you would do something like that for someone who was a stranger," he said. "More to the point, that person was my father."

"Your dad wasn't a stranger to me," she said with confusion. "I knew him growing up."

"Why? How?" he asked.

"He worked at the lab, and I had to drop things off there sometimes for the cattle ranch," she said. "Your dad always greeted me with a warm smile and a wave. He was one of the nicest people." She paused after her voice cracked on those last few words. Next, she cleared her throat and sat up a little straighter. "He was just a good person and was always kind to me when I saw him around town."

Dillen didn't know what to say to that. Was there more to Liz than met the eye?

Before he went too far down the rabbit hole of caring, he pulled into the parking lot of the trailer park where he'd grown up. It wasn't a fancy ranch like the Hayes home. This was Cider Creek Park, but there wasn't anything park-like about the area. In fact, it was more gravel than anything else, which crunched underneath the car's tires at the moment.

"Not exactly the palace where you grew up," he quipped. "Think you can manage sticking around for a night here?"

Liz took in a slow breath.

"We should stick to the real reason we're being forced together instead of these backhanded insults you've been lobbing," she said with finality.

Had Dillen just been put in his place? He was partially amused.

"Sounds like a plan to me, princess," he quipped.

"Good. Then learn your place. And don't call me princess," she shot back. He'd riled her up. Good. She shouldn't get too comfortable around him because he'd just end up disappointing her much in the same way he'd done with his father.

An ache formed in his chest the size of the Grand Canyon and with the force of a hurricane as it sucked water out to sea. The water never came back in the same way it had left. It battered. It bruised. It flooded.

And that was exactly what Dillen would be to Liz. He would be trouble times ten. He would destroy her heart and her trust in all men. He would be the disappointment he'd always been to his own father.

Dillen parked next to the trailer he'd grown up in. This had been his childhood. It hadn't been filled with ponies and fancy birthday parties. It hadn't been filled with more friends than he'd known what to do with. It hadn't been filled with the kind of love Liz had surely experienced growing up a Hayes. It was a piece of...

He decided it was best not to say the word that would come next. It was probably better for everyone involved if he stuffed those thoughts down deep instead. This was the time he would normally hit the gym and get in a good workout to burn off much of his frustration. Talking had never been his thing. Lifting, pushing his body to the limit was the only time he got tired enough to relax, let alone sleep.

The trailer looked the same on the outside. It was white with neon-green trim like the relic from the eighties it was. Embarrassment flooded him. Why had he brought Liz Hayes here?

"This was a mistake," he said, reversing course. "You would probably be more comfortable in a hotel. There's one not too far from here off the highway."

"Why?" she asked as he put the gearshift in Park. "You think I'm too good to sleep in a trailer?" She issued a disgusted grunt. "Watch me."

Liz opened the car door and exited the Honda while the engine was still running. He cut it off, hopped out of the vehicle and hit the key fob to lock the doors.

"Look, you don't have to prove a point to me," he started. "I'm sure that you're fully capable of suffering a night or two inside a trailer just to prove you're one of the 'little' people."

She whirled around on him and poked a finger in his chest.

"Look here," she said. "I'm getting a little tired of this self-pity routine you have going. The one where you're a victim because you didn't grow up with money. Guess what? It's not the treat you think it is to be a Hayes. So, congratulations. You're just like everyone else in town who believes we're all entitled brats. Good for you. You figured us out. Do you want a prize now?"

He stood there for a long second dumbfounded.

Dillen knew exactly what he wanted. It wasn't a prize. It was a kiss. The way her gaze lingered on his lips while she slicked her tongue across hers said she did, too. So that was exactly what he did. He leaned in and pressed his lips to hers, waiting for the slap that might come next.

Chapter Four

Liz grabbed fistfuls of Dillen's shirt and then pulled him closer until his body was flush with hers. His lips tasted like fresh coffee, dark roast—her favorite—as all kinds of sensations lit her nerve endings on fire. Realizing her mouth was presently moving against Dillen's, she pulled back, wishing she could think of something snappy to say. Nothing came to mind because she'd wanted it to happen, too.

Taking in a deep breath only ushered in more of his spicy male scent. She chalked the kiss up to exhaustion. "That won't happen again."

"Good that you're not denying that you were a willing participant," he quipped, but she could tell by the huskiness in his voice the kiss had affected him more than he probably wanted to admit.

"No," she said. The infuriating part was that he might have started it, but she'd wanted it to happen just as much as he had. "But everyone has a lapse in judgment every once in a while. Doesn't mean it'll ever happen again." She balled her fist and then planted it on her hip. "Why don't you open the door so I can get some sleep. I must be delirious."

"Yes, ma'am," he said as he saluted. He was pushing her buttons, trying to get a reaction out of her.

Rather than go down that rabbit hole, she released a long,

slow breath and then followed him to the door. The key was tucked underneath the mat—not exactly a secure place. Then again, folks out here didn't usually worry about security as much as those from a big city. Having a key at all was something.

Once inside, Dillen flipped on a light in the cozy living room. The place was clean. *Preserved* might've been a better word. There were plastic covers on the sofa and matching love seat. There weren't many decorations aside from matching lamps and several framed photos. The red brick fireplace had a wooden mantle painted white with several school photos of Dillen on top at various stages of childhood. Mr. Bullard had bought every grade and framed the five-by-sevens. It was sweet.

A rancid smell came from the kitchen area. Dillen immediately turned left and stomped over to investigate. His nose wrinkled as Liz pulled her shirt up over hers to buffer some of the odor.

Dillen muttered a curse after he opened the trash can lid. He immediately pulled the trash bag out and then closed it up. He held his arm out as he exited through the back door, propping it open, no doubt, to neutralize the smell as quickly as possible. She followed suit, turning on the vent over the stove before waving her arms in the air to dispel the stench.

Well, now she was awake.

Dillen joined her, opening windows. He grabbed a dish towel from the dishwasher handle and then waved it around. With the frigid temperatures and wind, the place was aired out in no time. Dillen replaced the trash bag with a new one before, one by one, closing the windows again. He left the one over the sink cracked.

"Sorry about that," he finally said. She couldn't be certain if he was referring to the smell or the kiss from earlier.

Asking might've put them in territory she wasn't ready to explore. Plus, if it was the kiss, how awful would it be for someone to apologize after? She would have to be one terrible kisser for that to happen. Was she? Couldn't say she'd had any complaints up to now.

Get a grip. Liz's thoughts were spiraling because she was exhausted despite the recent surge of energy. Even so, she was running on fumes and didn't appreciate the timing of her second wind.

"Why don't you take the main bedroom?" Dillen asked. "My old room turned into a hobby room years ago."

When she lifted her eyes to meet his, she realized he'd been studying her.

"I don't think I could," she said. The thought of sleeping in Mr. Bullard's bed didn't sit right. Dillen might've been a class-A jerk, but his father had been nothing but kind to Liz. It didn't seem right to take over his room. "The couch looks comfy. Can we just throw a pillow and blanket over there?"

"Wouldn't you be more comfortable in a bed?"

Liz pushed away all thoughts of the word *bed* in the same sentence as Dillen. She was genuinely exhausted and standing upright solely due to a second wind as her thoughts kept circling back to the same topic...him. The man might've had a soft side—which he hid very well—and kissable lips, but that was no reason to keep thinking about him.

"I'll do fine on the sofa," she insisted. "Believe it or not, I won't find a pea under a mattress. I can sleep pretty much anywhere and have ever since business picked up. I can't tell you how many times I've fallen asleep with my head on my desk."

She was overexplaining, which didn't make sense, either. When had she started caring what Dillen Bullard thought about her?

"Have it your way," he said before disappearing into a back room. She assumed the main bedroom was there.

Examining the living room situation, she wondered if it would be all right to take the plastic covers off the furniture. The love seat was fine, as was the recliner that faced the TV, but she didn't want to make a crinkle noise every time she moved or sleep on top of plastic. It would get too hot. At least the smell was gone.

Liz bit back a yawn.

"Can I remove the couch cover?" she asked, shouting into the other room.

"Be my guest," came the response.

After taking the cover off, folding it and tucking it away in the corner of the room, she moved to the kitchen, located a glass and filled it with water. On top of being slaphappy, she was thirsty.

The water helped ease some of the dryness in her throat. By the time she finished the drink, Dillen returned with folded up blankets stacked on his right shoulder and a pillow on top. He walked over to the couch and had it looking like a proper bed in the matter of a minute. The man had serious skills. How?

Right. The military.

How could she have forgotten, considering he had on fatigues?

Liz could admit Dillen Bullard had grown into a fine-looking man. She didn't remember much about him from school other than the fact he'd kept to himself. He'd been the only one who could climb the rope ladder in PE by the time high school had rolled around. That should have told her something about where he'd been headed.

"Thank you," she said as a wave of exhaustion struck. "Is there a place I can shower?"

"This way," Dillen said, leading her to a small hallway off the living room. There were three doors. Two on the left and one at the end of the hallway. "The first one here is the bathroom. The second one is my dad's home office, and the last one used to be where I slept when I was a kid that is now a hobby room." His chest was puffed out like he was prepared to take a punch. Did he really think so little of her that he believed she would judge a person for growing up in a trailer? The place had everything anyone would need to make a home.

Dillen opened the first door before taking a step inside. The bathroom had all the necessary equipment, including a stand-up shower. The floor creaked, and the bathmat was clean but worn. It looked original and was the color of dirt, but the whole color scheme was neutral, so it fit.

"Pop always kept toothbrushes from dentist trips in here," he said, opening a drawer in the cabinet. There were rows of toothbrushes, neatly lined up. "Feel free to use whatever you need."

She thanked him again, wishing her body didn't react every time he brushed past her.

DILLEN WASN'T READY to let Liz off the hook for being a snob just yet despite the fact she hadn't turned her nose up at the family trailer. He assumed she was silently judging his upbringing. Maybe the question was Why did he care? She was nobody to him and Pop. Well, that wasn't exactly true. She'd spent Pop's last moments with him despite not having a memory of what those had been.

After a good night of sleep, he intended to talk to her in the morning. He stepped out into the hallway. "Holler if you need anything. I'll drop a robe outside the door if you want to wash your clothes."

"Will do," she said, looking like she couldn't shut the door fast enough. "And thanks."

He walked into the living room and then grabbed the plastic wrapper she'd taken off the couch. He pulled the others off before folding them up. After depositing those in a closet, he wrangled a blanket. His rucksack had all the supplies he'd need to stay for the week while he handled Pop's affairs. Dillen had every intention of figuring out if foul play had been involved as Liz suspected.

He grabbed the robe while she showered, and then hooked it onto the door handle of the bathroom.

Rage heated the blood in his veins at the thought. His hands fisted at his sides. He flexed and released his fingers a couple of times to work off some of the tension before heading out to the Honda, where he'd left his rucksack in the back seat.

After retrieving his supplies, he scanned the area. Pop had lived on half an acre but owned the property behind his trailer, so there were no neighbors right on top of his place. There were several, smaller plots of land with trailers on his lane. Across the street and down a bit had a small plot of land where Rosa and Macy lived. They were sisters who looked in on Pop from time to time. The man had lived a simple life. He hadn't been wealthy. What could anyone have possibly wanted from him? Why would anyone have wanted to hurt him? Pop wouldn't have killed a bee, even if it had stung him. And he wouldn't go to the construction site on his own. Did someone lure him there? Drop him there?

Shouldering his rucksack, Dillen headed back inside. Liz was sitting on the couch.

"I'll be right back," he said, heading toward his father's bathroom.

Liz stood up and made a beeline for the door, locking it.

Whatever had happened clearly had her riled up because folks didn't do that in these parts. It wasn't uncommon for someone to leave their keys in the drink holder, so they didn't have to carry them around, so locking their home wasn't normal behavior when there weren't many neighbors or main roads out here.

Dillen needed to get his bearings. Being back at the trailer without Pop had him off kilter. Memories engulfed him, threatening to suck him under and hold him there until he could no longer breathe. Since he hadn't slept in the main bedroom since he was five years old, and only when he'd had a bad dream, staying in there now was out of the question. He would rest in the recliner in the living room. Talk about memories. Glancing over at the bed now made his eyes water.

A quick shower later, he'd brushed his teeth and thrown on sweatpants and a cotton T-shirt. Normally he slept in boxers, but he didn't figure Liz would appreciate him walking around with almost no clothes on. Thinking about the kiss from earlier was enough to heat his blood. Bad idea. He didn't want something that had happened in a flash to occupy this much of his brain power. Still, he couldn't ignore the sizzle.

But Liz Hayes was off-limits. At the end of the day, she was a spoiled princess and Dillen's feet were firmly planted on the ground. They were from different worlds and had already clashed because of it. Right now, she was putting on a good show of being comfortable in the small trailer. How long could she keep it up?

On that note, he joined her in the living room and made himself comfortable on the recliner. She'd closed the window over the kitchen sink and was on her side, facing the room and softly snoring despite the lamp being on.

The warm glow from the microwave offered enough light for him to walk back over to the recliner without fear of stubbing his toe. Although he couldn't forget the layout since every piece of furniture sat in its exact same spot from the day it showed up.

Dillen let those thoughts carry him to sleep after he got comfortable on the recliner.

Not an hour later, wind howled loud enough to wake him. Liz sat bolt upright, searching the room as she clutched covers all the way up to her chest.

"It's just the wind," he said, rubbing his eyes with one hand as he searched for the recliner's lever with the other. His fingers curled around the wood before he tugged at it, causing the recliner to return to an upright position. He studied Liz to see if she was cognizant of what was happening or sitting up while still asleep. One of his buddies in his unit had a terrible habit of doing the same. He never spoke, just shot up to a sitting position in the middle of the night.

"You're okay." He tried to make his voice as soothing as possible, wondering if he was the last person on earth she wanted comforting her.

Liz nodded before crumpling onto her side again. Her eyelids fluttered before closing.

"Liz," he said quietly.

There was no response. The problem was he was awake. Going back to sleep would be impossible, but he'd gotten in a solid forty-five minutes. He'd survived on less sleep for longer amounts of time. Then again, since hearing the news Pop was in the hospital, he hadn't really slept.

What the hell was he supposed to do while he sat there? Making noise might wake Liz. She needed sleep. No, she deserved sleep.

Pop had a desktop computer in his home office. Dillen

could start there and poke around to see if he found anything suspicious.

Dillen threw the covers off. He knew exactly where to step so the floor wouldn't creak underneath his weight. The wind, however, had a mind of its own. It howled, shaking the double wide. He stopped halfway across the room mid-step.

Liz's steady breathing said she was still asleep. Good.

He crossed the room and entered the hallway without making a sound. The door to Pop's office was closed. Dillen stood there, holding on to the door handle, unable to make his hand move. He leaned his shoulder against the door and then the side of his head.

Why was walking inside harder than any mission he'd ever been on?

Chapter Five

The walls shook, causing Liz to sit bolt upright. She glanced around the room, trying to gain her bearings. Nothing looked familiar.

Shaking her head to break through the fog, she remembered. Dillen had brought her here to rest before they dissected what had actually happened to his father and why she'd woken up in a hospital after stopping at an intersection during a freak ice storm. A weather system had been moving in, and she'd heard cries for help, or so she'd been told.

The recliner had a blanket draped over it. Where was Dillen?

Liz stretched her arms out and released a yawn. She pushed to standing, got a little woozy and almost immediately sat right back down. She took a minute to regroup and heard clicking noises coming from down the hall. Was Dillen on the computer?

The second attempt at standing produced far better results. She took a couple of steps toward the hallway, and the flooring creaked underneath her weight.

"I'm in here," Dillen said. His masculine voice slid over her and through her despite her best efforts to reject it. Goose bumps formed on her arms as she thought about what else those lips of his were good for. This seemed like a good time to remind herself that she wasn't here for a social call. No matter how hot the man was, he was off-limits. Not that she needed to worry, considering the only reason he was able to be in the same room with her was to find answers about his father's death. Murder?

Liz took in a deep breath. *Murder* was a strong word. And yet it resonated.

Had Mr. Bullard said something to her? She pushed for answers but only managed to cause an ache to form in the spot right between her eyes.

After issuing a sharp sigh, she headed toward the clicking sound of fingers on a keyboard. Another deep breath later, she walked inside the office. The room had a desk pushed up against the wall to her right. There was a plastic floor mat underneath a leather chair on wheels, taking up much of the middle of the room. A framed American flag along with a picture of a young Dillen in his army uniform was on the wall. And then another picture of him in salute as a Green Beret, which she recognized as the army's Special Forces soldiers. An old metal filing cabinet that stood five feet tall was pushed up against the left back corner of the room.

"Did the wind wake you up again?" Dillen asked, nodding toward the chair in the corner next to the desk.

"Again?" she parroted.

"I thought you might have been asleep last time," he said as he stared at the monitor. "The wind was something last night."

Liz took a seat, perching on the edge of the chair, and yawned. "I have no recollection of being awake before, but I'll take your word for it."

"Are you hungry?" he asked, his tone and demeanor much

softer than last night. Then again, he deserved a break considering he'd just learned the news his father was gone.

"Maybe in a few minutes," she said. "I'm currently in that sleep-fog where it feels like you're moving outside your body."

He nodded before clicking the tab closed and then swiveling the chair around toward her. He leaned forward and clasped his hands together. "I had no idea there would be so many decisions to make after..."

"My grandfather died a few months back, and I bet my mother is still drowning in paperwork," she admitted.

"You don't know for certain?" he asked with a cocked eyebrow.

"I run my own business, so, no, I haven't been home or checking in much," she said by way of explanation. It was a cop-out, but she wasn't quite ready to examine the reasoning.

Dillen opened his mouth to speak, but she cut him off. "By the way, Hayes family members work their backsides off making their own businesses, so don't look so surprised that I built one from the ground up."

His questioning expression morphed into a small smile. "Sorry. Note taken."

"It's just you seemed to be confusing me with some entitled princess last night, and reality couldn't be further from it," she continued while she had his ear.

The smile widened, and she didn't want to notice how full his lips were or how much more attractive the man was when he smiled.

He opened his mouth to speak again before clamping his lips shut.

"What?" she asked. "Did you have something to add?"

"Are you finished?" he asked with that bemused smile

planted on lips that covered perfectly white and almost perfectly straight teeth.

A solid reason for that statement being infuriating to her wasn't readily available, but there she was angry anyway. And then it came to her. It was the tone more than the words. Mocking?

"I'm just saying that you were a jerk last night," she defended, hugging her arms across her chest.

"Hey, that's personal," he teased, tensing up like he'd just taken a punch.

"Dillen, can we be serious for a minute?" she broke down and asked on an exhale.

"Yes, ma'am," he said, sitting up a little straighter and removing the smile.

"Good," she said.

"Before you say anything else, I do recognize that you are here out of the goodness of your heart, prince—"

She shot him a look that stopped him cold.

"Liz," he corrected. "And I do appreciate the fact you stayed with Pop...not to mention the fact you're here now trying to help sort this out. I was going on emotion last night and probably a few preconceived notions about you. No matter what, I had no right. I'd like to offer an apology if you're willing to accept it."

"Done," she said, studying him. His demeanor had softened, or maybe it was just his face muscles that looked less tense. In fact, a deep sadness set in his eyes that formed an ache in her chest. Kindred spirits? "Now we can get down to business."

An emotion flashed behind his eyes now that she didn't want to analyze because it looked a whole lot like desire. Couldn't be, though. Dillen Bullard could barely stand the ground she walked on. Clearly.

But she wasn't here for him. She felt bad for Mr. Bullard. The sweet older man hadn't deserved what had happened to him.

"We have to go back there," she said. "To the site, so I can retrace my steps and maybe get a memory or two back of what actually happened." She would prefer to remember everything, but what if her brain was protecting her from information so horrific that knowing would cause nightmares or a major depression? Fear? Should she be afraid that whoever tried to kill her would come back to finish the job?

For Mr. Bullard's sake, she needed to know what had happened.

"Okay," Dillen said. "I'll be right there with you in case the bastard or bastards who did this to you and Pop come back."

Did he sense her fears? A highly person trained like him would probably be able to read someone with one look.

Or maybe a better question would be to ask why she cared what he thought in the first place.

DILLEN'S AMUSEMENT FADED the second he realized Liz was afraid to go back to the site on her own. Being here in the home where he'd grown up probably wasn't high on the list of places she wanted to visit. He needed to remember that and hold his tongue on the sharp digs. Being glued to her meant finding out what really happened to his father. This was his new mantra. It would keep him focused on what was important instead of slipping into the past. And besides, he appreciated her help.

Somewhere locked inside her brain might've been the key to figuring out what had really happened. Dillen had only so much time on leave. Time was of the essence.

"Thank you," she said on an exhale. "I wish I could remember." She brought her hands up to rub her temples. "All I get is a headache and no answers."

"You've been through a lot," he said, trying his best to find a way to reassure her. "Don't be too hard on yourself."

She nodded. The acknowledgment followed by the look of relief in her eyes shouldn't have caused his chest to swell with pride as much as it did.

"It's frustrating to feel like I might have answers locked away inside here," she admitted.

"I imagine it is," he said. "Trust the memories will come back. Do your best not to fixate on them."

"Okay," she said. "I'll do my best. Relaxing isn't exactly my forte."

"Can I ask a question?" One had been burning in the back of his mind.

"Sure."

"Why not call your family to stay at the hospital with you?" he asked.

"How do you know I didn't?" she asked, her eyebrow shooting up.

"They would have still been there," he said. "You guys were like a clan in school, always protecting one another and having each other's backs."

"They brought food, but we didn't always get along when we were younger," she pointed out. "There were four strong-willed boys in the house along with me and my sister."

"Only child," he said on a shrug.

"Then let me fill you in," she said. "My brothers and sister might have had my back, but they were also pains in the neck. No one could talk to me or about me when they were within earshot."

"I could see why they might've wanted to protect you

against high school boys," he said. "Most of the ones in our school were all testosterone and little brains."

"It didn't seem to matter that I could handle myself," she continued. "I'm pretty certain they threatened anyone who got within five feet of me."

"Never thought about it like that," he said. It could explain why she'd been so standoffish back in school. She hadn't wanted her brothers interrogating anyone.

"High school was a lonely time," she said. The admission surprised him given her family's popular status.

"The teachers had high expectations of me being a Hayes," she said. "I couldn't step out of line in the slightest."

He hadn't thought about the pressure that might come with a famous last name. Then again, he'd had bigger fish to fry. Like being able to keep food on the table in his youth. His father's paycheck had barely covered essentials, not that Dillen should complain. Looking back, Pop had done the best he could with what he had to work with. "Living under a microscope couldn't have been fun."

"It was miserable," she said. "Why do you think I bolted the day after graduation like my siblings?"

"You moved away from Cider Creek?" he asked, incredulous. His jaw shouldn't have dropped, but it did. Why would a princess like Liz leave town? Because a few people had kept an eye on her every move? When he heard himself say it like that, it didn't sound great. In fact, it felt stifling.

"Why does that surprise you so much?" she asked with more than a little indignation in his tone. Fair.

"I just realized what you were saying, and it sounds like its own hell to be a Hayes in this town." He wasn't one hundred percent on board with changing his opinions, but he was starting to see that her last name could have been an albatross around her neck.

"Honestly, I had a roof over my head and food on the table," she said. "My mother and Granny loved us, and they did the best they could after my father died. The fact that Duncan Hayes existed to make our lives a living hell shouldn't taint everything good."

Dillen had forgotten about the fact her father had died when she was young. He also hadn't thought about how terrible it might've been to live under the iron fist of Duncan Hayes. His image in Cider Creek might have been as town savior, but Dillen had never liked the man. Was he beginning to see Liz in a different light?

"Your grandfather was a piece of work," he agreed.

"You better believe it," she snapped. "What happened at home didn't fit the good family man image he portrayed in public. But how did you see it when no one else in town seemed to?"

"I was never enamored by all of his donations and money," he said point-blank.

"Good that someone in town could see through him," she said. It was the first time he realized her disdain for Duncan Hayes might've been on par with his. "I shouldn't speak ill of the dead, but the only positive that I got from my grandfather was his work ethic."

"At least something good came from being related to the man," he conceded, figuring a trust fund was probably another benefit. All grown up, she didn't fit the trust-fund bill. There wasn't anything about her that said she was lazy or entitled like he imagined most rich kids were. He wouldn't know firsthand because he didn't hang out with trust-fund babies. In fact, this was the closest he'd ever been to one.

"Working on a ranch didn't exactly jive with manicured nails or high heels," she continued, like she had something to prove. He should know. He recognized the defense mechanism since it was his go-to.

Damn. Was he admitting the two of them might be alike in some way?

Dillen sat up a little straighter, rejecting the idea before it took hold. Liz Hayes didn't need anyone's pity, especially not his. So why was he softening toward her?

Chapter Six

Liz's stomach growled. "I guess I'm hungrier than I realized."

"Let's get something to eat," Dillen said, immediately standing. He waited for her as she pushed up, got a little woozy and then pulled it together. "You need food, but I can't make any promises."

"I'd eat crackers at this point," she admitted. The thought of coffee had her feet moving faster toward the kitchen. Could she, though? Would caffeine make her headache worse or better? It dawned on her that caffeine might actually solve her headache. She hadn't had a cup in days. "I saw a coffee maker on the counter."

"Coffee is guaranteed in this house," he said as they cut across the living room and walked into the kitchen.

The pantry was stocked. Overstocked, in fact.

"It's not like Pop to have more than he needed for a week," Dillen said as he appraised the cabinet. There had to be five bags of coffee grounds, all the same dark-roast flavor. "This isn't like him."

"Your father liked his routines," she said. "I'm guessing shopping is one of many."

Dillen nodded. "He doesn't—*didn't*—do anything out of the ordinary. Stocking up on supplies like coffee doesn't make sense."

"Here, let's check the expiration dates," she offered. "Maybe he just didn't like to throw anything away."

They checked each bag one by one. The dates were all similar, meaning the coffee had been bought at roughly the same time.

"Pop must have been off lately," he deduced. "Maybe his memory was starting to fade."

She opened the fridge. "Did he normally drink wine?"

"Pop? No," he said as he turned around. His gaze landed hard on the half-empty bottle in the fridge along with several unopened bottles in the door. Dillen scratched his head. "I have no idea when this started."

"Was it possible he was dating someone?" she asked.

"No, but then I didn't think he drank wine or stocked up on coffee, either," he admitted with a shrug. "I'm in new territory here."

Her mind immediately snapped to Mr. Bullard dating a married woman. Weren't passion killings one of the top reasons for murder? "What about a new friend?"

"That I do not know," he said. "Again, I would have said no to that question before. In all my years growing up here, the man never once went on a date or brought home a buddy to watch a game or have a beer."

"You joined the military and left home," she pointed out. "Is it possible he was lonely?"

Dillen shrugged. "Anything is possible at this point. Is it probable? I don't think so. But what do I know?" He issued a sharp sigh. "TV used to be company enough for him. Believe me when I say he watched certain shows every night my entire childhood."

"What would cause him to change his routine?" she asked.

"That's the sixty-four-thousand-dollar question." Dillen

grabbed coffee before closing the cabinet. "Do you see anything edible in the fridge?"

"The eggs haven't expired," she said before opening the freezer. "I can use these tater tots to make something that resembles hash browns."

"Sounds like a plan," he said as he went to work on a pot of coffee. There were no fancy pods. Just a good old reliable Mr. Coffee machine that had been around since the dawn of time. Filters were not in short supply, either.

Had Mr. Bullard been sick? Was that the reason he'd stockpiled? Had he been dating?

Questions piled up as she pulled out the ingredients to make breakfast. The milk was fresh, so she poured a glass to calm her stomach before whipping up fried eggs and makeshift hash browns.

"I'm surprised a Hayes knows how to cook," Dillen said, breaking the good vibes they'd had going while working together in the kitchen.

This time, she let the comment roll right off her. If he was trying to get a rise out of her, it wouldn't work.

The eggs came out nicely, as did the hash browns. Before she could ask for a plate, two appeared next to the stove on the counter. She could feel Dillen's masculine presence without glancing in his direction. The man was also stealthy, so he was out of the way pouring coffee before she had a chance to thank him for the plates.

After dividing up the food, she brought the dishes over to the table. Dillen brought mugs and then silverware.

"Smells good," he practically grunted. Was he upset with her for not responding to his dig? He'd corrected himself, but it was clear his impression of her and her family was the same despite her opening up about what life was really like for her growing up a Hayes. So be it. She wanted answers to who would have wanted to murder a kind older man like Mr. Bullard. Secondly, she needed to know if someone was coming after her. And third, she didn't want to care why Dillen's opinion mattered so much to her.

They'd shared one good kiss. It barely qualified, and yet her heart argued the opposite. Her lips still sizzled from the contact. Even though their lips had barely touched, this would be the new benchmark for every future kiss.

"What kind of work do you do?" Dillen broke the silence.

"I run an accessory business over the internet," she supplied, figuring that was enough information for him to stop asking questions.

"Does that mean jewelry?" he asked.

"No," she stated before stabbing a piece of tater tot with her fork. She took a bite and then chewed. Since talking about her personal life hadn't gone so well earlier, she didn't plan to go there again.

"Are any other memories coming back?" he asked, breaking eye contact.

"I wish I did," she said. "All I keep thinking is that your dad didn't deserve what happened to him."

"We're in agreement there," he said. "I should check out his bathroom a little closer to see if there's any hint of a woman having been here."

"They might have gone to her place," she offered.

"True," he agreed. "Plus, Pop would have cleaned up right after she left here, so there won't likely be any traces left behind."

"We could ask neighbors," she said.

Dillen snapped his fingers. "You know what? I remember seeing one of Pop's neighbors at the hospital. Mr. Martin. We should definitely drive around and ask questions. I don't know the guy very well. It's not like we had neighborhood parties or broke out the grill. Pop kept to himself mostly, but there was a man…"

"Wish I could help with names, but I haven't lived in Cider Creek in forever," she said.

"I doubt you made it over to this side of the tracks much anyway," he commented.

Later today she would think of a great zinger in response. But right now, nothing came to mind. Why did that always happen? The minute she laid her head down on the pillow at night, she thought of every great comeback. But now? Speechless.

THE LAST THING Dillen needed was to get close to a Hayes. They couldn't be trusted, no matter how soft their skin was or how sincere those eyes were.

"All done?" he asked, figuring his contribution to the meal would be clearing the table and throwing the dishes into the dishwasher.

"Yes," Liz said with a back stiffer than a corpse.

He cleared the table as she sat and sipped from her coffee mug. The meal had been good. Better than good. He'd been utterly shocked a Hayes could pull off a decent breakfast. Didn't they all have hired help even as adults?

"I doubt you guys have the work ethic of ranchers on this side of the tracks, but I imagine most folks rise with the sun," Liz said after taking another sip.

Shots fired.

Dillen cracked a smile because her zinger was a good one.

"The neighbors should be up," he said. "They're good folks. You should pop over here and get to know how the other half lives."

"Really? Why would I do that when I can hang out with one percenters all day?" she asked dismissively.

The caffeine must've been kicking in was all he could think because her comebacks were getting snappier each time. The banter proved she wasn't a complete uptight princess.

"Good point," he said before placing the last dish in the machine. "I'll try to remember that when I'm throwing my next hoedown."

Liz laughed. The sound was like music filling the air.

"I have brothers who gave me a hard time growing up," she said by way of explanation. "And I don't normally get insulted by the opposite sex, but I haven't spoken to them in years other than an occasional text check-in, so I'm rusty with the insults."

He had to give it to her. She was taking his jabs better than he expected for a spoiled trust-fund baby. "They trained you well."

"A lifetime with four brothers should do something besides drive me up the wall," she commented, rolling her eyes. "You would probably get along with them pretty well."

"I doubt it," he said reflexively.

"Why?"

"They never spoke a word to me in high school. Why would they start now?" he asked, hearing the defensiveness in his own voice.

"They didn't know you back then," she said. "As memory serves, you were in my grade."

"That's right."

"Were they awful to you?" she asked.

"No. Can't say they were," he responded.

"Okay, then I guess I don't understand why you hate us so much," she stated with a raised eyebrow.

"Duncan Hayes," he said, surprised by his own honesty.

"That makes sense to me," she quipped. "But I'm not sure

why you think it's a good idea to judge the whole family based on one person's actions. We're all different, and no one disliked Duncan Hayes more than me and my siblings."

"Is that why you didn't go straight home from the hospital or call your family?" he asked, using the mention of her grandfather to switch topics.

"I'm not ready to face them until I've figured out what happened to Mr. Bullard," she said honestly. "My family is a whole thing that sucks you in." She shook her head. "Once I step inside the door, I'll be sucked in."

"Everyone knows your family, right?" he asked.

"Just about everyone," she responded. "Though, to be honest, I haven't been home in so long I doubt anyone would recognize me."

"Despite more than a decade passing since you were last here, you haven't changed a bit."

"Oh, I've changed," she countered with a grunt of disapproval. "I'm not at all the scared kid that I used to be."

Dillen studied her as the dots seemed to be connecting in her brain. She frowned.

"I should probably call them again to let them know I made it here," she said on a sigh.

"I'm surprised they haven't blown up your phone already," he admitted.

"They respect my wishes," she said. "Since I didn't reach out to them, they'll assume I want space. Plus, they're busy with their own lives and work."

"Doesn't sound like the same group who wouldn't let a guy get close to you in high school," he said.

"Like I said, we've all grown up since then," she defended. "You're not exactly the same tall, skinny kid I remember, either."

"I'm surprised you noticed me at all," he quipped. He'd

changed since high school in more ways than he could count, and yet one thing had remained a constant. Anger. The military had given him better coping mechanisms for it. But it had never subsided. The fact that Pop was gone struck like a physical blow, exploding inside his body with nowhere for it to exit. No release. Now all that anger balled inside him, forming a hard knot in the center of his chest.

Dillen issued a sharp sigh. Going down that road always led to the same result. More frustration.

"Come on," she said. "Our school wasn't that big. You might have always kept to yourself, but that didn't mean I wouldn't have talked to you if you'd seem the least bit interested in a conversation."

"I'm pretty sure everyone wanted your attention," he said. "But you always sat alone. I'm guessing it has more to do with what you wanted versus your brothers being overprotective."

"I won't lie. High school was brutal," she admitted, catching him off guard.

"Even for a princess like you?" he asked, immediately regretting his word choice. Words meant to mask the simple fact that he wanted to kiss her like they'd invented the idea.

Chapter Seven

Dillen Bullard was infuriating. His opinion would never change, so why bother correcting him again?

Liz stood, crossed her arms over her chest and tapped her toe on the vinyl flooring in the kitchen. "I'm ready if you want to go speak to the neighbors and then visit the construction site together."

He glanced out of the curtain over the kitchen window and nodded. "It didn't dawn on me last night that Pop's car is here."

"Could mean he was taken from here to the site," she reasoned.

"Or that he went for a walk and was grabbed," he said.

"True," she said, taking a mental note of the recent supply hoarding activities. The rest of Mr. Bullard's trailer was just like usual according to Dillen, who'd disappeared into the main bedroom after excusing himself and mumbling something about throwing a sweater on.

The wind had calmed down, and it wasn't raining. The weather conditions might have had an impact on the construction site. A growing piece of her wanted to swing by there first before evidence could be blown away by the wind if it hadn't already. As heavy as those winds were last night, debris might have been tossed around, too.

Liz had been in the hospital for five days. Today counted six since the so-called accident. Again, she wondered why Mr. Bullard would've been wandering around during an ice storm. Wouldn't he have driven? His home was on the outskirts of town, too far to walk. He hadn't seemed to be a runner. She didn't figure he'd changed his habits.

Dillen entered the room as he pulled a sweater on over his head.

"I've never seen your father run," she said.

"Pop? No," he confirmed. "That's because he didn't exercise other than walk. I bought weights and put a bench out in the shed but never could convince him to use them. He didn't like workouts and could be as stubborn as a mule when he didn't want to do something."

"The site is far from here," she continued. "I'm wondering how he got there if his car is still here. Did he ride a bike?"

He shook his head. "He wouldn't have taken one out in bad weather even if he did own one, and there was no getting him on the back of a motorcycle. Believe me, I tried once. It was a disaster."

"Was he ever diagnosed as autistic?" she asked.

"No," he said. "Not that I'm aware of."

"So, you don't know exactly what you're dealing with?" she asked.

"He was different," Dillen said with fire in his eyes. "He liked his routines more than most. It's no different than me being in the military. I've seen guys who thrive on routine, waking up at five thirty every morning so they can go through the same motions every day. Doesn't mean they need a diagnosis."

"Okay," she said, realizing she'd just hit on a sore spot. "I wasn't saying there was anything wrong with your father."

Dillen moved to the coffee maker, poured another cup

and then turned off the machine. "Do you want more before we head out?"

"No, thanks," she said, realizing a wall had just come up
between them. "I've had enough for one morning."

Her statement covered more than she planned to discuss
right now.

"Do you want to go to the construction site first?" she
asked. "I was thinking the longer we wait the colder the
crime scene becomes."

"The neighbors can wait," he said before throwing a couple of ice cubes into the mug. After stirring, he drained the
contents. "If we find anything, we go to the sheriff and ask
him to open a criminal case."

Good. The thought of revisiting the crime scene, if it
could be called that, had her nerves on edge. A growing part
of her wanted to face it and get it over with. Right now, her
hands were trembling at the thought of going back there.
At the thought of what she might find. And at the thought
of what she might remember.

Anticipation was the absolute worst. At this point, she
needed to get the visit over with even if it stirred up a flood
of memories she couldn't handle. Correction, she would
find a way to cope with whatever came her way. She always did. History would repeat itself, and she would find
a way to deal.

Again, the thought her brain might be protecting her from
something potentially devastating hit her.

You got this.

If she could leave home after graduation at eighteen years
old, survive on her own and start a successful business, she
could handle anything.

After putting on her coat and shoes, she walked out to
her Honda with Dillen. "Do you mind driving?"

Dillen said he didn't before opening the door for her and then claiming the driver's seat for himself. "I almost thought about taking out Pop's vehicle. I don't know how many folks know about his passing. The grapevine is strong in these parts, if memory serves."

"It sure used to be," she said. "Couldn't tell you what has changed since I last lived here considering next year marks my fifteenth year away from Cider Creek."

"You really hated it that bad?" he asked as he navigated onto the roadway.

"Couldn't wait to get out, and never looked back," she admitted. "So, yes, you could say that it wasn't my cup of tea."

The rest of the drive to the construction site was spent in quiet contemplation. Every muscle in Liz's body tensed a little more as they neared the intersection. It was the last place in her memory of that night.

She located her cell inside her purse and then sent a text to her oldest brother, Callum, letting him know where she was and what she was up to. He'd stepped into the role of family caregiver after their dad had died despite how much she'd fought him on it.

A response came back almost immediately. Come home when UR ready. B Careful.

"All good," she said out loud as she responded with a thank U. Thinking back, she'd always been able to talk to Callum. Then there was her younger sister, Reese, a sister who'd just decided to get married according to the sibling group chat.

In fact, all of her siblings had found love and happiness right here in or near Cider Creek upon their return. The last thing Liz needed to complicate her life was a relationship. She shuttered thinking about how possessive her last boyfriend had become when she couldn't tear herself away from a business that was flying high. She'd worked too hard to get where she was to have anyone derail her. Having to choose between a man and the business she'd built from the ground up had been a no-brainer.

The right man would understand her well enough to know better than to draw a line in the sand. Hell, he'd even support her rather than complain that making a living was taking too much time away from the relationship.

"Do they want you to come home?" he asked. She noticed he gripped the steering wheel a little tighter when he asked the question.

"When I'm ready," she said. "Callum understands." And then it dawned on her that her sister was marrying one of Dillen's old friends. "I'm guessing you already know this, but Reese and Darren are getting married."

"Darren Pierce?" he asked.

The incredulous note to his tone put her off.

"What? You don't think my sister is good enough to marry him?" she asked.

"I never thought he'd end up with a Hayes, if that's what you're asking," he said like it should've been a known fact.

"You may not like my family but, you know, not everyone automatically hates us because my grandfather was a jerk," she quipped. "Some folks actually give us the benefit of the doubt."

"Everyone sucked up to your grandfather," he responded.

"Clearly not *everyone*."

DARREN NEEDED TO have his head examined for getting romantically involved with a Hayes after it hadn't worked out the first time, as far as Dillen was concerned. Darren and Liz Hayes had been high school sweethearts years ago before she broke his heart, left town and didn't look back.

Dillen hadn't thought about his old friend in years. Back in high school, teachers used to mix the two of them up based on their names despite the fact they'd looked nothing alike. The similarities ended with the alphabet. Their taste in women couldn't have been more different, even though Dillen could admit to feeling a pull toward Liz like nothing he'd ever experienced in the past.

That wasn't entirely true. He'd had a severe crush on her during high school, and those old feelings must've been resurfacing now. If someone had told seventeen-year-old him that he would kiss Liz Hayes at some point in the future, he might have laughed. Or punched them. Thankfully, he'd gotten a tighter grip on his anger since then.

Liz's cell phone buzzed. He caught her staring at the screen out of the corner of his eye.

"The family meeting is being put on hold indefinitely," she said to him. "And my sister is asking how you're doing, so I guess the whole town knows we're spending time together."

"What meeting?" he asked.

"One my mother called to discuss next steps with the family ranch," she said. "Now that Duncan is gone and a little time has passed, I imagine she wants to know where we stand on the family business."

The cell buzzed again before he had a chance to respond.

"Everyone sends their condolences and wants to know if there's anything you need," she continued. "Darren doesn't have your contact information any longer, or he would reach out himself."

Well, damn. He'd be a jerk to pop off at the mouth when people were offering sympathy. He wasn't. And, honestly, he appreciated their sentiment. Now that Pop was gone, Darren had no family left to speak of. His mother had ditched when he'd been a kid, too young to remember her. He had no siblings that he knew of. He'd grown up an only child who'd learned to depend on himself from an early age.

"Tell them I appreciate their offer," he said, stopping himself before saying he was fine. He wasn't fine. In fact, he'd never been less fine in his life. "If I think of anything, I'll reach out."

She nodded and typed on the screen.

"Can I give them your cell number?" she asked.

"Why not," he said, glancing up at the sky to see if pigs were flying. There was a time when he'd believed he would witness that before he'd be in contact with a Hayes. Maybe he should start believing in miracles after all. He fished his cell phone out of his pocket before handing it over.

Liz took it, and their fingers grazed. He didn't want to think about the jolt of electricity or the tension that seemed to sit thickly between them, charging the air. She immediately looked away from him after taking the offering and intensely focused on the screen.

"Mind if I put you in my contacts?" she asked without looking up.

"No, go ahead," he said. "Do you mind making sure I have your information?"

"Sure," she said after clearing her throat.

Dillen pulled up to the construction site. The sun was shining, which made the forty-eight-degree temperatures feel a whole lot warmer inside the vehicle. They would be hit with the cold again the second they opened the doors.

After taking in a deep breath, Liz shifted her gaze from the phones. He sat with her car idling at the same red light she'd mentioned, but they were coming from the opposite side. Her mind was blocking out the memories. Protecting her? He wanted to do the same, even though he realized bringing her here to get answers might create more stress.

It was an impossible situation. He could shield her from this place and, possibly, keep her from remembering. Or he could confine his anger and help her face whatever came next. Since he didn't intend to let her out of his sight until they found answers, he had no choice but to walk her through this place.

"Let me know whenever you're ready," he said, idling the engine at the light. "Take your time."

"I came from the opposite side of the street," she said, pointing. "It was getting hard to see out of my front windshield while I sat at the light because the cold front came in so quickly. Everything started fogging up, so I rolled down my window. That's when I heard a noise." She flashed eyes at him. "I thought it sounded like a wounded animal."

A coil tightened in his chest at thinking of his father being left out here alone to die.

"The last thing I remember is getting out of my vehicle and running toward the sound," she said before pinching the bridge of her nose. There was still a bandage on her head. She would need to follow up with the doctor at some point. "This is so frustrating. My head hurts when I focus on recall too much. It's like the next few minutes of what happened are locked inside a vault in my brain and I can't break in no matter how hard I try. In fact, trying seems to make it worse."

"It'll be all right," he soothed, reaching for her hand while readying himself for the now-familiar jolt. "We'll find answers. I promise you."

It was a promise he intended to keep even if it killed him.

"Are you ready to park?" he asked when she didn't respond.

Her lips curled down at the edges, frowning. "We can't

sit here forever. This might be a small town, but someone will come roaring up here eventually."

It dawned on him that someone might have come up on the scene during the ice storm. Then again, folks hunkered down in times like those, not wanting to venture out into the streets past dark. Towns like Cider Creek shut down as soon as the sun dropped below the horizon. Plus, it was the holidays, so workers would have been sent home. Most construction sites in small towns were staffed with out of town folks.

"We can take it slow," he said. "Other people will have to get over themselves if they show up here."

Liz squeezed his hand. "Thank you. That means a lot."

Those words shouldn't have made him want to open his heart to her. But they did.

Chapter Eight

The compassionate side to Dillen wasn't something Liz was used to. It made him even more attractive. She didn't need to be more attracted to him, so she shut down her feelings, let go of his hand and threw up a boundary. Dillen Bullard was off-limits. It would be a mistake to lean into his comfort. Because he would leave town once he'd handled his father's affairs and she would never see the man again. She needed to keep their interactions in perspective, which wasn't something she was used to forcing. Normally, it came naturally.

Being here at the site wasn't helping with her memory, so they needed to hunt for clues. "I think it's safe to pull onto the side of the road and park."

Dillen did as requested. His change in demeanor was nice.

He was on her side of the Honda in a matter of seconds, opening the door for her and offering a hand up. She accepted the help, doing her best to ignore the way his touch made her feel and all the senses he awakened in her.

Walking around the Honda…there was still nothing. No memory of what had happened after exiting her vehicle at the light. Construction seemed to have stopped. Was it the weather or the holidays?

Looking down, she retraced what might have been her

steps. The freezing rain had helped with footprints on the cold, unforgiving earth. She followed a trail that looked like it might have been her shoe size.

The case was dismissed as an accident, and yet everything inside her screamed this was anything but. Getting the law to believe her considering she had memory loss was another story altogether.

"Are you okay?" Dillen asked. She appreciated the fact he was checking in with her.

"So far," she said. "But I'm frustrated as all get-out that I can't remember. I feel so close to the information. It's almost taunting me."

"Have faith in yourself," he said. "Relax, if at all possible. It'll come back."

She took those words to heart, wishing they were true. "What if it doesn't? What if I can't remember?" A few beats passed. "What if I'm the reason you have no closure on your father's murder?"

"Then we'll find the answers another way," he admitted. "Your memory is only one possibility. We have others. We have the crime scene, for starters. This is significant."

He was right. So, why wasn't she ready to let herself forgive herself?

Was it because she'd always taken everything personally?

Liz took in a breath and regrouped. Focusing on work was so much easier than dealing with the real world. Had she been hiding, like her last boyfriend had suggested?

Well, hell. She wasn't here to solve her personal problems. She'd come here to find a murderer.

"Those are my footprints," she said. "Watch this." She took a step beside one of the prints. The imprint was a perfect match.

"Let's follow your walking pattern, then," he said, hot

on the trail. They walked past the porta potty, and around a cone before stopping in front of a stack of Sheetrock that towered over both of them. "Look at this."

He pointed toward an area that looked like a body had been pulled out from underneath a stack of Sheetrock. An image scorched her brain. A trembling hand. A cry for help.

A gasp escaped before she covered her mouth with her hand to suppress it. "I remember this."

After telling Dillen what she recalled, he stood there quiet, studying the area.

"Look at this," he said, pointing toward footsteps walking away from the area. There were two distinct sets of tracks. "The frozen ground kept the prints intact. These should be work boots, but they're not."

"Those tips look like cowboy boots," she agreed.

"Not the usual footwear for a job site," he continued. Were they onto something big? Something that could break this case wide open?

It felt right. And then unfamiliar voices stirred in her memory bank. They were muffled. It was almost like trying to listen to someone in a tunnel, just out of reach. "No, it isn't. Why would anyone wear cowboy boots?"

"There are two sets of tracks here," he continued, clearly on a trail. He followed them to where they stopped. "It looks like whatever they were carrying got dropped right here."

The imprint in the earth seemed to agree with his assessment.

"I hear voices in the back of my head," she said. "Male, and at least two of them. But I can't make them out."

"Meaning you don't recognize them?" he asked.

"Right, but then I haven't been home in fourteen years," she said.

"Do you think you would be able to identify them if you heard them again?" he asked.

"It's possible," she said. "I'm not getting anything clearly right now, though. I'd be guessing, which could implicate an innocent man, and there's no way I could live with myself if I pinned the wrong person to a crime like murder."

"Or you might lead the sheriff's office in the right direction," he said, pulling out his cell phone and taking pictures of the site.

"The cowboy boot prints leave in this direction," she said, following the trail. "There are men-size tennis shoe imprints going back the other way."

"I'm guessing these belong to the EMTs on the scene," he said, motioning toward the footprints. "And these could belong to a deputy or the sheriff."

"A gurney probably wouldn't be able to roll across this terrain, so they would have carried your father," she continued before making eye contact with Dillen. "I remember a hand coming out of this pile of broken Sheetrock. And then another cry for help."

Her heart ached at the look on his face at hearing his father had been abandoned, left to die and in pain. His hands fisted at his sides, and tension rolled off him in palpable waves.

"I'm so sorry," she said, hating to be the one who put the look there. "He didn't deserve this." A rogue tear escaped, running down her cheek.

Dillen's hand came up immediately before thumbing the tear away. He dropped his balled fist to rest on her shoulder. She took a step toward him, closing the distance between them.

Their gazes locked, and she knew in an instant her heart was in trouble. Doing her best to set personal feelings aside, she leaned into Dillen. His strong arms looped around her waist as she buried her head in his chest, unable and unwilling to maintain eye contact when she was this close to him.

Besides, she wanted to be here for him in what must've been one of the worst moments of his life. Facing down the spot where his father's life had been essentially snubbed out practically gutted her, so she could only imagine the effect it was having on Dillen.

"Your father was a good man," she said when she could finally find her voice. "He didn't deserve this."

"I know," he said, his voice husky and raw with emotion—emotion removed from all anger. In that moment, he was just a man, not a seasoned soldier, who was trying to cope with unimaginable loss.

"We'll figure this out," she said, stopping herself before saying the word *together*. When they were standing with bodies flush, heat flooding her, she needed to stay as far away from that word as possible. It was dangerous to think it, let alone speak it out loud.

"I hope so," came the response. There was a desperation in his tone like she'd never heard from the normally arrogant-to-the-point-of-almost-cocky man. She reminded herself that underneath all the anger was a human, just like everyone else. Dillen was hurting, his heart broken, and he was letting down his guard for what she was certain would be a few brief moments.

He needed to know someone cared. Cared about his father. Cared about the murder. And cared about Dillen.

"He wouldn't have gone out. Thursday is always TV night," Dillen said, his voice still raw with emotion. He took a step back and dropped his hands to his sides before fishing out his cell phone. "Maybe pictures will convince the sheriff to open an investigation."

The absence of Dillen was immediately felt as a frigid wind whipped her hair around. She hoped he was right.

They were about to find out.

DILLEN SQUARED HIS SHOULDERS. Going down a road where he told Liz his deepest fears or let her into places that hadn't seen the light in forever wasn't a good idea. So, he distracted himself by taking pictures of where Pop had been found.

Liz did the same.

"There are no work-boot imprints in this entire section," she finally said after dropping her cell into her handbag. Wind whipped her hair around, and her teeth chattered despite wearing a coat.

He needed to get her out of here before she froze. "I think we have enough to take to the sheriff."

"Okay," she said, taking a few steps toward the Honda. She paused when he didn't immediately follow. "Do you need a few minutes alone?"

"Do you mind?" he asked. As far as he was concerned, this was sacred ground. This was where his father had taken some of his last breaths on his own before being hooked up to a ventilator in the hospital.

"Not at all," she said.

He pulled out the keys and tossed it over to her. She caught it like a baseball. Was that part of the benefit of growing up with four brothers?

His mind drifted off topic, wishing he could think about anything else right now. As long as he was wishing, he might as well go all in and wish Pop was still alive. There was so much Dillen would say to his father now that he was a grown man.

A tear pushed through and fell onto his sherpa-lined denim coat. The thought of some bastard walking away and leaving Pop out here in the cold caused Dillen's jaw to clench so tight he thought a tooth might crack.

Glancing around, he took note of how isolated this construction area was. Whoever was responsible for Pop's murder had wanted to make sure he hadn't been found right away.

This was a time when folks went home to see their families. Construction workers came in from all over Texas, Oklahoma and Louisiana to work on crews in these parts. There were never enough young locals for a project the scale of this one.

Had one of the men who worked here come across Pop? Had Pop put someone off without realizing he was being offensive? Being on the spectrum could come off different if someone didn't know what was really going on in his brain. He could be obstinate to the point of frustrating. Had he argued with someone over a parking spot? Someone who was angry enough to track Pop down?

Dillen shook his head. Didn't sound right. Who would become so upset with an older man who was on the autism spectrum they would murder him in cold blood? It didn't scan right. No, there had to be a reason someone would decide to end a life in this manner.

For one, this looked like an accident in the sheriff's point of view. Did someone go to great lengths to make it seem so? Dillen hadn't lived in Cider Creek in a long time. Was the sheriff lazy or incompetent? As an elected official, the spot had political implications. Folks were placed in certain positions because certain constituents needed law enforcement to look the other way. As much as he didn't believe Cider Creek was that kind of town, sheriff positions covered the county. Dillen couldn't speak for the rest of the county as to whether or not the law was above board.

Folks moved to rural places for all kinds of reasons, some of them bad. There were meth lab busts in the country as well as human-trafficking rings.

His thoughts were all over the place.

It occurred to him that his father might have stumbled upon something he shouldn't have. Being a witness could've gotten him in trouble. He might not have even realized what he'd seen, but a criminal wouldn't have known that. Pop might have been out in his old truck, and the bastards might have driven it home. A quick check of his wallet would've given away his address.

Now Dillen's mind was firing on more possibilities. Any of these reasons made more sense to him than Pop wandering onto a construction site during an ice storm and being pinned by debris.

Maybe Mr. Martin, who'd been at the hospital last night, would know something about Pop's comings and goings. Plus, where was his cell phone? Was it around the jobsite?

Using care, Dillen shifted a few pieces of Sheetrock around, searching for a cell phone. He didn't immediately find anything. Since he didn't want to disturb a possible crime scene more than he had to, he stood up, checked on Liz in the car and then headed her way.

The photos should've been enough to convince law enforcement to open a case. As he rejoined Liz in the car, the heater blasted him.

"What were you looking for?" she asked, cutting down the temp.

"Pop's cell phone," he said, pulling out his own and looking up directions to the sheriff's office.

"Why didn't you try to call it while we were out here?" she asked.

"The battery would long be dead by now." He propped his phone inside the drink holder.

"Did the hospital give you his personal effects?" she asked.

"Now that you mention it, no," he stated. "They didn't, and I didn't think to ask for them, either."

"You'll have to go back and give them instructions on what to do with…"

Her voice trailed off. This situation had her choked up.

"I'm sorry," she said again.

"You can stop apologizing," he offered. "There's no need. You weren't the one who did this."

"True. But I'm not helping much, either, and I can't shake the feeling the information is right there, like when a word is on the tip of your tongue but you just can't seem to find it," she said.

"Still not your fault," he said, reaching for her hand. "I don't blame you. In fact, the only reason Pop had a prayer at living is because of you. Without you, he would have died out here in the cold ground. He was still alive when he was taken to the hospital because of you. The doctor had a chance to save him, it just didn't go Pop's way at the end of the day."

He hoped like hell she took every word to heart because he meant them.

"No more saying *I'm sorry*," she said with commitment. Good.

Dillen smiled at her as he navigated onto the road toward the sheriff's office. She didn't deserve to be sorry. In his book, she was a hero. "You don't need to beat yourself up any longer. You did what you could."

"I just wish I could recall what happened," she said on an exhale. "But I'm sure it'll come back to me at some point."

He hoped the information came before it was too late to do anything about it. His time in Cider Creek was limited. Now maybe the sheriff could answer the mounting questions.

Chapter Nine

As Dillen parked in a spot at the sheriff's office, Liz checked her cell phone. There were a couple of messages from the family, who were checking on her. She would respond to those later. It was a strange feeling to have a family again after cutting herself off from hers for so long. She couldn't help but wonder who Dillen had now that his father was gone.

What about when he returned to his military service? Who would he have to lean on then? She had a feeling men who worked in Special Forces didn't sit around and share their feelings. Of course, she might be surprised to find out what truly went on while the men were out on missions or back at the barracks, but she suspected there was a lot of lifting weights and sports involved. Dillen had the kind of chiseled body to support her theory.

Neither one of them had talked about having anyone special in their lives.

Could the two of them stay in touch? Would he allow her into his life? Even if it was just to check up on him every once in a while.

He came around the front of the Honda to open the door for her. She took the hand being offered, ignoring the frissons of electricity traveling through her fingers and up her arm. It provided more comfort than shock at this point now that she'd become accustomed to the sensations. Now it was more like warmth from a campfire on a cold night outdoors.

"How long do you have before you have to go back to work?" she asked as they walked toward the red-brick building.

"I'm on emergency leave. I can take long enough to deal with Pop's affairs," he said. "But I can't be gone forever."

Liz had no idea what that meant. She could only hope it would be enough time to convince him to let her stay in his life.

"It should be said that I have no beef against your mother, by the way," Dillen said. His statement came out of the blue. "She was always a sweet lady."

The admission caught her off guard. Liz was also beginning to realize how fortunate she was to have a family who cared about her and how unfair her actions might have been to her mother and granny. They hadn't deserved for her to turn her back on them.

There was so much trauma at the ranch. Between losing her father and then watching the pressure Duncan had put on the family to be perfect. She didn't understand why her mother had put up with him for all these years. To her thinking, her mother had been weak. Lately, she was beginning to believe her mother possessed a strength like no one else to be able to hold her head up high and keep fighting after losing the love of her life.

Liz might go to her grave never knowing the kind of romantic love her parents had experienced. It made her sad when she really thought about it. Not that she needed someone to complete her. She was a whole person as it was. Period. And yet she couldn't deny her heart was starting to ache at the idea of being fully loved by someone.

Those thoughts took a back seat the second Dillen opened the door to the sheriff's office. An older woman who sat behind a desk stood up to greet them, no doubt the clerical side of the office.

"May I help you?" the woman asked. She had a full head of gray hair cut short and teased up. She had on iron-pressed blue jeans and a white blouse with ribbons in front.

"We're looking for Sheriff Courtright," Dillen said as the woman smiled at him.

"My name is Eleanor," she said with a nod. "May I ask what this is about?"

Eleanor motioned toward a pair of chairs sitting across from her desk. Liz and Dillen walked the few steps over and took seats.

"I have evidence that will prove my father, William Bullard, was murdered," Dillen said, looking Eleanor straight in the eye.

Her lips compressed, forming a thin line. "I'm sorry to hear about your father, Mr. Bullard." She flashed eyes at him. "I'm assuming you share the same last name."

He nodded that he did.

"Okay, then," Eleanor said before her gaze shifted to Liz.

"Liz Hayes," she supplied.

"I know who you are," Eleanor said, wrinkling her nose like a skunk had just sprayed the room. "I just thought I might be seeing a ghost seeing as how you haven't seen fit to show your face around town."

Liz smiled awkwardly. Being called out for the fact she hadn't been home in far more than a decade didn't make her feel any better about her life choices. Dillen, on the other hand, reached for her hand and then squeezed. His reassurance worked. Her stress level dialed down several notches.

"Nope, it's me. In the flesh," she said with an equally awkward smile.

"Good to see you," Eleanor said in a condescending tone.

Since Liz had no idea who the woman was, she assumed this was one of Duncan's acquaintances. His reputation as a family man was all over town. He hadn't been. She would've thought people might have figured it by now considering every last one of his grandchildren had moved away at their earliest opportunity. People believed what they wanted. "Same."

Eleanor clasped her hands together and placed them on top of her desk. "May I see the evidence?"

"I'd rather discuss this with the sheriff personally," Dillen said.

"It's just that I usually brief the sheriff on what's about to walk inside his office door," she continued. She was probably used to being the gatekeeper.

"Tell him Dillen Bullard is here to discuss his father's murder," he said without missing a beat.

Eleanor stood up with a curt smile. "I'll see if he's available."

"Much appreciated," Dillen said. His gaze could cut right through a person when he needed it to.

"Coffee is over there," she said, motioning toward a credenza with a machine and pods next to it. "Help yourself."

"Yes, ma'am," Dillen said in a tone of voice that was military stiff.

"I'll be right back," Eleanor said before disappearing behind a door she opened using an ID badge.

"Now I see what you're talking about," Dillen said out of the side of his mouth with disgust. "I thought you were being dramatic about being a Hayes before. Looks like I owe you an apology. You have no idea who that woman is, do you?"

"No, I do not," she said, appreciating his disdain for the situation.

"And this happens all the time?" he asked.

"It used to," she said. "I honestly thought it might die down now that we've been gone for so many years. So much for that idea."

"It's like being under a microscope," he said. "Who is she to look down her nose at you for making a decision to strike out on your own? It was a gutsy move that should be applauded, not condemned. How old did you say you were when you booked out of town?"

"Same age as you," she pointed out. There were a few other similarities between them that probably didn't need to be discussed while she was feeling an even stronger connection to the man.

"Eighteen," he said. "I enlisted the day after graduation."

"That's when I moved," she said. "And I did it with money I'd saved. I refused to ask anyone for a dime."

"You started a business that young?" he asked.

"No, I had to work odd jobs to make ends meet while saving up enough money to buy supplies. Then it took another couple of years to decide exactly what I wanted to do and become good at it. Overnight successes usually take years."

He chuckled, and the sound made her heart sing.

DILLEN KNEW HE could be bullheaded, but this might've taken the cake.

"Sticking with a dream can't be easy when the odds are stacked against you," he finally said, ready to acknowledge he'd made snap judgments back in high school. He should have known better than to hang on to old notions, but here they were and he was doing just that.

"I started small," she said. "That helped."

His respect for Liz Hayes was growing by the hour.

"Funny because my business didn't really take off until I got picked up by a major store and now it has gone bonkers," she said.

"Who is tending to the orders?" he asked.

"I finally hired a second-in-command and brought in several temp workers to help handle things while I'm gone," she said. "I only planned to be away from work for a week or two."

"How many people did you say you brought on board?" he asked.

"One full-time person, who has been with me for a year now, and three temps to cover while I'm out," she said, holding up four fingers.

"Look at your hand," he instructed. "That's how many people it takes to replace you. That's incredible." He wanted to say *she* was incredible but stopped himself. He was, however, beginning to see her in a new light. And he felt pretty damn bad about casting her in the old one.

The door opened, and then Eleanor's head peeked out. "The sheriff will see you now."

Dillen stood and held his arm out for Liz to take the lead. She did, walking in front of him and toward the door. He reached over her head to grab the door and hold it open for her. When she turned and smiled, a bomb detonated inside his chest.

What could he say? She had the kind of smile that could start wars.

Three doors down the hallway, Eleanor stopped and held her arm out like she was urging them to go inside. "I'll be at my desk if anyone needs me."

"Thank you, Eleanor," Sheriff Courtright said as he stared at the screen on his desktop computer. He stood up, introduced himself and then shook each of their hands. "Eleanor said you have evidence that you'd like to bring to my attention."

Sheriff Courtright leaned over his desk, his knuckles balancing him on the oak. The man looked the part of small-town law enforcement. He was tall and slim, wore a Stetson and was in head-to-toe khaki-colored clothing.

Dillen fished out his cell phone and pulled up the proof. "Take a look at these from the construction site where my father was found." He pointed to the cowboy boots walking away from the scene.

"May I?" the sheriff asked, nodding toward the cell.

"Be my guest," Dillen stated, offering it. "We just came from the construction site."

"How do you know these boots don't belong to workers?" the sheriff asked as he flipped through the images. He seemed distracted and unimpressed, two things Dillen didn't want to see from the man.

"As you can see, there are work-boot imprints around the site, none of which lead to where my father was found," Dillen continued.

"I was sorry to hear of your father's passing," Courtright said warmly. There might've been sincerity in his tone, but he wasn't hearing the implication of what Dillen was hinting at.

Dillen also took note of the sheriff's word choice.

"Thank you," he said, figuring anger wouldn't do any good in this situation. To be fair, he couldn't think of a time when he'd been trying to sway someone's opinion intellectually and it had worked. When he was trying to get information out of someone on a mission was a different story. Then his anger was one of his biggest assets. The men in his unit hadn't nicknamed him Pit Bull for nothing. "If you take a look at the evidence here—"

"I understand your concerns and I sympathize, but what motive would anyone have for murdering your father?" Courtright asked. It was a fair question.

"That's something I would hope to uncover during an investigation," Dillen explained.

"What about these pictures and the fact that I have unexplained bruises?" Liz piped up. She dug around in her purse until she located her cell phone.

This was the first he heard about her bruises. The information caused more of his protective instincts to kick in where she was concerned.

"Can you show me these bruises?" Courtright asked.

Liz took off her coat and rolled up her sleeve. Around her left arm, bruises formed finger outlines as though someone had grabbed her and squeezed. "How do you explain this?"

"Could have been the EMTs," the sheriff said after a thoughtful pause.

"And what about this?" she asked with a little more frustration in her tone, exposing her hip to reveal a massive bruise.

"Again, you could have been dropped by an EMT on the scene," the sheriff said. "The driver who pulled up behind the car you left running at the red light called in a suspicious vehicle. It's how my deputy found you and Mr. Bullard."

"Which doesn't mean she didn't walk up on someone who knocked her out," Dillen added.

"True," Courtright said. "But there are other, easier explanations for the bruising and the vehicle. In my experience, the simple answer is usually the correct one." He handed back Liz's cell after glancing through the photos. "Plus, we need a reliable witness or motive in order to open a murder investigation."

"I hear what you're saying," Liz said, sounding more than a little annoyed. "My head injury and lack of memory doesn't qualify me as a witness despite what I know in my gut."

"There was a citizen in here the other day who said lightning struck his dairy cow and now it won't give any milk," Courtright said. "Claims his neighbor manufactured the lightning. Said his gut instinct told him the man was after his business."

Liz issued a sharp sigh, and Dillen didn't blame her. The implication would make any honest person want to throw a dart between someone's eyes.

"Are you calling me a liar?" she asked, locking gazes with Courtright.

"No," he defended. "But I am realistic."

Before Liz could snap at Courtright, he put a hand up to stop her.

"Apologies if I'm coming across the wrong way, Ms. Hayes," he said, softening his tone considerably. "The message that I'm honestly trying to convey is that the mind is a tricky piece of equipment. Even when folks believe theirs is functioning full force, mistakes can be made. Folks can lock onto an idea, and reality escapes them."

"I understand where you're coming from," Liz continued, pushing her agenda. "Believe me, I do. However, my brain is solid and I know these bruises didn't come from EMTs. But let's just say they did. What harm would it do to open an investigation into Mr. Bullard's death? He was an upstanding citizen of Cider Creek my entire life, and I suspect his, too. He deserves justice if there was wrongdoing. Can you explain how his vehicle is still at the trailer considering the construction site is too far to walk, especially in the kind of weather they had that night?"

"He might have caught a ride with someone," Courtright offered.

Dillen shook his head.

There were times to speak up and times to sit back and listen. This was time for the latter.

"I've heard good things about you," she continued as though she realized she was making headway. "You're fair, and you care about everyone in your jurisdiction."

Courtright gave a slight nod of approval.

"I fully believe with every fiber of my being that Mr. Bullard was murdered," she said. Hearing those words caused Dillen's muscles to tense. No matter how many times he heard them, the response would be the same. "You can find the person and bring them to justice before anyone else gets hurt. Because Mr. Bullard figured something out or was in the way of someone wanting to do harm to the community you've been sworn to protect. I'm sure of it."

"Even if I did open an investigation, I'd have no idea where to start," Courtright said on a resigned sounding sigh. "Boots at a crime scene don't exactly make for the kind of evidence that warrants opening a murder investigation." He looked straight into her eyes. "Your family has been through a lot. More than any family should have to endure." His gaze shifted to Dillen. "It's not easy losing a parent. I know firsthand."

"Then do something about it," Liz urged. "Don't let Mr. Bullard die in vain."

"What other proof do you have?" Courtright asked.

"It was TV night," Dillen supplied. "Pop never left home on TV night."

"Doesn't prove he was murdered." Courtright stabbed his

fingers through his hair. "His mind could have been slipping for a long time. How often did you come home to visit?"

Dillen was ashamed to admit the last time he was home. "Not often."

"Then how do you know his mind was solid or his routine stayed the same?" Courtright asked.

"All I have is the knowledge Pop didn't alter his routine," Dillen said, hearing the defeat in his own voice.

"If you can bring me solid evidence, we can talk about opening up an investigation," Courtright said. "Right now, we have nothing to go on." He clamped his lips together like he was stopping himself from making another comment.

Dillen locked gazes, daring him to say what was on his mind.

Courtright relented. "Your father had been keeping to himself more than usual lately. A group from the church stopped by to visit him on Wednesday evening out of concern. Talk was that Mr. Bullard was losing his mind."

"He wouldn't have answered the door on Wednesday. Anyone who really knew him would know that. He had a lineup of shows that he binge watched every week." This couldn't be right. Dillen intended to prove his father was murdered. The prints might not have been proof enough for Courtright, but they screamed *murder* to Dillen.

"That's all well and good, but folks change their habits," Courtright continued. The man's mind was made up. Unless Dillen and Liz could present new evidence, this conversation would continue going around in circles. In the sheriff's mind, Liz wasn't a reliable witness and Pop had been losing his marbles.

"We'll be back," he said to Courtright before leading Liz out of the office, through the lobby and out the front door.

Dillen intended to deliver on the promise.

Chapter Ten

"Why is he being so stubborn?" Liz asked Dillen the second they were safely inside the Honda.

"Good question," Dillen said.

"You must be good at reading people," she continued. "Do you think he's dirty?"

"No," he said, navigating onto the roadway. "But I want to ask neighbors about Pop's recent behavior. I'd like to know if anyone new has been hanging around the trailer."

"Do you think they *would* know?" she asked.

"Folks in Cider Creek know each other's business," he said. "I highly doubt any of that has changed over the years."

"Good point," she said on a frustrated sigh. "I know your father was murdered. I have no doubt in my mind. After visiting the construction site, I'm even more sure than I was before. Something bad is in the air. I can feel it."

"I can, too," he said.

Liz reached over and touched his forearm. "There's no way we're allowing a good man's murder to go unpunished."

"The sheriff will get on board as soon as we can offer proof," he said. "I got the sense he wished there was more he could do. Without a reason to change his mind, I can see his point that an investigation might be seen as a frivolous use of resources."

"You got all that from being in the room with him?" she asked.

"Last night, while you were sleeping, I pulled up an article that said the public wasn't thrilled with him," he admitted. "Folks have been in an uproar about how their tax dollars are being used since taxes were raised."

"He did seem awfully hesitant to step up without overwhelming evidence," she admitted.

"All he needs is a good reason, and we didn't supply one," he stated. "But we're on the right track and his mind is changeable."

"He thinks I'm reaching for evidence when I talk about my bruises," she said, wishing there was more she could do. "And then he dismissed anything I had to say that relied on my memory."

"It's to be expected, I guess," he said. "Shouldn't be that way, but I can see how folks might be swayed into thinking you can't remember anything or any of your memories might not be dependable."

"Is that what you think?" she asked a little more defensively than intended.

"No," he said. "I believe you saw Pop's hand coming out of that pile of broken Sheetrock."

His voice was more mechanical now, like he'd distanced himself from all emotion.

"Your father wouldn't have changed his habits, either," she continued.

"You and I seem to be the only two who believe that statement," he said as he headed back toward the trailer.

"At this point, I'm not sure how much help I am," she said, not wanting to leave but needing to go home for the family meeting that was on hold until she arrived since she was the last sibling to return, and then head back to work.

She missed being so busy that her mind had no time to wander or think about things like how much she was going to miss Dillen.

"Go on," he said, gripping the steering wheel until his knuckles turned white.

"I came home for a reason," she started. "When I checked my phone earlier, I saw a long list of work emails. I can't run my business from here and I've already been gone seven days. Temps can't pick up the slack forever. And you said it yourself, I do the work of four people when I'm in the office. Orders are stacking up, and production can't slip. I can't afford to lose my business. And let's face it, I'm no closer to remembering what happened."

"Like it or not, you've picked up a shadow until you get your memories back," he said with the kind of finite tone that said it was useless to argue.

Except that he didn't get to decide who followed her around.

"As much as I respect that you need to get to the bottom of—"

"That wasn't a question," he said, interrupting her. "Wherever you go, I go."

"Until what?"

"The truth comes out," he stated. "Besides, you need me."

"What makes you say that?" Now, she really was interested in hearing his answer.

He loosened his grip enough to thump his thumb on the wheel. "You can't be certain you're out of danger."

"No one has tried anything so far," she pointed out.

"Because you've been with me," he said like everyone should've been on the same page.

She wasn't. Being with him caused her to want things she knew better than to want, and she'd only been around the man roughly twenty-four hours. Imagine how she would feel if she spent days or weeks alone with Dillen.

"That's a fair point, but it doesn't prove anything," she said.

"You have a shadow whether you like it or not," he insisted, clearly digging his heels in.

Liz crossed her arms over her chest. "I'm fairly certain there are stalking laws even in a small town like Cider Creek."

"They won't apply," he said.

"How so?"

She couldn't wait to hear his response.

"You want me beside you until you get your memory back," he said.

"Really? And I don't know this already because…?"

"You know as well as I do that whoever murdered my father is still out there," he said.

"They could be long gone by now," she stated. "It wouldn't do any good to stay in town anyway. Plus, it could be someone who worked the construction site and has already left Cider Creek. There's no progress being made on the site right now."

"You saw the boot prints."

"What if the sheriff is right?" she asked.

"You saw the boot prints."

"Doesn't mean we know what we're talking about," she said. "They aren't definitive proof that someone murdered your father."

"Why are you doing an about-face now?" he asked, agitation in his tone.

"Because what if we're wrong and we spend days together before we figure it out? I lose time with my business, not to mention the fact my family is waiting on me to get home," she said. "I'm just delaying the inevitable."

"It doesn't have to be," he said.

"Inevitable?" she asked, but it was a rhetorical question. "Yes, it does. Your life is overseas, but while you're here, you have to take care of your father's affairs.

"I have a family waiting on making a big announcement that I'm avoiding," she said. "Because I don't want to go home and face that house."

"Is that what you think you're doing? Avoiding responsibility?" he asked. "Because someone who leaves home at eighteen years old and ends up starting a successful business doesn't seem like the kind of person who runs from duty."

The fact he made good points only frustrated her more.

"Life is easy for a broke solider," she quipped, wishing she could reel those words back in the moment they left her mouth. It was a jerk move on her part.

Liz tensed, waiting for the backlash.

DILLEN DIDN'T NORMALLY get caught up in emotions. Taking a calmer tact, he tried to focus on what she'd meant rather than what she'd said. It didn't take long.

"You don't have to be scared," he finally said, realizing comments like hers were coming from a place of fear.

"I'm not," she defended, rubbing her hands up and down her arms like there was a sudden chill in the air. Like he said…fear.

"You wouldn't be human if you weren't at least a little bit afraid," he soothed. She didn't need him griping at her. She needed a calm, steady voice. He could be that for her.

Her chin jutted out in defiance. "I'm good."

"I hope that's true," he said. "Because if anyone deserves to be, it's you."

Arms still folded across her chest, she turned to face the passenger window. Was she avoiding making eye contact? His focus had to be on the road except for the few times he was stopped at a red light, but he could feel the sudden chill in the air.

The rest of the ride was filled with silence. Her wheels were turning, he could almost hear them.

"Mind if we stop off at Rosa and Macy's house before we head home?" he asked since they had to drive right past the sisters' place.

"I guess it couldn't hurt," she said.

"We can swing home for lunch after," he said. "You have to be starving by now."

"I could eat," she said. Her answers were short, which wasn't a good sign.

He parked on the gravel road in front of the Brown sisters' double wide. They were both divorced now and had reclaimed their last name from before marriage. Neither had children, so the sisters had gotten a place together to live out their golden years.

Liz got out of the passenger side before he had a chance to come around and open the door for her. Another bad sign. They were racking up. He wasn't ready to give up just yet. She'd agreed to have lunch together. He could work on her then.

Before they hopped onto the wooden deck, the front door swung wide open. Rosa stood there in a flannel nightgown that covered her from neck to toe. Her hair was up in pink curlers, and she had on matching fuzzy slippers.

"Macy," Rosa shouted. "Come look at what the cat dragged in." She opened the screen door, letting her yippy dog loose to run around Dillen's ankles. "And he brought a Hayes girl with him."

Damn. Everyone really did know the family. He was see-ing what a nuisance that could be, especially when she'd been away for fourteen years. Folks in Cider Creek had long memories. Maybe his investigation would benefit from it.

Rosa's gaze zeroed in on him. "How long has it been?"

"Too many years," he said with a smile meant to disarm the sixty-plus-year-old neighbor.

"Where are my manners?" she asked, throwing up her hands. "Come on in."

The little dog continued its yipping.

"Chauncy," Rosa chided. "Get in here."

Dillen stepped over the dog and led the way inside the double wide. Liz followed, reaching for his hand. He clasped their fingers together as they walked inside. The decor looked like a time warp from the seventies. There was wall-to-wall burnt-orange carpeting, Formica countertops with vinyl flooring in the kitchen and doilies on almost every other surface. The furniture looked handed down from a grandmother. It was ornate and didn't look comfortable to sit on, more like a place someone sat to sip tea. There was a sizable flat-screen on a hutch. The TV was on with the sound muted.

Macy stood at the kitchen sink, water running with her hands buried in soap. The two might've been three years apart in age, but they could pass for twins. The older sister, Macy, had on a flannel shirt and jeans with the same pink slippers as her sister. "Well, I'll be. You're a sight for sore eyes, Dillen Bullard."

She turned off the water, shook water off her hands and then finished the drying job with a hand towel.

"Good to see you, Ms. Macy," he said.

"And who is that behind you?" Macy walked over,

squinting her eyes at Liz. "I recognize you. You're Duncan Hayes's granddaughter."

"Yes, ma'am," Liz said with a warm smile.

Macy exchanged glances with her sister before offering sincere condolences. "I was real sorry to hear about your dad's passing," she said to Dillen.

Rosa motioned toward the sitting area, so everyone claimed a spot. Dillen and Liz sat side by side on the sofa. She sat so close, their outer thighs touched, sending heat rocketing through him.

"We'd been worried about your dad," Macy said.

"Sister," Rosa warned.

"What?" she quickly said.

"We should mind our own business," Rosa warned. But why?

"Pop's death might not have been an accident," Dillen said, figuring he needed to lay his cards on the table. "If you two know something, I sure would appreciate an update."

Rosa gasped before covering her mouth. "I'm so sorry, Dillen. I really am. Your dad was the sweetest man and…"

She stopped herself as she became too choked up.

"If this wasn't an accident, my sister and I want to help," Macy clarified.

"Thank you," he said.

"Have you talked to his lady friend?" Macy asked.

"I would if I knew who she was," he stated. "Pop's phone is missing, so I can't look through it. There wasn't anything on his computer hinting at a relationship, but I guess folks don't exactly send emails anymore."

"The best way to describe her is…" Macy stopped herself.

"Be blunt," he said. "There's no need to mince words with me."

"She was blonde, for starters," Macy said.

"Big hair teased out and bleached," Rosa added.

Macy nodded agreement. "She was busty and wore her skirts a little too short."

"They were hiked up her backside," Rosa said. "You could see cheek if you looked hard enough."

"Not that we did," Macy said. "The blonde was hard to miss when she got out of her vehicle."

"What did she drive?" Dillen asked.

"A fire-engine-red Jetta," Rosa said.

"I'm guessing you didn't get a license plate," he said, figuring it was a Hail Mary question that needed to be asked anyway.

"No, we didn't," Macy said with a note of self-recrimination.

"I only asked on the off chance you did," he said. "You probably would only have noticed if the license plate was original or unique in some way."

She nodded. "There wasn't anything special except for the vehicle. But she didn't always drive here. That was only a couple of times, and she never stayed."

"He picked her up?" Dillen asked.

"We assumed so," Macy said. "But then we were trying not to be nosy neighbors." She exhaled like she'd been holding in a breath for two days. "It's just we always paid attention to your dad since he was...*special* to us. Once you left, he didn't have anybody, so we cooked for him and took over plates."

Dillen chuckled. "I'm guessing he didn't like that too much."

"Not until we got the routine down," Macy said. "Once we knew to make lasagna on Tuesdays, he started accepting the food."

"He was a stickler," he agreed.

"But a good person," Rosa chimed in.

"That he was," Dillen said, wishing he'd spent more time with Pop over the past few years. "I should have come home more. Then I would have known about the blonde and anything else going on in his life." He put his hand up to stop the ladies from letting him off the hook. "He liked to video chat on the first of every month, but there were times when I was deployed that he didn't hear from me for several months."

"You were a good son, Dillen. Don't let anyone tell you different," Macy scolded, wagging her finger at him.

Was he?

"Wouldn't a good son be here to protect his father?" Dillen asked as more guilt surfaced. Could the blonde lead to answers?

Chapter Eleven

Liz squeezed Dillen's hand in a show of support. Beating himself up wouldn't change the past. She needed to remind herself of the fact every day, or she would be the biggest hypocrite. She was still conflicted over whether or not to call it a day with the investigation. Curiosity had her wanting to follow through, but this could take days or weeks and she had a life to get back to.

The bigger issue was feeling like she was somehow letting down Mr. Bullard, who'd been the nicest, purest-hearted man in Cider Creek. He'd been different but never looked down on her for being a Hayes. In fact, he'd always had a kind smile on the occasions when she'd run into him at the store or gas station. He'd always said hello to her and never judged her. The gentle soul hadn't care one way or the other about her grandfather or his money, power or influence. It was rare to know someone so untainted by life. Being a single parent couldn't have been easy.

"Don't you dare blame yourself, Dillen Bullard," Macy warned. "Your father wouldn't have wanted you to do that."

Dillen issued a sharp sigh before slowly nodding.

"What about others?" he asked, redirecting the conversation back on track. "Did anyone else stop by that you knew of?"

Macy placed the flat of her palm on her thigh like she was needing to prop herself up as though life was almost too heavy to bear. She locked eyes with her sister. "I never saw anybody."

"Same," Rosa said before wrinkling her nose like she'd just walked into skunk spray. "Just the blonde, and she was all wrong for your dad."

Based on the description, the blonde didn't seem like someone Mr. Bullard would've dated. But what else would the wine be for? And what about the coffee? Had he bought more out of routine but stayed the night at his girlfriend's house so often his supply had built up?

"We would have been happy for your dad if the blonde hadn't been so out of place here," Macy said. "Maybe we should have checked on William more often. He might have gotten so lonely that he was willing to spend time with the first person who showed him attention."

"If I'm not allowed to beat myself up, neither are you," Dillen piped in.

"Well, that's certainly fair," Rosa said, giving her sister a disapproving look. "We all did our best. No one knew what was really going on, and it's none of our business who your dad dated. I'm just sorry he's gone."

"Has she been by in the past couple of days?" Liz finally asked. "The blonde?"

"Come to think of it, no," Macy said. "Not that I'm aware of anyway."

The red vehicle would have stood out.

Dillen stood, thanked the ladies for their time and then led the way outside. He opened the car door for Liz. She got in, and they drove the short way across the road to get to Mr. Bullard's trailer.

Once inside, Dillen walked straight to the fridge and started rummaging around for food.

"Don't you think it's strange the blonde hasn't been here in days?" she asked him as she poured two glasses of water and then set them on the table before taking a seat.

He stopped what he was doing. "Yes, I do."

Based on his non-shocked reaction, he'd already caught on.

"The reason might be that she knew he wasn't going to be home," she continued, checking for a reaction.

"I had the same thought," he said. "If I had Pop's cell phone, I could figure out the nature of their relationship quicker."

"You don't think it was romantic?" she asked.

"On Pop's part? Yes. On her part? I have questions." He shut the fridge door a little hard. "There's nothing inside here to eat unless you want another breakfast."

"Let me check," she said, joining him.

He stepped aside and let her have a look while he checked his phone.

"The diner is still in business," he said. "We could swing by there for lunch."

She hesitated only because being recognized as a Hayes was getting old. "Let me check the freezer."

"We could order online and swing by to pick it up if you don't want to go inside and sit down," he said with a raised eyebrow.

"How about these frozen pizzas?" she asked, motioning toward the boxes. "They look good to me, and they'll be faster."

"Okay," he said, but the question was still clearly on his mind.

"I'm tired of being treated like Duncan Hayes's granddaughter everywhere I go," she conceded. "It's nicer if we stay in. At least for me."

"Understood," he said, reaching around her to grab the pizza boxes.

"We can go out for dinner if you'd like," she offered.

"I'll pick up food," he said. "I've been watching the way people treat you, and I'm starting to understand why you left fourteen years ago."

"Folks have it worse," she said. "I shouldn't complain."

"Feeling isolated in your own hometown is a pretty good reason," he said as she checked the box and then preheated the oven.

He pulled out a round pizza pan after she took the box and opened it.

"We might as well take a seat while we wait," he said, motioning toward the table once the pizza was cooking.

Liz sat across the small table from him.

"The military saved my life," he started. "I had to get out of Cider Creek. My earliest memories in school are being teased about Pop. I was a scrawny runt back then and got my backside handed to me for sticking up for him."

"That didn't last long because by middle school you were the tallest kid in our grade," she said. Her heart went out to him for the bullying he'd experienced. Kids could be jerks to each other.

"I filled out by high school, but by then everyone had left me alone," he said. "I'd developed a hothead reputation, according to the school counselor."

"You had good reason after being bullied."

"I ended up with a chip on my shoulder that not even fourteen years in the military spent fighting a real enemy could fix," he continued. "If I'm honest, it's still there."

"Seems like you have it under control," she said. Although to be fair, he'd been hard on her recently.

"I'm trying," he said before taking a sip of water. "It's not always easy, though."

"Must have been difficult on your relationships," she said.

"What relationships?" he countered with a half-cocked smile.

"Come on, Dillen. A hot guy like you must have been with plenty of women," she continued, half wanting to know the answer and half not.

"Not really," he said on a shrug. "I'm deployed a lot, so I'm fighting most of the time."

"What's the saying about soldiers? A girl in every port?"

"It's partially true," he said. "But not for me. There are people I see on a regular basis when I'm on base. They don't need to be in a relationship any more than I do."

"What makes you say that?"

She really was curious.

"What about you?" he asked, turning the tables at the moment the oven timer dinged.

"Saved by the bell," she said, hopping up to get the pizzas.

He joined her, opening a drawer and pulling out a pizza cutter. He cut slices, then she placed them on plates before he slid a second pizza in the oven. They made a good team in the kitchen.

What about in the bedroom?

Liz's cheeks flamed just thinking about the two of them in bed together. She needed to redirect her thoughts before she ended up down the rabbit hole.

DILLEN GRABBED BOTH plates and headed back to the table while the second pizza did its thing. "You were just about to tell me about your relationship status."

"Single," she said. The red flush to her cheeks made her even more beautiful if that was possible. "I was in a relationship that became suffocating."

"I'm guessing he wanted to spend twenty-four seven together," he said.

"Not that bad," she said. "But he did ask for space in my closet."

"What an awful request," he teased. "I thought women wanted to be asked those questions."

"What about the women you spend time with?" she quipped.

"You got me there," he said. "I shouldn't group everyone into the same category."

"There are women who want husbands and children," she said. "There's nothing wrong with those things. They just aren't for everyone."

"Amen," he said a little too enthusiastically.

Her gaze immediately popped up to meet his. "You don't ever want children?"

"I could do without them," he admitted, thinking it would take a special person to make him want to settle down. Someone intelligent and funny. Someone beautiful inside and out. Someone he wanted to spend all day in bed with on a Sunday morning.

Someone like Liz?

Dillen smirked. He must've been exhausted because he'd just thought of Liz Hayes as someone he could see himself locking down with in a real relationship.

"What's so funny?" she asked.

He realized she was studying him.

"Nothing," he said. "Tell me about this guy. Why did you break up with him?"

"Kevin gave me an ultimatum about work," she said.

"Why would anyone draw a line in the sand like that?" he asked. "Plus, why wouldn't he be damn proud of you? I know I would be if my lady was crushing a business."

"Apparently I wasn't spending enough time with him, and he thought I was in a bigger relationship with my business than I was with him," she said on a shrug. "Demanding that I choose between a guy and my livelihood wasn't the best play."

"Sounds like a losing proposition," Dillen confirmed. It was a mistake he would never make with someone like Liz. Her business was her independence. It had been hard fought, and she'd done an amazing job. Any man should've been proud to be by her side, not whine because she couldn't coddle him every five minutes. "I'm guessing he wasn't as driven as you are."

She shook her head. "He had a trust fund to back him up."

"So? You could have one, too," he defended.

"I mean, sure, I guess that's true," she said. "But why would I want Duncan Hayes's money? He would have held it over my head and ruled my life."

"I'm guessing your siblings felt the same way or they would have stuck around town," he said.

"We're all so independent. I can't imagine anyone being happy under Duncan's thumb," she said. "I'll never know how my mom put up with him for so many years."

"She had six mouths to feed after losing her husband," he said. "I'm one hundred percent certain she did it for you guys."

Liz compressed her lips into a frown.

"You're right," she said after a thoughtful pause. "And that's probably the real reason I've been determined not to let anyone in. I saw the hurt in her eyes when my father died. I witnessed how Duncan took over. And the spark in her just died for a long time."

"Losing someone you truly love can knock the wind out of you," he said. He and Liz weren't so different after all. Both kept everyone at arm's length as a survival tactic.

"What about your mom?" Liz asked, turning the tables. "Do you mind if I ask what happened to her?"

The timer dinged, so he took a break from the conversation and cut the second pizza. After filling their plates with round two, he sat down and contemplated whether or not he wanted to discuss his mother.

Why the hell not? They'd talked about a host of other subjects. He realized Liz was a good listener and he actually liked talking to her. He'd never really opened up about his past before. There was something special about Liz he couldn't quite put his finger on.

"My mother left after dropping me off to my first day of kindergarten," he began. A sharp pain in the center of his chest had him wondering if talking about his mother was a good idea. He didn't go there with anyone. Not even Pop had talked about her after that day. "She said all these things to me that my five-year-old brain thought was to comfort me to get through that day. But no, she had other plans."

"That's so unfair," Liz said with the kind of compassion that was balm to a wounded heart. "You didn't deserve to have that happen to you."

"I appreciate it," he said, getting choked up talking about the past. "But it's good to finally tell someone. It's like this has been bottled up inside me for so long that I've become used to living with the anger."

"What did your mother say, if you don't mind my asking?" she said, reaching across the table to touch his hand.

"That I should be brave," he said. Liz's touch had a soothing effect like he'd never experienced before. "That it didn't matter what else happened, I was going to be okay. I could handle whatever came my way. She'd said she was certain of it."

"You were five years old," she said, twisting up her face in disgust. "You needed a mother."

"Someone forgot to tell her that," he said. "The funny thing is she never said that it wasn't my fault. So, when she wasn't there to pick me up after school and the office had to call Pop, I blamed myself."

"It wasn't your fault," she said with the kind of conviction that said she believed every word. "You deserved so much more from her."

"Apparently five years was all she had in her as a mother," he said.

"Have you tried to locate her now?" she asked.

"Why would I?" he asked. "You don't have to tell me twice that you don't want me in your life. Once is all it takes."

"No one could blame you for feeling that way," she said. "Even though you deserved so much more."

"Looking back, she must have realized Pop was on the spectrum," he said. "I always wondered if she was afraid that I was different, too. If that was the reason she didn't love me enough to stick around."

"That's a horrible burden for any child to carry alone," Liz said, standing up and moving around the table. She brought her hands up to cup his face while locking gazes. His heart practically exploded in his chest.

He stared into the most beautiful eyes he'd ever seen. The fact he could look into those eyes all day wasn't something he wanted to think about right now. All he really wanted to do was bury himself inside her and get lost.

His pulse thumped. His heart pounded. His breath quickened.

"I figured it out," he finally said, hearing the huskiness in his own voice.

"Sure," she said. "But that's a lot of trauma for a kid to handle. What did your dad say?"

"That's the funny part," he continued. "We never brought her up again."

"So you spent your entire childhood believing you did something to run your mother off," she stated. "Is that right?"

Denying it would do no good. So he didn't.

"The only thing I'd like to do right now is kiss you," he said. "But I won't do that unless you ask me to."

"Dillen Bullard," she started, leaning toward him, "I'd very much like for you to kiss me."

Chapter Twelve

Liz was used to asking for exactly what she wanted in every area of her life, except relationships. Until Dillen. Until now.

Placing his hands on her hips, his fingers dug into her sensitized skin as he pulled her on top of him. She straddled his thighs, all while locking gazes. Her heart had never pounded so hard against her rib cage. Her lips had never burned to kiss someone so much. Her body had never ached to feel someone moving inside her to this degree. To say she was stepping into foreign waters was an understatement.

Rather than run away from her feelings, she embraced them. There would be consequences, but she couldn't focus on those right now. All she could do was surrender to the tide washing over her and through her.

Dillen's lips were tender against hers at first, right up until his tongue slipped inside her mouth. Then his mouth covered hers with bruising need. Their breaths came out in gasps as she brought her hands up to his shoulders to anchor herself, digging her fingernails into his skin.

Her body hummed with need.

The air in the room crackled with electricity as he drove his tongue deeper. She bit down on his bottom lip, scraping her teeth across it as she released it. He groaned with pleasure, egging her on. Her full breasts were flush against a solid wall of muscle.

Tension between them escalated pretty damn fast. Another minute of this and she would definitely pass the point of no return.

Pulling on every ounce of willpower, Liz pushed off his shoulders and stood up. She shook her hands and paced a couple of laps around the small space, willing her pulse to return to normal.

She risked a glance at Dillen. The smirk on his face was a mile wide. He looked to be struggling about as much as she was.

"That can't happen again," she said, realizing kissing Dillen was dangerous territory.

"It probably shouldn't," he said, sounding less determined than she was to keep this relationship platonic. But then he was used to casual relationships. Liz might not go all in with the men she dated, but she gave as much as she could with her obligations. Running her business was her first priority. A man like Dillen could derail her focus.

Liz released a slow breath, trying to steady her racing pulse.

"You have to admit, that was a damn good kiss," he said, the corners of his mouth still upturned.

"No one's denying that," she said. "It's a good part of the reason it can't happen again." It would ruin her for other men, but she wasn't quite ready to own up to the fact to Dillen. He didn't need to know the full effect he was having on her body and soul.

It was most likely the circumstances surrounding them. Emotions were heightened overall, and they were both looking for some form of release. Sex with Dillen would do the trick. She had no doubt it would blow her mind. But that would make it worse when she walked out the door and returned to her normal life.

"We can't afford the distraction," she finally argued. No one, not even Dillen, could disagree with that.

"No," he said on a sharp exhale. "We probably can't."

Besides, sex would be a form of blowing off steam for both of them, and she wanted it to be more special with Dillen.

Did she just say she wanted to have sex with the man?

Her brain was playing tricks on her. She searched for a distraction. Her gaze landed on the table. Food. Right. Pizza. "Our meal is getting cold."

"So it is," he agreed with a long, slow nod.

A quick headshake later, and he repositioned to face the table, picked up a slice and chewed on it. His expression turned serious after clearing his throat.

"We need a way to find this blonde," he finally said. "I didn't see anything on Pop's computer."

"Now you know what to look for," she pointed out. "What about pictures from his phone? Mine sync up automatically with my computer."

"I'll check, but Pop hated being on the computer," he said. "I highly doubt he took selfies with a lady love, but it never hurts to investigate."

"Considering the fact that much of my sales are online, I don't know what I'd do without my technology," she admitted.

"I could do without most of it, honestly," he said. "I hate the thought of being glued to a device."

His line of work wasn't exactly tech friendly.

"I can imagine being out on a mission might make for bad internet connections," she said.

"I'd tell you, but then I'd have to kill you," he said with the kind of seriousness that made a shudder run through her. Then his face broke into a wide smile. "Military joke."

She smiled back, making eye contact, which wasn't the best of ideas. As long as she kept a healthy distance from the man, she'd be fine. Being close to him was a different story.

Liz reclaimed her seat and finished off the last bites of pizza on her plate. After, she stood up and moved to the sink with her dish. Dillen joined her, standing beside her. She took a wide sidestep to put some distance between them. Being flooded with his spicy male scent was a bad idea while she was still feeling vulnerable to him. Give her a few more minutes, an hour, and she'd be good to go. Right now, though, it took an enormous amount of restraint not to lean into the man and pull from his strength.

Since he didn't seem as bothered, she figured the pull was much stronger for her. Her self-control needed to be on point from here on out. Besides, he would always see her as a Hayes, a princess.

"The past few days are really hitting. Do you mind if I wash up and take a nap?" she asked, suppressing a yawn. More caffeine wouldn't help in a time like this. Stepping away from the attraction with Dillen, she felt tired in her bones.

"Go ahead," he said. "The shower in the main bedroom is nicer. You might want to use that one."

She nodded, remembering she had suitcases in her trunk. "I totally forgot about having clothes and toiletries in my car."

"Where?" he asked. "I didn't see anything. Since you were going home, I figured you already had supplies waiting there."

"My trunk, but I'll—"

"Don't sweat it," he said, pulling out her key. "I'll just grab your stuff and be right back."

Part of her wondered if it was a good idea to bring everything inside. This was a temporary stop on her way home.

Before she could mount a protest, Dillen was heading for the front door. He returned as she finished loading the dishwasher and set the pair of suitcases down in the kitchen.

"I'll be in the office if you need anything," he said before turning toward the hallway.

She wasn't touching that statement with a ten-foot pole. *Need* was a tricky word when it came to Dillen. Besides, she'd vowed not to need anyone a long time ago.

FOCUS WASN'T NORMALLY a problem for Dillen. Shifting his thoughts to more productive ones had been his lifeline on missions. So why did he keep circling back to the kisses he'd shared with Liz?

They'd been hot, came the quick response from a voice in the back of his mind. They had been—he couldn't deny it. What he couldn't understand was why they trumped all others. Liz was beautiful, there was no disputing that. And sexy as hell. There was a strong but vulnerable quality in her that drew him in. She could handle herself. And yet he wanted to step in and be her hero.

He needed to remind himself of the fact she was as close to royalty as one could be in these parts. Except after getting to know the real her, the word didn't ring true any longer.

Booting up the computer, he took a seat and rolled the chair closer to the monitor. What had he missed before?

After spending the next hour digging around, he realized this was probably a dead end. For one, Pop hadn't had an automatic picture sync, like Liz had mentioned. Secondly, Pop had rarely sent emails. His inbox, however, was full of ads for services like treatments for a larger sex organ and women who wanted to satisfy him.

Dillen blinked a couple of times at the brazenness in some of the scams.

Pop had had the internet along with a camera and microphone, which was how he'd taken calls from Dillen. The equipment was old but had gotten the job done. Dillen had been on Pop to upgrade for a few years now, but Pop could be stubborn when he'd really wanted to be.

His cell phone might provide better answers, but it was lost. Was there a way to recapture the data?

There had to be.

Dillen glanced at the clock. It was after hours on a Wednesday night. The call center for Pop's cell service was open twenty-four hours a day, seven days a week. Dillen grabbed his own cell and made the call.

"This is Jordan, how may I help you?" the perky male voice answered after he'd sat in the queue for a long wait for a representative.

"I'm trying to access cell phone data for my father's phone," Dillen explained.

"And what is the phone number on that account?" Jordan asked.

Dillen supplied the number and waited.

"Are you a primary account holder, sir?" Jordan asked.

"No, I'm not."

"Oh," he replied, sounding a little deflated. "I'm sorry. I won't be able to share any account information with anyone who isn't primary on the account."

Dillen muttered a curse underneath his breath. "Is there a supervisor I can talk to?"

"I'm afraid she will give you the same answer, sir," Jordan said. "Is there any chance you have a court order or power of attorney?"

How did Dillen say he hadn't expected his father to die?

"No," he stated.

"Then I'm afraid there isn't much I can do to help you," Jordan said. "Is your father available? I can give the information to him."

"No," Dillen repeated, not wanting to go into detail with Jordan about a suspected murder. "My father passed away unexpectedly."

"I'm sorry for your loss," Jordan said with compassion in his voice. "I really wish there was more I could do. Unless you have documentation and then I can direct you to our website, where you can make a formal request."

"It just happened, so it'll take a minute to get my ducks in a row. I appreciate you trying to help," Dillen said. The customer service rep had gone out of his way to be friendly.

"You're welcome," Jordan said, his voice returning to a level of perky Dillen would never achieve even if he tried. "It was my pleasure."

Dillen ended the call before smacking the flat of his palm on the desk. What else could he do to get the information? Calling back and pretending to be his father came to mind. Of course, he would need to have a lot of information on hand. They would most likely want a social security number, possibly an account password. That's where he came up empty. The other information was probably here in the metal filing cabinets. He would need to dig around and find it anyway now that Pop was gone.

A shot of caffeine would be nice about now. He'd been in the office for two hours hunting for a break. It was getting dark outside. Their late lunch probably qualified as dinner, but he wanted to have something in the house just in case Liz woke up hungry.

He had a hunch she wouldn't appreciate waking up to an empty trailer. She'd been through a lot in a short amount of time. Again, her loyalty to Pop came to mind. Sticking around when she'd easily could have left Pop alone in the hospital wasn't something a self-absorbed princess would do.

All his preconceived notions about Liz Hayes were breaking down when he looked at her actions.

Dillen put on a pot of coffee. There was something comforting about the smell of dark roast. Being here in the trailer made him feel closer to Pop. His heart clenched at the thought that his only family was gone, and his mind started spinning out when it came to taking the next steps. Would he sell the trailer? It seemed wrong since this was the only home he'd ever known. But why would he keep the place? Leave it here, empty, and who knew what would happen.

Rosa and Macy would keep an eye on the place. He could count on them to keep watch. But what practical reason could he have for staying put?

The sound of gravel crunching underneath boots out front caught his attention. Dillen moved to the living room window since the light was off. He leaned his back against the door and peeked outside.

The neighbor from the hospital walked up and tapped on the door. Dillen's gaze flew to Liz, who was asleep on the sofa. Thankfully, she didn't stir.

He moved to the door, opened it and stepped outside into the frigid evening air.

"You sure have grown up since last time I saw you," the familiar man said, sticking his hand out in between them. Dillen must have shot a look as he took the offering because the older man said, "Theodore Martin. You probably don't remember me, but my friends call me Teddy."

"Mr. Martin," Dillen said as he drew his hand back and stuffed both inside his jeans pockets. "I'm not sure if you've heard the news but Pop passed away."

"I'd heard," Mr. Martin said, his face twisting in sympathy. "Saw the lights on as I drove by and decided to swing by to offer my condolences to you and your family."

"Thank you for stopping by," Dillen said, not bothering to correct the man about the fact that he was single and his only family was gone. "Did you stop by the hospital?"

"Me? No," Mr. Martin said. "And, please, call me Teddy."

Dillen could have sworn he saw the man. Then again, Dillen could have been mistaken.

"I'm sure your head is spinning over all the decisions that need to be made, so I won't keep you," Teddy said. "If there's anything you need, I hope you'll call."

Dillen highly doubted Teddy Martin was a good friend of Pop's. So, he wondered if the nosy neighbor was here snooping around for a story. Folks could be like that in these parts. They sniffed out gossip and wanted to dig around for something to talk about over a beer.

He dismissed the older man as wanting news to feed the rumor mill.

"Your dad and I had been talking," Teddy said as his face twisted into a constipated expression. He put his hands on his hips like he was debating whether or not he should continue. "We signed some papers, but I don't want you worrying about that right now. We'll get it all figured out soon enough."

"What papers?" Dillen asked, concerned.

"It has to do with water rights," Teddy said, "but it can—"

"A big part of my job while I'm home is finalizing Pop's

affairs," Dillen stated. "I can't do that if I don't know what we're talking about here."

"That's a good point, son." Teddy threw his hands in the air with dramatic flair.

"Is a lawyer involved?" Dillen asked.

"It was more like a handshake deal," Teddy continued. "There are papers but nothing on me." He dropped his hands to his waist. "I just wanted to put that on your radar. I'll drop off the document."

"What are they going to say?" Dillen pushed.

"Oh, just that we made a deal for me to use a little bit of water supply on his property," Teddy explained. "Nothing to get too worked up about." Teddy put his hands up in the surrender position. "I bet you have a lot on your plate already."

"I'm just getting started but this sounds important," he said, figuring he was going to be buried in paperwork.

"Have arrangements been made, or are those still in the works?" Teddy asked. Dillen noticed the change in subject. "The wife would like us to pay our respects."

He issued a sharp sigh. "It's in the works."

"I'll leave you to it, then," Teddy said. "I didn't intend to take up this much of your time. I'm back there in case you need me."

His land was directly behind Pop's, where he had a small family-owned cattle ranch. The connection was coming back the more time Dillen spent with the neighbor.

"Will do," he said to Teddy before the man turned and walked away. Had he come all this way on foot?

Cold air cut right through Dillen's shirt, so he headed back inside, locking the door behind him. More of that anger surfaced—anger he needed to get a grip on because the last thing he should do was unleash it on a civilian.

A few deep breaths later, he turned around and leaned his

back against the front door. Eyes closed, he tried to force a calm that he didn't feel. Feelings were the brain's tricks. Their hardwiring could be changed. He'd become an expert at compartmentalizing his when he needed to complete a mission.

"Hey," Liz said. The sound of her sleepy voice opened his eyes.

"Hey back," he said.

"I heard voices outside," she said, shifting the covers and sitting upright. She crossed her legs and wrapped the blanket around her shoulders.

"A neighbor stopped by," he said. "Teddy Martin. He lives behind us."

"Did he want something?" she asked, cocking her head to one side. The move shouldn't have been sexy on her, but it was. It wouldn't be on anyone else. There was something special about the way she moved.

"Just stopped by to offer his condolences," he supplied as he moved to the coffee machine.

"Ranching communities are good about taking care of their own," she said.

He nodded as he poured a cup. "Do you want coffee?"

"I'd take a cup if you're offering." Her sleepy voice tugged at his heartstrings.

There was something off about the exchange with Teddy. Dillen didn't like it.

Chapter Thirteen

There was something different about Dillen's voice. A distance to his tone now. He sounded deep in thought. Or just plain old tired.

"One cup of coffee," he said as he walked over and placed hers on the table in front of her.

"Thank you," she said, leaning forward to pick up the mug. She rolled it around in her hands, enjoying the warmth on her palms. "How long was I out?"

"A few hours," he said, taking a seat on the recliner. He sat with his torso pitched forward, elbows on his knees, as he held onto his coffee. In that moment, he resembled a man who'd suffered a great loss. All the hard casing normally surrounding him seemed to peel away, and he was just a son missing his father. Would it help ease some of the pain if they talked about him?

"What's your favorite memory growing up here with your dad?" she asked before taking a sip of fresh brew.

Dillen thought about it for a long moment in silence.

"Come on," she urged. "There has to be something."

He kept his head bowed as though in reverence to the memory.

"There is this one thing we used to do together," he started. "But it's just stupid guy stuff."

"I'd like to hear about it," she continued pressing. Keeping everything bottled up inside was a lot like holding a rocket in hand. A spark could light the fuse, blowing up everything within spitting distance.

"It's not that big a deal," he said. "When I was little, on the first night of summer break we used to go camping in the backyard. But I was afraid of the sound of crickets chirping, so Pop made up this story about the cricket king and how it was his job to save little boys like me. So, every time I heard the chirps, it was a signal to tell me the king was out making sure nothing bad could happen to me."

"That's the sweetest story I've ever heard," she said, surprised his father had offered so much comfort when it came to emotions.

Dillen shrugged like it was nothing, but his eyes told a different story when they locked onto hers and held. Their depths were like rivers with so much brimming underneath the surface. "We had a whole routine of going to a store after school to get batteries for our lanterns. I could pick out any kind of candy I wanted. It was usually something sour. And then we would make pizza once we got home. He always took that day off from work so he could pick me up from school."

"I'm sure you looked forward to it for weeks," she said. "It probably made the end of the school year even more special."

"Pop kept up the tradition even when I outgrew it," Dillen said with shame in his voice. "I begged him to come inside, but he refused." His voice cracked, raw with emotion. "I was embarrassed by him. Can you believe that? What a jerk."

"No, you were a normal teenager," she said. "We all went through the same things."

"Yeah? Well, I'd give my right arm to have one more

night underneath the stars with Pop," he said, standing up and turning his back to her as he walked into the kitchen and headed straight to the coffee pot to top off his cup.

Liz set hers down and then joined him in the kitchen. She put her hand up on his shoulder. He whirled around and caught her wrists so fast she didn't have time to blink. He immediately released them and took a step back.

"Piece of advice," he said, "don't sneak up on a soldier."

Dillen excused himself and walked straight out the front door. Liz knew in her heart of hearts that he wouldn't do anything to hurt her. But he looked angry with himself for his reaction.

She returned to the sofa and her still-warm coffee mug. Rolling it around in her palms brought on a wave of calm. A few deep breaths later, her heart rate returned to a reasonable level.

The front door opened and Dillen walked in. He closed and locked the door behind him before making a beeline to her. He took a knee on the opposite side of the coffee table. She was grateful to have a little distance between them.

"I'm sorry," he said to her with remorse in his eyes and more of that shame in his voice. "I came straight to the hospital from a war zone with no cool-down time in between, so I apologize for what just happened."

"Nothing did," she said, holding up her wrists. "Not even a thumb print. See?"

"It could have and that's not me," he continued. "It's not who I want to be."

"Okay," she said, still processing what just happened. "Surprising a Green Beret probably wasn't my best idea."

"It shouldn't matter," he said. "I should have had better control." He shook his head like he could shake off some of his frustration. "I'm sorry that happened." It was obvious how twisted up he was about what he'd done. Of course, he'd stopped himself from actually hurting her other than the equivalent of rug burns on her wrists from his tight grip.

"No more apologies, remember?" she said with a small smile. Dillen was far from an abusive person, so she wasn't worried about that. She was, however, concerned about his mental state. Was he in the right frame of mind to deal with the grief of losing his family?

Dillen dropped his head. "I would never forgive myself if I hurt you."

"You didn't," she soothed, remembering the tortured look in his eyes after he realized what he'd done. It must've been hell living inside his head. The man could have easily snapped her in two, but he hadn't. "You stopped yourself. *You* did that."

"Yeah, but what if I hadn't," he said low and under his breath.

"Wasn't an option, Dillen," she said, responding even if he hadn't intended for her to hear him. "You wouldn't have hurt me."

"How do you know?" he asked, briefly lifting his head enough to lock gazes for a few seconds. The uncertainty in his eyes was a knife stab to her chest.

She didn't have a solid reason to offer except to say, "You just wouldn't have done it."

"I'm glad you believe that," he said through clenched teeth, adding, "because I don't, and what just happened scares the hell out of me."

"That's just the thing," she countered. "Nothing *did* happen."

He just looked at her. "You have no idea what you just escaped, do you?"

"I'm right here," she said. "Alive. Fine. Unhurt."

"Your wrists might argue differently," he said.

She held them up. "They're a little red."

"I hurt you," he said.

Her wrists were nothing compared to the kind of hurt a man like Dillen could inflict on her heart. This wasn't the time to point it out, though.

"I'm fine," she argued. "Look at me."

He didn't seem able to make eye contact this time.

"ON SECOND THOUGHT, it might be best for you to head over to your family ranch tomorrow," Dillen said, still shocked at his own behavior. She was letting him off too easily because she had no idea what he was capable of. He did, which was exactly the reason she should go.

"What if I've changed my mind?" Liz asked, curling her legs up on the couch and then wrapping her arms around them. "What if I want to stick around?"

Her comment surprised him because he figured she would jump at the chance to be rid of him. Did he want her to go? No. Should he push her to leave? Hell yes.

"It's your call, Liz," he said as calmly as he could. She was clearly digging her heels in the more he fought her on this. The woman could be infuriatingly stubborn when she wanted to be. And even when she didn't. "I won't force you to go, but I think it's best if you do."

"You're giving me whiplash, Dillen," she said, studying him. "Earlier, you didn't want me to leave, and now you're practically forcing me to. I shouldn't have caught you off guard. I won't do it again. Problem solved."

If only she knew how dangerous a soldier coming in hot like him could be. She was right about one thing, though. He would cut his arm off before he would do anything to hurt her intentionally. It was the unintentional that had him concerned.

Liz patted the spot on the couch next to her. "Sit with me?"

He shouldn't. He should get up and walk into the bedroom and lock himself inside. But what did he do? He got up and took a seat next to her.

Why? Because she'd asked him to and he figured he owed her at least that much after what had happened. If she was willing to stay, he wasn't going to be the one to tell her not to. Not anymore. Besides, his willpower was fading when it came to her. The kisses they'd shared had been burned into his memory. Tension tightened his muscles just thinking about it. Sex…well hell, he couldn't even go there. Suffice it to say, it would be the best sex he'd ever experienced. Their connection was too deep for anything less.

But damn, fighting his own demons wasn't making life easier.

"Hey," she said.

He turned to look at her as she brought her fingers up to graze his jawline. She dropped her hand to his, and he linked their fingers.

Dillen had no idea how long they sat there, but it was the most peaceful he'd been in far too long. There was something basic and simple about sitting on the couch, almost like they were back in high school.

"What's on the agenda for tomorrow?" she finally asked, leaning her head on his shoulder while getting more comfortable.

"Should you stop by to see your family?" he asked, thinking they could work it in.

"That might be nice," she said. "Did you know Darren has twins?"

"With your sister?" he asked, not hiding his shock.

"No," she said with a smile that could light a cave on a cloudless day. "He was married before but lost his wife in an accident. I've seen pictures of his twins. They're adorable."

"Damn," he said, thinking he'd been so wrapped up in his own problems that he'd neglected his friend. "I haven't see or spoken to Darren in years."

"A lot has happened since the two of you talked then," she said. "But he and Reese are happy as larks, according to the family."

"Good for him," Dillen said. He couldn't imagine falling in love, getting married, starting a family and then losing the key figure in his life. And he felt like a crappy friend for not knowing any of this until now. "He deserves to be happy."

"They seem like a great couple," Liz said.

"Is he at the ranch? Does he live there?"

"Honestly, we can figure that out when we drop by tomorrow," she said. "I've been dreading this trip, putting it off, but it'll be nice to see everyone in person."

"It's easy to take family for granted," he said. "You think they're always going to be there, and then life makes a different decision and you just have to figure out a way to learn to roll with it."

She nodded, and he realized she of all people would understand. She'd lost her father at a young age. Was that the reason she'd kept to herself all those years?

"I might drop you off tomorrow so I can keep the investigation going," he said, changing the subject. "After Teddy's visit, I'm also realizing that I need to make arrangements for Pop plus start taking care of his affairs—starting with what I'm going to do with this place."

"Have you given it any thought?" she asked, shifting to a more upright position. He liked the way she'd relaxed into him a few minutes ago. But this was probably better for both their sakes.

"Not really," he admitted. "Which is why I need to start."

"You could always talk it through with my family," she offered. "They're knowledgeable about Cider Creek and could probably give you the best advice as to whether to hold on or sell." She exhaled a slow breath as she looked around. "I'm not sure how you'd be able to get rid of this place, though."

"Don't tell me you like it here," he quipped, wishing he could reel those words back in. Too late.

"Because I'm a princess?" she retorted with indignation and hurt in her voice.

"No," he countered. "Because it's masculine. There's nothing soft about it."

"And…what? You picture me sitting in a purple room with nothing but fluffy pillows around?"

Liz leaned away from him now, propping herself up on a throw pillow.

"That didn't come out right," he said, reaching for her and tugging her over to him again. "This place is too simple and brown."

"It's calming here," she said after a few beats of silence. "There's something warm and homey about the place." She shrugged. "And it reflects your father, who was a very good man who never treated me any different because of my last name."

Those words made it click in Dillen's brain as to why she had such an affinity for his father. It wasn't because she'd pitied Pop. Dillen could be a real jerk sometimes.

A loud boom shook the walls. An explosion?

Dillen hadn't expected to hear an all-too-familiar sound like that one back at home. What the hell had just happened?

Chapter Fourteen

Liz hopped to her feet at the same moment as Dillen. He bolted toward the front window, moving faster than a gazelle with a lion on its tail.

Dillen muttered a curse. "Rosa and Macy."

The bright orange glow shone brightly through the slats in the mini blinds.

"How bad is it?" she asked as she caught up to him.

"The worst," he said.

He was outside and gunning toward the massive blaze engulfing the double-wide in two shakes. Liz grabbed the blanket on her way out after feeling the blast of cold air from the door being opened. She threw it around her shoulders as she ran barefooted across the gravel.

Rocks cut into the bottoms of her feet. The wind slammed into her.

Where was rain when they needed it?

Another explosion knocked Dillen backward and off his feet as he neared their trailer. Nothing stopped him from getting right back up and running toward danger. He disappeared around the side of the double-wide, giving the fire engulfing it a wide berth.

Liz started to follow, then realized she didn't have her phone with her. She circled back to get it, praying Dillen would be okay. Her cell was sitting on the table next to her coffee. With trembling hands, she picked it up and managed to call 911.

"What's your emergency?" the dispatcher said after answering on the third ring.

"Fire at the neighbor's home after an explosion," Liz supplied, gasping for air from the run back, the cold and the stress. She glanced at the gas stove in the kitchen and then said a silent prayer for the sisters.

"What's the address, ma'am?" the dispatcher asked.

"Hold on," Liz said, needing to go check outside. There was nothing on the door, so she ran to the mailbox, ignoring the painful stabs to the bottom of her feet. She opened the metal box and retrieved a piece of mail. The flashlight app on her cell phone provided the light she needed to read the address. She rattled it off.

"And your name?" the dispatcher said.

"Liz Hayes," she supplied.

"And you said there is a fire following an explosion at your home?" the dispatcher asked.

"No, it's across the street at Rosa and Macy's home," she supplied, realizing she didn't know their last names.

"Please hold," the dispatcher said. After what seemed like an eternity, she returned to the call. "I have alerted the volunteer fire department. Please stay on the line while they arrive."

"Do you know how long it's going to take?" she asked.

"Fifteen minutes," the dispatcher supplied.

"The whole trailer will be gone by then," Liz stated. She couldn't stand here and do nothing. "I have to go."

Before the dispatcher could argue, Liz ended the call. There was no way she could stand idly by while watching Rosa and Macy go up in flames. She set her cell on top of the mailbox and bolted in the direction Dillen had gone a few moments ago.

Heart pounding, adrenaline kicked in. The rush had her pulse skyrocketing and her breath coming out in gasps. *Breathe.*

As she rounded the corner, she saw legs sprawled out. It wasn't immediately clear which sister they belonged to. The answer came a couple of seconds later as she neared. Macy's lifeless body lay there.

Liz choked back a scream, bringing her hand up to cover her mouth.

The back door slammed against the wall. Dillen appeared, walking backward, dragging a second lifeless body. Rosa. Her flannel nightgown was on fire.

Hopping onto the wood deck, Liz pulled the blanket from her shoulders and wrapped it around the small blaze. Then she helped get Rosa safely away from the burning trailer. Dillen's shirt was up over his nose and throat, but he was coughing the entire time. It was a scary, barky, dry-sounding cough.

"Go get fresh air," she said to him, shoving him away from the smoke.

Wind whipped it around, but it was clearly fueling the blaze.

Liz dropped down to her knees beside Rosa. The older woman's pupils were fixed and her chest didn't rise or fall. Liz dropped her head onto Rosa's chest and listened for any sign of a heartbeat. She got nothing.

Scooting over to Macy, Liz repeated the vitals check. Macy was gone, too.

Tears blurred Liz's vision as she placed her hands on top of one another on the center of Macy's chest and started pumping. It had been years since she'd taken a CPR class, so she pulled on the only information she remembered and pumped after clearing Macy's airway. Thirty chest compressions. Liz dropped her head down, placing her ear against Macy's heart. Nothing.

She pinched the woman's nose and then gave two breaths.

A few seconds later, Dillen was behind her, working on Rosa. Neither stopped until the thunder of footsteps filled the air.

Liz looked up and saw a pair of EMTs, one tall and thin while the other was short and stocky. Thin went to Dillen while Stocky came straight to her.

"How long have you been performing CPR?" Stocky asked as he took a knee beside her. He set his medical bag down and opened it while waiting for an answer.

"Almost since I called 911, so about fifteen minutes," she said.

"And how is the patient?" he asked, taking a read of her pulse.

"Not responding," she said as the first tear fell.

Liz wiped it away, tucking her chin to her chest.

"I got this now," Stocky said. "You did everything you could to help."

She was being gently dismissed. If anyone could save Macy, it would be Stocky. So, Liz stood up and took a walk to clear her mind and her lungs.

Within minutes, the place swarmed with firefighters and law enforcement personnel. Liz sat down, leaning against a tool shed, exhausted.

After what seemed like an eternity, but was probably less than half an hour, the blaze was out. Dillen walked over and sat next to her after being given oxygen by one of the EMTs. She'd overheard him refusing to get checked out at the hospital. At least the coughing had stopped.

Her nose and throat burned.

As she sat there, quiet, Dillen's hand found hers. There was something comforting about his touch.

Sheriff Courtright walked over to them and then crouched down to meet them as close to eye level as he could without sitting on the ground. "Are you okay?"

"Yes," Liz responded as Dillen nodded.

"What happened in there?" Dillen immediately asked, nodding toward the back of the trailer.

"The fire started from the gas being left on the stove," Courtright said.

"Neither of the sisters smoked to my knowledge," Dillen said. "I was inside and didn't see any signs of vaping, either."

Liz nodded as Dillen sat motionless, staring at a point over the sheriff's left shoulder.

"You're saying this wasn't an accident," Courtright said.

"I'm certain it was arson," Dillen said.

"How do you know?" Courtright asked.

"Turning on the stove doesn't lead to fire otherwise we'd all be dead." Dillen's lips formed a thin line like they did when he was angry and holding back a remark. "Someone lit a match or something like that. Plus, the glass on the kitchen door was broken. Someone came in from the back and turned on the gas stove."

"The glass might have been broken after the fact," Courtright pointed out as he studied Dillen.

"We visited Rosa and Macy earlier today," Dillen said, his voice scratchy. "They told us about a blonde woman who visited Pop. They were suspicious of the woman. And now they're both dead."

Liz bit down on a gasp. It was true. She suspected murder, too.

Courtright's gaze bounced from Dillen to her and back. "Is that right?"

"Yes," she managed to croak out with a cough.

Dillen pushed to standing, pulling her up along with him. "I'm taking Liz across the street to Pop's house, Sheriff. I need to get her away from all this."

He held tight to her hand.

"You're welcome to come there for a statement, but she needs to change clothes to get away from the smoke smell," he said plain as the nose on his face. "We'll be there when you're ready for our statements." He started toward the house and then stopped. "But unless you want to treat this like a murder investigation, we don't have a whole lot to add other than the fact I ran in through the back and pulled each of the sisters out."

"I called 911," Liz added, but the sheriff would already know that.

Before Courtright could complain, Dillen had them leaving the scene. He was right. Unless Courtright wanted to take them seriously, there was no use wasting their breath.

"Hold on a minute," the sheriff ordered.

DILLEN KEPT RIGHT on walking. He'd said all he'd needed to and had no plans to waste his breath or his time if Courtright wasn't going to take him seriously about opening a murder investigation.

Liz tugged at his hand to veer over to the mailbox. She grabbed her cell phone from on top of it before walking inside Pop's home. "I'm glad I have a suitcase full of clothes with me."

"Take them off, and I'll throw in a load of wash," he said, pulling his shirt over his head. He stripped out of his jeans before he realized Liz was watching.

She turned her head away the second she got caught, mumbling something about going to shower and change before disappearing into the main bedroom.

Dillen took the opportunity to grab a shower, too. He grabbed his rucksack from beside the kitchen door and headed toward the bathroom.

Fifteen minutes later, Liz joined him in the kitchen holding out a ball of smoke-smelling clothes in hand. He took them and threw them into the wash with his own.

After pouring two fresh cups of coffee, he set them down on the table almost the moment a knock sounded at the door. After exchanging glances with Liz, he walked over and opened it.

"Sheriff," he managed to get out despite the frog in his throat. Dillen stood at the door, taking up the entire frame and blocking the sheriff's view.

Courtright's hands went up in the surrender position, palms facing Dillen. "I'm not making any promises, but I'm inclined to believe you and I'd like to hear more about what happened across the street."

Dillen studied the sheriff for a long moment. The muscles around his eyes pulled taut. Worry lines etched his forehead. He appeared sincere.

"Come inside," Dillen said, stepping back to make room.

"Thank you," Courtright said, following Dillen into the kitchen, where greetings were exchanged between the sheriff and Liz.

"Would you like a cup of coffee, Sheriff?" Dillen asked.

"No, thank you," Courtright said, joining Liz at the table, where all three sat down.

Dillen went first detailing what happened from his point of view. Liz recounted her side of the story, which was similar in the beginning to the point where he ran round the trailer and she retrieved her cell phone to call 911.

"Don't you think it's suspicious there was an explosion in Rosa and Macy's home following our visit?" Dillen asked.

"It's all circumstantial evidence," Courtright said, but his tone revealed he was just as skeptical as they were about the explosion being accidental. "If you're asking me as a person, I agree with you. As a law enforcement officer who can't act on intuition, I need proof."

"What about the fire marshal?" Dillen asked. "Will he investigate?"

"I put in a request before I came over here," Courtright admitted. "It'll be up to him whether or not he proceeds with an investigation."

"How do these things normally go?" Liz asked, her voice still as scratchy as Dillen's.

"The fire marshal usually goes with my requests," he explained. "Doesn't mean he will every time, especially since the last one didn't go my way. He might not want to commit the resources."

"Is there any way we can talk to him?" Liz asked.

"He'll get a copy of my report," Courtright said. "Your statement might make a difference."

Dillen noticed the sheriff didn't include him. "Because her last name is Hayes? Is that why the fire marshal will listen to her and not me?"

"I didn't mean to insinuate—"

"You didn't have to," Dillen interrupted. "The whole town cowers to the Hayes name. My family might not have the kind of money they do, but that doesn't mean we aren't trustworthy."

"It's been pointed out that you've been in trouble with the law in the past before you signed up for the military,"

Courtright said. "That doesn't bode well for me using you as a means to get folks to do things for me."

Dillen shouldn't have been surprised that once a label was placed on someone no matter how young, it stuck. The fact that he'd straightened up his act and had been serving his country for the past fourteen years should've counted for something. "As much as I'd love to be your 'selling point,' any logical person can see suspicious activity is going on here."

"I'm not disagreeing with you," Courtright said. "And I'd personally like to thank you for your service. You're doing this country proud. This town should be damn proud of you. But the Hayes name gets results. We don't have time to worry about whose word we use to convince folks to do the right thing."

Courtright was right. Still, it burned Dillen up.

He was more determined than ever to find the blonde woman with the red Jetta.

Chapter Fifteen

"I have enough to go on," Sheriff Courtright said as he stood. "I'll be in touch if I need anything else." He looked directly at Liz. "Will you be here if I need to speak to you again?"

Her cheeks flamed at the insinuation she and Dillen were a couple.

"I'll be around," she said. "You have my cell phone number if you need to reach me." She'd given it to him as part of her statement along with her address in Houston and information about her business.

On paper, she could admit to looking like a dependable witness. But so was Dillen. Just because he'd gotten into trouble years ago didn't mean folks should continue to look down on him.

Courtright nodded before letting himself out. She immediately got up and locked the door, realizing the threat was still out there. An ominous feeling settled over her at the thought. Was she safe? Had Dillen been right all along? Would the same person who'd blown up Macy and Rosa's trailer come after the two of them?

"Why Rosa and Macy?" she asked Dillen after a few more sips of coffee to relieve some of the dryness in her throat. "Why not come after us?"

"You heard the sheriff," he said. "It's all circumstantial evidence at this point. Rosa and Macy could potentially identify the blonde who'd been visiting Pop. We stopped over there to talk to them, which could mean someone is watching."

Liz involuntarily shivered.

"No one will hurt you on my watch," he promised.

Could he deliver? Even Dillen Bullard was human, capable of making mistakes despite being a highly trained soldier.

The determined look in his eyes said he wouldn't let harm come to her on purpose.

"We're going to have to watch each other's backs from now on," she said. "Three people are dead, and we still don't know why."

Dillen drained his coffee cup. "It's late. We should get ready for bed."

Despite the caffeine, she was so tired her bones ached. Even the nap earlier couldn't put a dent in her exhaustion. It was Dillen. He made her feel safe enough to finally rest after being in the hospital keeping watch over his father for five days straight. She'd scarcely slept the entire time except for grabbing an hour here and there.

"I need sleep," she said before excusing herself to go to the bathroom.

Her thoughts were spinning to the point that her head hurt. The headache between her eyes returned. Sleep sounded like magic at this point. Had she eaten dinner? Could she choke anything down if she tried?

Probably not. The image of the sisters' lifeless bodies would stay stamped in her thoughts for a very long time.

Liz scrubbed her teeth. And then she threw on a soft T-shirt and sweatpants. Fuzzy socks finished off the outfit.

Purple. Comfortable. She could use as many comforts as possible right now.

Her thoughts kept shifting back to the sisters, to Mr. Bullard's trembling hand and to the feeling they were missing something right under their noses.

She needed sleep to stop the hamster wheel of questions circling through her thoughts.

Dillen was sitting at the kitchen table with a stack of papers and his cell phone out while he studied the screen. She cleared her throat so as not to surprise him again. Liz was no match for his fast reflexes.

"Hey," he said as he looked up at her, his voice still gruff and his eyes red rimmed. "I just got off the phone with the morgue."

Liz walked over to the table and took a seat. "What did you decide to do?"

"Cremation," he said. "Pop left a copy of a will in the desk drawer, but he didn't have instructions for when the time came. I figure this is a way to bring him back here, where he was most at home."

She nodded before reaching out to touch his hand. The electrical current that came with contact felt reassuring to her now. "I bet he would like that very much."

"I need to decide what I'm going to do with this place now that he's gone," he said. "I let my unit leader know this was going to take longer than I thought."

"Does that mean you're staying for a while?" she asked, thinking she needed to deal with work now that he brought up the subject. She'd barely checked in since arriving in Cider Creek.

"Looks like it," he said. "Not more than a couple of weeks, unless…"

He didn't have to finish the sentence for her to realize

he was talking about finding the person responsible and bringing them to justice. She could only hope that he would allow the law to do its job instead of meting out justice on his terms. She pitied the person on the receiving end of Dillen's wrath.

And yet she also realized how much he walked the line. Despite the sheriff not being cooperative at first, Dillen hadn't crossed any illegal lines. He obeyed the law down to speed limits and stop signs.

"Did you get approval to take the time?" she finally asked after getting lost in her own thoughts for a minute.

He nodded.

"Even without the investigation, I would need more time," he said. "I haven't even thought about what I'm going to do with his clothes, but there's no reason to keep them."

"You don't have to make those decisions all at once," she said. "Just start with the essential ones, and then figure out the small details. Besides, you might want to keep the clothes around for memories sake."

Maybe it was just that she'd been around too much death lately, but she was starting to wonder how much she was really living. Her business was thriving, and she was proud of herself for her accomplishments. Wouldn't they mean more if she had someone to share them with? Maybe Kevin had had a point. Maybe she was married to her work.

"We should try to sleep," he said. Dillen looked tired. He needed sleep. She couldn't imagine him trying to spend another night on the recliner. And to be honest, she didn't want to be alone right now.

"I just need to brush my teeth," he said.

"Mind if I curl up in bed in the main bedroom while you do?" she asked, putting her hand up to stop him from thinking she wanted more than to be close to him. "The thought of being alone with my thoughts isn't doing good things to my brain."

He nodded, looking like he understood more than he wanted to. "Do what you need to. You won't bother me."

Liz followed him into the bedroom and then curled up on top of his bed.

"Do you want your blanket?" he asked, standing at the bathroom door, looking better than anyone had a right to while standing there.

She shook her head. "I used it to…"

Recognition dawned. He nodded before half jogging into the living room. He returned a few moments later with the blanket he'd used.

"Thank you," she said, taking the offering and fanning the blanket out over her body. She was touched by the gesture and grateful for the warmth. She didn't want to climb underneath the covers on his father's bed, but she could curl up on top.

Dillen left the door cracked, another move she appreciated.

Liz closed her eyes. The image of the dead sisters stamped Liz's thoughts. She sat up and rubbed her eyes. Would she ever be able to shut them again?

By THE TIME Dillen had finished in the bathroom, he expected Liz to be asleep. He was surprised to find her sitting up with the lights on.

"I can't close my eyes," she said as a tear rolled down her cheek.

He moved to the bed and sat down on the edge, thumbing the rogue tear away. "What is it?"

"The sisters," she said, twisting the edge of the blanket between her fingers. She shook her head as though trying to shake off the images. "I just keep seeing them. Macy with her blank look. Rosa as you were pulling her from the house." More tears fell.

Liz turned her face away from him. Was she embarrassed?

"Hey," he said in as soothing manner as possible. "It's okay not to be all right."

His training kicked in, and he compartmentalized the losses, focusing instead on finding the truth. But if he let those emotions bubble to the surface, he would feel just as awful.

"You don't have to be ashamed of crying," he said quietly, reaching for her chin and then slowly turning her to face him. "It just means you're alive, real."

She took in a deep breath.

"There's so much pent up back there—I'm afraid if I let it go, I won't stop," she admitted. Liz was the most real, most honest person he'd ever met.

"I'll be right here," he said. "I'm not going anywhere."

Liz pulled him all the way onto the bed, where he positioned himself beside her, backs against the headboard. She tugged his hand until his arm was around her, and then she burrowed into him.

He pressed a kiss to the top of her head before he could stop himself. She reacted by looking up at him with those big, beautiful eyes. It would be so easy to dip his head down and claim those pink lips, but she didn't need that from him right now. Right now, she needed to feel protected, safe.

So, he forced his gaze away from her beautiful face and just held on to her. He had no idea how much time had passed before she rolled onto her side and curled her body around his. Her steady, even breathing said she'd fallen asleep. Since he didn't want to disturb her, he grabbed a blanket to put over them. Then, he leaned his head to one side and fell asleep.

The sun didn't shine brightly the next morning. Instead, clouds covered the sky as Dillen opened his eyes and realized he'd slept until noon.

Liz was still curled around him, and he didn't have it in him to move her when she looked so comfortable. Without his phone, he eased to sitting so he could at least run through the events in his mind.

"Hey," Liz said, stirring. Her sleepy voice tugged at his heartstrings.

"Good morning," he said, needing to put up more of a wall when it came to her. As it was, he was starting to lose grip on his emotions, which was not a good thing.

Dillen needed to put some physical distance between them. Besides, he couldn't remember the last time he'd slept a straight eight let alone more than twelve hours. But that was exactly what he'd done last night.

He pushed off the covers and slid out of bed.

"I'll throw on a pot of coffee," he said before heading into the bathroom to brush his teeth.

Liz followed, keeping her distance. She must have gotten the hint, and he hated the look of confusion in her eyes—confusion she tried to mask. If he didn't know her so well at this point, she would have gotten away with it, too.

Dillen sighed sharply before heading into the kitchen. He needed to refocus. A quick glance at the stack of papers he'd pulled, which included everything from the title to Pop's truck to his cable bill, did the trick. He put on a pot of coffee and then pulled out breakfast supplies.

Liz had to be as hungry as him.

She joined him as he started cracking eggs. "Move over. I can do that." There was a hint of hurt in her voice. She tried to cover that, too. Again, if she'd been talking to anyone else she might have gotten away with it. Not him. Not when he was so tuned into her that he could practically read her thoughts.

Dillen took a step back. "Mind if I take another look at the papers while you do your thing?"

"Not at all," she said. "I prefer it that way. You'll just be in my way if you stand here."

There was a sharp edge to her voice now that said she didn't appreciate the about-face. Damn. If life was different...if *he* was different, he might have something to offer a woman like Liz.

Sifting through the stack of papers, he remembered something Teddy had said yesterday. "Apparently Teddy and Pop had some kind of agreement. I looked all over the office while you were in the shower yesterday and couldn't find anything. That's when I came across the will."

"An agreement? Did he say what kind?" she half turned as the topic of conversation seemed to interest her.

Dillen shrugged. "Said this wasn't the time to bring it up, but he wanted me to know about it before I sold the property."

"Well, now I'm curious," she said. "Maybe we can swing by later and ask for a copy. There might be legal issues involved in selling the property if the two of them have a binding agreement in place."

Dillen didn't like the fact his father might've made a decision about the land or trailer without first consulting him. More evidence of him being a bad son. It was mounting. He should have asked. He should have known. He should have visited more.

Had Teddy taken advantage of Pop?

Chapter Sixteen

The afternoon zoomed by while Liz answered work emails and fielded questions. Dillen kept his face buried in paperwork, tearing apart his father's office while searching for additional documents he might need. His search wasn't fruitless. He came up with his dad's passwords in the form of a sheet of paper taped to the inside of one of the metal drawers.

Before she realized the time, her stomach growled to tell her it was past dinner. She pushed up to standing from the kitchen table and then walked down the hallway, making as much noise as possible so she didn't catch Dillen off guard again.

"Hey," she said as she stepped inside the office.

His back was to her, his gaze fixed on the computer screen. He swiveled around in the chair, and it was like the sun hitting her full force with its warmth on a spring afternoon. "Are you hungry?"

"You read my mind," she said. "We could do the diner" It might be good for them to get out of the trailer and talk to folks.

He wiped a hand over his face. "Sounds good. I've been staring at a screen far too long today."

Dillen stood up and then followed her into the living

room, where they split up. She grabbed jeans and a sweater and then disappeared into the bedroom. After changing, she met Dillen in the kitchen. He'd done the same, having thrown on a sweater.

After slipping into shoes and putting on a coat, she followed him outside. He stopped on the front porch.

"I'm wondering if we should take Pop's truck," he said. "See if it throws anyone off to see it parked at the restaurant."

"Okay," she said, thinking it was a good idea. While he drove, she could scan reactions.

They moved to the truck and then drove to the diner. It was half past seven o'clock by the time they arrived. Business was slow, so there was plenty of open street parking.

Dillen had been quiet on the ride over. Was the reality of settling his father's affairs sinking in? Or was it being in his dad's vehicle again? Or both?

At least the fireworks show he'd been setting off inside when she'd woken up next to him had finally subsided. Dillen might've had it all, but he fell under the category of *complicated men*. She'd sworn those off years ago to pursue her business. Complicated men were distractions. Case in point, the way she felt about Dillen didn't match up with the short amount of time they'd spent together. Her heart had her wanting to go all in despite how much her brain protested. Didn't real feelings take years to develop? Didn't real relationships unfold over time?

Dillen parked in an open spot as close to the front doors of the diner as possible. The gray truck was visible on the main drag, so they were covered there. He exited the vehicle first and then came around the front to open her door.

He immediately reached for her hand and then linked their fingers. She pulled back, releasing his hand.

"People will talk," she said by way of explanation, hating the hurt look in his eyes. "Everyone knows me. It's not like you can walk in there anonymously as long as I'm with you."

Dillen stopped and stood there, studying her. "I don't care what people say or don't say, and I sure as hell don't care what they think."

"It'll draw more attention, and you don't need that right now," she said, twisting her fingers together.

"You mean *you* don't need that right now," he said through clenched teeth.

She stopped herself from making an apology. "It's in the best interest of the investigation."

He opened his mouth to speak and then clamped it shut before holding his hand out to indicate she should lead the way.

Liz did but felt like a jerk. Did he think she didn't want to hold his hand in public because she thought she was too good for him? Because the assumption couldn't have been further from the truth. She bit back a curse. This wasn't the time, but she intended to clarify the misunderstanding the minute they were alone.

Dillen held the door open for her.

"Liz Hayes?" Georgina Baldwin came rushing over. What was she doing here? Liz had thought most of their classmates had moved to Austin, Houston or San Antonio after graduation. Some had gone off to colleges. Others had spread their wings and left the small town behind.

"Georgina," Liz said as she was brought into a hug.

Georgina's gaze bounced from Liz to Dillen and back. She smiled and her cheeks flushed with attraction. "I didn't realize the two of you were friends."

"What are you still doing in town?" Liz asked, distracting her former classmate.

"My parents bought this place a couple of years back," she said, tucking strands of her long brunette hair behind her ear. "I imagine they did it so I would come back home and help run it." She shrugged in dramatic fashion. "Guess it worked."

Her gaze zeroed in on Dillen.

"Sorry to hear about your daddy," she said.

He thanked her and then asked for a table in the corner.

"Sure thing," she said, recovering her bouncy personality after a moment of sincerity. "You can sit wherever you want."

Liz reached for Dillen's hand before she could stop herself and linked their fingers. He smirked.

Yes, she was jealous. Fine.

"Well, that was a distraction," she said after Georgina bounced back to get water, promising to return in a jiffy. "And who says 'jiffy' anymore?"

Dillen's smile widened.

"I just thought she might leave us alone faster if she thought we were a couple," she defended.

He put his hands in the air in the surrender position, palms out. "No skin off my nose. I would like to point out, however, that you were the one who dropped my hand outside."

"Good of you to point that out," she quipped, knowing full well what had just happened.

Georgina bounced back to the table with two waters in her hands. She set them down, and Liz couldn't help but notice how closely she stood to Dillen, especially when she bent over to set Liz's water down across the table.

The table wasn't *that* big.

"Are you back for good?" Georgina asked, directing the question at Liz.

"No," she said. "Just passing through for a family meeting."

"And what about you?" she asked Dillen. Could she bat her eyelashes a little harder?

Liz was getting snippy. She blamed it on stress and hunger.

"I'm out of here as soon as possible," he supplied.

"Oh, well then, point your phones right here for the menus," Georgina said, looking caught off guard at his curt response. His tone of voice had said he was ready to leave more than his words ever could. "I'll be right back to take your orders."

With that, Georgina disappeared back in the kitchen.

"She got out of here fast," Liz said with a self-satisfied grin. She retrieved her cell and aimed the camera at the QR code taped to the corner of the table.

"You're welcome," he said so low she almost didn't hear him.

Liz couldn't afford to get attached to Dillen, so someone flirting with him shouldn't have mattered one way or the other.

DILLEN PERUSED THE MENU, unable to hold back a smirk. He needed to wipe it off his face because Liz had been clear there would be nothing between them. She was right. He just kept forgetting the fact.

"What looks good?" she asked as she studied the screen on her phone. "I know I'm hungry, but it's hard to think about eating after what happened last night."

"You need to keep up your strength," he said.

She looked directly at him. "How do you do it?"

He shot a puzzled look.

"Do what you do and still sleep at night. Still eat?"

"You do what you can to shut it off so you can still function," he said.

"Sounds tiring," she admitted.

"It is" was all he said before dropping his gaze to the screen. "Fried chicken."

Liz nodded, but he could tell she was studying him. No, it hadn't been easy in the beginning. After fourteen years of being a soldier, he'd learned how to shift his focus away from the things that gutted him. But were they still there?

Hell yes.

Was it the reason he kept everyone at a safe distance?

Hell yes.

Was it the only way he could do his job and keep going?

Hell yes.

The problem was that his usual coping mechanisms weren't working so well when it came to losing his father or containing his feelings for Liz.

"Fried chicken looks good," she finally said. "Definitely with mashed potatoes and gravy."

"I was thinking the same," he said.

"I should probably do a salad to pretend I've eaten healthy today," she continued as her gaze stayed steady on the screen.

He nodded. "Collard greens look good to me."

"Oh, those do look good," she agreed. "Okay. I'll have what you're having."

Georgina came back and took their orders. He remembered her from high school. She'd been one of the "popular" group who hadn't given him the time of day. Funny how things changed as he'd gotten older.

"Why not come after me directly?" Liz finally asked when Georgina disappeared for the second time. The corner where they sat was quiet. There was a dotting of four-top tables with a row of booths along the wall. And there was counter service to the right in retro diner furnishings. It didn't look like much had changed except ownership and some of the menu to add a few healthier options.

"We already talked about that," he said. "You've been with me."

"I've been with you for the past couple of days," she pointed out. "But I was in the hospital alone before that, and no one tried anything."

He shrugged his shoulders. "Could be there were too many witnesses around."

"I guess so."

"Harder to burn down an entire hospital," he reasoned.

"Sure," she agreed. "I see your point there."

"But you're not convinced those are the only reasons."

"Whoever is behind your father's murder went to great lengths to make it look like an accident on his part." She tapped her fingers on the table, a sure sign she was deep in thought. "Someone must have either circled back or was hiding, waiting until he…"

She shook her head like she could shake off the mental image.

"You know what I mean," she continued after a deep breath.

"The person might think you don't remember," he said. "Which doesn't mean you won't."

"I would think that would make me a liability in their eyes," she said.

"Maybe we're not dealing with memory loss with me because I really don't know what happened," she said. "The doctor said I hit the back of my head on flying debris or tripped and fell. I don't remember that, but it's possible someone came up from behind and struck me."

"What about the bruising?" he asked.

"The person might have gripped me to keep me from falling down," she said. "They may have been planning to set up an 'accident' for me, too."

Dillen took a minute to consider her points. She made a good argument.

"Plus, now, like you said before, it's too risky to come after me while I'm with you," she stated.

Georgina approached the table holding a server tray loaded with dinner plates and a breadbasket.

She managed to open a tray stand and then place the over-size tray that had been on her shoulder on top.

"Here you go," she said, placing Liz's plate down first and then Dillen's. The bread went in the center of the table. He took note of the fact that Georgina stood a little too close to him. So much so, she rubbed up against his outer arm when she moved. A quick glance at Liz said she noticed, too. He shouldn't have been happy about the fact even though he most definitely was.

What did he intend to do about it?

Chapter Seventeen

Liz did her best to ignore Georgina's flirting. It was a losing battle.

"Can I have a Coke?" she asked, figuring it would be a good reason to shoo the woman away from Dillen.

"Sure thing," Georgina said, whirling around and heading back the way she came.

The thought of someone lying in wait, ready and willing to hurt her—kill her?—wasn't doing good things to her mind.

Rather than go there, she picked up her fork and dug into her vegetables, giving the fried chicken a minute to cool down.

Georgina returned with the Coke, moving over to Liz's side of the table this time. She thanked her.

"If there's anything else you need, just let me know," Georgina said before adding, "It's good seeing you again. I hope you won't be a stranger while you're in town." The comments were directed at Liz, but she had a sneaky suspicion Dillen was the one Georgina hoped would come back. Alone?

"We will," Liz said, taking in a slow breath to calm frazzled nerves. She was getting upset over someone flirting with a man who didn't belong to her in the first place.

The food hit the spot, and Liz was surprised she cleaned her entire plate. She must have needed to eat more than she'd realized. Of course, the pizza last night hadn't been enough to hold her over until dinner today.

She thought about the past, about Kevin. Life had come easy to him. All he'd had to do was step into his family's furniture business. Hell, he didn't even have to work all that hard since his sister worked there, too. Renee would cover for her brother in a heartbeat. In fact, she'd called Liz after the breakup and told her she would regret walking away from the relationship one day. Renee had reminded Liz how awful it would be to wake up fifty years old and alone with no one to share her life with.

Renee had accepted Liz into the family with open arms, so it probably stood to reason she would be upset with the breakup. Renee had taken it too far, giving Liz a hard time. Liz hadn't expected the two of them to be friends after the relationship ended, but she hadn't expected Renee to chew her out, either.

The fact that her ex couldn't stand up for himself and needed his sister to step in for him was another red flag and clear indication Liz had made the right call in walking away. Besides, he had too much free time. The man barely had to clock in any hours and was perfectly content to ride the family money. He was good looking and charming and could be fun. Liz had liked those aspects of him when they first started dating.

Being with him reminded her to take a day off once in a while and go out on his yacht on a Tuesday for no reason other than the fact the sun was shining. Ultimately, her need to be successful on her own and create something from scratch had driven a wedge between them. The fact that she couldn't go out every Saturday night, especially once her business had grown, had upset him more and more. His response had been to tell her to hire someone to handle "all that" so she could go out and play.

Liz just wasn't built that way. She was a Hayes through and through, a person who thrived when she was busy and took a great deal of pride in what she was accomplishing. He'd become jealous of her work, and she'd looked down on him for "coasting" on his family's funds.

The breaking point for her had been the yacht. The morning after the breakup, she'd had a change of heart and decided to join him on the yacht. Finding him passed out with Renee's best friend wrapped around him on deck had been the incentive she'd needed to walk away for good. They'd been clothed, albeit in swimsuits with barely enough material to cover, but it still had felt like a betrayal. He'd sworn nothing had happened "that time," but that wasn't even the point. The two of them had drifted apart, and she couldn't go back.

After him, she'd doubled down on her career, and suddenly two years had gone by without a relationship. She could admit that, lately, she was beginning to feel like it might be nice to have someone to share her accomplishments and life with.

She looked up from her reverie to find Dillen studying her. And then, out of the corner of her eye, she saw the widow Margaret Coker take one look at Dillen, perform a double take and then bolt in the opposite direction.

"I'll be right back." Liz got up from her seat and headed toward the door. By the time she managed to step onto the concrete sidewalk and locate the widow, Ms. Coker had managed to hop into the driver's seat of her sedan, start the engine and was already pulling out of her parking spot.

Weird.

Liz took note as she turned and walked back into the restaurant.

"What was that all about?" Dillen asked. The check sat on the table, so she grabbed her purse to chip in her portion of the bill.

He covered the paper slip with his hand. "Not in a million years. This one's on me."

Liz nodded and smiled. She could tell when she was going to lose a fight. She'd grab the next check to keep them on solid friendship footing.

"Do you remember the widow Margaret Coker?" she asked before finishing off the Coke she didn't especially want but felt obligated to drink now that she'd ordered it.

"I guess so," he said, his gaze shifting out the window. Recognition dawned. "Yes. I do remember her. Why?"

"Did you have a disagreement with her fourteen years ago when you last lived here or on one of your visits home?" she asked.

"No," he said. "Why would I?"

"You tell me," she said. "I'm only asking because she just took one look at you and bolted. I couldn't get outside fast enough to ask before she was in her car and pulling out of her parking spot."

"That's strange," he said, shaking his head and bringing his elbow up to rest on the table. "I haven't had any interactions with her in years. In fact, I don't remember doing anything that might have upset her back in the day. And that's the only time I would have offended anyone."

"There's no way she's connected to your father's..." Liz glanced up and saw Georgina heading toward them. She nodded, giving Dillen a heads-up that their former schoolmate was almost right behind him.

Dillen reached for his wallet, pulled out cash and set a

few twenties on the receipt. "That should cover it. We don't need change."

The new information about Coker had his mind whirring—she could almost see the wheels turning.

It made no sense why the widow would be scared of running into him. Unless she had information. Or was hiding something.

DILLEN STOOD, ready to go. "Do you have any idea where Ms. Coker lives?"

"No," Liz said. "I don't have the first clue. Maybe someone in my family will know? Granny or my mom might be our best bet since they are the only two who stayed in Cider Creek with Duncan."

He nodded as his thoughts went down a dark path. How would Ms. Coker be involved in murder? It wasn't logical. She worked for the county.

"Let's head that way so we can ask," he said as he followed Liz outside.

In the truck, he glanced at the gas gauge as he started the engine. The damn thing floated, and they didn't have as much fuel as he'd first thought. "We should probably stop for gas while we're in town."

"Okay," Liz agreed. "There aren't any stations by the ranch, so it's now or never."

Dillen located a station on his cell phone and drove there. He got out and pumped gas. He realized Liz had picked up on the fact Pop had been on the autism spectrum. Looking back, he wondered if it was the reason his mother had walked out and never looked back. He had no plans to have kids, but if he did, he would be there for them every step of the way. The woman had turned her back on a husband

and son. Was that part of the anger inside him that was always so readily available?

Opening up to Liz, talking about what happened was the first time he'd ever spoken to anyone about the past. The boulder that had been docked on his shoulders for what had seemed like his entire life was being chipped away the more he talked to her. Was that the reason he kept going when he normally pulled back?

He was beginning to realize the two of them had more in common than he'd ever thought. Both had been brought up by single parents. Both couldn't wait to get out of Cider Creek the second they'd been old enough. Both had a deep-seated need to prove to themselves and the world around them that they could succeed under any and all conditions.

Who would have thought?

Dillen's wisecracks about her bring a princess had grated on her nerves. Now that he'd seen a different side to her—the real side—he wished he could take those words back. He couldn't have been more off base about calling her a trust-fund baby.

He could admit to being wrong. His feelings for Liz had caught him off guard. The attraction had been instant and undeniable. And despite him being a complete jerk, she was still talking to him. That was something.

It was clear that she took a great deal of pride in all her accomplishments. Hell, she should be proud. Not many folks started a successful business, let alone kept one going.

Dillen walked inside to pay for his gas as another vehicle pulled up. He glanced back and saw there was an elderly woman at the wheel and no passengers. There was clearly no threat, so he kept going. There was no line inside, but the attendant was busy in the stockroom.

"I'll be right with you," the young male voice called out.

So, he stood there, waiting.

A few minutes later, the attendant came jogging to the cash register, apologizing for keeping Dillen waiting. He paid with cash, which was his habit. He'd never like the idea of the government being able to track his every move when he used a credit card, despite working for one of its branches in the military.

Plus, he didn't like using plastic to pay for anything. It could get him into trouble if he wasn't careful.

A gas station attendant might notice if someone unusual came to town so Dillen decided to ask about the blonde. "Any chance a woman with platinum-blond hair who wore her miniskirts a little too short and drove a red car ever stopped by to fill up her tank?"

"Um, no," the male attendant said, looking like he was doing his best to recall the information. He shook his head. "I definitely would have noticed someone like that."

She would have stuck out in a town of blue jeans and ponytails.

It dawned on him someone wearing a ton of makeup and with platinum-blond hair might be covering up their real looks. Hiding?

"Thanks," he said to the attendant.

"No problem," the guy said before heading back toward the stockroom.

The bell rang on the door as Dillen walked outside. The sedan pulled away, and Liz stood at the gas pump with her arms folded across her chest. She was leaning against the truck and had a serious look on her face.

"What happened while I was inside?" he asked.

"I just called Ms. Coker," she supplied.

He shot a confused look.

"Got the number from my mom just now," Liz explained.

"What did she say?" he asked.

Liz moved around to the passenger side and reclaimed her seat. He did the same on the driver's side.

"I couldn't get her to talk," Liz said. "But she's holding back on something."

"Maybe we should stop by her house," he said, starting the engine.

"It might scare her even more," she said. "By now, the whole town must know about the sisters."

"I didn't think about how that might scare someone into going into hiding if they had information," he said, navigating back onto the roadway, heading to the one place he never believed he would be going... Hayes Ranch.

"She was off," Liz said. "I could feel it. But she swore nothing was wrong and that she suddenly remembered she had to run an errand when she saw us a little while ago."

"What are the odds?"

"Not high," she admitted. "No. She's hiding something, and I can't for the life of me figure out what it is."

At this point, someone had answers. They were close to finding them. He could feel it.

Chapter Eighteen

Liz didn't like the interaction with Ms. Coker one bit. It had left a sour taste in her mouth. With Dillen's background as a Green Beret, she had no doubt he could force the truth out of anyone. Ms. Coker was going to take a lot more finessing, which was something they didn't have time to do.

"Your silence makes me believe Ms. Coker doesn't like me," he said.

"Does she like anyone?" she asked. How did she tell him that the woman thought he was trouble? How did she tell him that the woman had warned Liz to stay far away from a man like him? How did she tell him that the woman had said a man like Dillen Bullard would only drag her down with him?

"Fair point," he conceded. "But my guess is that she especially doesn't like me."

"Said she was concerned about your type, whatever that means," she said. "Do you ever think that some people never leave high school?"

"It's part of the reason I got out of here as fast as I could," he stated. "Folks don't ever seem to change. At least in the military, I meet different people. People who don't know squat about me or my background."

"Same here, except I moved to Houston," she agreed.

"But I'm also thinking that maybe folks still treat us like we're the people we used to be because we haven't been around to show them any different."

Dillen stared out the front windshield like he did when he was contemplating a new idea but didn't respond. Liz refocused since they were getting close to the ranch.

Facing down the ranch with him gone shouldn't have affected her as much as it was. "How many of my family members do you know personally?"

"I haven't held a conversation that lasted longer than two minutes with anyone in your family but you," he admitted. "And that's only recently."

This family could be intimidating based on size alone. Six kids, with four of them being boys, was a lot.

As they pulled onto the gated ranch drive, he stopped at the security booth. The main house wasn't visible from the street. It was large, though, with eight bedrooms along with a guest suite on the first floor.

"Liz Hayes is home," Dillen said to the attendant as the man stepped outside.

"ID, please," he said.

Liz was already on the phone with her mother. She handed over the cell.

The security guard nodded a couple of times and said a few *yes, ma'am*s into the phone before handing it back.

"All clear," he said before tapping a button that opened the gate to the long drive.

Dillen parked before exiting the truck first. He came around the front of the vehicle to open her door. There was something comforting about this routine. Chivalry was ingrained in Texas folks, but their routine brought a sense of calm over her.

"I've been thinking about what you said on the ride over," he said after opening her door.

She shot him a questioning look. She'd said a lot and didn't know what he was referring to.

"About how folks can't change their opinion of someone if all they knew of them was the past," he stated. "I realized it's true because I expected everyone to still be eighteen years old, like when I last left. I've been back and forth a few times but never saw anyone from our year. I was shocked at how fast some folks had aged, like our old history teacher in tenth grade."

"Ah, Mr. Swinson," she recalled. "I haven't seen him recently, either."

"You might not recognize him if you did," Dillen said. "He has a full head of gray hair now and looks like he's aged twenty years."

"See what I mean," she said. "Our minds get fixed on our last memory of a person. If there's no new information to counter it, we stick to the same old ideas."

He nodded before placing his hand on the small of her back and walking beside her to the back door.

"Are you ready for this?" she asked him, but the same question could be asked of her.

"Ready if you are," he said after taking in a deep breath.

Their gazes locked, and then he broke into a wide smile. "You're going to do fine."

"Yeah?" she said. "So are you."

He pretended to slick his hair back and straighten his make-believe collar. "We got this."

The gesture was sweet and counter to his tough-guy image. Liz appreciated his sense of humor. Given the circumstances, it hadn't come out much. It would have been nice to have met up again under different conditions. Would they have spoken to each other? Or would those old opinions of each other have gotten in the way?

Liz opened the back door and walked into the kitchen of the main house. A hundred-pound Akita mix came bolting toward them along with an unfamiliar person trailing behind.

"Atlas, sit," came the command. Surprisingly, the dog obeyed. The unfamiliar face was framed by long straight dark brown hair with caramel highlights and bangs. "I'm Payton, your brother Callum's wife." She smiled a warm smile. "This is Atlas. Based on all the pictures I've seen, you must be Liz." Payton's gaze bounced from Liz to Dillen.

"Dillen Bullard," he said, taking a step forward with an outstretched hand.

Atlas growled from deep and low in his throat.

"Sorry—he's a work in progress when it comes to trusting men," Payton explained. "Best to keep a distance."

"Nice to meet you," Liz said to Payton as her older brother Callum joined them. He had dark hair that was not quite brown and hinted at their Scottish-Irish heritage with natural reddish-blond highlights. He was forty-two but didn't look at day over thirty-five.

Liz broke into a wide smile at the sight of her brother. "Wow, I've missed seeing your face outside of a hospital lobby."

"Right back atcha, kid. Got your text saying you were coming, so I let a few people know," Callum said before studying Dillen.

"You remember Dillen Bullard," Liz said.

"Right, of course, how could I forget?" Callum said, recognition dawned as he connected the dots this was Mr. Bullard's son. "I'm sincerely sorry for your loss. Your father was a good man."

"Thank you," Dillen said, shaking Callum's extended hand. "It means a lot to hear you say that."

Callum's gaze bounced back to Liz and the bandage on her head. "How's the healing? Getting better?"

"So far, so good," she said. "I have to go back to the doctor in a few days but I'm doing okay."

"That's good to hear," Callum said, some of the tension eased in the muscles in his forehead. "We need you around here."

Callum fired off a text, and then siblings started filing in.

"You know Darren and his twins, right?" Callum said to Dillen as activity in the room spiked.

"Darren, yes," Dillen said. "Not the twins, though. I've been overseas for a long time and am afraid I'm not up to speed on life in Cider Creek."

"Don't worry," Callum said, blowing it off like it was nothing. "You'll catch up quick. Not a whole lot of new stuff goes on around here. But that's probably why you left in the first place."

Dillen grinned, and it was about the sexiest thing Liz had seen all day.

Rory filed in next with a girl who looked to be entering her teen years and was undeniably a Hayes.

"You must be Livia," Liz said to the niece she'd never met. "I'm your aunt."

"Dad has shown me, like, a ton of pictures of you guys," Livia said. "I recognized you right away."

Tiernan and Sean came strolling in next, phones in hand. A redhead introduced as Raelynn followed Sean, and another with long russet hair came in behind Liz's other brother. She must've been Melody.

A female with long blond hair walked over to stand beside Rory. She must've been Emerson.

"Where's Reese?" Liz asked after introductions were made.

"Around here somewhere," Callum said. He'd stepped into the role of taking care of the younger kids after their father had died. Liz had been young, but she still had memories of their father. Being here, seeing family pictures sprinkled around made her feel like she'd come home.

She reached for Dillen's hand, and he linked their fingers. To her family's credit, no one so much as raised an eyebrow.

After condolences were doled out and Liz explained the bandage and that she would be fine what felt like a dozen times, everyone settled around the oversize dining table. And then Granny walked in. Eyes wide, mouth agape, she couldn't get to Liz fast enough. She met Granny halfway across the room and was pulled into the kind of embrace Liz had been missing for fourteen years.

Granny tilted her head back and just looked at Liz as though taking her in for the first time. "You're grown."

"Yes, ma'am," Liz said.

"But I hope you haven't changed too much," Granny said with a wink.

"I wouldn't dare," Liz stated with that Hayes pride that caused her chest to puff up a little.

Granny was followed by a sight for sore eyes… Liz's mother.

"Mom," Liz said, turning toward her mother as she entered the room from the back door.

"I came as soon as I heard you were here," Marla Hayes said. She was five-feet-two-inches of kind eyes and warmth.

The two embraced as Granny turned her attention toward Dillen. Reese filed in next with a toddler on each hip. Liz never thought she'd see the day her sister looked like a natural mother, but the proof was standing right in front of her.

"I must be seeing things because I know Dillen Bullard isn't here in front of—"

"It's Pit Bull now," Dillen said to Darren as his former high school friend entered on the heels of Reese and the babies.

"Damn, you look the same," Darren said before giving his friend a bear hug.

"Yeah? You look a helluva lot older," Dillen teased. "What are you? Fifty?"

Darren belly-laughed before introducing his family, his pride evident in his eyes. Could Liz ever change her mind about kids?

She would consider it with someone like Dillen.

DILLEN DESERVED TO be called a hypocrite and a jerk for the assumptions he'd made about the Hayes family.

There was another news flash—being around Liz's big family was nice. The jokes, the laughter, the love the Hayes siblings obviously shared for each was beyond anything he'd ever experienced in his thirty-two years.

"We came here to ask a few questions about Ms. Coker," Liz started.

"Can it wait a few more minutes?" Marla Hayes asked. "We've all been waiting a long time to be together under one roof and I'd like to make the announcement you've all been waiting for."

Deacon, the ranch foreman quietly slipped inside the kitchen.

Liz nodded. Everyone returned to their seat at the table. Even the children quieted down.

"As you all know, your grandfather is gone," Marla started. "So, I thought about what to do with the ranch and the land, but it seemed wrong to walk away from the one good thing Duncan built. Then there was all that vandalism going on, which seems to have stopped now that many of you have moved home or are in process."

Did Liz ever think about moving back to the ranch now that many of her siblings were doing the same?

"When everyone is together, we're a strong bunch," Marla continued. "However, I don't want the responsibility of running this place on my own, but someone in this room does."

Gazes shifted all around, searching each other's faces. Right up until the ranch foreman Deacon stepped up to the island. Heads nodded and smiles abounded.

"Deacon has been the glue holding this place together for a long time, even when your grandfather was alive," Marla continued. "It only seems right to hand over the reins."

"I couldn't agree more," Callum said. "My only concern is this is your home. Where would you and Granny go if not here?"

Deacon shook his head and put his hand in the air. "I have no rights to the family home. This is Ms. Marla's home, and I would never dream of taking that away from her or anyone in the family."

"Which is why Deacon will work the cattle and own the land beyond this backyard," Marla said. "We'll share the barn and pitch in whenever Deacon needs us or as all of your schedules allow."

"I don't need much space," Deacon added. "I'm plenty happy in the bunkhouse with my guys." He took a few seconds to look each Hayes sibling in the eye. "But I won't take the deal if any one of you is against it."

Callum looked at each sibling individually, no doubt looking for a nod or head shake. The nods were unanimous. "Everyone here thinks it's a great idea."

Deacon put his hands together in prayer position. "This

means the world to me. This land and the cattle mean everything." The older man wiped at a tear that broke loose, running down his cheek. "I consider every last one of you my family."

"You've always been one of us," Callum said. Those words shouldn't have choked Dillen up like they did. "You deserve this."

Deacon saluted before excusing himself. He was clearly uncomfortable in the main house.

"Granny and I will keep this house, and it'll be handed down to you guys once we're no longer here," Marla continued.

Dillen coughed to clear the sudden frog in his throat.

"Now that many of you are married, engaged and have children, it's my hope that you'll consider coming back home for big family Christmases," Marla said. The comment got heads nodding and put big smiles on faces.

"A few of us were going to suggest the same thing," Callum said, glancing over at Liz. "You were missed this past holiday."

"You brought a dinner plate to the hospital for me," she said with a smile before asking if he'd seen a blonde driving around in a red Jetta.

Callum shook his head.

Dillen felt like a jerk for making all those assumptions about the family in high school and then holding on to them.

He looked at Liz and, much to his surprise, a real future sprang to mind.

Dillen mentally shook it off. He was getting caught up in the moment, in the idea of family. He didn't deserve one of his own.

Chapter Nineteen

"I have one more announcement to make."

Liz's thoughts still reeled from the first one her mother had made. She couldn't imagine what a second one might be. Although she couldn't be happier for Deacon. He deserved the world after all his years here, looking after the cattle and the kids while she and her siblings had been growing up.

"I've sold mineral rights to a trustworthy investor who will ensure no one ever does anything to harm this place again," her mother said. "I know each of you is self-made, and I couldn't be prouder of you for it. Your father, if he was here, would be bursting with pride the way each and every one of you have turned out as people." Her mom got choked up, and there wasn't a dry eye in the room.

Her mother recovered with one of her warm smiles, the kind that radiated from across the room. Mineral rights on the kind of acreage the Hayes family owned would be worth a fortune. The only thing that came close in value to a rancher was water rights. Those could be sold or leased for big money.

"You can do what you want with the money, but it's far too much for me or Granny to spend on our own, so we've decided to spit it eight ways to get the number down to something more manageable per person," her mother continued.

Liz really was curious where this was going, not that she cared about more zeroes in a bank account. It occurred to her that she could do a lot of good in the community with more funds.

"The number will hit your bank accounts today, but it's well into eight figures," her mother said. "Donate it. Keep it. Let it grow. Build a monument. Feed the hungry. I don't care what you decide to do with the money as long as you keep it in perspective, which doesn't seem like a problem for any one of you guys."

"I'm already doing what I love," Callum said. "So, there's no reason to rush into spending anything for me. But I'd like to start a family charity so we can pull some of it together and help the community."

"We sorely need a new recreation center with a decent basketball hoop," Sean chimed in.

"We can start there and figure out the rest as we go," Callum said. "As long as everyone agrees and feels good about what's happening."

"I don't have a problem with it," Reese said. "I can already think of half of dozen ways to use some of the money to help single parents."

Heads nodded.

Liz was proud of her family for putting others first. The stubborn trait from Duncan Hayes would pay off in the end. They would all dig their heels in when it came to making sure something good came out of all the money their grandfather had made. Something that made Cider Creek a better place to live.

She instinctively reached for Dillen's hand. He didn't move out of the way or link their fingers. But his muscles tensed. Was he pulling away? Why?

"Who can stay for coffee?" her mother asked.

Easy chatter filled the kitchen. Liz remembered the same thing happening in this room a long time ago when her father had been alive. Dinners together at the table came back. As did the spark that used to be in her mother's eyes. It was replaced with warmth and the remnants of grief, along with a twinge of sadness. Liz knew her mother was patiently waiting for the day she would join her husband. But right now she had a lot of living to do.

Her mother beamed while looking around the room. Another twinge of guilt struck. Liz reminded herself that she was here now. That was all that mattered. Her siblings were home. And life was coming full circle with her siblings finding the loves of their lives and becoming or starting families.

Warmth filled her, and she forgot about her problems for a little while. If she'd known home would feel this magical, she would have come here a long time ago.

No. It wouldn't have been the same. The air was lighter now that Duncan was gone. It was awful to think but true. He'd cast a heavy cloud over the family for far too long. And seeing her mother's spark return gave Liz hope for the future.

"We should probably go," she said to Dillen.

He shook his head as his lips compressed into a frown. "You belong here. I don't. You should stay while I find the bastard who killed my father."

"You're not leaving without me," she insisted.

But he got up and walked out anyway.

Liz heaved a sigh. She couldn't…*wouldn't* force Dillen to be with her no matter how much the fact that he'd just left had shattered her heart. For the first time in Liz's life, she looked around a room and felt an ache in her chest… she felt an aloneness she'd never experienced before, and she feared it had everything to do with Dillen.

DILLEN STARTED TOWARD the truck, veered right for reasons he couldn't explain and ended up in the barn. Being around animals was a helluva lot easier than people. People were complicated.

"Who's there?" Deacon asked as he came out of the office.

Dillen bit back a curse. "Sorry. I didn't realize anyone was in here."

"You're welcome to stick around," Deacon said, leaning against a post. "Just me and the animals in here most of the time."

"Congratulations, by the way," he stated. "You've worked here for as long as I can remember."

The older man cracked a smile. "You turned me down when I offered you a job back in high school."

"Couldn't stand the thought of working on Hayes property," Dillen admitted. "I'm not proud of the fact now—because I probably needed that job."

"We all do stupid things from time to time," Deacon said. His expression turned serious. "I'm sorry to hear about your pop."

The sincerity in his voice touched Dillen. "Thank you."

"He was a good man," Deacon said, crossing his legs at the ankles and looking down at his boots. "The world needs more good men like him."

"How well did you know Pop?" Dillen asked, hoping the foreman might know something about the blonde.

"Not very," Deacon admitted. "But he always had a quick smile and a wave every time we passed each other no matter what else was going on."

"I used to joke Pop had one mood," he said, smiling at the recollection.

"Your pop was always in a good mood. Didn't know a stranger and was happy to be alive. Never complained."

Didn't know a stranger. Those words resonated. It would've been easy for the blonde woman to take advantage of Pop. But what had she wanted from him?

"No, he didn't," Dillen said. "I took that for granted when I was kid. Somehow only saw his faults."

"Easy to do," Deacon said. "Plus, you shouldn't be so hard on yourself. You were just a kid thrown into a circumstance not many would handle well with your mom leaving the way she did."

Since Deacon hadn't known Pop, Dillen figured the foreman hadn't known his mother, either. But it was nice of him to offer his sympathy.

"Well, I've got work to do," Deacon said. "Stay as long as you'd like. It's always nice to have company around."

"I appreciate it," Dillen said, but he needed to circle back and apologize to Liz for snapping at her a few minutes ago. He couldn't think straight in the kitchen with all the family around. It made him want something he knew better than to expect...a family of his own.

Since he'd never wanted a wife and kids, he'd been thrown for a loop, and his anger had momentarily taken the wheel. It was the reason he'd decided to get some fresh air. Because it had also occurred to him that after Macy and Rosa being murdered, Liz might be a whole lot safer here at the ranch with full-time security while surrounded by family. He couldn't selfishly put her at risk.

Footsteps behind him caught his attention. They were light enough to be female, and the gait sounded like Liz.

"Hey," came the familiar voice from behind.

Dillen turned around and issued a sharp sigh. "I pushed you away in there because I don't know if I can keep you safe."

"I'm a grown woman, Dillen. Don't you think I deserve a say?"

He nodded. "That's the reason I'm in here and not in Pop's truck headed back home." He took a step toward her to close the gap between them. "The thing is I'd never be able to forgive myself if anything bad happened to you."

"I feel the same way about you," she said, meeting his gaze and holding on to it. "If we're together, we can watch each other's backs. If we're apart, the risk goes up. That's the way I see it."

He listened because she was right. She deserved to have a say.

"Okay," he said. "If you want to come with me, I have no plans to stop you." He didn't add the part about not being able to resist her in more ways than he cared to count. That realization was best kept to himself.

Deacon emerged from the office again. "Good to see you here, Liz."

She ran over and gave the foreman a hug. "I didn't realize how much I'd missed this place."

"Does that mean you're thinking about sticking around?" he asked.

Liz twisted her fingers together like she did when she was nervous or on the verge of making a decision. "I'm definitely planning to be more of a fixture around here. Beyond that, I haven't decided yet."

"I miss saddling up with you," Deacon said with a smile, his sun-worn skin making him all that much more real as a human.

"We will definitely ride together again soon," she said, her face bright with a smile. "I promise."

"Bring this guy around, too," Deacon said. "I'm guessing he can handle his own on a horse. We can all go out together."

As much as Dillen appreciated the invitation, he'd be shipping off soon enough to a place where he'd be riding shotgun in a Humvee instead of on the back of a horse. "I'll keep it in mind."

Liz must have read between the lines because she frowned but quickly recovered. "We should probably get going back to your dad's place."

"Drive careful," Deacon said. Then his gaze widened. "That's across the way from Rosa and Macy's place, isn't it?"

"Yes, sir," Dillen supplied.

A look of fear crossed Deacon's features. "Be careful. Both of you. You hear?"

"We do, and we will," Liz supplied before giving another brief hug. "Thanks for caring about this family over the years. I know my brothers looked up to you after our father..."

Liz tucked her chin to her chest and sniffled. She brought her hand up to discreetly wipe away rogue tears. "You know what I mean."

"I do," he said before adding, "and I will continue to do so."

This time as they left the barn, Dillen reached for Liz's hand. He had nothing more to promise her than right here, right now. Could it be enough?

Hand in hand, they walked to the truck. Marla came running out the back door holding a stack of plastic containers in her hand.

"Take these," she said, handing them over. "And come back soon. Okay?"

Her gaze bounced from Liz to Dillen and back. "I mean both of you, in case that wasn't clear."

"Yes, ma'am," Dillen said with a smile. He took the offerings and then placed them on the small bench seat in back of the truck before shutting the door.

"Good," Marla said before bringing each one into a hug. She headed back inside after excusing herself with a self-satisfied smile.

Dillen stopped himself from opening the passenger door mid-reach. "Are you one-hundred-percent certain this is what you want to do? Because you have a family who loves you in there and you don't have to go home with me. We can still work on the investigation together using our phones. You don't have to physically be with me." He turned around to face Liz.

"Are you trying to push me away again, Dillen Bullard?" she asked, balled fist on her hip.

"No," he said. "But you should think about what you're getting into with me."

"You don't think I already have?"

"I didn't say that exactly," he admitted with a smirk. She wasn't backing down, and it was just one of many qualities he loved about her. Loved?

It was too soon for the *L* word. Dillen backed off, taking a physical step to the side.

"Good," she said before opening the door and then sliding into the passenger seat before he could say another word. By the time Dillen had claimed the driver's side, she was belted in.

Being around her family, even for a little while, had showed him how good a family could be. He was beginning to rethink all his preconceived notions about what it would be like to settle down. He could see himself with Liz, surrounded by all her brothers, sister and sisters-in-law.

Liz's cell phone rang. She checked the screen. "Granny?"

She answered on the second ring. "Okay. I'll see if he's... No, he's right here." There was a pause. "I don't think so."

He glanced over and shot a quizzical look.

"She wants to speak to you," Liz said.

"You can put the call on speaker," he offered, wondering if he'd left something behind. His phone, wallet, keys were on him, so...

"Dillen?" Granny's voice sounded deceptively sweet.

"Yes, ma'am," Dillen said, a little scared of the senior citizen for reasons he didn't care to examine.

"I want you to listen real close to what I have to say," Granny said.

"Yes, ma'am." Why did he feel like he was about to be dressed down by his old drill sergeant?

"You take good care of my granddaughter. You hear?" Granny continued.

"I can take care of myself, thank you very much," Liz interjected.

"Lizzie," Granny scolded. "Was I talking to you?"

Dillen would laugh if he didn't think he would end up in the doghouse with Liz.

"No, ma'am," Liz said like a kindergartner who'd just been scolded on the playground.

Granny was a force to be reckoned with.

"Okay, then," she said. "Let me continue speaking to Dillen."

"I'm right here and can hear everything you say, Granny. So, watch it," Liz warned.

"Well, then, I stand corrected," Granny said, a playful hint to her tone. "I'd better mind my p's and q's."

"Yes, you better," Liz stated, unfazed but also kidding.

"Dillen," Granny started again.

"Yes, ma'am."

"You have to stop calling me ma'am because I keep looking over my shoulder for my mother-in-law," Granny quipped. "She was a mean old bitty."

Well, now Dillen really laughed. He couldn't help it. Granny was a cutup. "I can't imagine anyone who wouldn't love you."

"She didn't think I was good enough for her son," Granny said, muttering a curse.

"Granny!" Liz interjected. "Keep it PG-13, okay?"

"I'm too old to have my mouth washed out with soap," Granny said before issuing a loaded sigh. "But all right. I'm an old woman who doesn't have much time left on this earth, so I'll cut to the chase."

Dillen couldn't help but smile. "Go on."

"You hurt my grandbaby, and I'll have to hunt you down and—"

"Granny!" Liz shook her head but laughed.

"I got it," Dillen said. "Don't worry about me."

"Good," Granny said before making an excuse and hanging up before Liz could get on her case again.

"Gotta love Granny," Liz quipped as she tucked her cell phone inside her purse.

He wasn't so worried about hurting Liz as much as the other way around at this point. Because leaving her to go back overseas was going to kill him.

Chapter Twenty

Liz would've been mortified except it wouldn't do any good. Granny was her own phenomenon, and there was no going up against a machine like her.

"Well, that was fun," Dillen said. Thankfully, his sense of humor was intact.

"You know, as wild as this might sound, I miss that," she admitted. "All of it. Even the ridiculous things I never thought I'd miss like my brothers being overprotective."

"They seemed all right to me," he said.

"Because you haven't seen all the text messages I've received since leaving the ranch," she said before realizing how that might come across. "They're just concerned about me and wanted to—"

"Don't worry about it," he said like it was nothing. "What kind of big brothers would they be if they didn't try to protect you?"

"I mean, technically, I'm the third oldest in the whole family, but whatever," she said.

"You're so old," he quipped. "I should have realized it when you whipped out your AARP card at lunch."

"Funny guy," she said. "You do realize we're the same age."

"I was just saying how young you are," he said with a

chuckle. "You have a good family, by the way." His comment came out of the blue.

"I've been wondering why we allowed one poison to destroy the whole family unit," she admitted.

"Your mother was grieving, and the rest of you were kids when your father died," he pointed out.

He was right.

"Still, why is it so easy to fixate on the one bad thing instead of staying focused on the good we do have?"

"If you figure that out, you deserve a medal," he said with half smile. "Your inheritance means you don't have to work again if you don't want to. That's definitely a good thing."

"Yep," she said. "Still doesn't change anything for me."

"I thought you might see it as a way to back off work some," he said. "You can afford to hire more folks now."

"Work has always been my escape," she said, astonishing herself with the admission. She hadn't really realized it until now. "It's more to me than a paycheck."

"That's fair."

"Building the business proved to me that I could take care of myself no matter what else was going on in life," she continued. "That has always been important to me."

"I can see why," he said. "You're amazing, Liz. You've created a successful business on your own. Few folks can say that. I imagine you'll find some charity to give a good portion of your inheritance to."

She nodded. "I plan to let the rest sit for a little while and, to be honest, forget it's even there. The last thing I want to do is focus on it."

"Sounds like a good plan," he said. The fact that he sounded impressed brought on a sense of pride. She didn't need his approval, or anyone else's for that matter, but it still felt good. In the short time they'd known each other, his opinion had come to matter more than most. Then again, in a way they'd known each other nearly two decades.

Driving back to the trailer meant going past Rosa and Macy's house. She hoped the fire marshal found evidence to prove the explosion had been a crime and not an accident. Her heart hurt at the thought of the sisters being gone. It all happened so suddenly. The fixed pupils were burned into Liz's memory. They'd been nothing but kind to her. They'd welcomed her into their home.

"Do they have any family?" she asked as they drove past.

"No children or husbands," he supplied. "The only reason I know is because Pop talked about them after they visited him. There were times when he had them stop by when we were on a call so they could say hello."

He pulled onto the parking pad behind Liz's sedan. It was already dark outside and getting late. It had been a full day. Liz's stomach picked that moment to remind her they hadn't eaten dinner yet. At least they had plenty of food now that her mother had loaded them up with meals.

There wasn't much better than home cooking. Being able to heat something up in the microwave sounded perfect at the moment.

Dillen made his way around the front of the truck to open her door. They both carried a stack of plastic containers. There was enough food here to get by on for a solid week at least. Liz had been afraid to go home for the big announcement on so many levels because she'd feared her mother was going to deliver bad news about her health. A weight was lifting from Liz's shoulders now that she knew her mother was going to be fine.

Liz was surprisingly happy to be home in Cider Creek. She'd forgotten what it was like to be around her siblings, her mother and Granny. It was good.

Stepping onto the porch, there was a large yellow envelope on the doormat with a fist-size rock sitting on top to hold it in place. The winds had died down today and the sun had shone, but the cold front lingered.

"What is this?" Dillen asked, balancing the containers with one hand and his chin while dipping down to retrieve the envelope. He tucked that underneath his arm as he fished out the key and then opened the door.

Liz followed him inside, setting her containers on the kitchen counter while he did the same. He ripped open the envelope as she stacked the meals inside the fridge.

And then he released a string of swear words that would make a sailor blush.

"What is it, Dillen?" she asked and grew even more concerned when he didn't respond.

"TEDDY." DILLEN BIT the name out through clenched teeth. The document he'd stopped by to talk to Dillen about would complicate trying to sell the place.

"The neighbor?" Liz asked, moving beside him. It was always more difficult to think straight when she was close.

"Apparently Pop wrote a note saying he would sell water rights on this land to Teddy," Dillen supplied.

"That might make it difficult to sell," she stated what he already knew. She studied him. "Are you planning to get rid of the place?"

"I haven't gotten that far," Dillen admitted. "This was my home. It houses all my memories of Pop, which up until recently I wouldn't have thought of as a good thing. This was the only stability I had in life. The thought of letting it go feels like pulling up anchor."

"Makes sense," she said with a tone that soothed his soul. "Which is why you don't have to make a decision right now.

Think about it. Let it sit for a while. See how you feel in a few weeks or a month. Unless there's a pressing need to decide, but it sounds like you have time."

Dillen understood why Teddy would want to make him aware of the agreement, but he really didn't want to deal with it right now. All he wanted to do was bring his father's ashes home.

A Post-it fell out of the envelope when Dillen turned it upside down. "What's this?"

It landed on the counter.

"Good question," she said as he turned it over to read the handwritten scribbles.

Please talk to me before selling. I'd like to make an offer. —Teddy

"I guess people have to get in quick when it comes to real estate, but this just creeps me out," Liz stated.

"He probably thinks I'll wrap everything up fast so I can head back overseas," Dillen explained.

"I mean, that is very logical," she said. "Looks like he wants to make an offer on the place before it goes on the market, though." She heaved a sigh. "I guess you are neighbors, and he might have been eyeing this place for a long time. If he and your dad already came to an agreement on water rights, it might make more sense for him to buy the property outright. That way he would have both."

"I was thinking along those same lines," Dillen admitted. "It's a practical solution." So, why did it make his chest fist?

"It might be hard to let go," Liz stated.

He felt that on more than one level, but her stomach growled again and he needed to feed her. "Let's figure out what to heat up so you can eat."

After a moment of standing there, still, she nodded. "My

mother and Granny are the best cooks, and I haven't had their food in far too long."

"My mouth is already watering," he said, needing to change the subject from the heaviness of loss. Dillen could only think about Pop being gone for so long before he had to refocus or get sucked down a hole he might never be able to pull himself out of again. "What's the specialty?"

Liz opened the fridge door and started picking through the containers. She made little mewls of pleasure as she looked at each one. The sounds stirred his heart and made him want to hear those same sounds while doing other things with him besides eating.

"I can't decide," she finally said.

"What are the top two?" he asked, appreciating the break in tension.

"There's a ham-and-potato soup that's literally to die for," she said before shooting a glance in his direction that said she wished she'd used a different word. "It comes with fresh chives on top."

"Sounds good," he admitted. "And what's the other?"

"Beef and mushrooms with mashed potatoes," she said before adding, "You know what, I'm in the mood for mushrooms. How does that sound to you?"

"Like heaven," he said, pulling a pair of plates from the cupboard. He wasn't any closer to figuring out who would want to murder his father and why, but at least the sheriff was working on it now, either officially or not. Seeds of doubt had been planted after Rosa and Macy's murders.

Dillen still couldn't believe the sisters were gone. They'd been a fixture on this street for years. They hadn't had any family to speak of. It had only been the two of them after their mother had passed away and their relatives had banded against the sisters over a small inheritance. Rosa and Macy had formed a tighter bond, and they'd lived together peacefully ever since.

Their deaths had made three folks in the same neighborhood days apart from each other. How could anyone deny that the casualties were connected?

Liz heated the container while he set the table and poured water. He threw on a pot of coffee for good measure, figuring he could dig around in Pop's finances now that he had all the passwords to see if there were any red flags there. At this point, he regretted not installing a security camera at the front door. The sisters had looked out for Pop.

The microwave beeped as an incredible smell filled the kitchen. Liz spooned portions onto the plates at the table with a satisfied smile.

"I haven't had this dish is so long my mouth is practically watering at the smell," she said, inhaling a breath. She picked up a fork and dug in.

Dillen couldn't agree more. The smell was one thing—it was on a whole other level. But the taste went above and beyond. "I never knew I'd been missing out on this until now."

"This is one of my mom's specialties," Liz practically beamed. "This tastes like home."

He could think of someone who felt like home but couldn't let himself go there right now.

"I never would have moved away if anyone in this house could cook half as good as this," he said. "This is amazing."

There was something niggling at the back of Dillen's mind that he couldn't quite put his finger on. He chalked it up to the day he was having. The last few days, when he really thought about it. Not to mention the fact Pop was about to be cremated and his ashes brought home. Those events alone would throw any normal person off balance. Right?

The thing was that when he was anywhere close to Liz,

the world righted itself and he felt a sense of comfort like he'd never known. Desire, too. Need. And don't get him started about how much he wanted to kiss the little spot of mashed potatoes off the corner of her mouth right now.

Being with her family had opened his eyes to what having siblings and female influences around was like. This place had been a bachelor pad, as Pop had liked to call it. There'd been no female touch since his mother had walked out. Even before, he didn't remember his mother putting any feminine touches on the place. Forget either of his parents cooking anything from scratch. It had been boxed pizzas and corn dogs in this house. If it could be heated in the microwave, it was golden around here. And now Dillen was wondering what it might have been like to grow up in a family of more than two. He couldn't begin to understand what it was like to have siblings. It might not have been awful to have a little brother or sister running around. Someone built-in to buddy around with during Pop's long hours or late nights at work.

Regret was a waste of time, so Dillen didn't go there. But he couldn't help but wonder what having a big family would have been like.

"What are you thinking about?" Liz interrupted his revelry.

"Families," he supplied.

"Mine can be a handful, but I wouldn't trade any one of them for the world," she said. "You know?"

"I wish I did," he said. "Almost all my memories are of me and Pop."

It occurred to him that his mother had at least had the courtesy to wait until Dillen had been old enough to go to school during the day before she'd disappeared. Had that been the plan all along once she'd realized married life was going to be way harder than she'd expected?

There were times when he wished he could sit her down and drill her with question, ask why she'd felt the need to walk out on him and Pop. But he wasn't into wasting his time, and she'd been clear that she wasn't coming back.

What about Liz? If he was willing to risk his heart, could he trust her to stick around?

Chapter Twenty-One

After dinner, Liz helped with dishes. She then took a shower and got ready for bed. But before getting under the covers, she joined Dillen in the office, where he sat studying the computer. "Find any unusual activity?"

He brought his hands up to rub his temples. "Nothing but a few extra ATM withdrawals," he said, leaning back.

"Date nights?" she asked.

"Could be," he said.

"We should take note of the dates and then ask around town if anyone saw him out on those evenings," she offered. It wasn't much to go on, but any shred of potential evidence was welcome at this point.

He nodded.

"I'm guessing you haven't heard from the sheriff about the red Jetta," Liz continued.

"Not a word," he said. "But investigations take time, and he has a whole lot more bureaucracy to contend with."

"True," she said on a sigh.

"I've been staring at this screen until my eyes are burning," he stated. "I'm going to take a shower and then let all the information simmer."

"Thinking too hard on a problem usually ends in a headache for me," she said.

Dillen followed Liz into the living room area, where they parted ways. She grabbed her phone and charger, then headed to the sofa. This seemed like a good time to respond to a few work emails and texts.

Liz made it halfway through her inbox by the time Dillen returned. He took a seat next to her, so she set her phone on the side table to charge.

"Don't stop working on my account," he said, looking content to sit beside her.

"I dealt with all the emergencies first," she said. "Plus, I could use a break."

"How about a movie?" he asked.

She needed a good distraction. "Sounds like a plan to me."

"What do you like?" he asked as he picked up the remote from the coffee table.

"Could you go for a comedy?" she asked. "I've had enough action for a while."

He seemed to pick up on the reference to explosions and fire because he gave a knowing look. "Comedy it is."

Dillen found the silliest movie on the list. Liz laughed. And laughed. It felt so good to laugh. She couldn't remember the last time she'd let go and enjoyed herself. Work gave a sense of purpose and accomplishment. She wouldn't exactly call it fun.

Tomorrow would be another heavy day of digging into everything that was happening and, hopefully, starting to find answers.

Liz wasn't sure when she fell asleep, but she woke the next morning in bed tucked underneath covers with Dillen curled up as far away from her as possible without actually falling off the bed. The second she stirred, though, he sat up.

"Hey," she said. "How did I end up here?"

"Carried you," he said, rubbing his eyes.

"What time did I crash?" she asked.

"Halfway into the movie," he said. "One minute you were laughing. The next, you were out. You fell asleep on my shoulder. I didn't want to disturb you, so I finished the movie and then picked you up. You didn't so much as blink."

"I'm not surprised," she said. "I've never slept better than when I'm with you."

She probably shouldn't have admitted that to him.

"Same here," he said so low she almost didn't hear him. It gave her a sense of satisfaction to know she had a similar effect on him. He threw the covers off and got up.

Liz could get used to this. She'd refused to live with any of her boyfriends in the past but being with Dillen twenty-four /seven was different. He felt surprisingly like she'd come home to a place she'd never known before, a place she never realized she missed until now.

She freshened up and met him in the kitchen. "I think we should do breakfast in town."

"Okay," he said.

Liz threw on jeans and pulled her hair back into a ponytail. Going into town yesterday had been productive. They needed to ask more folks about the blonde. "Where can we stop to ask about the red Jetta?"

"Post office might be a good place to start," he said before disappearing to get dressed.

Too bad her family didn't recognize anyone with a red Jetta who was blonde and looked bigger than life. Could the blonde bit be a wig?

Why not?

It would be a great way to conceal someone's appearance.

She briefed Dillen on her thoughts on the way into town. Halfway there, a call came in from Callum.

"Were you asking about a red Jetta yesterday?" her brother asked.

"Yes, why? Have you seen one?"

"I'm at the market on Fourth, and there's one parked in the lot," Callum said. "It sticks out in a sea of trucks, especially the color."

"We're on our way," she said. "Could you do me a huge favor?"

"Anything."

"Stick around in case the driver returns to the Jetta before we make it there," she said. "If they beat us, can you sneak a picture? It can be from a distance."

"You bet," he said.

"Thank you," she said. "I'll owe you one."

"No return favor needed," he stated. "It's what we do for each other, right?"

"Right," she confirmed, realizing once again how much she'd missed her brother as she ended the call.

"So that's what it's like," Dillen said.

"What?" Liz asked.

"To have siblings."

"That's when it's good," she said with a smile. "You should see when we fight."

"Fighting is better than silence," Dillen said.

She realized more and more how lucky she'd been growing up. Duncan Hayes might have been a jerk, but the rest of her family wasn't, and everyone had suffered because of him. She could honestly say that she genuinely liked each and every one of her family members. They each seemed happy and in love.

The Hayes family was growing, a new generation emerging. One she hoped could learn lessons from the past and build a better future. One they could all be proud of. One that was good both inside than out.

They were several minutes away from the market when her phone rang again. She checked the screen before answering. "Hey, Callum."

"The driver slipped past me, but I got a picture as she was exiting the parking lot," Callum said with frustration in his voice. "It's grainy."

"I appreciate you for trying," Liz said.

"I just turned down Maple," he said. "Heading northbound."

"You're following her?"

"Yes," he confirmed.

LIZ DIDN'T BOTHER to mask her shock as she put the call on speaker. "Dillen can hear you now."

After perfunctory greetings, Callum continued.

"Thought I might be able to get an address for you," he said. "People usually head home after a grocery trip. She only had one bag, so I might be running her errands with her instead of unloading groceries."

Dillen shifted their direction so they could cut the vehicles off at the light between Fourth and Oleander Street. "We'll join you and then you can break off to get back to what you were doing."

"Sounds like a plan," Callum stated. "We are continuing northbound."

"Okay," Liz said.

Dillen sped up. "If I take Elmhurst, I should be able to catch up."

"Elmhurst is good," Callum said. "The driver is checking me out in her rearview mirror. She might have caught onto me."

"Be careful, Callum," Liz said. "Lives have been lost over this—whatever *this* is."

"Always," he reassured.

"How is the driver reacting to being concerned about you following her?" Dillen asked.

"She seems mildly concerned over my presence," he responded. "Then again, I'm trying not to read too much it. Of course, a woman would be suspicious if a vehicle followed her out of the grocery store parking lot. Let me know when you get close, and I'll back way off."

"If she isn't turning, then we should be there in a minute, give or take," Dillen said.

"We seem to be circling back to the market," Callum said. "Hold on."

Liz held her phone in a death grip.

"Okay, we're back on Fourth heading toward the market again," Callum said. "Now she's on Farm Road 62."

"That leads nowhere," Dillen observed. "You may as well go straight. There's not really anywhere else she can go, so following will give you away."

Callum issued a sharp sigh. It was obvious he didn't want to break off.

"She'll figure you out, and that will alert her to us," Dillen continued. "Trust me—I'll find her. Besides, we appreciate everything you've already done. We wouldn't be this far without you. Breaking off now helps us the most."

"Will do," Callum said, "I'll keep on straight so I can circle back around to the market."

"Thank you, Callum," Liz said before Dillen could chime in.

"I'm just glad you're home, Liz," her brother said. "I hope you'll consider sticking around, or at least visit more often."

"Actually, we can talk about this later, but I'm thinking about relocating my headquarters to the ranch," she said.

Dillen was caught off guard by the revelation. He wouldn't have guessed in a million years Liz would consider moving back to Cider Creek.

"Let me know whatever I can do to help with the transition," Callum said. "It'll be good to have the family back together."

"I'm still thinking about it, but I'll let you know as soon as I decide," she said to her brother. "Being home has been nice, and it's because of you and the others. I didn't realize how much I missed Mom's cooking until recently."

"We've all gone our separate ways," he said. "But I'm splitting my time between Houston and Cider Creek now even though I'm at the ranch and across the street at Payton's more than not."

Dillen turned onto Farm Road 62. He didn't want to interrupt the moment happening between siblings, so he didn't say anything.

"I gotta go," Liz said. "We'll talk about this later. Okay?"

"You bet," Callum said. "Be careful out there."

"I won't let anything happen to her," Dillen said. It was a promise he intended to keep.

"I'll hold you to it," Callum said before exchanging goodbyes and ending the call.

A couple of minutes later, a red Jetta was visible up ahead. Dillen had been trained in evasive measures, but being on a straight country road with little to no hills didn't provide for a whole lot of places to hide.

There were open fields lining both sides at this point. Down the road were clusters of trees that looked to be at the entrance of someone's home.

The red Jetta hung a right and then disappeared in the

thicket. Dillen turned right to follow. He slowed his speed to a near crawl, surveying all around and checking for danger.

A second too late, he looked up and spotted a dark figure sitting on a tree branch with his back against the trunk while holding a saw. The guy made one deeper cut, and then the thick branch came crashing down on the truck's windshield, hitting hard enough to shatter the glass. Dillen jerked forward from the impact. His airbag deployed as did Liz's. And then his door opened followed by hers.

Before Dillen could get his bearings and shake off the momentary shock, a fist slammed into the left side of his jaw. His head snapped right, and then he answered with a hard left. His fist connected with what felt like a tank of a person. Big meaty hands grabbed at Dillen as he threw another punch.

Out of the corner of his eye, he saw Liz fighting back as a guy jerked her from her seat belt.

Dillen spun around the second he was free from his seat belt, drew his knees up to his chest and then unleashed hell, knocking Tank back a few steps. Dillen used the momentary advantage to pop out of the truck and dive into Tank.

The guy looked to be in his early twenties. Despite the cold, he had on a flannel shirt with cut-off sleeves. He had the face of a blond Frankenstein along with a thick neck. He'd most likely spent high school on the front line of a football field.

Dillen snapped off several punches in a row as the two tumbled to the ground. He rolled like an alligator with prey in its mouth, came up on top of Tank. Dillen squeezed his thighs, pinning Tank's arms to his sides. Tank bucked.

It wasn't enough to knock Dillen off balance.

Tank grunted, tried again. This time, Dillen had to put his hand down to keep from being bucked off.

Liz screamed. Dillen had never felt so helpless in his entire life. Tank used the distraction to buck Dillen off. The bigger guy landed a few punches in Dillen's torso and a knee in his rib cage that might have snapped a lower rib.

But glancing over at Liz to see if she was all right cost him a face punch. Tank had created enough space to wiggle an arm free without Dillen realizing.

The punch was so hard, he had to fight to stay conscious.

Chapter Twenty-Two

Liz dug her nails into her red-haired attacker's face and clawed. Her memory came back from the construction site. She'd turned from Mr. Bullard in time to see his face as he slammed a piece of Sheetrock into her head. It was the last thing she remembered before she was knocked unconscious. She brought her knee up to the sonofabitch's groin as fast and hard as she could, trying to drive her knee up to his throat.

Red doubled over, dropped to his knees and coughed.

She bolted in the opposite direction but was stopped short on her second step. Red's lanky fingers wrapped around her ankle like a vise. She stumbled forward with her other foot before face-planting onto the unforgiving dirt.

Liz sucked in a breath and let out a scream, using all her energy to kick so she could break free from the man's grip. His hand was on her like glue. There was no room to move.

She curled up and then twisted around, trying anything to break his grip. That didn't work, either.

There was no time to give up. She clawed her fingers into the back of Red's hand. He sneered at her, and the image would be burned into her memory for many years to come. His canines looked like a wolf's, and his beady eyes were intense.

Red threw his other arm up, gripping her ankle with two hands now. There was no breaking free. He was too strong.

The next thing she knew, he was dragging her toward him as he propped up on his elbows. "You just won't die."

"Nope," she bit back. One leg was free, so she rammed it toward his face. She heard a crack, and blood shot from his nose.

"You should be buried just like the old man," he said through gritted teeth.

But he didn't stop. Now he was climbing her legs like a ladder, his bony fingers digging into her thighs. He captured her free leg and forced hers together just as the sound of a vehicle turning onto the gravel drive caught her attention. Red didn't seem to notice. At this point, he was breathing so hard he was practically growling.

Blood splattered across his face, dripping in his mouth and covering his front teeth. He looked like something out of a zombie movie as he inched toward her waist.

The sound of heavy feet on gravel came next as Dillen continued to fight with the second attacker.

"Get the hell off my sister," Callum said. In the next second, Red went flying. He slammed against a tree. The skinny guy was no match for Callum. Her brother studied her for a second before his gaze bounced back and forth from her to Red. "Are you okay?"

"Go," she said, waving for Callum to make sure Red couldn't be a threat. She rolled onto her back and tried to catch her breath enough to move, turning her head toward Dillen. "It's him. These are the men who killed your father."

The second attacker was pinned underneath Dillen but still fighting with everything he had. Dillen was big. This guy was a tank.

Liz looked around for something to help as Callum literally sat on Red.

"Call 911," Callum instructed.

She gave a quick nod before running her hand on the ground, determined to find something to use as a weapon. Her fingers grazed something sharp. A rock?

She gripped the fist-size rock and managed to push to standing in between gasps for air. It felt a lot like she'd just run laps around a football field for half the morning. Her ribs ached when she took in air. Red might have cracked one or more of them.

But she couldn't care about that right now. Not while Dillen was in the fight of his life.

The bigger guy bucked, and Dillen responded with a jab to his jaw. Dillen drew back his hand and shook it. His knuckles were bloody, and she had no idea if that was his blood or the other guy's. She could only hope it belonged to the other guy.

Because nothing could happen to Dillen.

"I remember the redhead from that night," she said through labored breaths as she walked around the pair, giving a wide berth in case the bigger guy bucked loose. "He's the one who knocked me out."

While Callum continued to hold Red down, she needed to call 911, but she might be able to neutralize the threat before making the call. She couldn't risk the bigger guy getting the upper hand.

Dillen wrangled the man's arms against his body with renewed anger and then squeezed with his powerful thighs. The guy grunted and then went crazy, bucking and trying to roll. His efforts were in vain. Dillen had a strong grip on the guy. Angry words tore from Dillen's mouth as he strengthened his grip.

"You need to die just like those old women from across the street," Tank bit out.

Liz made it around to the guy's head, closed her eyes and then slammed the rock down. Warm liquid squirted.

She opened her eyes enough to see the guy blacked out. "I'll call 911."

Dillen couldn't afford to relax. Rather, he tightened his grip on the guy's torso, pinning his arms to his sides. "Good." He sounded exhausted from battling the bigger guy.

Liz ran to the vehicle on the passenger side and dug around for her cell. She located it on the floorboard and then palmed it.

"No. No. No."

"What is it?" Callum asked before Dillen had a chance to respond.

"No cell coverage out there," she said.

"I should have known," Callum stated. Red was pinned underneath her brother.

"How are you here?" she asked.

"Check your phone," he said. "I panicked when I tried to reach you and couldn't."

"No bars," she explained. It hurt every time she took in a breath. "What should we do now?"

"Find them," Callum instructed. "Take my ride. I know I could call a few minutes down the road."

Liz panicked. How could she leave them?

"We'll be all right," Dillen urged her to go.

"My vehicle is still running," Callum said. "Go."

Leaving them behind to drive down the street was the opposite of what Liz wanted to do. But there was no choice. She ran to her brother's vehicle and claimed the driver's seat.

Phone in hand, she backed out of the drive and then sped down the farm road.

Every few seconds, Liz glanced down and checked her phone.

A minute passed. Then two.

And then bars.

Liz stopped in the middle of the road and called 911.

"I can't pinpoint the exact address," she began, rattling off the farm road where she was and approximately how far down the road emergency vehicles would have to go in order to find the house.

"Got it," the dispatcher said. "Wait right where you are for emergency vehicles to arrive."

Absolutely not.

Liz dropped the cell phone into the cup holder, made a U-turn and then sped back to the scene. The call dropped, but she'd done her part there.

She rummaged around in Callum's back seat.

There was rope and duct tape. She could use either or both. She grabbed supplies and then brought them first to Dillen. She helped him tie off the unconscious man while he was still out.

"Let's toss him in the back of Pop's truck," Dillen said. He took the heavy end, and she took the feet. With some effort, they hoisted the attacker up and into the bed of the vehicle.

She immediately shifted to Callum, taking supplies there. All three of them went to work on Red. He was tied up and in the truck bed in a matter of a minute.

"Help is on the way," she said.

Then Liz looked down the lane at the red Jetta parked at the small two-story farmhouse.

"How much time do we really have?" she asked, shifting her gaze to Callum and then Dillen.

"I HAVE NO plans to sit around and wait," Dillen said.

Callum's vehicle was being blocked by Dillen's and a tree trunk, so they had to hoof it. It would be quieter that way, but there was no other advantage because he could see the farmhouse windows from here. Which meant that anyone on the other side could, too.

"I have no idea what we're walking into," Dillen said. "I'd like to go ahead for recon."

"I'll come with you," Callum started, but Dillen was already shaking his head. "I don't want her anywhere near the house until I know it's clear. Plus, I'll move faster and easier on my own."

Callum clamped his lips shut like he was stopping himself from mounting an argument. Good. He wouldn't win this one. After a quick glance in Liz's direction, Callum gave a slight nod.

Dillen looked to her for confirmation. She walked straight up to him and kissed him.

"We need to talk when you get back. Okay?" she asked.

He couldn't agree more. There was a lot he wanted to say to her. This wasn't the time.

Dillen crouched low, ignoring the pain in his ribs and thighs. He could add his face to the list of things damaged. He kept as much to the tree line as possible leading up to the house, unsure of what he was about to find. This place could be any number of things. For all he knew folks could be running weapons or drugs out of here. This area was remote, and anything was possible.

A person could come charging out the front door right now with an AR15 and spray bullets across the lawn. Or there could be hostages inside. A family being held against their will. Children with guns to their heads.

His mind snapped to all possibilities. He'd seen just about everything during his military tenure. While back home, he didn't make it a habit to carry.

Rather than go to the front door, he moved to the side of the house, grateful no one had started firing from inside. He peeked in the first window. It was a bedroom. No one was inside.

Methodically, he moved around the perimeter of the house, checking each window as he went. There were more rooms with no one visible. Beds were made in the pair of bedrooms. An office was neat enough.

His concern grew about this being a family in trouble.

Dillen checked the window of the office. It was no surprise the window wasn't locked in these parts. He opened it and slipped inside the home.

On top of the desk was a stack of papers.

There were several versions of a handwritten note, not unlike the one Teddy had left in an envelope. Was someone setting up Teddy?

Dillen moved through the home without a floorboard so much as creaking underneath his shoe. He moved to the back of the house to the kitchen. Back against the wall, he surveyed the room.

A blonde female sat with her back against a cabinet and her knees pulled up to her chest. The sink was above her head.

She was crying. Her arms were extended in front of her with her wrists tied. Big tears rolled down her cheeks. He didn't recognize her, but that didn't mean anything. She could be reasonably new in town. She fit the description of the person they were looking for. And she drove the red Jetta.

But had she been doing any of this of her own free will?

Dillen moved his hand around to get her attention. Then he brought his finger up to his lips, telling her to be quiet as she looked up at him.

She nodded.

He gave a thumbs-up as he looked around, didn't see anyone else in the room. Had the person who'd done this to her fled?

She nodded again, indicating it was safe to come to her. So, he did.

The knot tying her hands together was loose enough that he realized his mistake. Dillen stood up and took a step back. The window reflected the image of a person about to attack him from behind.

Dillen dropped down and spun with one of his legs extended. The move was effective. It swept the would-be attacker off his feet. The guy landed in a thud behind him, then immediately spun around and jumped on top of the…

"Teddy," Dillen said as the blonde scooted against the cabinet.

She folded her arms over her knees, hugging them into her chest. "It was a bad idea from the start but my uncle talked me and my boyfriend into helping him."

It dawned on Dillen what Teddy wanted had from his father. Water rights.

Sirens sounded outside in the distance.

"He owed them to me," Teddy said. "What was he doing with them anyway? I tried to pressure him to sell the property to me, and he wouldn't."

"The men outside," Dillen started, needing to know. "Did they kill my father?"

"It was supposed to look like an accident," Teddy said as the blonde cried so hard she hiccupped. "Pull yourself together, Helen."

She shook her head and cried harder. "I never should have got Jimmy and his best friend Benji involved."

"You killed my father to have access to the water on his land?" Dillen said to Teddy, almost not believing the words despite them coming out of his mouth. "You took away my only family for what...water?"

"There's been a drought," Teddy stated like it explained everything. "Small ranchers have to do whatever it takes to stay alive. We're not like that bastard Duncan Hayes, who has all the resources at his fingertips."

"You sonofabitch," Dillen said, firing off a punch that knocked Teddy unconscious. He wouldn't kill the man no matter how much he wanted to. No, Teddy was going to jail for the rest of his days, where the only water he was going to see on a daily basis was in the toilet.

"I'll talk," Helen said. "I never wanted to get involved in this in the first place. It's my fault Jimmy and Benji hooked up with my uncle. You can bet you'll have my full cooperation."

She threw her hands into the air about the same time the sheriff came through the back door along with a deputy.

It only took five minutes to update Sheriff Courtright.

"I interviewed Ms. Coker, and she said a blonde came into the government offices looking for property deeds to check property lines," Courtright said as Liz joined them.

She was a sight for sore eyes.

"I'd bet money she can identify this woman as the blonde in question," Dillen said, disgusted.

"When they couldn't take the water rights in court, they must have gotten desperate," the sheriff said.

"He did," Helen said. "Jimmy and me were going to get enough money to run away together so he could leave his wife." She stood up. "I'll tell you everything I know. I never wanted to get involved in murder."

Courtright nodded. "You'll all be heading down to the station with me and my deputy."

Liz walked straight over to Dillen and wrapped her arms around his waist. She burrowed her head into his chest, and he never wanted her to leave. She fit perfectly right there.

"I'm guess we'll get a match with footprints on the scene," Courtright said. The sheriff took their statements. "That's all I need from you right now. You're free to go. Rest assured justice will be served."

"Thank you," Dillen said to Courtright after shaking the man's hand. "Pop didn't die in vain. This bastard isn't getting away with his crimes."

"No, he isn't and neither are the others involved," Courtright said.

A wave of relief washed over Dillen. He looked at Liz, and one word came to mind...*home*.

"Callum said he could take us home since your truck needs to be towed," she said to him, looking up at him with eyes he could look into for days.

He walked her out the back door, needing to be out of the building for what he had to say. When they cleared the yard, he took a knee.

"Liz, I underestimated you from day one, even when we were kids," he started. "But I've finally figured out something about myself. I'm in love with you. Probably have been since we first met when I was too stubborn to acknowledge it."

Her face gave away nothing.

So, he had no choice but to keep going.

"I thought you were a princess, and that meant out of reach for a guy like me," he continued. "But I'm here to say that I love you with all my heart. I may not be much of a prince, and you sure as hell deserve better than anything I can give you. But if you'll have me, princess, I promise to stick by your side through thick and thin until I take my last breath."

Tears welled in her eyes, but he couldn't tell if that was a good or bad thing.

"I feel like I've known you my entire life, and in some ways, I have," he continued, figuring he needed to go for broke at this point. "It would be an incredible honor to call you my girlfriend, and someday, when and if you're ever ready, I'd like to call you my wife."

"Dillen," she started, but emotions seemed to get the best of her, so she stopped to catch her breath.

A few tears spilled out of her eyes, and he started to worry. Was she trying to find a way to let him down easy?

"In finding you again, I've finally found where I belong. You're the great love of my life. You're my place to call home. So, yes, I'll be your girlfriend because I love you. I'm in love with you. And I will love you until my heart stops beating. I would love to be your wife someday when we get settled into our new lives here in Cider Creek. You have to finish up time in the military, and I need to relocate a business. But I fully intend to make us official. And until then, I'm still calling you mine."

He picked her up off her feet as he stood up, ignoring the pain in his ribs and more body parts than he cared to count. And then he kissed the absolute love of his life, his future bride, his everything.

Real love was almost impossible to find. And he was the luckiest bastard on earth for finding it with Liz Hayes. She was kind, smart and beautiful inside and out. There would never be another person who could measure up to her.

"Sounds like a plan to me," he said, referring to her comment. "I intend to give you a ring before I head back overseas. Consider it something to remember me by."

"It will never come off my finger," she said, pressing a kiss to his lips.

"Good," he said. "And if you don't mind, I need to pit stop some place on the way home."

"I'm sure Callum won't mind," she said. "What's the errand you need to run?"

She skimmed him with her gaze, and he could see that she was confused as to what couldn't wait while they both looked like they were coming from a fight and had lost.

"The hospital left a message for me earlier," he said. "Pop is ready. And it's time to finally bring him home."

* * * * *

COMING SOON!

We really hope you enjoyed reading this book.
If you're looking for more romance
be sure to head to the shops when
new books are available on

Thursday 7th December

MILLS & BOON

LET'S TALK
Romance

For exclusive extracts, competitions and special offers, find us online:

f MillsandBoon

𝕏 @MillsandBoon

◉ @MillsandBoonUK

♪ @MillsandBoonUK

Get in touch on 01413 063 232